THE

UNFORGIVEN

THE
UNFORGIVEN

DANIEL H. MURPHY

Title spread original artwork by Licarto

99designs.com/profiles/1851594

Cover design by Bob

99designs.com/profiles/1253957

kpgs.design@gmail.com

Images provided through BigStock

Published in the United States by Three Cord Press

www.threecordpress.com

For My Grace

– PROLOGUE –

Sharp morning light slanted through a curtainless window, illuminating dust floating in the sparsely furnished room. In the middle, a chair, table, and sofa stood alone, islands in the otherwise stark residence.

The room felt empty, between the heavy air and unbroken quiet. He twisted his hands, tracing patterns of stained dirt, the nails rough and scored with marks. Short stubble covered his head above a face shaved clean. He still smelled of dirt and smoke.

So much depended on words. Words said, and those unsaid. He was not ready.

The walls, too, were bare; the kind that would throw back whispers and laughter if there were any, anything at all. The walls reflected only silence and sunlight, stark and white. There was a chair, there were his hands. There was her.

"I know I caused you grief…"

Grief. Loneliness. Anger. Hollow words to name the unnamable. Other words were needed.

He tried again.

"I left you alone…"

She sat across from him, wrapped in the silence. He shifted where he sat and took his cup.

No, these words were not right. Too few, too small. He closed his eyes, wiping away unwritten speeches, and took up the thread of the story instead.

"Let me tell you everything."

– ONE –

I stood before the three Arbiters.

I felt I'd been standing for months. Before the Arbiters. Before the Speakers. Before the wreckage and smoke.

The Arbiters had sifted each grain, each minute and moment, looking for what they called *evidence* or *motive*. Blame is what they sought.

I had sifted through more, through our life and my life before that. Moments in the dark, at my bench in the foundations of Abbey Spire. Moments alone together, when we retreated to the farthest corners of the house. Days in the long grass beside the lake water, building towers out of sticks and woven grass. The day we met.

I held my answers tightly. Blame was theirs, to paint as they wished. The rest was mine.

The Arbiter in the middle, sitting in the largest chair, leaned forward. His scalp, devoid of hair or eyebrows, reflected the lights from above. His lips moved little when he spoke, his body beneath the black robe not at all.

"We have heard your story."

"Have you understood it?" I asked. Some would have called it rash, others bold. It was reflex.

3

"We have heard your story," he repeated, the ceremony inviolable.

I knew my part and did not speak again.

"You are Unforgiven."

My eyes widened. I had expected their disfavor. I had not expected this.

"It was an accident!" I cried out, again. Again, no one listened.

Two men at my shoulders seized my arms. I fell from my shackled feet when they pulled me, and they took my weight. They dragged me, still facing the three Arbiters, to the doors.

As the wreckage of our life receded, one thought consumed me: *I have to go back*.

*

They dragged me through the great doors. The corridor beyond echoed like dull thunder when the doors shut, then emptied of all but our footsteps. The guards pushed me into a railcar and chained me to a seat. One lit a pipe, and we left.

The track twisted ahead of us, disappearing in the sparse light of a maintenance tunnel.

Rails. I had not ridden the rails since the day they took me. On that morning, it had been the train I rode six days a week to Abbey Spire. The trees out the window had been cold and bare. The train had been hot.

Too many bodies, all traveling in from the communes. Most were head down, a few had talked. I'd looked out the window. As a child, I'd stared at the Spires rising from the horizon. I'd gazed at the lights at night from the top of the neighbor's tree, while my father's voice, mingled with yellow light, quietly spilled from a window.

Then, the Spires had held mystery and promise. As I grew, I'd chased them, and they'd taken me in. And I'd discovered the Spires were no more than this: kilometer high buildings of stone, metal, glass, and wire. Full of people. Full of people just like us, with all their pettiness and ambition. And occasional magnificence.

That last morning, I'd gazed at the trees instead. They remained beautiful.

But these were not those rails. This was not that train. This was a car for eight, holding three. I was inside a Spire, sweeping past access hatches and bundled cables. I was cold.

The younger guard looked to the man with the pipe, then back at me.

"Why'd you do it?"

I held my tongue and held his gaze. There is no way to explain to a man whose job is to drag you by your armpit what happens when your life is taken away at the word of another.

He turned away, unanswered, and whispered something. The guard with the pipe huffed out his nose and looked back.

"Think you'll get out?"

I tried to stare him down as well, but his nerves ran deeper than the first's.

"No one gets out."

"Then I'll get through," I said.

The railcar approached an outer archway and stopped. There was a bar across the tracks, between us and the night.

5

Pipe huffed again. A guard with a gun approached, and Pipe gave him a stack of uniflex sheets, exchanging low words.

The guard waved us on, and the car accelerated, faster than before. Pipe turned back to me.

"They don't want you back."

They don't want you back.

A part of me, the part that lies, didn't believe him. But this time I was the one to look away. He laughed, underwhelmed by his victory, and took his pipe in his palm.

As we slipped through the magnetic field at the exit arch, the taut air pulled each hair on my arms and head with a familiar tug. And then we were out, truly outside.

The echoing rumble of the corridors changed to a new song, the simple turbulence of wind, as we sped along the rail high above the earth. The State smelled of city, of thermal exhaust and stagnant messes, of wet metal and mulched wood, of ten million bodies and all their possessions. It smelled like home.

I breathed deeply, feeling the damp air of early evening a last time, savoring the fog in my lungs.

The Spires loomed around us, the towering buildings rising in the dusk from the unbroken gardens below. Only the patchwork of lights marked the great walls.

With a set jaw I sat back. I pretended to sleep as the young man in front watched. Alone in my thoughts, I relived the last hour, the last day, the last year. Mumbled words escaped me as I tried to speak into the memories, but I could not change a thing.

*

I opened my eyes when the wind changed, softening and slowing. The young guard in front still watched.

"Welcome home," he said.

My eyes slid to the building beyond. It didn't loom like the Spires. Shorter, a few lights, nothing special apart from an intangible weight. It might have been the shadow in the evening gloom or maybe just thin windows and thick walls. Maybe the place really is soaked with inescapable melancholy.

The Hall of the Unforgiven.

The railcar slowed, following a wide curve in the bridgetrack toward the center of a landing dock. Figures stood on an open platform before the Hall, beneath tall metal floodlights that seared the shadows from the concrete.

*

It was more open, though less crowded, than the courtyard I'd crossed each morning at Abbey Spire. Six days a week, I'd left my train, full of Communers like me, and trudged my way to the lockers, full of my tunnel rats that kept the Spire standing.

Abbey courtyard had sprawled like a snake pit in my path. It milled with those using the front door, with clean coats, matching hats. Their door led to the *other* Spire. The one with carpets and art-bedecked walls, the one with wooden tables and screens covered in words and numbers. The one full of suits and haircuts.

It was my daily reminder of them and us. Them and us. I hated the way they looked at us. Rather, the way they didn't look at us. Pride and shame, two sides of a coin, one the broken shards of the other. Daily, that courtyard asked me which I would choose.

Daily, I'd skirted the edge of the courtyard in moments when fewer people walked by. They rarely noticed me anyway, in my ever-brown coat and the stained coveralls where my legs poked out. I slipped quietly through the sidegate to the other door, the smaller door marked "Engineering," and passed in like a shadow.

This dock was not Abbey. There were no walls, and it held only three figures. All in grey coveralls, two with firearms slung on their shoulders. No suits, but that held little comfort. It was still them. It was their front door that I was corralled toward as the railcar glided to a stop.

A figure approached where we parked. He leaned his weight on the railcar's door as if the muscles in his body mutinied after a day of needless patrol and spoke to the others in low tones. The young guard laughed. The new guard's eyes fixed on me, and he regarded me with narrowed eyes, the barest hint of a squint.

*

In Abbey Spire, there had been a door separating our lockers from the carpeted hallways. It was marked 1106. The man inside had been there longer than me. His office sat beneath a kilometer of Spire and was less useful than one of the foundation stones.

We called him the Desk Janitor, and I didn't know if he was the janitor who sat at the desk, or the man whose only true job was to keep that one-by-one-and-a-half-meter space clean. I did know we kept that door closed, a few centimeters separating us from him. Five dozen men and women on my side knew how to weld, seal, fasten, or lock that thing shut for good. And we would have if we thought it could actually keep him on the carpets.

Most days, I went in.

The Desk Janitor had raised his voice, that last day, as soon as the door started moving. As if he'd been staring at it, waiting for his moment. "There's six floors without water! Six!"

I stepped inside, pulling door 1106 shut behind me. "Which floors?" Though I already knew.

I believe my daily calm rattled him. He understood little, but me least of all. He could not do my work. I was persistent with quiet reminders that I could do his. He blamed me for his mistakes and oversights, and I took ownership of none of it. And yet he was paid three, maybe four times my rate. He was consumed by the fear that I would take his job, and so he dedicated himself to these daily rituals of putting me in my place. I, for my part, played my role to keep this dance going from day to day, keeping his fury and fear smoldering. I didn't enjoy it. It just seemed the right thing to do.

I rarely listened. He meant no harm, or none he could make good on. If he was terrified of me taking his desk, he was more terrified of running the place without me. It may have meant a suit and a paycheck, but I never wanted that desk. I didn't want to be a desk cleaner and list maker. I wanted a screwdriver and the hidden dark inside the Spire-walls, metal and water and sparks.

He never understood me, but I understood him. And I understood the squint in his eye – the fear that comes when hiding behind unearned authority.

It was the squint that lay in this new guard's eye. Yet, this time, I was the one afraid.

*

Light spilled into the open car, glinting on my restraints. I studied them to avoid meeting his gaze. The metal was light, perhaps reinforced aluminum. The devices were quaint, with actual keyholes and an exposed hinge that could have been clipped or forced with simple tools and another pair of hands.

Unremarkable. Inescapable.

Each time I glanced, he was still squinting at me. When Pipe rapped his head with the bowl of his pipe, the new guard broke gaze to swipe at his hand.

Then he finally spoke to me. "Hey!" he said. "Read the reports today?"

He retrieved a handheld from his pocket. "*Speakers say: Judgment Expected Today.* Got that one right." He looked at me for this, then back to the unit in his hand. "*Sordid details emerged over the last two months as Speakers and Arbiter agents together dug into the explosion in the West Commune.*"

He looked at me over the handheld. "How big was it?"

"Amos!" A woman's voice carried from a grated window at the base of the building.

"Nedder," he muttered before calling back, "What do you need, Shea?"

"Not a thing. You have a man to process."

This Amos re-engaged his body, lifting his bulk from the car, and looked at me more closely.

"Nedder," he muttered again. "How many locks is that? They have to do this every time? Hey, Shea!"

She was no longer at the window.

10

"Woman, we need those keys!"

Her voice carried across the platform. "Well, I'm putting tea on."

Amos shook his head. "Nothing but the State's finest out here."

I snorted.

He paused.

I wiped my nose. Satisfied, he moved on. Before ambling to the building, he favored me with a conspiratorial grin. "Big fireball, huh? Wish I'd seen it."

He soon returned, gun hanging at his back, keys spinning on a finger. He jumped into the open car and began tugging on my chains and my arms. I could smell his breath as he muttered to himself.

When the last key snagged, he asked, "Modern locktags, would that be too hard? You still sharpening pencils and recycling paper over at the Hall of Judgment?"

"They got pencils at the museum," the young guard said.

"Well, this spragging Hall must be the only thing between the State's last locksmith and starvation."

Pipe grunted; it may have been another laugh. "Hall of Sanitation has openings. Want a change of scenery?"

Amos looked at them sideways. "I'll keep to the fresh air."

His hand grasped my shirt, and I was yanked to my feet and onto the dock. Amos gave a light push that sent me stumbling toward the building, though his attention never drifted from his friends.

When I caught my balance, his back was again turned. I searched the three of them, but they could have been on lunch break for all the attention they now gave me. Shea's window was still empty.

"What am I supposed to do?" I asked. No response.

The men laughed, and Amos raised his heavy arm to slap Pipe on the back, though it came more like a blow than a pat.

*

My foreman Simmon had a daily ritual of slapping my back. It was his way of greeting. And, though he never left a bruise, it was also his way of reminding me that he could still hand-tighten a hex nut tighter than me.

"What is it, 17 finally go out?" he had asked, his arm falling heavily, when I stepped out of room 1106.

"Six floors without water," I had said.

"Whatever it takes to get his attention."

I'd extended a rueful smile. "The grout on 357 will have to wait."

"The grout." Simmon shook his head, a frustrated, patronizing smile. His outward condescension was the privilege of a man who did not have to face the Desk Janitor daily. "Yes, it will. I've got lighting flickers on the nineties. We need to get in the wiring before something goes out. There's a lab on 97 that can't lose power. I need your guys. Mine only follow directions; they don't think."

"Give me Jacks and New Jacks, I need to break them in. And Genkov; I need at least one who can fix a pump without questions. You can have the rest."

And so we had talked. Divided the crew, sent two to start the grout anyway. Asked about the family, asked about the shop.

And then Simmon, with a nod, had moved off, tapping shoulders. That was the last I saw him.

*

Now Amos's hand, unfamiliar, fell on my shoulder. It grabbed my collar, spinning me, and gave me a rough shove. "Let's go, Unforgiven."

It was enough to make me stumble toward the grated window. Shea had reappeared with two steaming mugs. I glanced back to Amos, who now wore a dashing but manufactured grin. Shea, with the barest trace of amusement, pushed the mugs under the grate.

"Welcome to the Hall, dear."

"Do you call everyone 'dear'?" I asked.

"Everyone but him," she replied dryly, nodding back toward Amos, who abandoned his smile in the other mug. "This you?" she asked, spinning a uniflex with a yellow form loaded on it across the counter.

My name was printed at the top.

"Should be," she said, pulling it back toward herself. "You're the only one checking in today."

"What time is check-out?" I asked.

Amos choked on his tea. I felt like I'd again violated some sacred gravity of the moment; there was no laughter in my heart.

Shea didn't smile. She only looked from under eyebrows and muttered, "Sooner than you'd like, dear." And then, more quietly, to her papers, "Sooner than you'd like."

She slid a now-organized stack of flexes back to me. "Sign here."

I looked at the papers. Name, date of birth. And below them, *Multiple Homicide.*

"No."

Shea spun the flex back to her. "You said this is you."

"I won't sign it."

Her fingers lingered on the flex as she sighed. "It's paperwork, not a confession."

"It was an accident."

As she looked at me, she didn't exactly smile. "Son, an accident is when your lunch falls on your shirt."

I placed my hand on the flex but wouldn't touch the pen. "I need to go back."

"Amos can sign. It's all the same. It's just me can't sign it."

"Please," I said.

She looked at the form, as if reading, as if there were something she could do. Amos reached past me to grab the pen, wrenching the flex free and signing on a dark line. "You old softie," he said.

"Don't call me soft you big thatcher!" Shea snapped. "You could use some softness past that gut of yours."

Amos assumed a mock horrified expression. "Forgive me, I am forgetting the hospitality of this Hall! Right this way, good sir, let me show you to your quarters." This with a half bow.

"And don't mock the Unforgiven," she said.

They were bickering. Like an old married couple. Had we ever looked like that? We had been two in lockstep, the shove and the countershove, rushing headlong toward disaster. Until we found it.

Now, the Arbiter in his large chair would have me believe it was too late. I was never one to accept that.

Name.

Date of Birth.

Signature.

The two continued to bicker. I made a quick inventory. Amos's gun. The railcar, still holding two men. The edge of the platform and a several-dozen-meter drop to the Earth. One door.

As tempting as the gun and a vainglorious suicide sounded, that was not the way back. Not the way through.

I have to go back.

Abruptly, I took and swallowed the tea in a burning gulp.

They fell silent.

Ignoring them, I scratched out Amos's name and signed my own. Then I escorted myself to the door. The door in.

The door through.

There I waited, my back to the silence of the interrupted argument behind. There was a curse. Then more silence, and a hum.

"Amos! Get on the phone," Shea's tired voice came. "Tell them to fix this door."

"They already fixed it."

"Well, it doesn't open!"

"Did you jiggle the button?"

"Get on the phone, thatcher!"

"Did you try holding it down?"

"I held it down!"

Amos took up the phone as Shea shouted, trying to have the conversation by proxy. Still squabbling like an old married couple. Maybe they were.

So, this was the displeasure of the State. They couldn't even incarcerate me properly. Not a grand display of discipline, but one of incompetence.

As it was ever. The State shouldered no blame when I was accused. They sat in their tall chairs, in their tall Spires, drinking the blood of we who labor in the communes. Because they are the lighthouse of civilization, and we need them. Because they know it.

They withhold technology, they undersupply, they construct dwellings without thought, and when the inevitable disasters come…

There I was. Their answer to their disaster. Their blame.

Unforgiven.

I could not escape this courtyard, not even into their prison. As it ever was, if I wanted the State to accomplish anything, I'd have to do it myself.

I studied the door. It throbbed lightly with the hum of failing electronics.

*

When I'd arrived in pump room 17 with Genkov and the two Jackses, only one pump still throbbed, weakly. Four were already silent.

Five pumps, four men. Genkov and I finished ours before lunch, filling the room once again with the pulse of the machine and the hush of water.

I found Jacks standing over a silent pump, staring at schematics on a handheld.

A man cannot divine the purpose of the machine from drawings, from scrutinizing its hard shell. If you build to spec, you will never make anything better than the "State's finest" who first built it. Someone who did not love it.

No, you must reach inside, fingers to be soiled and bled with each lesson. You must dismantle the machine, hold each piece, follow each thread and trail to see the flow, the whole. The purpose. Only then can you see.

Only then you can fix it.

Yet, Jacks stared at his drawing. I sent him to grout, a long suspicion of his mediocrity confirmed. As he left, he called me a perfectionist, as if it were an insult.

New Jacks stood over a dismantled pile of parts spread across the open floor. A more promising start.

Genkov quickly finished the third pump and went to see how Simmon fared with the flickering lights. I took New Jacks under my wing, and the two of us worked the last two pumps deep into the afternoon.

Perfection is the only satisfaction I ever got from the work. The State ignored us who lived in the bowels of their Spires, keeping them standing, keeping their systems running. They thought it was easy because I never let it break. It was my mistake. They had asked me to do miracles with nothing and gave me nothing for it.

They couldn't even keep a door working. It should be them before the man in his big chair, hearing his pronouncement on their failures and disappearing through the echoing doors.

I traced this new door's hum. A tube ran from the hinge to a cabinet, with a smaller tube then running along the wall toward Shea's booth.

Take it apart. Build it right.

I stepped to the cabinet, held shut by nothing but a friction catch. My hand faltered as I moved to pull it open, imagining a gunshot at my back. More likely the hand back at my collar, twisting me and shoving me State knows where.

Nothing came. There was no pause in the argument. I tugged the cabinet open.

The simplicity within was disappointing. It was a glorified relay switch, where Shea's button triggered another circuit to open the door. Still feeling the itch on my shoulder blades, I ran my fingers along a cable. I traced the crimps and the familiar friction of insulation.

My shoulders unknotted. Home was here, inside a box with wires and circuits pulsing with life. The belly of the machine.

It was obvious what was wrong. An audible buzz sounded from the top left of the box, where two wires nestled and the insulating plastic was frayed. A quick touch yielded the tickle of low current, so I pulled the wires with my hands, wedging another better insulated cable between the two. It wasn't elegant; it got the job done. Then I shorted the whole thing and, silently, the large door swung open.

They finally noticed. Hurried footsteps approached.

Amos shouldered me aside and peered into the box, as if he

might see something he understood. With a grunt, he closed the prison door. He called to Shea and the door swung open again. He slammed the cabinet shut, giving me a suspicious glance. Then he grabbed my shirt at the shoulder and shoved me through. I caught a last look at Shea through the closing door, still with pity in her eyes.

*

Again a closed door, a dim hall, footsteps and echoes. Again I was dragged. Amos was possibly twice my size, but I deemed him roughly half my intelligence. I was done being dragged for today. Certainly not by him.

"Anyone could hotwire that thing," I said, wrenching my shirt from Amos's grasp.

He let go. "Breaking in isn't the direction we worry about."

I smirked.

"Why are you smiling?" he asked.

Before I could answer, his fist sunk into my gut. I doubled over. I couldn't breathe.

"Because it's funny," I said anyway, my voice tight.

He moved quickly for his size. His eyes were still flat, still calm, as he grabbed the front of my shirt and drove me against the wall. The back of my head struck hard, and I saw lights.

I raised my hands, palms open, perhaps to ward him off or perhaps to placate him before the next blow. But he looked into my eyes, still calm, with utter apathy. He released my shirt, and I slumped on my feet.

"You can walk, Unforgiven. Let's go."

And he left me where I'd slumped, shrinking down the hallway without a backward glance.

The fear from the morning, the Hall, returned. I should not have let a few low-wage guards distract me from the weight of the Spires. Or the authority conferred by closed doors.

My head hurt. I leaned onto my knees, catching my breath, watching his back.

The door back to the courtyard was three unguarded meters away. Thoughts flooded in again, of dashing back outside, of snatching a gun from an unguarded shoulder. And then?

No one gets out.

My jaw worked unconsciously. No words came.

Amos turned a corner and was gone.

At the last, I hurried to catch up, falling in step behind him. I stared at a point on his brown shirt, halfway between his shoulder blades, until he pulled open a door and stepped aside. Without a word, the door closed behind me, and I never saw him again.

*

Waiting in the next room were a pair of men that had none of Shea's softness nor Amos's apathy. The floor and walls were tiled in a dirty white. A single light hung from the ceiling, illuminating a metal chair in the center, while the walls remained in comparative shadow. I stood close by the door, eyeing them uneasily across the room.

Then I'll get through.

The two men circled me like wild dogs. They led me, docile, to the lone chair. One of the men lowered his head and looked me in the eye.

Then I heard a hum, and a hand clamped over my eyes. Cold sweat slipped off the fingers and onto my eyelids. They pushed my head back even as I felt my body squirm, and clippers passed over my scalp, sending my hair to the floor.

I kept my eyes closed. The cold hands twisted my head left and right, folded my ears up and back as the clippers passed over. I flinched with each nick; one of them chuckled with each flinch.

Next came my nails as they clipped them far back, fingers and toes one at a time. They cleaned my ears and checked my mouth with gloved fingers. They pulled me to my feet and pulled my shirt off, then pulled everything off.

I was left in the cold light, once again eyeing them, and the two of them eyeing me. One grabbed a bucket off a table, just a man doing his job. The other smiled, almost a wink when I caught his eye.

Cold fluid broke over my head and shoulders. It stank. I squeezed my eyes shut and opened my mouth, wheezing from constricted lungs. Over my coarse breath and over the splash on the stone floor one of them laughed.

They turned a hose on me, on my ribs, on my face, on my thighs. When I raised my hands to guard my face, the spray moved to my stomach. My eyes were still squeezed shut and my mouth wide, trying to inhale without aspirating.

It continued until I was rinsed and the ground slick. I had fallen more than once. When it finally ended, I stood with my eyes closed and hands raised, dripping and contorted like a statue in the rain. But for the shivering.

The one who had fetched the bucket threw a towel and clothes over the wet chair, and the two of them left out another door. The new clothes were a uniform of pale blue and a pair of something more slippers than shoes. None of it did anything for the cold that now chilled me to my bones.

*

The men waited beyond the only unlocked door. I stepped before them, clean and shaven. If they hoped for some word, some reaction, they received none.

The one who had laughed reached forward, pretending to straighten my collar. I stood still, watching. He seemed disappointed, then spun on his heel to walk away.

The other guard jerked his head and said, "C'mon, son."

The two guards fell in step with each other but spoke little. We walked slowly. The corridors we passed were flooded with sterile light, long hallways of open doors with shadows spilling out. The place was eerily quiet apart from the echo of our steps, accompanied by random rattles and clinks from machinery in the walls.

*

There were few left on the train when I'd pulled into the West Commune Lake Station after fixing the pumps that last evening. Home. Fewer still got off, and none went my way.

I'd pulled my jacket close, cinching my pack to my back and tucking my hands beneath my arms, moving between the islands of light scattered down the street. Some light fell from overhead, more spilled out of windows where families worked late.

The wind off the lake filled my chest; cold, damp, and woody. The bakery still smelled of bread and fire, though its windows looked long dark.

This street had shrunk as I had grown. It had grown quieter as I'd aged, though perhaps that was more due to the hour. There was little laughter before sunrise and after dark.

I remembered it alive. What the West Commune lacked in Spires and postmodern antiques, it made up for in children and gossip. At least in daylight.

Our light was on at home. I stood outside on the doorstep, I don't know how long. I heard your footsteps moving nearer, then away. Quiet humming and the occasional words of your song.

You sounded happy.

It is hard to say what held me there, at the door. Perhaps it was fear. The house was full of whispers and loose threads now. I couldn't map or trace it any longer.

The doorstep, under my feet, felt solid. The strap of the pack on my back, now clenched tighter in my fist, was solid. Inside, I couldn't keep my feet.

With me outside, you sounded happy.

In the end, I was cold. I opened the door and stepped in for the last time.

*

My handlers stopped at an unmarked door in an empty corridor. They pulled it open and nodded me in.

The room inside was dark. Instead of your song, shadows and whispers spilled from this door. I stepped in, and the door closed.

"Aw hell," a voice rumbled out of the darkness.

"What is it?" another voice followed, higher pitched, from a different corner.

I peered into the darkness. It was impenetrable.

"It's thirteen," a third voice said.

"Thirteen? Can't be. Hey, you," the second voice said again. "You Unforgiven?"

"I am." The words fell without echo, without response.

Then the first voice rumbled back from the darkness, "Aw hell."

– TWO –

"Hey," another voice said in the darkness. "Over here."

I approached with an arm outstretched as my eyes adjusted to the near blackness. The outlines of bunks had begun to emerge when the voice spoke again right in front of me.

"This bunk's open."

"Thanks," I said. It sounded more invitation than order. I couldn't make out any face or figure, only a hand emerging from the shadow and pointing vaguely upward. I pulled off my slippers and climbed onto the upper bed.

"So, you're Thirteen," the voice said from below. Whispered conversations sprang up in the corners of the room, rising and falling and blending so I could not hear the words.

"What does 'thirteen' mean?" I whispered back, matching the murmur.

"Well, there's twelve of us. Was. We got Abel, Crow, Pope, Oyster, you know, all of us here. I'm Patches, by the way."

So I made thirteen.

"They said to us, 'Once we get Thirteen, we start the program.' I've been here about three months, and I wasn't the first. But Duck came in a week and a half ago, and then we've just been waiting.

And here you are. Thirteen. I guess the program's started."

"What duck came in?" I asked.

A muffled chuckle sounded below. "He's a kid, sleeps over there. Don't worry about it. You'll meet them tomorrow."

"What's the program?"

"The Forgiveness program."

I chewed on this for a moment. "Is that good or bad?"

"I never heard anything good about it but maybe better than staying here? We'll find out tomorrow. Unless the spraggers are stringing us along."

I scrutinized the ceiling, scanning small shadows in the plaster. "But I just got here."

"Go to sleep," Patches mumbled. The room had grown silent.

Blood pounded in my ear against my pillow as I thought. Unforgiven, the Forgiveness program… the whispered names the State gave to sanitize the rumors. Only whispers, though, few voices. No one knew what the program was because it seemed no one came out.

*

I was shocked awake by a wash of light, accompanied by the bang of the door and footsteps. "Up!" came a sharp command. Men scrambled out of bed, and I quickly followed. The man who'd called himself Patches rolled off the bunk beneath mine.

His hair was a motley mess with several spots, a couple black, one grey, but mostly different shades of brown. He met my eye and extended a hand, shaking mine with a smile and a single nod of his head.

26

A few bunks away I saw the kid who must have been Duck. He was tall and skinny and had the look of being all grown up but not yet "grown up." He was standing at a relaxed attention. In fact, everyone was: rigid, eyes forward. I quickly copied them.

"Boys!" the voice spoke. A woman's voice. It snapped like all the schoolteachers I'd ever hated. "There is a deviation from the schedule today." She spun on her heel and strode out of the room.

The others relaxed. I found her statement alarming, given what Patches had said. He again met my eye, arching his eyebrows suggestively.

The other Unforgiven began to move. The biggest man I had ever seen emerged from behind a stack of bunks, and my eyes followed him, wide. He was huge, all muscle and thick bone.

"Who's that?" I asked.

"Kodiak," Patches said, with a touch of a grin.

"Kodiak," I echoed. It made sense. I could imagine him trampling the forest, knocking trees flat. "What's he, uh…" I broke off. "Is he Unforgiven?"

Patches laughed. "By which you mean, 'What'd he do, and will he rip my arms off if I crank him up?'" He watched me, still with that half grin.

"Roughly," I said.

"Don't know!" Patches rejoined. Too quickly, as if he'd rehearsed the line on others before me. "Haven't cranked him yet. Don't be the first, though," he said, patting me on the shoulder as he squeezed past to join the exodus.

I followed, keeping close. Gentle giants don't live in the Hall of the Unforgiven. I scanned the rest of them, casing for other threats.

Most looked like the people I passed on the street. Some like Suits, some like Coveralls, but just people.

A small man watched me intently, as I'd just watched this Kodiak, from the corner of the room. He was grizzled with the hint of a beard that I'm sure the guards could not get ahead of, even if they shaved him every day. We made eye contact, and he just stared. I hurried to the door. At least he was small.

Another man stood in the doorway, half blocking the opening. At first I thought he was a guard, some kind of doorman, but he wore pale blue and his hair was cropped close.

Men squeezed past in the space he left, some exchanging a glance or a nod. The man directly in front of me shoved the doorman against the frame to make space and walked through with shoulders squared.

The doorman batted the back of his head as he passed, not entirely unfriendly. The one who had done the shoving walked on without a word.

I fixed my eyes on the wall beyond the hallway and hurried with deliberate steps, attempting my own passage. This was no longer The Outside, with tea and broken doors. Here, there were hoses and fists.

"Hey," the doorman said, raising a hand as if to grab my shoulder.

"No," I said, and kept walking. The doorman did not take hold of me, and he said nothing more.

*

The *clack clack clack* of the school teacher beat out a pace down the hall. She was far ahead, and I couldn't see her past Kodiak.

As I hurried to catch Patches, a hand grabbed my shoulder.

"No," I said again, attempting to shrug it off, but it clamped tighter.

"I didn't ask anything."

Turning, I found a man in grey, not pale blue, with a full head of hair and a moustache. A guard.

He held me as the rest of the Unforgiven streamed past. The Doorman caught my eye as he slipped by, but I read nothing in his face.

When we were alone, this guard guided me, by the shirt he still held in his hand, to a door leading off the hallway. I watched the backs of the other prisoners recede from me. None looked back.

The guard shoved me in.

Something rested on a table. An electrical device, probably a weapon. The guard shut the door behind me, and there was the click of a lock.

I spun. "Look, don't–"

"Amos said you can fix that," he interrupted.

Several heartbeats passed while my pulse spiraled back down. Only then did I notice the shelves; we were in a supply closet. I picked up the device.

"Procurement will take a day's wages if I turn it in broken."

I said nothing.

"I'd consider it a favor if you fix it."

I looked afresh at the man, leaning against the inside of the closed door. I didn't know my options, didn't know the consequence of any decision I now made. I took a screwdriver from a nearby shelf and sat.

For fifteen minutes, neither of us spoke. He stood behind me. When I finished, I rose and took the shock weapon in my hand, turning to the guard. His face was calm, but I found him with a matching weapon already in hand, pointed at my chest.

"Here," I said, handing it to him.

He took it, pocketing both once I was unarmed. Then he gave me a coin with a large 'P' written on it.

"Thanks," he said.

He unlatched the door and left.

*

I turned the coin in my hand, unsure what I had just earned. Evidently, something of value. *A favor*, he had said. In a passing thought, I wondered how many coins it would take to buy my way out.

I slipped back into the hallway and turned in the direction the others had last been heading, hoping to find them before someone found me alone and drew the wrong conclusion.

A p-coin. A barter system. Perhaps I could build a ladder out of this Hall, out of this *Program*. I would need friends, status, access... possibly some compromising information. There could be a way.

It was nothing more than a collection of idle thoughts by the time I heard voices and smelled butter in the air. A dozen meters later I found the Unforgiven in a mess hall.

Bright floodlights were spaced on the ceiling, marking the corners of squares with harsh light. Along one wall, and raised a few steps from the floor, men and women in grey were seated, eating with subdued conversation. Guards.

Along the opposite wall a set of tables were laid out with two piles, one of eggs and one of bread.

Between, Kodiak sat at a table with the Doorman and one other. They spoke quietly and sparsely, focused on eating. Patches sat at a table with three others, and the rest filled a larger table, also filling the room with their noise.

I walked toward the tables when my plate was covered, eggs over bread. Patches noticed and kicked out an empty chair. "Thirteen!" He called.

He pointed to a grey-headed man as I sat. "Stump." The man nodded. With the luster of his skin and the hard muscles in his jaw and neck, he was more hale than aged. The lights overhead reflected off his thick glasses.

"Nice to meet you," I said. Stump gave no further acknowledgement.

"Thatcher doesn't talk much," said another man. "Probably senile." The speaker was tall and wiry. He sat head and shoulders above me but probably weighed ten kilos less.

"Crow here talks plenty, though," Patches said, indicating the gangly man. "Plenty for all of us. I'd be indebted if you can get him to shut up."

"You out-talk me two-to-one," Crow said, stuffing a bite into his mouth. "But you babble. I say what everyone else is thinking.

Senile, right?"

"That's enough, Crow," Stump said.

"Huh. That's what your mother always said. Usually not till four in the morning, though."

The old man shook his head over his food, refusing the bait.

"So…" Patches drew out the word and turned back to me. "This is Scarecrow. A man who needs no introduction once he's opened his mouth. You can call him Crow. Or you can ignore him entirely."

I held my peace, not ready to pick sides.

Patches looked up and over my shoulder. "Can we help you?"

Another man had approached and now stood behind me, plate empty. He was broad shouldered and light haired. He stared into me with drawn brows as if I were one of the desk janitor's failure reports. He wore Unforgiven blues.

"What are you?" the man asked.

"What do you mean?" I said.

"What do you do?"

"I'm a janitor."

He frowned to himself as he stared over my head. Then he walked off without a word and began grabbing more eggs.

"His name's Thirteen!" Patches called after him, with no response.

"Stuck up Spire prick," Crow said.

"Five weeks and he never comes off it," Patches said, ignoring Crow. "You aren't Spire are you? You look like you're made of better stuff."

"I live in the communes," I said quickly, omitting my daily trip to the Spires for the last eight years.

"Communes," Patches said, with a gesture to his chest. "Stump here, Outskirts. He's practically still got thatch in his hair, but he's solid." A point with his fork indicated the last man at the table. "Now Oyster here, he grew up way outside. But he tried to go Spire. Didn't you?"

The last man at our table had been silent so far. He did not remind me of an Oyster, unless it was his round face, a touch shorter and touch wider than others at the table. He had short black hair growing in on his shorn head. His hand fidgeted on a fork, two more of which sat unused on a napkin by his plate. He narrowed his eyes.

"At least they had the foresight to save the world," Oyster said. "They're the ones who built the towers, got off the grid, tried to do something."

"Cocky spraggers," Crow talked over him. "So their great-great-great-grandparents did something right and yours burnt the world. Doesn't matter. Those guys didn't do anything. Those guys," he jabbed a fork and dropped egg on the table, "are an outsized bucket of buttpiss in a giant, Spire shaped bucket."

"Well, at least they kept blueprints of the toilet, so they can take care of themselves," I said. Crow cocked his head and stared me down.

I stared back.

Patches threw back his head and laughed. "I like him!"

I leveraged the interruption to break eye contact, even as my stomach slowly turned. *What am I doing?* I had no idea who these men were.

I thought I wasn't picking sides.

"Maybe that's exaggeration," Patches said, defusing the tension. "But be careful. Those Spire pricks did something real to get in here. Us from the outskirts, doesn't matter. You cough wrong you might end up in the Hall. Those guys," he indicated the other tables with a quick nod, "they done stuff."

Oyster and Crow both grunted at that. I surveyed the larger, louder table. The man who'd interrupted us before filling up on eggs was with them.

"What'd you do?" Patches asked. "Run over someone's dog?"

"Something like that," I said, hoping the moment's hesitation went unnoted.

Oyster and Crow grunted again. I didn't speak further, listening, eating, and contemplating my coin instead. Stump was as silent as I, while Patches, Oyster, and Crow talked about the inconsequential things that had happened in their world over the last twenty-four hours.

*

Breakfast ended when the schoolteacher clacked in and prodded us to another room. Four guards leaned on the back wall as they watched us enter, each holding a kind of large barreled gun. Thirteen chairs were set up in three rows, and a man in a uniform leaned against a table set before them.

His uniform was grey like the others but buttoned all the way to the neck. His hair was close-cropped, almost shaved like ours.

However, you would never mistake him for one of us – his back was straight. I immediately named him the Drill Sergeant.

The old man, Stump, put a hand on my back as I hesitated in the door, gently urging me forward. It was neither insistent nor impatient, but unexpectedly reassuring.

"What is this?" I asked as he stepped beside me.

"Don't know," he said.

I followed him into the back row. Crow sat on my other side. While the schoolteacher and drill sergeant conferred at the front, I again scouted the twelve Unforgiven confined with me.

The one with the unshaveable beard and the Spire man who'd asked about my profession were whispering with each other. The others sat quietly, watching the front of the room for something to happen, or speaking in small groups. All seemed agitated.

The Doorman who'd blocked my way in the bunk room sat alone at the end of a row, his chair pulled apart. He could have seemed bored, except for the way, like me, he studied each of us in turn. He alone did not seem lost or agitated. I tried to watch him surreptitiously. I wondered why he'd moved his chair out.

Eventually the schoolteacher retired to the wall. The one light hanging above spread wide enough only to cover the chairs, and she disappeared in the shadow with the guards. The drill sergeant straightened and cleared his throat.

"Unforgiven," he said, "you are here because of your violations against society and against the State, because you have been deemed an unworthy, unproductive, or destructive influence on the world outside this Hall."

There was a murmur.

"But everyone deserves a second chance. I am here today with an opportunity for you to redeem your value to the State."

The murmur became a rustle as men in light blue stopped whispering and sat up to listen.

"The Forgiveness Program is an opportunity to serve and sacrifice for the State. If you complete the program, you will be Forgiven."

"And if we're sacrificed?" an Unforgiven spoke from the other end of the chairs. There was nervous laughter. The joker was fine featured and moved with an expressive grace as he pressed the shoulder of the man next to him.

The drill sergeant waited for the room to quiet, then nodded. There was a muffled thud. A guard had quietly stepped forward from the wall and cuffed the joker's head with his forearm.

The drill sergeant waited longer in silence, then resumed abruptly. "If you complete the program, you will be Forgiven. If you do not, you will not. This will be your only opportunity."

The rustle returned, the murmur invisible, hidden beneath the surface.

"Refusing," he let the word hang, "will not be in your interest."

He pushed a button and the light dimmed. A projection plane appeared in the air, the image splitting the space between us and him. It was a map of the city. There were no lines or words, but I could see the gray sprawl and recognized ridges and lakes in the vicinity.

"You are here," he said. And then the map began to move,

panning down, south, and a little west. It accelerated until I couldn't estimate the kilometers. Where it slowed and stopped was entirely green.

"In 48 hours, you will be here." He strode around the projection to stand beside the image. "These are the Outlands," he continued, and the murmur broke the surface again. Unforgiven sank in chairs.

"Everything you have heard about the Outlands is true. There is no remnant of civilization. There is no one passing through, and there is nowhere to escape if you try to leave. Everything there can and will try to kill you. The water, the plants, and the animals. As well as the inhabitants."

"Inhabitants? You said there's no civilization." Crow said. I leaned into Stump, distancing myself.

The Drill Sergeant looked over Crow's head into the shadows beyond.

Crow raised his hands to protect himself. "Hey! It's an honest question!" His head swiveled left and right, hoping to see behind without turning away. The drill sergeant studied the gangly Unforgiven, assessing which side of impertinence he stood on. We watched for a nod.

"Outlanders," he said instead.

"No." Crow announced and stood up. There was the clatter of several chairs while inarticulate refusals echoed around me.

The guards stepped forward and, using their guns like riot staffs, began shoving Unforgiven back to their seats. In seconds the room collapsed into a tangle of blue and grey, limbs and curses, as fingers knotted into shirts and guards and prisoners strove for mastery. Crow was thrown on top of me, knocking us both to the floor. I stayed down, feeling each shove and blow transmitted through the tight knot of bodies above me, under the single, stark light.

"Silence!" the drill sergeant yelled, a sharp word that filled the room and brought a moment of hesitation into grey and blue alike.

Only the Doorman, in his pale Unforgiven blue, still sat in his chair. A little removed. His arms were crossed on his chest, his legs stretched in front of him. He still studied each of us with an impassive expression.

"I have been authorized to ensure you listen," the drill sergeant said. "Sit. This is your only warning."

A few men quickly righted chairs and sat down. Others moved more slowly. The chairs did not quite find their former, orderly rows.

Satisfied, the sergeant strode behind the plane to stand closer to where Stump, Crow, and I sat. He watched us as he spoke.

"You may have heard that Outlanders are nothing but men and women. By a strict definition, this is true," he said. "Or you may have heard they are something more or less than human. This is more true."

What I had heard were the bedtime stories – animals in the bodies of men, cannibals, wild things. They were the terrors in my closet; they were the reason to be indoors after midnight.

"Your objective," he continued, "is to locate a habitation or gathering ground of these Outlanders and inflict maximum casualties. If successful, you will be extracted. This is the Forgiveness program."

The room had become oppressively silent.

"Why would we…?" Stump mumbled beside me. I looked sideways at him without turning my head. Crow had mentioned he was from the Outskirts. He probably had his own opinions on Outlanders.

I felt a twisting in my stomach somewhere beneath cold ice. I wondered if this is how people feel before they were driven into the woods to be shot.

"Over the next 48 hours you will undergo a medical and skill evaluation. You will receive general and specific training for your assigned responsibilities. You will be equipped, briefed, and deployed. Any questions you have will be answered tomorrow."

He turned to the table and started spreading out some uniflex sheets. "Dismissed," he said over his shoulder as an afterthought.

– THREE –

As we shuffled toward the schoolteacher, the showman who had been cuffed for his joke spoke in animated undertones to the men beside. I followed Stump.

I felt the p-coin in my pocket, testing its weight, turning it from finger to finger. Forty-eight hours. I knew so little. I needed to buy my way off that flyer, out of this program.

As I left, I saw the Doorman standing at the other door with a woman in a skirt and suit. Her face was lined and her hair was pulled into a severe, grey bun. A boy and girl stood a few steps behind her with the look of aides. Access badges hung around all their necks.

She said something to the Doorman, who responded with an emphatic gesture. She spoke again, and he leaned forward, putting his hand on her forearm. I could not hear the words, only an edge in his tone. Her eyes narrowed, but she did not respond to him.

She glanced at me, and the Doorman turned to look as well. I stepped backwards and hurried to disappear into the ball of departing Unforgiven.

*

The room we arrived in was large and open, with concrete walls interrupted only by ancient water stains and exposed piping.

Thirteen folding tables were set out in a way that suggested an initial attempt at order that ended in impatience. Beside each table was a man or woman in a white coat. I felt, more than saw, the Doorman enter the room behind us, last to arrive.

The guards hung by the wall again. I could see more clearly now the large guns they held, low and casual.

"Would they kill us?" I asked, leaning close to Stump.

"Don't ask for trouble."

Whitecoats began peeling Unforgiven off the group, one by one. I made eye contact and a woman beckoned me with a curt gesture.

I stood before her while she marked lines and boxes on her datapad, never looking up. Finally, she glanced at me and said, "Strip."

She spoke the order as if it were a statement. When I didn't move; she simply looked at me, her single word hanging between us.

I glared at my reflection in her flat eyes as I stripped.

She poked and prodded, noting every bit of me on her datapad, inserting needles to pull things out and push other things in. I sat, stood, and laid down with my eyes fixed on infinity.

I felt the urge to flip the table. To shove her away from me. To yell that I was a man and not an animal, that I was not the defect in this machine. I was being sent to the Outlands, probably to die. I felt myself at the bottom of a deep well, looking up at faces peering down.

I saw the guards. I saw the Arbiter from the Hall of Judgment in his large chair. I saw those I'd left behind, those who had stood by while I was accused and condemned, all looking down.

They were up there and I was down here, where a cold woman with cold hands pulled my arms up to feel my lymph nodes.

She made a final note on her datapad and walked away.

Most other men were already done and dressed as I covered myself. I waited by my table, watching the guards at the back. Their guns had unusually large barrels. I wondered what was inside.

When all examinations were ended, the schoolteacher took us to a kind of lobby where we again clustered in murmurs and silence.

After only a minute a different lady entered the room. She tapped men one by one, telling me "room 27" and directing me down a hall. I went, and I opened the door marked 27 without knocking.

*

Bright sunlight streamed through two large windows and fell across the floor. A desk and two stuffed chairs occupied the room, and a tall plant with broad leaves stood in the corner. The room, from a bookshelf in the corner to the worn, brown carpet, had a dustiness that felt more warm than worn. There was something distinctly…un-Hall-ish about it.

I stopped one step inside the doorway, looking across the room and out the windows, to sunlight and the world outside. There were blue skies, white clouds, and birds, flying in line to cover the distance together.

I crossed the room and put a hand on the glass. A moment later, a voice at my shoulder said, "I love this window." I found a short man beside me. He was mostly bald and was wearing the same clothes he'd probably worn for thirty years, judging by the wrinkles and the palette. He was smiling.

I turned back to the window without response.

"Please sit with me." The man walked to one of the stuffed chairs, facing away from the window, and gestured to the chair with the view.

I schooled my face to cold impassivity. I owed the man nothing and planned to give him little more than that. He rifled through a folder full of actual papers instead of uniflex sheets. I sat.

"So," he asked without looking up, "what are they calling you?"

"Thirteen."

He grinned. "You could do worse. Thirteen, then," and he was already back in his papers. "I am Henry. You work as a building engineer?"

I didn't answer. It was written on his papers.

"Is that primarily a cleaning job?" he asked.

"I fix things."

He adjusted his glasses, looking up. "What sort of things?"

"Anything."

He flicked his pencil tip at me, remembering something, and walked to his desk to rummage through his drawers. He returned a moment later with a device.

He turned the object over in his hands. "This hyperphonic broke many, many years ago."

He handed me the box and sat down. "My son still has the working one. We have a lot of memories, just the two of us, talking over these boxes. But it's old now, and I haven't found anyone who can fix it anymore."

I turned the box over in my hands, only listening with half an ear now. "What tools do you have?"

I dimly thought of earning an H-coin, or stealing a wrench, but I really just wanted to open the box and see how it worked.

He returned to the desk and brought out a screwdriver and an antique letter opener. I quickly worked the pins and seams.

"I have wanted to give it to him, so he and my grandson can use them. Oh, I know there's a million new gadgets out there they could use instead, but there's something... personal... knowing your boxes connect directly and only to each other. I guess I'm sentimental."

I hadn't seen a hyperphonic before. I'd heard about them, basically secure point-to-point radios with generous line-of-sight and distance limitations, but the old man was right - there was a wealth of better tech now. Tech that passed through the State's network.

My fingers and eyes eagerly took in the parts, parsing the obvious before gingerly tracing the known right to the edge of the unknown. My eyes unfocused as my mind took over the map, linking each wire, divining function from form. Certain lumps of metal shone salient and others faded into the clean, crosshatched web of circuitry. The machine's flow coalesced, and it was beautiful. Beautiful old tech, like the dusty shelves and worn carpet. A few minutes more and I'd isolated the thin, loose spots where the electric flow ran dry.

"Can you fix it?" he asked, softly now, standing behind the chair.

"I can fix anything."

"What do you need?"

A moment later I was on the intercom with a "building engineer," with a list of tools and parts. I had meant to stonewall this man, but he had put a screwdriver in my hand.

As we waited for the materials to arrive, he sat back in his chair, no longer looking at the papers. "Can you really fix anything?"

"Yes," I said.

"Have you been inside a maglock generator?"

"I have."

"Hydraulics? Computers? A rehumidifier?"

"Anything that goes in a Spire," I said. "Give me a few minutes with it, and I'll figure it out."

"So you just see it, and you understand?"

"That's right."

"How?"

I leaned heavily onto my knees. Perhaps Henry's interest was curiosity, perhaps a challenge. Either way, we had entered my domain.

"Do you believe in chaos?" I asked.

Henry thought. "In a fashion, I suppose."

"No such thing," I said. "Everything has a reason for existing. This hyperphonic was *designed*, for a purpose. All the parts connect for that purpose, and they all flow from the source. Because no power, no purpose."

"Unless it's broken," Henry said.

"The world is a complicated place," I said. "Things wear out and get knocked, that's the *reality* but it isn't the *design*. You give me this box, I can start at the source and trace it until I find something I don't understand. But whatever sits in that gap, what I don't understand, is still there for a reason. It connects to the things designed around it. So I look, I push and pull and feel until I understand. And if it's broken – it was made once before. I can patch it or remake it. Whatever it needs."

Henry wore a curious smile. "You realize not everyone can see like that?"

I sat back and shrugged. I'd never had to think about *how* before or defend it. It simply worked.

"I suppose, but I don't know why. Whether it's a circuit or an engine, any system is just source, pathways, and purpose."

The door opened and a man entered with a proper toolbox. I took the tools and dug deeper into the hyperphonic as our conversation devolved into the trivial. Henry had dabbled in repairing his own plumbing or his vehicles but had broken more than he fixed and had a million questions.

I gave him half an ear, but this gift was better than the windows and sunlight. I scraped out the scoring and built new pathways of fresh, shining metal in the gaps. Minute by minute, the hyperphonic was remade.

Before long I handed him the box, resealed. "Turn it on."

He chuckled as he lugged the box back to his desk. He quickly connected it to a source and flipped the switch. There was a whine as it powered, growing higher and higher until it faded beyond audibility. And the running light was on. Henry looked up with glistening eyes. "Thank you," he said to me, before reverently putting the box down on his desk, walking back and sitting down again, repeating the words a little louder.

He took a moment, removing his glasses to wipe his eyes before settling himself. "Thank you, Thirteen," he said a final time. "My apologies, sorry, truly sorry. As I said, I'm sentimental."

I held up a hand but said nothing.

"To the business at hand, though." He laid the folder aside and placed his elbows on his knees, like a father preparing to lecture his son. "You said you fix anything and everything. Why a janitor?"

The question broke on me like the cold bucket the night before. "Is this relevant?"

"Yes, Thirteen. With this gift, why a janitor?"

"What are we doing here?" I asked.

"Ah," he said. "I am meant to evaluate your 'native skills and mental fitness in support of role allocation and materiel outfitting for the duration of the program,' is what it says."

He gave an apologetic smile at my confused expression. I studied the man sitting across from me, again letting myself wonder if he was worth the conversation. "What's wrong with being a janitor?" I asked.

"Nothing, there is nothing wrong," he said. "Objectively speaking, though, it is not the most... well, lucrative option available to you."

This was true.

"Don't you ever want to build something of your own, something new? Surely you'd be capable of such a task?"

"We're all capable," I said. Something sensitive twitched under the weight of his question. "You're a smart man. Why do you chat with Unforgiven for a living?"

Henry pulled his chin into his chest and looked at his lap, as if collecting his thoughts. Then he leaned in close.

"Yet here we are. Your time is short. If I can help you, at all, and the next Unforgiven, and the next, my work is worthwhile." He held my eyes for a moment, then sat back. "Tell me, why a janitor?"

I scrutinized his face. In the quiet I grew conscious of the sun warming my hand, where it fell on the chair.

"And this is help?" I asked.

He brought his hand up to his face, pushed his glasses up his nose, and curled a loose fist in front of his mouth.

"What's in that folder?" I asked.

"Name, age, weight. Birthdate, employment, former address, crime, sentence. Paperwork."

"Family?"

"Names."

I leaned into the chair and looked at the ceiling. The fabric was soft and smelled like the library room at the museum. I felt the space of the long years behind me.

"My father was a building engineer. A janitor."

"A talented one?" Henry asked.

"A dedicated one."

"Tell me about him."

"He worked lakeside." I could still hear his voice. Gruff but warm, always shouting but never angry. "Just a man keeping a tower clean and running for the State. Funny thing is, there are only three people with all the keys: the boss, the security man, and the janitor."

"What happened?"

"People asked to be let into certain rooms. He refused. So they asked him to leave the doors unlocked. Gave him guarantees."

"What were they after?" Henry asked.

I shrugged, eyes still on the ceiling.

"What did he do?" Henry asked.

"He always said you've got to do what's right. Seventeen days later, he walked home with a crushed hand and a small severance." I remembered sitting in the chair by the fireplace the day he came home, arm wrapped in red-stained white cloth.

"What had happened to him?" Henry asked.

"Circumstantial, they called it. I can read circumstance, though. But he was out, and someone else got the keys."

"What happened to your family after that?"

"We got hungry," I said. And we sat in silence for a time.

*

Henry was too polite to nudge me onward. But in the silence, I wandered through the memories and took up the thread at the next scene. "His hand healed. Good as new, but he never worked again."

"They wouldn't take him back?" Henry asked.

"Someone would have. But he wouldn't go. Stubborn thatcher. He did odd jobs around the community, anything to bring something home, food or money."

I smiled then. Despite everything, these were fond memories: the grey headed man in old worn shoes, a toolbox in one hand and a coterie of children following him around to see what was next.

"Winter and summer, he walked the town. He was a beggar, but he was beloved. People trusted him. When you needed a job done, when you needed your child looked after, you went to Dad."

"Was it enough?" Henry asked.

I began to shake my head. It hadn't been. I read the titles of the books on Henry's shelf while I told the rest. "When he got sick there was nothing we could do. Mother, she called him a fool. Told him none of it had to be that way. He was too proud, stubborn as the weeds. She walked out on him five days before he died.

"I stayed. It was fall, and we had the windows open so the leaves and rain on the air might cover his dying breath. I was in the chair in the corner, down past his feet. He couldn't lift his head, but he opened his eyes at the end and looked at me. 'Hold your head high,' he said. And he was gone. When we buried him, I couldn't see to the end of the crowd that gathered."

"I'm sorry," Henry said.

I waved my hand, brushing aside the sympathy.

Henry slowly turned the handful of pages in his folder. He placed a hand on one and studied it for a moment. "When did you decide to follow in his footsteps?"

"As soon as I could. I told you, we were hungry."

Henry laughed. It wasn't funny, just blunt. "Did you love him?"

There had been something beautiful in the disaster that had been my father. "I loved him for who he was and hated him for what he did to us. I made two promises the day he died: do what's right and take care of my own."

"Then what happened?"

"Nothing happened."

Henry's fingers lingered on another page. "How did you end up here?"

I turned my hand over, curling and uncurling the fingers. I reined in my temper, schooling my voice into an even monotone. "I'm not a murderer."

"What are you?"

"I'm a man who's lost his home. Ripped from my wife when she needs me most." I was leaning toward Henry, my voice raised. "My head is high. I've done what's right, everything I can."

I fell back and my voice dropped, now a bitter edged thing. "Just, one day, everything went wrong. And you brand me Unforgiven and sacrifice me in the name of your Justice." Henry flipped the page. I hardened my voice. "I am not the broken piece in this machine, Henry. I'm not a murderer."

He looked at the papers and spoke quietly. "Your wife spoke against you."

I stared at him, breathing heavily. It was a bitter twist.

A knock came at the door. A young man poked his head in and asked Henry if he was done. Henry looked at his watch and told him we'd finish in a moment.

"Thirteen?" he asked, now with a purposeful edge. "I need to ask you a few more specific questions."

I nodded, mute.

"Are you knowledgeable about guns or weaponry?"

I had trouble pivoting with him. My thoughts were in turmoil. "No," I said.

"Have you ever fired one? Or demolitions?"

"No."

"Any experience in outdoor survival?"

"No." My stomach began to turn.

"Emergency medicine? Field medicine? Anything at all?"

Nothing of the sort.

The questions continued. No to maps and orienteering. Never negotiated. No special education in chemistry, biology, botany, zoology. No professional or amateur athletics. In short, nothing they were looking for. Finally Henry laid his pen down and studied his papers, then gave me an inscrutable look.

"What now?" I asked, tired fear flowing past ebbing anger. Based on his hurried questions, I had no "native skills" outside a Spire basement, and he had given no window to his conclusion on my mental fitness. "Am I a dead man?"

It was the real question. Henry did not meet my eye. He shook his head almost imperceptibly, and his face softened.

"You have a gift. An invaluable one. Most squads don't have someone with your talents." But he faltered. "And Abel is a good man..."

That was the end of the skill evaluation. Henry wrote a few things, signed something and, closing the folder, handed it to me. I stood and took a long, last look out the window and the birds wheeling on the city's thermals.

As I left that office, all Henry said was, "Good luck, Thirteen."

In the silence that followed I heard one thing clearly; he had never answered my last question.

– FOUR –

I was led back to the mess hall where we had eaten breakfast. The guards' tables sat empty, and the room felt oppressive in the comparative quiet.

A handful of Unforgiven already sat at a table, leaning close, speaking low. The serving table that was full a few hours before now held only loaves of bread, thin cuts of meat, a block of cheese, and something green in a tray.

I took a plate and stared into the food.

"What's on your mind?"

Patches stood across from me, not exactly grinning. There was a tautness around his eyes as he speared a series of thin meat slices with a plastic fork.

"Scanning the menu, I guess."

He tossed a slice of bread neatly onto my plate. "Eat up."

"Yeah," I said. I spun the bread with my fingers so the flat side faced me, but made no further move toward the meal.

"Build your sandwich," Patches said, his voice lower, now devoid of play.

"Build my sandwich. That's what I do. I build a sandwich." I grabbed the fork and began spearing meat, one after another.

"You had other plans?" Patches asked.

"They asked me about my father in there," I said.

"They asked me about my allergies," Patches said, "and time in the Wilderness Scouts when I was ten."

I put a thumb on the cold meat and held it down to pull the fork out. I left it where it lay, bunched, spilling over the edges of the bread. "I just wanted a roof, a family, a safe street to walk down. Plants in the corner and a tank with a fish in it."

Patches slid a bottle with some pink sauce in it toward me, lost in thoughts of his own. "Seems far away now."

I left the bottle on my side of the serving table, unused. "Just a place to call home. Was that too much to ask?"

Patches gazed into his slice of meat, as if the lines and creases could reveal life and fortune. "It wasn't too much to ask. But it's gone."

I met his eye across the pile of meat and shook my head. He gave a weak smile, finding himself again, and puffed a laugh. "Guys like us, Unforgiven, you roll with it."

I jammed the vegetable spoon back into its tray. "Sounds like giving up."

Patches shrugged.

"You think you deserve this?"

He shrugged again.

"Well, I don't."

Patches grimaced at his plate and moved a few steps down the table. "What are you going to do?" he asked.

"Well, I've got this," I said, pulling out my p-coin. "It's a start."

Patches laughed, now a genuine laugh. "Ah, you met Piro! What's the master plan? A pack of cigarettes? Or a stick of nudies?"

"No," I growled, and shoved the coin deep in my pocket. Maybe he lacked the imagination to assemble the possibilities. Maybe he just knew what I didn't. "I'm going to figure out how this system works. Finish the program if I have to. I'm going home."

Patches stopped serving himself and let the large fork rest on his plate. He rubbed his ear, then looked at me. "Look, don't take this the wrong way."

"Take what?"

He paused to choose his words. "You're talking like this program is a ticket out? It's not that kind of ticket."

I stared him down, across the table.

"They don't print those tickets. Look, I can tell you how this thing works, if that's what you want."

"What?" I said. "It's cranked, we're spragged, oh well, stupid world?"

For the briefest moment, Patches was without a response.

"Yeah," is all he said, quietly, finding his feet.

I looked at my sandwich. I hated the thought.

"Hey," Patches said. He came around the end of the table and grabbed my shoulder, scooping up the unused bottle of sauce and turning me toward the chairs. "I know how you feel. Nedder, I wish I still felt like that." He let out a deep sigh and released my shoulder. "Let me know when you figure it out. The moment you figure it out, yeah?"

He didn't believe it. But there was kindness in his

condescension.

"Yeah," I said.

*

We took our plates and joined the others. The tables were pushed together to form a large clover shape. Six Unforgiven sat around the edge like a giant roundtable and argued in quiet voices.

I knew the faces by now but I was still gathering names. Duck, the youngest, was there, along with old Stump. Duck looked even smaller now, or they'd given him the wrong size pajamas, as his shirt hung loose around his frame. The Showman, who had incurred the wrath of the drill sergeant in the briefing, was balancing his chair on two legs. He had a sharp nose and a sharp jaw, fine features that cast shadows beneath the overhead lights.

There was also the one who'd asked me my profession before ignoring me, who I'd labeled "the Spire," and two others I knew not at all. One had thick glasses and the other was the bearded man who had so unsettled me in the bunkroom.

As I sat, Duck was lecturing his elders. "In the Outlands, the devil walks free. They say when the moon is full, they kill their own. Everybody, killed."

"Good," said the Showman. "So, no one left to bother us?"

"No!" said Duck. He gestured with his hands, pushing one loose sleeve up to his elbow. "The devil brings them back! But they come back twice as mean. The next time they get killed, they do it twice as dark and twice as mean, because the ones they bring back don't feel pain anymore."

"Less appealing," said the Showman, bringing his chair down

to all fours. The faces at the table were mixed, some smiling at the simpleminded superstition and others troubled, recalling stories they had heard.

"The only way to kill them for real is to eat them. So, they eat each other. That's why I said, 'they're going to eat us.'"

The Showman lifted his sandwich in the air and let it fall open, limp bread spilling a few small leaves of lettuce and the dry meat to his plate. His lips slid into a theatric, practiced grin. "Getting warmer again. You might sell me on this."

"Don't tease! I'm serious. It's the truth."

The man with the glasses leaned forward on his elbows. His body was still as he cleared his throat, the combination silencing the room as he drew all eyes. "The truth is much less macabre." He was not as old as Stump, but his hair was graying. He had fine features, nearly expressionless as he began to lecture.

Crow pulled up a chair at the table and dropped his plate with a clatter, popping Glasses' bubble of rapt attention. "You and your truth," he said. "It stinks like bullfart when you open your mouth."

Glasses directed a tight smile at Crow and continued.

"The seventeen technocracies saw it coming. They were already off-grid when the power went out and the Oil Wars began. Everyone else kept smoking and kept killing until the Earth finally turned on them. The technocracies shut out the smokers and hunkered down, and those left outside faced the Cataclysm."

"And ten years later," the Showman proclaimed, tilting his chair again, "the State and the sixteen other technocracies ushered in a golden era of prosperity and enlightenment!" He knocked his chair all the way backward as he stood and took in the room with a sweep of his plate, his bread and meat falling everywhere. "And then I made a better sandwich, because this one tasted like bedsheets."

There were a few chuckles.

"You still biting the pillows?" Crow asked.

"No, simply

Dreaming sweet dreams
of prettier things
entwined, enshrined above me"

The Showman hummed to himself at the serving table, making a sandwich identical to the one he'd destroyed.

"Everyone knows how they got there," Duck accused Glasses. "I'm telling you what they are now."

"No, the point is, 'Outlanders' are just what's left," said Glasses. "No infrastructure, no education, no power, no civilization. The rustics who survived – nothing more, nothing less."

"I'm telling you! They worship the devil. They'll eat you alive and wear your skin. They'll burn you under the full moon!" Duck cried, agitated.

The Doorman had quietly entered, and I wondered if he'd had a psychological evaluation like the rest of us or finished a closed-door conversation with the matriarch in grey. He moved among the bread and meat. His head was down, preparing a tower of three sandwiches, but his head was tilted, taking in every word at the table.

"They're all thatchers," the Spire said, waving a hand as if that ended the conversation. "We'll do for them whatever we need to."

"Hold on," Stump said. He dropped his fork with a clatter and placed a palm on the table, his temples bulging beneath his grey hair as he clenched his jaw before speaking. "These are people. So they don't have the Library, the Mainframe, or any of that State stuff, but they're people. They just don't live in Spires."

"And where did you live, grandpa?" the Spire asked.

"Rail commune," Stump said.

The Spire narrowed his eyes and studied the old man. Stump stared back. "You didn't grow up Rail."

Stump remained nonplussed. "No. I grew up in the outskirts. With the Families."

"Ha!" the Spire said, clapping his hands at the guess. "Family warboy. Bunch of rustic thatchers. We've got an Outlander right here!"

"I'm a Family man," Stump said, lacing the word with pride to replace the Spire's contempt.

"What was your roof made out of?"

"Thatch." There was no hesitation in Stump's response.

"A right thatcher. I don't know what this program is, but there's Outlander number one." He threw out a hand in a casual gesture and turned back to his food. A piece of beef slapped him across the head.

His eyes snapped up, glaring in the direction of the offending meat and finding Crow. He leapt to his feet and rushed at Crow, who was affectedly oblivious to the offense, trying to take a bite of his sandwich.

Stump and Glasses were too slow to intercept, and the two men grappled on the floor. A moment later the Spire was grabbed by his shoulders and hauled off the gangly man. Crow was left on the ground, cackling.

Without a word, the Spire straightened his shirt and walked back to his seat. He held his sandwich and took a large bite while staring down Crow.

"All this fuss. Over nothing. It's not real. It's never real," a new voice said in the ensuing silence. "You'll see."

The bearded man sat behind an empty plate, fingertips pressed together. He sat shorter than those beside him, but rounded shoulders and a sharp voice gave him presence nonetheless. He now took in the table with the same unblinking gaze I'd received in the bunkroom.

"We may never know what they truly wanted from us," he said. "But hear this, there is no such thing as the Forgiveness program."

Duck interrupted, "What if there is? Why would they do all this if they weren't sending us somewhere?"

"Oh, they may send us somewhere," the Beard said. "The question is whether you, or anyone else, could ever come back. The question is what game they are playing. And the real question, Duck, is whether you will play."

I was watching the Doorman, trying to divine what he thought of all this. He was chewing his sandwiches too deliberately, as if trying to look natural.

"Oh, drop it," Glasses said. "Look around you: they have us by the balls. They tell us to eat; we eat. They tell us to clean; we clean. They tell us to die; we die. Why fabricate all this drama?"

"Because," the Spire said, squinting at the Beard, as if seeing him for the first time, "the spraggers need a story to tell about why we disappeared."

The Beard inclined his head toward the Spire, like a king bestowing a favor on a subject.

"So they can experiment on us or sacrifice us to the volcano god, or whatever it is they do," the Showman added around a mouthful of food. He pointed at the Spire while nodding at Duck, an exhortation to listen.

"Explain: Why are they telling the story to *us*, then?" Glasses asked.

"Wait, we aren't going to the Outlands?" Duck asked before the Beard could answer.

"It would not surprise me if we did not go to the Outlands," the Beard said, not quite answering the question.

"Always the ominous hints," Glasses said. "You don't know anything."

A twinkle appeared in the Beard's eye, almost a wink. "I know I will not play their game."

This silenced the table for a time.

"I don't know. Seems either way, the spraggers mean to kill us," Crow said.

"But maybe not?" Duck asked.

"Have you ever met a Forgiven?" Crow countered.

"No one out there is Forgiven," Spire said, his tone wishing to disagree with his own words. "You heard them – unfit for society. What motive would they have to send us back out as if nothing had ever happened?"

He sat back. Most of the men examined their food; some pushed bits around with forks.

"It's real." The Doorman spoke, and all heads turned and looked at him.

"And what do you know?" Crow asked.

The Doorman looked at him, as if weighing him, but did not answer.

Finally Patches spoke, "I knew someone who was Forgiven." All heads swiveled again. "Well, a friend does. He says there's a guy who runs a hardware store over in the Cobalt district. My friend goes in there every week, knows the guy real well. Anyway, this guy came out of the Forgiveness program. He won't talk about it much, never told my friend what it was or how he did it. But he's a Forgiven, and now he runs a hardware store in the Cobalt district."

"What's his name?" the Doorman asked.

Patches didn't know.

More silence. A friend of a friend who didn't talk much about it. It was a spiderweb to grab at as you fell from a bridge. All around us were empty halls and empty rooms. What happened to those who came before? *Dead or Forgiven.* And only one of us had heard of a Forgiven.

Glasses cleared his throat. "Well, we'll know in 48 hours. No need to keep arguing about it."

For a long time after that, the only sound was the steady clink of Stump's fork, putting in one bite after another. Oyster entered with Kodiak, the two in animated discussion about what they would do after they were Forgiven, but when they sat and saw us, they too fell silent.

*

They put us outside for an hour after lunch. They called it "freshening." The door was locked behind us and three guards were left to watch the thirteen. One carried one of the large barreled guns; the others had things attached to their belts that I could not identify.

The yard was stone and concrete, with short weeds growing where the stonework cracked. Three sides were exterior walls of the buildings, while the fourth was a wire fence looking out beyond the border of the State proper.

The other Unforgiven wandered slowly, talking in groups. I walked to the fence and stuck my fingers through, to the outside. We were still high up, maybe fifty meters above true ground. I could see trees and, beyond them, a lake.

It wasn't our lake.

I remembered that day I was sick. I didn't go to Abbey Spire. You went to the bakery, as always. Left at sunrise to start the ovens. Midmorning I thought I needed sun, so I took a canteen and made my slow way to the lakeshore. I was lying under a tree, dozing in the shade, when our heavy, grey blanket fell on me.

"It's too cold out for you here today," you said.

"How did you find me?" I asked, opening my eyes.

You laughed and sat. You would have cuffed my head if you

didn't know I was ill. "I had you watched."

"What? How?" I asked, sitting up. Then, "Why?" That was probably the most pertinent.

"You honestly don't realize you sit by the lake every time you get sick?"

"I do?"

"You do, metalman."

You gave me tea and bread covered with herbed butter. You said the herbs would make me better. Then I slept with my head on your leg while you watched the breeze on the water into the afternoon.

*

I was still there at the fence, my fingers half free while the rest of me remained imprisoned, when Patches appeared. I felt him study me, but I did not want to come back from those memories.

He cleared his throat. "You're making them uncomfortable."

"Me?" I asked.

"It isn't normal. Everyone else – except Kodiak maybe – hung by the guards when they got here. Or followed someone around. They were nervous, started looking for friends. For protection. You didn't say a word all lunch, and now you're standing here at the fence. It isn't normal."

"I'm sorry," I said.

"So there's two schools of thought," Patches continued, leaning on the fence. "Some are saying you got whacked pretty hard by the greysuits on your way in, and you don't know where you are. The others are saying you're a crazed, homicidal maniac, and you're planning how you're going to kill us."

I looked at my fingertips, still hanging over the expanse. I had always thought they were for building, for fixing. "Which do you think?" I asked.

"I think you're planning to kill us," he said. "But they voted me over here. If you go all feral and start eating me or something, then the rest know to scatter."

I laughed. "I'm a janitor."

"Oh right, you said that. And this place is full of mops and buckets. They make us clean once a week. Is that how you'll do it? With two mops and a bucket?" He was smiling.

"I was looking at the lake."

"Don't," he said, his tone shifting. "That's not your life anymore. Better to face the wall. Then you won't be disappointed when you wake in the middle of the night."

I left my fingers poking through the fence. I breathed the air. I needed to remember. This was not my home.

"Why two mops?" I asked.

Patches laughed. "My imagination can run wild. Sorry. But are you a wizard with a mop? You could really help us out on Tuesdays. Not that we'll be here any more Tuesdays."

"I had people to do that for me."

"Ah," he said. "*Head* janitor."

"Yeah."

"Spire janitor?"

"Yeah."

"What does the head janitor do in a Spire?"

"Anything. They'd keep us in the basement as much as they could. Plenty of pumps, batteries, and generators down there. But when a building is a kilometer high, you can't stuff all the infrastructure at the bottom."

He exhaled, a gentle laugh, as if to acknowledge how little he knew of such things. "Ever go to the top?"

It was always the question.

"Twice," I said.

"Which one?"

"Abbey."

His eyes moved, but we couldn't see it from here. "What's it like?"

"A spotlight went out. Just an aged-out bulb. I could have sent anyone, but I told them I'd do it myself. Foreman's privilege. You get out there, in a harness, all ropes and clips. Doubled up. You wouldn't believe the wind – so cold and so strong. It tugs at you; it tells you you can fly if you'll just lean into it and… jump. And there's a primal terror that no amount of ropes and clips can whisper away.

"It was maybe ten minutes before I took my first step. Another 20 to climb the infrastructure and find the bulb. A minute to replace the bulb. Then three hours to *look*."

Despite his warnings, Patches now looked out over the trees with me. His eyes were distant, imagining.

"I swear the Earth curves up there. The whole State. Its Spires look like the tips of a mountain range. I saw the ocean. Water, right up to the curve. The other way, mountains. I'm not a poet; I can't tell you what it was like. Just…I spent three hours, looking."

"You said twice?"

I smiled at the memory. "I told them a bird had gotten into a circuit box. Pulled it apart and built a nest. That I needed more tools and parts. Went back up the next day."

Patches barked a laugh. "That settles it. You aren't a killer, just crazy."

"Crazy?" I asked.

"Yeah. I don't like heights."

– FIVE –

When an hour had passed, when we were "fresh," they herded us to general training. I found my way next to Stump again, as he plodded along. I couldn't tell if he didn't understand what was happening to us or didn't care, but his quiet presence was calming.

We filed into a gymnasium with a shapeless pile of fitness equipment heaped to the side. Tables were positioned around the floor, creating a series of stations. One held potted plants. Another held medical equipment. In the middle of the room was a wrestling mat and in the corner, a table of guns.

The list Henry had ticked down scrolled through my mind. These tables were my grid of empty checkboxes. Perhaps I could check some off today. Perhaps each table, every checked box, meant another day alive.

Twenty tables. One afternoon.

I was directed to the shooting range with three men I did not yet know. There was the one I'd named Glasses, not quite as old as Stump and seemingly fond of lectures, and Showman, the fine-featured joker. The third was a slender, dark man, coiled like a whip and gliding like a cat.

The instructor asked if any of us had shot a gun. This third man slid to the table and picked up some kind of rifle. He hefted the gun twice and turned to the instructor. "It isn't loaded."

"Not with real bullets."

He hefted the gun again, studying it more closely. He faced the targets and fired off three quick rounds. Three holes appeared, clustered in the middle of a bullseye.

"I'll move on," he said. And he was gone.

"Eyes of the State," I said to no one in particular.

The Showman stepped beside me put an arm around my shoulders, leaning on me, watching the man retreat.

"You haven't met Taj?" he asked.

"I've hardly met anyone," I said. I watched this "Taj" stalk, heading to another table, until a scuffle erupted in the center of the room. The giant, Kodiak, lifted one of the instructors over his head and threw him onto the mat on the floor. "Eyes of the State," I whispered again.

The Showman turned me back to the table and gave a quiet laugh when I shrugged his arm off. "Well, you can call me Pope."

I took his proffered hand.

Glasses held out his hand as well. "Happy."

"To meet me?"

The Showman barked a laugh.

"No. They call me Happy," the man with the glasses said.

So, the Showman was called 'Pope' and Glasses was called 'Happy.' I amended my mental list.

"I think I'm 'Thirteen,'" I said.

"And don't worry about Taj," Pope said, "he's a big kitten."

I didn't think that metaphor was good. He seemed more like a panther. "What is he?" I asked.

Pope leaned in conspiratorially, still putting theater into every word, and whispered in my ear, "Assassin."

"Are you serious?" I mirrored Pope's soft tone. He was already approaching the weapons on the table. "Why's he called Taj?"

"Doesn't matter," Happy said. He didn't look at all happy behind his glasses.

"What were you, Pope? Priest?" I asked.

Pope laughed again, hollow this time, and returned to a whisper. "Unforgiven don't speak of these things. We are what we are."

I looked questioningly at Happy. "He just likes speeches. Probably big hats, too, if he could get his hands on one."

Pope picked up a long rifle and lifted it up into the light, inspecting its angles. "I, however, was an artist. A painter, a sculptor, a creator."

He turned to the targets. "And I think that you and I, Doctor, may have the hands for these." He handed another of the long rifles to Happy. "Come. Let's see who can hit the eye of the bull."

The Showman and Glasses. An artist and a doctor. Derailed and Unforgiven.

I looked down at my own hands. I had good hands too, the hands of a builder. I left them to their game and walked to the table, and now it was just me and the weapons.

"What are these?" I asked.

The instructor, mercifully, did not say "guns." He lit up and described each piece in detail, like they were his children.

There was the sniping rifle, then several standard weapons. He tried to explain the difference between the automatic and semi-automatic variants, but he lost me until he simplified it as how much you have to pull the trigger. There was a shotgun and a couple of hand guns.

My attention drifted about halfway through. The table stretched two meters to my left and my right. Only one of us had heard of a Forgiven. If this was the training, I didn't want to go wherever they were sending me.

One table, one day alive.

The last piece, at the end, caught my attention again. It was different from the others. The instructor, seeing the question in my eyes, reverently picked it up. "I'm not sure if they'll send this with you."

"What is it?"

He studied me, then said to himself, "You don't look like the type."

"This is the Silent," he said, handing me the gun. "Careful. Real bullets."

The weapon felt warm and heavy, alive and dangerous, in my hands. "How silent?" I asked, turning it over.

"Completely," he said. "New technology. Special chamber, special rounds. No pop. They told me magnets."

I wanted to take it apart, State help me.

"Where is the power source?" I asked. "The barrel, it's too short."

The man spread his hands wide, beaming. "New technology."

He escorted me to the rail, where Pope the artist was congratulating Happy the doctor. I saw one hole, among many strays, in the middle of a target.

The Silent still felt alive in my grip. My heart raced. I lined up, pulled the trigger, and… nothing. I felt a jump but that was it, no pop, no zip. And no hole on the target.

"How do you aim?" I asked.

His eyes flashed as he hastily grabbed the live weapon from my hands. "Not the type at all," he mumbled to himself, putting a training gun in my hands as he surreptitiously glanced around the room to make sure none of his colleagues had noticed his indiscretion.

Nineteen more tables, I thought in the back of my head as each minute passed. As soon as I could at least hit the paper of the target consistently, I moved on.

*

Across the room, a station was piled with machines and gadgetry. My heart lifted. I skirted the hand-to-hand area in the middle, where Kodiak was watching two men sparring with spears. It juxtaposed oddly with the shooting range. It all seemed out of place, but it had to fit together somehow. Chaos was nothing more than a failure of perception.

As I crossed the room to the machines, the Doorman fell into step beside me. I sidled a half step away.

"They told me you know machines," he said.

"I do."

He pivoted in front of me then, walking backwards in stride. He had a sharp jawline, and his close-cropped hair had begun to grow in thickly, longer than the other Unforgiven. He stood half a head taller than me, broader as well, but it was his hard grey eyes that demanded attention.

I stopped up short.

"Go to medicine and shelter. And botany. You'll see the equipment tomorrow."

It was something more than a suggestion. My eyes narrowed. "Why? What do you know?"

He turned his head and let out a breath. Then he strode off. I looked again at the pile of machinery I'd been approaching, then at the retreating figure of the Doorman, who looked over his shoulder a last time to say, "Shelter."

When my gaze drifted, it landed on two guards against the wall with their large-barreled guns. They were watching me and commenting to each other. The Doorman's was the only advice I had. I scanned for a table that suggested shelter and began walking.

*

I was distracted the rest of the afternoon. I lit a fire but never learned how to build a tent. I did learn about botany; it was all about poisons and thorns, edible plants, useful plants. I tried to learn medicine but nothing beyond first aid made sense to me. I watched the hand-to-hand combat and observed how to hold a knife, how to stand when waiting for an attack. I didn't step up to try. Even if I'd been a larger man, I feared I couldn't learn fast enough to make it useful.

Too soon, the afternoon turned to evening, and they called us out of the gymnasium.

After dinner it was showers. The washroom tiled a white that was losing a long battle to yellow. The thing was long, built like an assembly line: door in, laundry, and at the far end sinks, mirrors and a door out. Between, the showerheads lined one wall, benches the opposite. Each man had a semblance of privacy as long as he looked only at the two walls.

As we threw our Unforgiven blues into the large hampers, the showers turned on all at once. I hid in the water for a brief five minutes, until they all shut off with a shuddering of pipes.

We received clean duplicates of our blues, and a guard nodded me to the last in a line of sinks, where I found what was needed for my hair and teeth. The others hurried about their routines, these motions familiar to them. I tried to shave but wasn't fast enough. I still had stubble on half a cheek when the same guard nudged me to towel off.

The men remained silent in the presence of our keepers as they marched us single file back to the dormitory. It was a stark contrast to the morning, and I wondered what had transpired on a past night to make the group so defeated.

The lights remained on for a half hour after the door was closed. The ceiling was littered with cameras and motion sensors. Conversation was bound to pockets of whispers between bunkmates, as if each night each man was reminded of his forced surrender and bowed back into silence and shame.

Several men removed books or stylus tablets from the cracks

between their mattress and bunk. I had not yet earned any of these. I ran the coin marked with a 'P' over my fingers, wondering how many were needed. Not for a book. How many coins would be needed to open the door from the inside.

– SIX –

When the door slammed open and the brisk, schoolteacher's voice ordered us up in the morning, I considered staying in bed. Yet I rolled to my feet a moment later as the tight brown bun bobbed out of the room.

The Doorman's unsolicited advice proved accurate. After breakfast, a guard led me, along with Stump and Oyster, to a room filled with the small machines I'd seen. It had grey carpet and no windows or chairs. The metal boxes were laid out like a row of young kids hoping for a dance.

The one technician looked past us to the hall, then gave a quick nod. A guard pulled the door shut from the outside.

"My name is Meeks," the tech said. "I'm to instruct you in the use and maintenance of this stuff. Yesterday, I guess you three were deemed the most competent of the bunch."

"Is this it?" I asked.

"Is this it?" he echoed, with a snort. Apparently, I was supposed to be impressed by this row of State toasters. "Be grateful there isn't more, you carry what you take." He added more quietly, "And you take what we can afford to lose."

Oyster looked at me, eyebrows arching. I, too, caught the hint. I glanced at Stump, but he either didn't care or didn't register.

"So, this is the menagerie. Your menagerie. You'll start over here." Meeks pointed at two pieces at the end of the row.

The first was a column with pipes and channels running vertical, along with what appeared to be a collapsed propeller. All this was mounted on a small console. The other was a box with shoulder straps and a screen, plus knobs and an earpiece on a lead.

"I imagine none of you are familiar with these?" Meeks asked.

Stump squatted down next to the boxy one, shifting it to face him. "Is this a short-range resonance sampler?"

"Mid-range." Meeks chuffed, as if he'd scored a point. "We call it the Ears."

"Never worked with one before," Stump said, standing back up. "But I handled them. Some came through my trainyard."

"Well, I won't confuse you with details," Meeks said. "All you need to know is that the Ears are a 'passive sensor system that will detect major objects and disturbances' around you. Heat, motion, scent, chemicals. Probably electromagnetism as well. Resonance. I didn't build it, I just run it. So you," he said, pointing to Stump, "push this button and start it up."

He ran through the details. You could adjust the range, but the wider the range, the less sensitive the Ears became. The box went on the shoulders while the earpiece looped up for the wearer. Primary feedback, audible. When things became interesting, the screen provided a map of the surroundings. Otherwise, it stayed off to conserve power.

I was engrossed, studying the screen and the dials. Meeks chuckled behind us. "*Resonance,*" he said again.

So I was a little impressed by this row of State toasters. But I wouldn't let it show. Meeks was too proud already.

He set two of us meandering around the room as targets to be tracked, while he instructed the third – on, off, range, and interpreting the earpiece's beeps and tones. Simple.

After we'd all pushed the buttons, we opened the Ears up and he demonstrated simple maintenance. He detailed water damage at length, which caused Oyster to catch my eye again. I shook my head.

He ended the instruction with two warnings: "This thing won't track through walls. If you have a solid wall, you need something big on the other side to trigger it. Any open space should work, though I guess you all will soon learn how dense the undergrowth can get before you lose resonance. Also, this thing stays on. You could power it down but I wouldn't recommend it. It carries about ten days of power under normal usage."

Something big. Ten days. Undergrowth. The hints were piling up. It did sound like Outlands.

"What about this one?" Stump asked. He was already squatting at the next machine.

"The Eyes. The Ears stay on, the Eyes are need *only*. You'll use them if things get… interesting."

Interesting, again. Oyster looked at me again. I looked back, hoping to communicate, *I was in the briefing, too.*

"Hold this," Meeks said, and detached the piped column I had noted when we entered, showing Oyster where to hold it. "Normally, one person can hold the Eyes and activate it by himself. In here we only have, what… four meters of ceiling? You two," he ordered, gesturing to Stump and me. "Hold onto this."

He spooled out some cable from the base and handed us a portion in the middle.

"Everyone stand back!" He flipped a switch on the base. The propeller whirled to life, the rotors snapping out. Thankfully, Oyster still held his arm exactly as he had been shown. The device took off with a gentle whir and rose quickly until it tugged at the cable in my hands.

"It's beautiful!" Oyster exclaimed. All of us stared upward at the miniature rotorcraft floating quietly above, gently tugging this way and that on its tether.

Meeks pushed another button on the console and a holographic display appeared. "The Eyes give you a detailed picture of your immediate surroundings," Meeks said as the rotor drifted. "Send it up and it'll give you a topographic view. You can adjust the opacity for your needs but generally rocks and hard obstacles appear close to solid while organic matter like trees will appear hazy."

The image showed the flat floor and the beginnings of the walls, although the hologram cut off abruptly before reaching the ceiling. So the frame was conical. There were rough bumps along the middle of the floor, not too granular, but enough to identify them as the pieces of the menagerie. In the middle of the room were three blue lumps and one red lump.

"We're the blue things?" I asked.

"Yes."

"Why are you red?" I asked.

Meeks paused, recalculating. These questions disrupted his patter. "We've loaded your biosignatures so the machine can distinguish your team."

"...And red is hostile," Stump finished for him.

"What's a hostile?" Oyster asked.

"Well, anyone not you," Meeks said. "In this case, me."

"Or Outlanders?" Stump asked.

Meeks pursed his lips. His cheek twitched. I'd seen it before, in the desk janitor. Too many questions, we weren't scared of him, we were too far ahead of him. That made him nervous.

He turned his attention back to the unit. "Ears are always red, but the Eyes give you the red and blue. Just remember, you're all red on the Ears. Don't get all jumpy the first time you turn the screen on."

I wanted to keep prodding him but, for the moment, I had enough sense not to. We each lofted the rotor once. Then we opened the console, and he pointed to easily repairable parts. He spoke more quickly now, started leaving things out. But I could fill in all his blanks. They were machines.

The morning settled into a cycle: demonstration, information, maintenance. We got stoves that made me question my time with a flint and tinder the day before. There was a water purifier which was purely mechanical. Nothing to break and, most importantly, no ten-day lifespan.

What I wasn't expecting was the Cloak. I'd seen projection screens ever since I'd entered my first State building, the projectors hanging images in the air, as we'd seen at the briefing. The picture looks solid until you put your hand through it.

They'd modified it to project in a sphere and added depth to the two-dimensional image. Essentially, this Cloak took a picture of the surroundings on one side and projected an opaque image on the other side, rendering invisible anyone and anything inside. It wasn't perfect. When I moved my head, I could tell the depth projection was off. But unless you were close, and unless you were looking for it, a person could walk right by.

"How long?" I asked. I liked the thought of having that on all night and day, like the Ears.

"About ten hours, cumulative," Meeks said. "Emergencies only."

There was one final piece before he turned us loose. "This is the device that will bring you home," he said. We circled around it.

He flipped a switch up and down. "On, off."

Then he pulled a slender cylinder from the unit and held his thumb above a button, careful not to press it, saying, "When it's time."

He picked up the box and placed it aside.

"Wait, that's all?" I asked.

"That's all you need for now."

*

Meeks held onto his mystery and his semblance of high ground. He sent us to explore as we liked, then he and Stump began discussing the Ears. I eyed the mysterious ticket home but Meeks had set it near him, off-limits. I couldn't fathom what in that box would bring us back from the Outlands. Maybe a bomb.

I gravitated back to the Eyes. The holographic projector had caught my interest earlier, and I had nothing else to do. I opened the casing and began taking them apart, while Oyster looked over my shoulder.

"Only what they can afford to lose?" he huffed as I worked. "I don't know anyone who could afford to even *have* this."

I grunted as I loosened a fastener. Maybe he'd never been inside a Spire.

"It almost makes me glad," Oyster said. "Almost."

"Bunking with Unforgiven. Waiting to be killed by their great machine. What's got you all excited about life?"

"I've still got dreams, Thirteen," he said.

"Alright," I said, hoping to mollify the edge that had entered his voice. "What do you dream about?"

Oyster didn't answer right away. I laid each part out cleanly, one by one, as I reduced the Eyes to pieces.

He sighed. "The town I was born in had a hill. You could see it from anywhere. There was a man, Old Man Horn. He lived at the top."

I disconnected the power source, which let me dig a little deeper. I hadn't worked on anything like it before.

"I met him," Oyster said. I'd located the projector by the time he continued, but it was trapped inside a metal cage.

"My family was not rich. We had enough to survive, no more.

One day Old Horn invited us up to his house."

"Your family?" I asked, interested again.

"All the families. He invited the whole town to the top of his hill. In the stories my mother told when I went to sleep, there were castles and fairs, lights and fires and spectacles. Feasts with an entire goat spit and roasted, feasts that lasted until morning. The night on Old Man Horn's hill - it was a story.

"Horn shot fireworks into the sky from sundown to sunup. I was a child, and I wonder sometimes if it would look as big now as it did then."

Then a voice squealed behind me, "What are you doing?"

The door slammed open and a large figure blocked the exit. One hand held the door open and the other held one of the large-barreled guns. "What's wrong?" the guard asked.

No one answered. I turned, slowly and smoothly, from the guard to look at Meeks. His face was pale white, and I traced his gaze over my shoulder to where the Eyes were lying, deconstructed.

"I wanted to hold the holographic projector," I said.

"You wanted to hold...?" Meeks spluttered. "Why would you want to hold the holographic projector?"

I didn't know. I just did. "I need to know how it works," I said.

"I told you how it works! Can you put it back together? Now?"

Meeks's shoulders rose and fell with hyperventilation. I looked from him back to the guard, who still stood in the doorway watching us. The Eyes were probably worth more than his job.

"Of course," I said. "I'm done now." Though I wasn't. But there wasn't a p-coin waiting for me at the bottom of this one. I'd learned from the desk janitor how far to push a nervous man before things stopped being fun.

Meeks wobbled off to pace in a corner of the room. The guard stepped inside and closed the door behind him, pulling in a chair and taking up post.

Stump settled down with us as I set to work. Oyster was nervously watching the guard, his hands fidgeting and grabbing at the fabric on his pants.

"What happened to him?" I asked.

"Who?" Oyster asked.

"The old man."

Oyster turned to me, his hands still fidgeting. His eyes drifted while he retraced his steps. "He died. He was old."

He shrugged and picked up a piece of the Eyes, rolling it across his fingers before I snatched it back to its place. "And I left and came to the Spires."

"Why?" Stump asked.

"I thought I would open a shop. Carry the finest, sell to the Horns. Become a Horn. But I couldn't afford the finest things. So I sold the mundane. And then..."

He trailed off. Stump picked up the thread, "...everything went wrong."

Oyster nodded.

I wondered, what counterfeit had Oyster passed to buy his dream? Maybe nothing. "Sometimes things go wrong," I said.

Oyster simply nodded again.

The vagaries of our stories seemed to connect somewhere in

this space. Things go wrong.

"But you asked me what I dream of," Oyster said. "I still dream of that night on the hill. I, *I* want to send the fireworks into the sky. Perhaps I'll begin again."

"Perhaps," Stump echoed.

I shook my head. It sounded tantalizing. But I'd heard well everything Meeks said and the things he had not.

I twisted the final bolt into place, handed the cable to Oyster, and flipped the switch. The Eyes fluttered to life and lifted toward the ceiling, and four sets of eyes rose as it lazily drifted back and forth near the ceiling.

*

The rest of the morning was tinkering, asking questions, modeling breakdowns and repairs. When the guard collected us, we rose to leave. Before we could get into the hallway, Meeks sounded another alarm.

We turned and the guard blocked the door. "What's wrong now?" he asked.

"We're a piece short," Meeks said. Tallying on his fingers and whispering to himself. "The…water purifier."

There was an awkward silence while he eyed us, the beginnings of panic rising in him again. Oyster shuffled back, embarrassed, and pulled the device out of his pocket. "There's no water in here," he said. "I wanted to try it."

Meeks snatched it out of his hand.

"I figured it was going with us anyway? So it wouldn't be a problem?"

"It is a problem!" Meeks growled.

Oyster held his hands up, but the guard grabbed Oyster's shirt behind the shoulder and shoved him into the hallway. "How many warnings you need before we cut off those fingers?" he demanded.

Oyster had no response. We walked the rest of the way to lunch in silence.

– SEVEN –

A few minutes after we'd joined the lunch table, the drill sergeant appeared and announced that, in five minutes, we would be next door.

Five minutes later, no one had moved. I glanced nervously from the different faces to the open door where he'd disappeared. I didn't want to be the first to break.

The drill sergeant appeared again in the doorway. "Drop it and move!"

"I've got this fine sandwich, Mom," Crow called, holding it above his shoulder. He left his back turned to the drill sergeant. "Just let me finish."

The scorned warden reached through the doorway behind him and pulled the large barreled gun from a guard. There was a screech of many chairs sliding backwards at once.

Crow turned, wide-eyed. There was a pop, and a dark object flew through the air. It caught him in the shoulder, sending both him and his chair tumbling to the ground.

"Augh! Spragging rustic!" Crow cursed in a now hoarse voice. When it was apparent no further discipline was forthcoming, Kodiak and the Doorman moved to pick him up.

"This is my Hall," the drill sergeant said with a stoic tone. He handed the spent gun back to a guard and disappeared into the dim room beyond.

Crow was pulled back into his chair. Kodiak dropped a heavy bag onto the table, a cloth satchel filled with loose, hard bits. Crow eyed it where it lay.

Two guards still stood by the doorway. One fingered another of the guns, the other held a long metal stick in his hand, something I hadn't seen before. Happy and Oyster were the first to stand. Others followed, uneaten sandwiches left on plates.

"Spragging rustic whore," Crow muttered as he rose. He rolled his shoulder and winced. His hand hung limp.

The briefing room was again lit by the single overhead light. A projected image already hung before us. More guards stood against the concrete wall. Maybe this was when they expected us to revolt. I found myself in the middle of the second row. Once the rustle of movement and scraping chairs ended, the underlying murmur of general dissatisfaction remained. No one more, though, gauged the cost of complaint worth a bag to the chest.

A point lit up on the screen. "This is your drop zone," the drill sergeant said, with no preamble. "There is a river here," and a box appeared.

He rolled on in a mass of words as he highlighted mountains, valleys, known landmarks and obstacles. The map panned and magnified until I was lost.

Taj, the assassin, leaned forward. The light from the projection reflected on his face as he studied each image, hardly blinking.

Happy, the doctor, slouched in his chair with arms crossed. He slowly shook his head.

The drill sergeant shaded seven areas on the map. Outlander activity had been noted. All I saw were trees. Duck had his eyes closed and a hand nervously rubbed, back and forth, across the top of his head.

These were details. As if they actually hoped to accomplish something with a janitor in the jungle. Meeks had said the Ears would die after ten days. I still estimated I might die after seven or eight, given what little I'd learned at the training tables. The jungle, a table of guns, sparks set loose in the forest. Wiping out a tribe of people, or sub-humans, or animals; whatever they were.

They called this Forgiveness.

The screen stopped moving. The drill sergeant spoke in shorter sentences, instructions I understood. Patches bowed toward his knees and gently rocked, fingers laced behind his head.

Don't touch or eat anything you didn't bring in your pack.

Don't spend a minute without repellant on your skin.

Two people awake at all times.

Don't try to conserve the Ears by powering down.

Seal all open wounds.

Don't ditch heavy equipment.

When he asked if anyone had any questions my thought was, "why me?" I had a thousand questions but none he would answer.

A hand raised. The drill sergeant fixed Stump in his gaze and for a moment nothing moved. He nodded.

"Why are you sending us to kill people in the Outlands?"

"Rich soil, good wood, biodiversity. Our scientists are confident there are medicines in that jungle, evolved biotechnology ripe for mimicking, Resource. In short, the Outlands hold a wealth that your city needs."

"But why are you sending us to kill people in the Outlands?" Stump repeated.

The sergeant's eyes narrowed. Neither spoke, neither blinked. "Do your job."

Stump lowered his hand, though his gaze didn't waver. The drill sergeant strode to the table at the front of the room without inviting further question. The screen faded and the lights rose. He reached down and lifted Meeks's mysterious device onto the table, the box that would bring us home. I sat up straighter.

"Note this, Unforgiven. The man sitting next to you may not be present to remind you."

He unfastened a few clips and opened a panel.

"This is the Beacon. Once you have reached an objective and identified your target, you will activate it," here he flipped a switch, "and position it undetected for maximum effect. Within thirty minutes a satellite will be positioned and targeted directly at this beacon."

Duck and several others glanced at the ceiling. The drill sergeant flipped the switch off. "The area of effect is approximately 150 meters from epicenter. Orient with the Outlanders inside this radius. I suggest you position yourself at least twice that from the beacon. And when the timing is right," he paused to lift the cylinder from the case and held his thumb above its button, "desolation."

There was a clatter to the side. Several Unforgiven jumped. The schoolteacher stepped into the light with an open box and began handing something to the men at the ends of the row.

"Your squad's objective is 500 Outlanders," the drill sergeant said. "You are being provided a transmitter. If your objective is achieved, depress the blue button and you will be extracted. Depress the blue button without achieving your objective, and you will be executed."

The open box came to me, and I lifted out a smaller cylinder with no markings. It fit in the palm of my hand, silver with a blue button at the end. There was a small swivel to lock the button. No mistakes.

He ended as he had started. "No one will come to your assistance. There is nowhere to escape. Do your job."

The drill sergeant's gaze drifted over me. I spoke. "You need us to position a satellite? Why not just do this from an office somewhere and call it a day?"

His eyes drilled into me in the dim light. "You are Unforgiven."

*

The silver cylinder rolled back and forth across my palms as I walked alone to the bunk room, between quiet clusters of blue-clad figures.

I thought of Oyster and his innocent hope. I thought of Patches and his quiet insistence, *they don't print those tickets.* I thought of life outside the walls and all I'd been unable to fix. I thought of the satellite and 500 monsters, of Henry and his persistent questions.

The weight of Piro's coin tapped my leg with each step. This machine ran crooked. Nothing connected, nothing made sense. I couldn't divine a purpose. I didn't like that.

The coin or the cylinder. Time was short, or maybe it was out, and I didn't know it yet.

Plans scattered past me like dust from a vent. I would break things when no one was looking, then fix them for favors. I'd get inside the walls, hide until they forgot me. I'd sabotage the guards' weapons and organize a revolt.

I would kill 500 beasts in a jungle.

Tomorrow. Tomorrow was a fixed point. The cylinder or the coin. The Outlands or a pack of cigarettes.

I put Piro's coin beneath my bunk's mattress before I fell asleep. For all I know, it is still there.

*

I cornered Patches at breakfast, dragging him to a table for two. "You need those two mops and a bucket?" he asked.

"What?"

"You look ready to do some…business," he said. He laughed, a little forced.

"No, I–" I softened my face and shoved his earlier jokes back out of mind. There was no time for banter.

"Look, when they did that interview before the medical exam, I asked my interviewer if I was a dead man."

"What'd he say?" Patches asked, rolling with my shift.

"Something strange. He said, 'Abel is a good man.'"

"Hm. I guess," Patches said.

I glanced around the room. I knew most of the names by now. "Which one's Abel?"

Patches pointed his plastic fork past my shoulder. There sat the Doorman.

"Him?"

"Yeah." Patches said. "Good man."

"I…" I started but shut my mouth. I'd begun to suspect as much. And yet…

"I'm not sure he's one of us."

"He's in blue."

I forced down my food and thought. I'd lost my appetite sometime in the last day. Abel.

"I don't know," Patches said, softening his assertion. "I gather he's been here a long time."

"Well, why do people keep calling him a 'good man'?"

Patches shrugged and took another bite.

"Why do you?" I pressed.

Patches thought. "It was morning when Kodiak got here. We heard noises, clanging through the building. A few hours later, they led him in. A big man with terrified eyes.

"Later, we pieced it together. They'd tried to strip, wash, and shear him – like they always do – and Kodiak broke the place up. Chairs in pieces; he even ripped the shower out of the wall. We placed bets on if anyone died, and we still don't know. No one wants to ask, you know?

"Anyway, when he showed up in the dormitory there wasn't a mark on him. But he was quiet, arms wrapped around himself. Like a caged bear, only no cage. We don't know what they did. Don't know what they *can* do. Kody won't talk about it."

Patches's eyes wandered to where Kodiak sat, eating. I turned to look at the man, full of vigor and noise. I couldn't picture it.

"Or maybe he would. I'm not asking."

"What'd Abel do?" I asked.

"What'd *I* do?" Patches corrected. "I backed away. Stray fish die in the net, right? I saw a giant, terrified man. I saw the hand of the State. I'm not a good man."

Patches turned his full attention to his remaining breakfast, avoiding my eyes.

"Abel saw… I don't know. He laid him on a bunk. Put his hand on Kodiak's head, like he was a child, and spoke softly until the bear fell asleep. The greysuits hovered, stared him down the whole time, with those big sticks. Abel just finished and stared back. So tell me, what makes a man do that?"

I shrugged.

"Better man than I," Patches said.

"I think he's dangerous," I said.

"Sometimes you need dangerous."

Good, dangerous; blades cut both ways. I rested my head in my hands, unable to force more food down.

"You going to make it?" Patches asked.

"I'm a janitor going to the jungle," I said.

"Head janitor," Patches corrected.

"Head janitor," I echoed. For all the difference it made.

"What do we do, Patches? I just got here. I don't…I don't

95

know what to do."

And there it was. I hadn't planned to lay out my cards like that, but this thread, from Henry to Patches to Abel, was leading nowhere.

I felt, more than saw, Patches looking at the top of my head. He leaned in close.

"Look," he said. "You keep the menagerie running. You stay behind Taj, Kodiak, Stump, Crisp; the soldiers and the warboys. Let them handle the jungle and the savages. In the end, you push your button."

"Who's Crisp?" I asked, head still bowed. "The one with the beard?"

"Ah, no. That's Ivan the Terrible. We call the big, pompous one Crisp. He doesn't call us anything, don't think he knows my name."

"The one with a Spire up his–?"

"Yeah," Patches laughed before I finished. "The one who still folds his clothes. I hear he was an executive, outside. But they're both thatchers."

"But Crisp is useful?"

"Well, he's big. And, in theory, he should know how to lead or some such."

I stared at my uneaten food, head still in hands, thinking. A human wall. Let men like Kodiak the giant and Taj the assassin, men more Unforgiven than I, do the work of survival and massacre. Let me as ever do the work of maintenance. Patches's machine had a logic to it, and I had a place in it.

"Can we trust them?" I asked. "I mean, will they protect us out there?"

Patches had been ready to speak, then his mouth snapped shut. "What?"

"Us. Well, I don't think…" Patches said slowly. "Kodiak doesn't like me."

"Who cares if he likes you?" I asked.

Patches's mouth twitched at the corner.

"I mean, what does it matter?"

"Look," Patches said, leaning in. "There's a core to this *team* or whatever you want to call it. Taj; that man knows what he's about. Kodiak, because I don't think anything in the Outlands could bring that animal down. Abel; I don't know what he's for but trust my gut he fits in there somehow. Anyone who knows how to stab or shoot someone. Then they need *you* to keep all the stuff working just like they need Happy to keep them from dying at the first poison thorn or killer butterfly."

Patches stopped there and nodded to himself. "They'll protect you because they need you. Stick to your place. Push your button."

"It's a cold plan."

"Don't sweat it. Everyone's thinking it. Just be useful while you use everyone else, right? That's life."

Useful. The word put a fingertip on another inarticulable problem I had with this whole situation.

"What are the chances?" I asked.

"Chances of what?"

"One doctor, one mechanic, an executive type, a bunch of

soldiers and fighters, does that make sense to you?"

Patches tilted his chair back and laughed a quiet, grim laugh. "I've been here three months, and I wasn't the first. There's thirteen of us. You think the State only incarcerates two or three people a month?"

I tapped my fork on the plate. It was a long time and not many Unforgiven.

"Listen. Other guys show up, we see them at breakfast a day or two, and they're gone. I don't know what kind of program they're on. Forced labor? Most of the people who come in here disappear. Then there's us."

"Who are we?"

"The way I see it, there's only two groups of people left: those they handpicked, and those they couldn't find a better use for."

"What are you for?"

Patches grimaced. "I'm baggage."

I didn't believe it. It was a system, a machine. You don't put extra metal in the machine. You don't put extra bodies to clothe and mouths to feed in one either. Patches had a purpose, too.

I leaned forward and spoke low. "No. They're dropping a pile of Unforgiven off in the middle of nowhere and shoving live guns into our hands."

Now it was Patches who scraped food across his empty plate, watching the spirals.

"What do you think is going to happen?" I pressed. "What, you think five minutes? Maybe a whole day? We're already picking at each other."

"They'll keep you safe," Patches reasserted. "But I... Like I said, I don't think Kodiak likes me."

The words took a darker tone in this new context. "Wait," I asked. "How much are we talking about here?"

"Heh. How much are we talking?" Patches rubbed his nose. "That's what he says. He says I talk too much. I can't help it."

"What's he going to do about it?" I asked.

The pause was pregnant.

"I still don't know really anything about him," Patches said.

Gentle giants don't end up in the hall, the thought came to me again.

"Someone needs to hold us together," I tried again.

"Yeah, I think that's meant to be Crisp."

"Half of them hate Crisp. But they sent *you* over when they thought I was a killer, right? You're the ambassador. Everyone likes you."

"Maybe. At least everyone but–"

"Look," I interrupted. "Keep your distance if you have to. Let Abel keep ahold of him. The rest of us need *you*."

Patches gave a quiet laugh. "Stop encouraging me. I almost believe you."

I smiled and shrugged, but before I could press him further he grabbed my plate, stacking it on his own. "And your pretty words won't stop me pissing my blue pants when they fly us out there. I don't like heights."

I snorted as he left to bus our dishes. It wasn't much, but I had something now, more than when I'd woken up. Stay close to Taj and Kodiak. Make friends with Happy. Fix the gear. And keep an eye on Abel and Ivan, the Beard. Patches was the glue. And I'd be his glue if that's what was needed.

– EIGHT –

The drill sergeant and the schoolteacher entered before we finished breakfast. The instructions were short once again: Get outfitted. It put a dull ache in my stomach.

Pockets of quiet chatter rose as the thirteen Unforgiven stretched into a jumbled line in the hallway, marching past the rows of ever-dark doors. I maneuvered myself next to Happy, Patches's plan at the front of my mind, and quietly asked how he was doing.

"Same as everyone else," was all I could get. Further questions elicited one-word answers. By the time we arrived at a locker room we, and everyone else, walked in silence.

The locker room wasn't meant for us. Padded benches with soft fabric stood over a thick, red carpet. Wooden doors covered floor-to-head lockers, and warm overheads shone over all with a soft light. The smell of cleaning agent lingered in the air.

I found myself before a door with the numeral 13. Inside was what was needed. Good pants, good boots, good socks, and a strong belt. There was a shirt made of some engineered fabric, smooth to the touch and skin-tight.

A few doors down I heard Crow say, "They always bury you in your best, right?" It was the nicest clothing I had ever worn. I tried not to chuckle. I didn't like Crow.

Behind the clothing, I found a large knife and a rifle. The rifle was one of the weapons I'd fired in training. The knife was foreign.

The gun wasn't loaded, and the locker held no ammunition. Bullets would probably be provided five minutes after we landed, once the only things to shoot were Unforgiven or Outlander.

The knife, on the other hand, had a smooth edge and a serrated edge that needed nothing further in order to kill.

Last in the locker was a pack. Inside was dense, packaged food – dry, heavy, but with varied colors hinting at vague flavors. I also found a thin tarp, one of the water purifiers, and a tube of bug repellant "juice." There was a second pair of socks and underwear and a small kit with first aid essentials.

And, at the bottom, a box of tools.

That last I opened eagerly. The pieces were hard as rock but light as plastic. I laid out four screwdrivers: the king of tools, simple yet necessary, and endlessly repurposable. I shoved the sheathed knife to the bottom of my pack, beneath the socks and underwear, and let my fingers rest on the textured case of the toolbox. I breathed, taking in the faint scent of composite plastic.

There were two flathead and two crosshead drivers. I felt the grip and the balance, then slid a flathead into a pocket for quick retrieval. The toolbox took its place at the top of my pack, and the three remaining screwdrivers in the top of the box.

I stood. Around me, men still dug into their lockers and changed out of their Unforgiven blues. Pope had a sniping weapon alongside his rifle. He'd pulled a small box of dyes from somewhere and was decorating the barrel with purple lines and spirals rather than dressing himself. At least he'd found a use for his p-coin, or whatever favor he'd traded, before time ran out.

Old Stump grunted next to me.

"How are you doing?" I asked.

"Pack fits. Boots fit." He stomped his heel on the ground as if to prove the point.

"No, how do you feel?"

He paused in his work, then dropped his laces and raised his head, adjusting his glasses. "We'll get through."

Patches thudded onto the seat next to me. Stump turned back to tightening his laces. "Do you need help with anything?" Patches asked.

I told him I was fine.

"Then why the frown, Unforgiven?" His earlier shadow had passed. Obviously, mine had not.

I ran my fingers through the stubble on my head, tasting the word again. It was still bitter in my mouth. But he meant it to be comforting, and, in a way, it was.

Across the room, Taj checked the chamber on a Silent, the magnetic gun from training. He looked calm and relaxed, shouting at Pope, who laughed and called back without looking up from his painting. Their relaxation, or courage, or fatalism, or escapism - whatever it was - was alien to me.

There was a shout and clatter as Kodiak shoved the Spire-executive, Crisp, against a locker. Other men, half dressed in black fatigues and half in blue Hall pajamas, halfheartedly pulled them apart, the angry words spilling to the floor between them.

I fingered the flathead in my pocket.

"I had a workbench," I said.

"Back before?" Patches asked.

"Back before."

Nothing but my eyes moved, flicking from stranger to stranger in this room of handpicked rejects.

"Down below Abbey," I said. "Every day at noon, when the gangs stopped to eat, I would go. Close the door. And I'd work."

"What on?" Patches asked.

"Boxes of broken circuits and metal. Screws. Wood they'd thrown away. I just built."

Patches sat beside me, quiet, and we watched the tense drama of men around backpacks and machines from our red velvet bench. Taj slammed his knife through a locker door, grunted in satisfaction, and began to work it free.

"And now?"

"And now."

Somehow, we both knew what I meant.

Patches spoke in a lower voice. "Still think you'll go home?"

I closed my eyes. Thirteen blue buttons, a crate of guns, and a one-way air ticket. I wanted to believe the good story. I wanted to live. "I don't know if I have a home."

"What happened?" he asked.

"A chain of accidents," I said.

"Ha," Patches laughed quietly. "Just a never-ending chain of accidents. That's all we are."

*

By the time gear was inspected, curiosity sated, and packs zipped, the drill sergeant came and called us to the center of the room where the menagerie was piled. He dragged Pope, half dressed and fingers wet with paint.

It lacked ceremony. I received some odds and ends along with the Eyes. They put the Ears on Stump.

We each hoisted the full packs onto our shoulders, testing the weight and adjusting straps.

"You?" I asked Patches.

"You what?"

"You think you'll go home?"

A sad look crossed his face. "If I can get through the next few hours, I think I can handle anything. Eyes of the State, I hate flying."

I smiled, despite an effort not to. "Need someone to hold your hand?"

"Hush." He smiled. But tightness remained around his eyes.

More guards came to march us back to the hallways, now shoving us into a strict line. I walked behind Patches, who muttered under his breath. He was stumbling, trying to keep in line. Praying, I figured.

Our line passed through another door, the same as all those we'd passed, except this one held white sunlight on the other side. Blowing wind struck at the door, catching our packs so each man stumbled as he emerged. The bright sky was a deep blue, with a towering thunderhead on the horizon. Grey concrete stretched in all directions, flat and unbroken. No weeds here. Behind us, the Spires rose to the heavens. Before us, treetops carpeted the land into the distance. In the middle of the platform was a small rotorcraft, its great fans swiveled to point directly at the ground.

We shuffled to a disordered stop as our keepers slowed. Two guards walked ahead and conferred with the technicians still scrambling around the small craft.

"I don't like this," Patches said next to me. "Small craft don't fly smooth."

"It's too small!" a deep voice shouted from the end of the line, at almost the same time. We leaned forward to see around the other Unforgiven and found Kodiak growling at the Drill Sergeant.

"Looks like you two have something in common," I said.

"This doesn't help."

"Sounds like he doesn't like flying either."

"I know what you're saying!" Patches ground out at me. "It doesn't help!"

The Drill Sergeant stood, brows drawn. He was leaning away from Kodiak but clearly unwilling to give ground. I could not hear all of Kodiak's words in the wind but his tone, and the spit flying from his mouth, were enough.

"No. This doesn't help," Patches moaned as the Drill Sergeant shouted back at Kodiak. He jabbed the big man in the chest with two fingers. Kodiak didn't flinch.

"Where is this going," I wondered out loud.

"We're going to die," Patches said beside me, his eyes squeezed shut.

"No!" Kodiak roared. And he lifted the Drill Sergeant by the front of his jacket and threw him a full three meters.

Patches moaned.

The guards, who had spread out, all raised their weapons and began closing in in a circle.

Before they could reach either man, Abel, the Doorman, swiftly stepped in. He stood before Kodiak, who was breathing heavily and glaring at the Drill Sergeant where he had rolled to a knee.

Abel scanned the guards, then held up a single finger. The guards hesitated, big-barreled guns and sticks held ready, looking between Abel and the Drill Sergeant.

The latter man rose to his feet and, after a moment, also waved a hand at the guards that looked like a "stand down." They did, a little, taking one or two steps back. They only half lowered their weapons.

"I don't like this," I muttered.

"What part?" Patches asked, interrupting his ongoing nervous mumbling to himself.

"All of it," I said.

Kodiak still glared at the Drill Sergeant as Abel spoke to him, a hand yanking on the big man's shoulder strap. "Kody," I heard. "This doesn't help anything. Trust me. This doesn't help. Trust me."

Kodiak finally turned his head and looked down at Abel. Abel continued speaking, more quietly now. He was large enough himself, but his eyes only reached Kodiak's chin.

When Abel stopped talking, Kodiak considered him for a long

moment. Then he shoved Abel to the ground and walked to the rotorcraft by himself, climbing on as the techs paused to watch him pass.

Happy and Pope helped Abel to his feet, balancing his heavy pack. The Drill Sergeant shifted his murderous glare to him, now. Abel looked back with an unreadable expression.

"So board that thing," the Drill Sergeant bit out to no one in particular.

The guards hung back as the remaining twelve of us followed his last order.

*

I slowed as I approached the rear door. Large hydraulics extended from the body of the craft, supporting a ramp. Several boxes holding levers and buttons were on the wall, just inside the door, and the telltale piping ran out, to the door, to the cockpit, and down into the floor. Inside, two rows of seats, maybe twenty in all, lined the sides. Kodiak was already sitting in the one farthest from the ramp, with his pack on the floor in front of him as he worked the restraints. As my eyes traced the lines and cables exposed on the craft's ceiling, some of the men pressed by me, untroubled by the affliction of curiosity.

Patches also loitered by the ramp, stricken by something other than curiosity. I grabbed him and guided him to a seat halfway down the left row and buckled in next to him. Before we were all settled, the sergeant came and stood at the bottom of the ramp.

"I hope I never see you again," he barked. Then he turned on his heel and walked from our line of sight. Pope saluted the now empty space where he had stood, and Oyster said, softly enough that the drill sergeant wouldn't hear, "Feeling's mutual!"

A pilot came back and quickly oriented us. Three hour flight, lavatory, no moving around, that sort of thing. He checked that we were buckled properly and disappeared into the cockpit. The thirteen of us were alone.

Patches had closed his eyes again, and again was whispering words I couldn't hear. The fans roared to life. His prayer spiked into audibility for a pitiful moment when the aircraft lurched to life and jolted the first few meters up from the ground. We wobbled as we ascended, rising several hundred meters straight into the air before leveling out. The wobbling was more than I was used to from flying in larger rotorcraft. Across from us, at the front of the plane, Kodiak was ashen faced.

"Abel," he said, "If I die up here, I'll kill you."

*

The fans rotated to propel us forward across the land.

The flight began calm, a proper anticlimax. We sat, the rotors hummed on, taking us State knew where. If I closed my eyes, I could almost imagine that the hum was the wind on the lake, and the molded seat the roots of our tree.

Pope told stories about women he had known, stories that twisted and turned with everything except credibility. When Duck tried to join the banter, they got into an argument about whether or not he could call himself a man yet. I found out he was only seventeen. So young to be sent to the Outlands. With his usual diffidence, Crisp made a comment about how young a boy could "become a man," in that sense, and then the doctor Happy contributed a more medical opinion.

Apart from the palpable silence surrounding both Kodiak and Patches, things felt almost convivial for more than an hour. Then a voice interrupted from the cockpit, "Hang on!"

The craft shook. Then it dropped, leaving us weightless, before catching loft again. The pilot veered into a sharp bank and I felt myself tilting, pressed into my seat. When we finally leveled out, the plane began jumping like a drunken bee.

Wordless shouts resolved into curses as shock wore off. Patches began wailing, "Oh nedder, we're cranked!"

"Shut him up," Kodiak ordered, speaking to no one, but glaring at Patches.

But Patches had grown wild. Something wordless, halfway between a wail and a whimper, streamed out of him.

"Look at me, Kodiak," Abel said from across the cabin. "Kodiak, look at me."

Kodiak did not. "Shut him up!" Spit flew from his mouth.

Then Abel turned to me, his eyes fixed on mine. He said no word, and his face did not so much as twitch. But I knew, in that moment, I'd been commissioned. It was us or nothing.

I nodded.

I turned as much as I could in my seat. "Patches, calm down. We're alright."

"We're alright. We're alright! We're all right here! We're falling!"

I grabbed his shoulder and he swiveled his eyes toward mine, but he went on.

"You talk too much!" Kodiak shouted.

"Mother help me but I can't help it, I never could. Oh no. My Dad used to tell me about flying in craft like these–"

"Shut him up!" Kodiak now yelled, the whites of his eyes showing around his irises. The craft rocked hard and half of us smacked our heads into the back wall. The other half were thrown forward against their restraints.

"Shut him up or I'll kill him!"

I couldn't, and Kodiak was disintegrating before my eyes. Suddenly I could see the scared, silent man that Patches had described being led in by the greysuits. Somewhere in those wide eyes wasn't a bear, or an Unforgiven – it was a boy who wanted out.

I wriggled free of one of my straps and twisted farther, grabbing Patches by the arm. His eyes snapped to me again but he still kept talking.

"–If you hit a bad storm, the craft can drop. When it catches the loft again, the seat–"

Here the craft rocked and the story was broken by a whimper and several curses.

"The seat crushes your testicles!" The last word came out like an animal yelp as the craft was tossed upwards. I looked down at the bulge in the seat, sculpted to hold my legs in place.

"Oh State, I need my balls!" Kodiak howled from the front. Now he began muttering and chanting just as Patches had before, in a kind of singsong prayer. I wriggled back into my restraints and held them tightly. Every lurch made my heart skip.

I studied the group. More faces were infected with fear. Duck had paled and might have been crying. Men were shouting down whoever was cursing loudest.

The craft took a sickening turn as the pilot shouted something about getting out of the worst of it, even as I felt the blood drain from my face to my feet. The storm was still tossing the craft about like a buoy weathering a squall.

I turned my head and tried again. "Patches!"

He ignored me. "I have this dream! I put my hand into the fans and it chops it up!" That was as far as he got.

"What are you talking about?" yelled Oyster.

Duck also shouted, "Bad luck to say it out loud!"

"Close your eyes, Patches," I ordered. "One step at a time. We're fine."

"I'm sorry, Thirteen, I'm sorry I'm sorry. I can't help it. It's just, my fingers! I can feel it, I can actually feel it!" Kodiak was looking at Patches now, not even blinking.

Someone retched, maybe from the image, maybe from the rocking. Patches continued, "I'm sorry, Thirteen, I'm sorry! I'm trying. I can't help it. I'm just talking! Oh State shut up I'm still talking…"

Abel was talking to Kodiak but Kodiak wasn't looking at Abel. The little boy was gone, and the big man had settled into a kind of stony calm. Not calm, more like a man having a tooth pulled. He was fixated on Patches and had found something to hold his center. If anything, this seemed worse.

It went on for much too long, and I thought to myself, *we've just got to make it to the jungle. Then we'll be alright.* Something deeper inside me laughed at this.

When the craft slowed to a hover, I let out a long-held breath. The buffeting continued. A pilot came back from the cockpit and started shouting orders.

"Quickly. Unstrap and come aft!" The ramp opened. We hadn't landed.

Wet wind and air came rushing in, and I saw grey clouds out the back hatch along with the tops of trees.

Abel was the first to move, taking off his restraints and moving to the back after leaning over and shouting something in Stump's ear. Stump held back while Taj quickly moved in behind Abel. There was a shouted conversation in the roar of the wind, and I caught only snippets, "Moving around too much!" and "Best we can do!"

Then, suddenly, Abel leapt out the back of the aircraft. The general dread of dying in the Outlands gave way to a more immediate panic. Taj stepped to the ramp as well, but now I saw a cord attached to his backpack. He leapt out and the cord played out behind him until it suddenly pulled taut.

People passed me and, with shaking hands, I began removing my restraints. Stump was trying to help Kodiak up but Kodiak pushed him off and shoved by everyone, saying to himself, "Getting off. I'm getting off. Off, off, getting off." I now saw the man from the cockpit was holding a line with an open hook, though he barely had time to secure it to Kodiak's pack before the big man stepped out the back.

People kept jumping, or being pushed, until there was no one between the chasm and me. "Won't the rope break my neck when it pulls tight?" I shouted.

"It stretches."

Suddenly it all made sense, in a horrible way. "It's set for a fixed length?"

"Yes sir."

"Then you need to hold a fixed altitude!" I shouted over the wind.

"We're doing the best we can!" he shouted back and slapped me twice on the shoulder. I think that was my signal to jump but I didn't get a chance. The craft suddenly dropped and the ramp disappeared under my feet. I vaguely heard the man curse as he swung out over the open air, now above me and hanging on to the craft with one hand. And then I was falling and my stomach surged into my throat.

The rope snapped tight. Rather than jerking me to a halt, it began to stretch and slow my descent. I had just enough time to think, *how wonderful,* before something slammed into my back, knocking the wind out of me. The ground. Before I could recover, the rope went taut again and I was lugged back into the air. Out of the corner of my eye I saw trees.

Voices shouted, "Grab him! Grab him!" And then a pair of hands were on me. They tugged my pack as they cut through the rope, and then I landed back on the ground again.

Taj's face appeared between me and the sky long enough for him to ask, "Alright?" I nodded, and he rushed off. Above me, the aircraft careened as another tethered man fell out the back. And then another horrifying thought came. *The equipment.* I wriggled out of my pack and turned it over. The Eyes. There were ominous rattles of loose metal as I shifted the bag.

Oh no, I thought. *No, no, no.* We needed the menagerie to survive. *I* needed the menagerie, or I would be expendable.

I looked up as another man jumped out of the aircraft, but his rope pulled him to a stop before he touched the ground. After that, he pendulumed into a tree as the aircraft tossed about, and I heard a crunch as his pack, too, was crushed. Taj and Crisp got their hands on him and cut him free.

Most of us were on the ground then, some people looking at their packs, like me. Others rushing around to collect the latest jumper, and a few starting to congregate and get bearings. One last man jumped out and landed almost perfectly, dragged only a few steps before he reached back and released the rope cleanly himself. Stump. Then the aircraft pulled the ropes in, closed the ramp, and zoomed off over the trees as it picked up altitude.

I don't know what I was expecting. Maybe one last salute or a farewell wave out the back of the aircraft. Maybe one circle before they left to make sure we were all right. Inside of a minute, though, the drone of the engines was gone. We were alone with the Outlands, the wind, and clouds that looked like heavy rain.

And with each other.

I heard a scuffle from the main center where others had gathered and then a crescendo to an outcry. I rushed over to see what was happening. When I got there, five men were holding

Kodiak by the arms and chest, but he wasn't straining against them.

On the ground was Patches, blood running from a gash in his neck out across the long grass where he had fallen. The matching knife, still wet, was clenched in Kodiak's hand. Happy was on his knees next to Patches, whose eyes were moving from face to face, terrified, and pleading for help as he gasped for air.

And then he was still.

Happy held his head for a few moments in a tender grip, cradling the still clean cheek in a bloodied hand. Then he let out a long breath and closed the eyes.

Abel stood off to the side, studying the scene with a blank face and crossed arms.

I fell to my knees, unable to look away.

– NINE –

I was dimly aware of voices and motion around me. Also of a sickening feeling in my gut. Not anger, nor fear. Confusion? Shock. Shock at the pool spreading through the broken blades of grass. Patches didn't deserve this.

I looked up at the men who were supposed to be my allies and saw only Unforgiven.

Through the shock, I began to hear voices. Someone, shouting, *gather my things, get to cover*. Another voice, something about the clearing. From my knees, I saw people scurrying, scrambling into their pack straps and filling their arms with loose gear.

Cover.

I jerked back to the present, and my gaze moved from Patches to his backpack. I rolled him over, repeating, "Sorry, sorry, sorry," softly. Once I'd extricated his arms from the pack, I rolled him back onto his back and looked at him again, at his re-opened eyes this time and not at the horrible puddle next to him. "Good luck," I said, not knowing if he was starting a new adventure, or if all his stories had now come to an end.

I slung my own abandoned pack on my other shoulder. The only thing I had removed was the broken Eyes, so I grabbed them, one part in each hand, one pack on each shoulder, and followed the others into the undergrowth. Crisp stood with his pack, watching the disappearing men with exasperation.

It wasn't until I found the rest of the men forming a small cluster in a space among the trees that I realized how hard I was breathing. I almost dropped the packs to the ground but remembered the horrible clinking of broken metal and placed them down gently. Then I collapsed.

The treetops were high above, their trunks rising like bundles of roots. Everything was covered with moss or fern, be it tree or rock or dirt. The ground was flat and soft, except where the trees cast up great ridges to bury their roots. The grey clouds of the sky showed through a hole perhaps ten meters wide, where the branch tips whipped in the wind.

The small space felt full. Happy stood at the center, where he was yelling at Abel. "I'm not doing anything until we deal with that animal!"

Kodiak was standing apart. His knife was gone but he held his rifle across his chest, defiantly nonchalant, though shuffling more than a calm man would.

Abel spoke more quietly, but also forcefully. "We don't have time for this. Kodiak is not what may kill you in the next ten minutes. "

"Abel, he just murdered–" Happy said, quietly urgent.

"Ten minutes," Abel repeated.

Happy relented, reluctantly, as Crisp straggled into our little space in the jungle. He dropped his pack, hard, and it disappeared into the ferns around his feet. We looked like guerrillas in our black suits, unloaded guns held tightly. Abel began rattling off questions and orders.

"Who has the Bugwall? Where are the Ears?"

Duck began to search his pack but then whined, "This isn't my pack! Who has my pack?"

Crisp interrupted before anyone answered. "We need to head back to the clearing. It's dark, it's crowded, we don't know what's in the undergrowth. Let's move!"

"This is safer," Abel said.

The two faced each other, and neither spoke.

"Juice up!" Abel barked to the larger group, without looking away. "Use any tube."

I scrabbled in my pack for the bug repellant. Abel's words brought to mind fifty different ways the bugs could kill me.

Crisp shook his head. "That is exactly the point. We need to reorganize the gear, assess damage, get these spragging weapons loaded…we need a plan. If we get to the open–"

"Bugwall!" Stump shouted as he held the device triumphantly over his head. It was in a pack next to Crow, who was simply slouching and watching the rest of us.

"Switch it on," Abel said. Stump turned it over in his hands until he found the switch, then flipped the device upright.

"No good," he said with a little shake. "No running light."

"Nedder," Abel muttered. "Thirteen!"

I jerked to attention.

"Can you fix it?"

"Yes." I could never answer that question otherwise.

Abel nodded. "Stump, get on those Ears."

Crisp was pulling Pope to his feet, and Oyster was already up and following.

"Hold," Abel called.

"You aren't in charge here," Crisp said.

The flurry of activity slowed as we again fell silent. There was a click as Taj slid a magazine into his rifle, pulled from an open sack at his feet.

Patches was still warm.

Abel approached Crisp's little group. "The Outlands are in charge here. And the Outlanders." He emphasized the "*ers.*" "We were just dropped in the middle of this spragging wilderness by an aircraft audible for a kilometer or two and visible for more. That means that between 5 minutes and two days from now someone or something will come to investigate."

Crisp studied Abel but held his tongue.

"We need to be where that thing or, State forbid it, that mob of things, won't find us unless they trip on us."

"We'll organize faster out there," he said. "Thirty minutes. What are the chances that something–"

Abel held up a hand. "Small. Maybe small. But the cost of being wrong is not. Just juice up."

Abel made sense. Still, Crisp looked at him suspiciously. I don't know if he was evaluating Abel's logic or what response at this point would most harm his authority. Pope and Oyster sat back down even before Crisp nodded.

Activity resumed.

I finished smearing my hands, face, and neck, and set my toolkit in front of the Bugwall. Then I uprooted at least six ferns that were in my way. Crisp was right, this would have been easier in the open light of the clearing. Though it was less windy here. I wanted my workbench.

The Bugwall was a small piece, a kind of sonic generator that vibrated the air in a ten-meter radius. We wouldn't notice, but insects would scatter or hole up. I wanted it working.

As I opened it, I heard Happy roaming and inquiring about injuries. I rolled my shoulders: banged up but not bad. He moved from man to man checking joints, pupils, and heads. Crisp directed men to make a pile out of the gear and evaluate what was broken, along with redistributing the necessities from Patches's pack.

A shadow beyond the corner of my eye, I felt the presence of Kodiak. He stood apart from the work, a gun, a knife, two huge arms. Stained hands. Abel and Crisp prowled through it all, pretenders to the throne of overseer. Of King. With click after click, the guns were loaded. I heard the whine of the Ears spinning up into service, with Stump at the earpiece listening for the first blip or beep telling us the promise of *visitors* had come due.

The wind whipped a murmur through the treetops. Just like the wind off the lake, beneath our tree at the shore.

The juice was still wet on my skin. What feeble protection it offered my neck and the life that still ran through it.

So I pressed further into the broken machine before me, my eyes tracing the screws, circuits, and wires. There was no exit on the other side, but there were clean lines and metal walls that could hide me, if only for a short breath. Patches, Kodiak, and the rotting jungle faded, far away.

I set to work with my fingertips, probing and pulling, the pressure quietly whispering the moment before a part would give. The lines and circuits untangled and laid out before me; order, perfection, all constructed in accord. The clean lines were always the same: power to processor to purpose. I breathed the metal dust and closed my eyes, mentally stepping inside the machine. It coalesced into its beautiful whole.

There, in the middle, hung the sonic generator, a locked box. I had worried that it might be the problem. I could not peer inside that box here in the Outlands, it was too fine for my eyes to decipher and too small for my fingers to work. But there was no need. The fault was elsewhere; the casing had been warped and cracked in the fall and the board inside had been dislodged, with a gash across the circuitry and a few wires loose.

"I can fix it," I muttered, mostly to myself.

"Good," a voice responded, close to my ear, and for a moment I imagined it was yours. Back before, when you would watch me work. Back before you wanted half a room of distance between us.

In the toolkit was a soldering iron. It had no visible power source but heated instantly. I carved a groove in the substrate and laid a conductive, metal path across the cut traces, flowing like a river into its bed. My work wasn't pretty, but it wouldn't short out. I moved on.

Repairing the pulled wires was no more complicated than

untangling a child's hair after the wind. I laid each in place, wrapping insulation with a steady hand. The rest was purely mechanical work, sealing and securing it all.

How easily some things repair.

As I tightened the last screw, I heard the voice at my shoulder again, "They should shoot him."

This time I jumped and turned, and my nose brushed against Ivan's beard.

"What in State are you doing?" I asked, jerking away and losing my balance.

"So you're the mechanic," is all he said. "I was watching your remarkable work."

"Alright," I said, uncertain.

"Things got a little *exciting* while you were…away."

I scanned the group. Abel, Happy, and Crisp were standing in a semi-circle arguing, a little apart from Kodiak, who stood with Taj. Taj stood in front, as if he were protecting the bigger man.

"Son of a rutting thatcher," I muttered.

Ivan pressed a magazine full of bullets into the dirt in front of me. I looked at it there and hated it. But I took it and slid it into the rifle beside me until something clicked.

"You aren't listening," Taj said to the other three.

"I'm listening–" Happy said, but Taj talked over him.

"This is the Outlands. Kody is worth three or four of you and we need him. The rules don't apply."

"He just opened Patches's carotid!" Happy said. "Outlands or no, it's murder."

"It's done," Crisp said. "What's important—"

"It doesn't matter," Taj interrupted. "We need him."

"That's quite a precedent!" Happy exclaimed. "So, what? He can shoot Duck? But if he cuts off your hand he gets a reprimand?"

Duck looked scared more than insulted. Ivan drew a breath next to me. I glanced at my hands before mastering my imagination. He'd just drawn his knife and… and I didn't want to think about it.

"He deserved it," Kodiak said quietly, perhaps to himself alone. Taj opened his mouth, but Abel held up a hand, and the conversation stopped. Abel stepped past Taj and looked into Kodiak's face.

"What was that, Kody?"

Crisp stepped behind Abel and spoke in his ear, raising his voice. "He's dead, we have a mission, we're wasting time! What about your *mob of things* now, eh?" Abel twisted, placed an open hand on Crisp's chest, and pushed him back.

He repeated his question.

Kodiak's whole posture shifted. His hands fidgeted. After a moment, he looked away from Abel but repeated in a mumble, "I said he deserved it."

Abel reached up to force Kodiak's eyes back to his. He looked furious.

"What do you think about them?" Ivan said quietly, for my ears alone. "Tight as testicles, those two." I shifted a few centimeters farther from him.

Taj stood at ease, but, despite his posture, still appeared on guard.

124

Abel still glared into Kodiak's face, and the big man, stony, looked at the ground past his shoulder rather than lock eyes.

Happy's agitated indignation burst out before Abel or Kodiak could speak again. "Deserved it? What happens when I 'deserve it'?"

Crisp's voice turned hard. "What are you going to do, Happy? Tie him up and shoot him?"

"If we must," Happy said. "I will do it. Or he can go off to the jungle to die naturally. He isn't coming with us."

"He's coming with me," Taj said quietly.

"He's dangerous," Happy said.

"He's necessary," Taj said.

"I don't care!" Crisp shouted. "Kodiak, you done killing?"

Kodiak looked at the barrel of his gun, fingers fidgeting on the hand grips. Abel didn't move at all.

"Alright then," Crisp said. "We have work to do. Let's plant that beacon and go home."

Happy and Taj glared, each measuring the other. No one responded.

"I don't have time for this," Crisp said, and stalked off. On the edge of the group, he began noisily rummaging in his pack and making ready to go.

"It won't happen again," Kodiak said, in the following silence.

"It was the flight," Taj said. "It's done now."

Abel remained silent.

"Flying?" Happy exclaimed, his voice high and strained. "What else, then? What else sets you off?" He took a step back and raised his gun. The barrel quivered. "I'm not going to discover your triggers one by one as you kill us! I won't!"

Taj took a step. He struck like a snake, and in a blur of motion his knife rested against Happy's throat. "Only one of us is not in control, now. It isn't Kodiak." His voice was low and terrifying. "Calm yourself, Doctor."

"Not yet," Abel said softly.

"Not what?" Happy rasped. His eyes wide and white behind his thin-framed glasses, gun and chin alike frozen in place.

Abel turned away from Kodiak. He shook his head. "Peace, Taj. Peace, Happy."

Taj stepped back and sheathed his knife. Happy did keep his peace, although his chest continued to heave. I let out a breath, and I heard nervous coughs from around the clearing.

Kodiak stood straight, but he didn't loom over the rest of them as he used to. Abel covered his eyes and rubbed his temples as he began speaking.

"Don't tell us you didn't mean to, Kody. You meant it." Kodiak tried to protest, but Abel held up his hand again. "You lost control up there. You lost control down here. You got scared."

"I don't scare," Kodiak said. "And I don't lose control."

"You aren't afraid of anything you can fight," Abel interrupted, now looking at the man. "But you were strapped to a seat in the air, and all the thick arms and all the thick skull in the world couldn't help you. You got scared." Abel emphasized each of those three words, and Kodiak flinched. There was no retort.

Abel was truly angry. He studied Kodiak until he was satisfied that, in the silence, the point was conceded. He stepped toward Kodiak again, inside arm's reach, and Kodiak looked away.

"What do you want, Abel?"

"Why did you blame Patches?"

In the silent space between question and answer a hundred empty answers flashed across Kodiak's face. The flushed skin, the flashing eyes, faded in an instant. He looked to the trees, hoping to pull out something, anything to throw back at that question, but the trees only whipped back and forth, reeling in the wind.

He let out a groan and dropped to a squat, his head tucked and hands laced behind his neck. His gun hung free around his shoulders now, resting in his lap.

"I don't know, I don't know," he began muttering.

"He was a scared man, just like you." Abel squatted down before him.

"I know, I know. I don't know. I did it again."

Abel studied the top of the head.

"Give me your gun."

That quieted the muttering for a moment. Then Kodiak simply said, "No."

Beside me, Ivan took a sharp breath. "This is where it begins."

I put a hand on my rifle, though I was unsure what I could do with it.

Abel waited. When the silence became uncomfortable, Kodiak spoke again. "Do I have to?"

"You do."

"Are you going to shoot me?"

"Not today."

Kodiak reached up and pulled off his rifle. Abel took it in one hand.

Happy blinked incredulously. "That's it? Take his gun? What about his knife? What about Patches? What about us?"

Abel stood. "Taj is right. We need every man. I take responsibility. You have your gun."

Happy spluttered, "Have my gun? What... what are you doing now?"

Abel looked on Kodiak, still squatting. "What I can. Come on, Kodiak, I'm not done with you."

"Where are you taking him?" Taj asked.

"Patches."

Kodiak struck a tree with his fist as he passed, but dutifully followed Abel away. The shaking branches quickly fell back into the rhythm of the wind.

"You said you aren't going to shoot me?" Kodiak asked as they disappeared.

"Not today," Abel said again, and they were gone.

– TEN –

"Let's get to the business at hand," Crisp said when they disappeared.

"No one's going to pleasure you out here, Spire-man," Crow said, still lounging in the roots of his tree.

Crisp's eyes flashed. Taj interrupted quickly, "We wait."

"We wait," Stump said as well.

"Well, apparently the clearing isn't too dangerous for a little funeral and reception," Crisp muttered quietly. He stood before the piles he'd created, fingers run through what little hair the Hall had left him. For a moment, just a moment, I saw a man, lost, trying to do what he could to get through.

Only a moment. Then he disappeared, the little king again in his place. Crisp hauled Oyster to his feet and began directing him around the piles. Pope and Duck were dragged in as well, and soon all were busy, trampling flat space among the ferns to spread out ammunition and other sundry.

Stump sat with me. He looked through the trees where Abel and Kodiak had disappeared. "He has a power over the beast."

"Over the monster," I said.

"I don't know," Ivan said, rising from his place and pivoting to face us. He put his hands in his pockets and blew out a puff of air. "That didn't seem quite… how do I put this? Not justice. We're making sure Kodiak is 'sorry?' Does that cover it?"

"It's a start," Stump said.

I silently disagreed. Kodiak killed Patches. This was more like getting away with it. And, of all of us, Kodiak seemed most likely to go home and get away with whatever got him here in the first place. Nothing was alright.

"No," Ivan answered his own question. "It doesn't, Stump. A man is dead." He dropped his voice. "Something is going on with those two."

He raised his eyebrows, giving a searching look. He looked from face to face, expectantly, as if he were waiting for an answer. I didn't know the question. He squatted.

"I don't like how things are going. I think we can do better."

Again, the searching look. Again an unasked question.

"Well, think about it," Ivan finally said. "And, Thirteen… Don't let anyone push you around. Know your opinion counts with me." He looked at us both for a moment and then excused himself.

"No one's pushing me around," I muttered once he was gone.

Across the clearing Ivan approached Crisp, who stopped his work, and the two conferred. Something about it reminded me of Abel and the woman in the grey suit. I clicked the safety on my rifle off and on, and off and on.

Stump was rubbing his ankles aggressively. "You alright?" I asked.

"Me? Fine, fine. Getting old. You'll understand one day." He paused and peered at me for a moment. "Lord willing. Don't let Ivan bother you, son," he said. "He's mostly harmless. He just has a nose for mischief. Hands too. If he doesn't smell any, he'll cook some up."

"What's he getting at, though?" I asked.

"Hm? He's unhappy. Trying to find someone to be unhappy with."

"Everyone's unhappy," I said, watching Crisp, who was watching the equipment while Ivan spoke into his ear.

Stump continued to work his ankles. I clicked the safety on and set about my pack, seeing if anything else needed fixing.

*

Taj busied himself with his own pack. He was now inspecting the barrel of his rifle, which he had separated from the rest of the weapon. He kept twisting it, a few millimeters, holding up to his eye, and twisting again, unsatisfied with something.

Oyster had taken to Crisp's inventory with delight and was now subdividing piles into smaller piles. Pope had wandered into the trees. Watching him, I saw he was collecting different shaped leaves.

Abel and Kodiak returned before long, Kodiak still walking behind. His hands were restless without the rifle. He walked with hung head, and his eyes looked red. Yet his face was hard as he glanced from man to man, daring each to acknowledge his shame.

I fingered the broken equipment in front of me, ignoring him so he could continue to pretend he was invisible. Ivan had never made me anything but uncomfortable, but in my heart I agreed with him. "Sorry" might be true, but it wasn't worth one barrel of rustic's oil. Kodiak was a problem.

This was the crux: Taj and Happy were both right. We couldn't sacrifice him – yet. There was a time for necessity and a time for justice. There would be a time to set things right for Patches. There would be no blue button in Kodiak's future. I would fix that, too, before all was done. Fix it myself if needed.

Abel nodded at Crisp and Oyster's piles, then called everyone together. Most looked, but no one really moved. Crisp eyed him before turning back to his lackeys to relay a few orders in a low voice. Only then did he square his shoulders at Abel.

So there we were, floating among the ferns. Abel, with Kodiak at his shoulder, and Crisp, with Ivan in his shadow, stood over us. Prepared to hash out boundary lines in this little kingdom. To decide what little fate was still left to us. Happy leaned on a tree, scowling, to the side.

"Thirteen's fixing what needs fixing," Abel said loudly. "We need a bearing that might find what needs finding. We need to move by morning. Sooner if possible."

Crisp looked left and right, then stepped forward. But before he got a word out, Abel said, "Happy, can we move?"

Crisp's jaw muscle bulged. He held eye contact with Abel, but ceded the floor, letting things play out a few more beats.

After a moment's consideration, Happy spat loudly. "As long as I walk behind Kodiak." After a pause, he added, "Everyone's fit to travel."

"Taj, you have a bearing?" Abel asked.

"Animals need water. There's a valley dug northwest from here, should have a river. Should be Outlanders." At least half his attention remained on the detached barrel. He couldn't see more than twenty meters through this undergrowth, so when had he learned the topography? Maybe the maps in the briefing. Maybe as he fell from the aircraft. "And if we stick to the valley walls, we'll be defensible and mostly hidden."

"Yes, Crisp?" Abel asked. Crisp dropped his head and looked at Abel under furrowed eyebrows, hands on hips. He waited a space, long enough that when he spoke, it gave the impression he was reluctantly advising men seeking his help.

"I think that sounds a little…narrow. I agree so far as we should fix what we can and move soon."

He shifted his attention, now speaking to the seated Unforgiven.

Rather, taking ownership of us.

"But you neglect two things: first, there are thirteen… twelve of us, and at least 500 of them. Think about that.

"But more importantly, the idea that the State is going to count bodies and pick us up is only an assumption, a bad one. I shouldn't be alone in thinking that. We travel in a direction that will benefit us. Not them."

"I don't want to find Outlanders," Duck said. He was looking at Ivan rather than Crisp. Ivan nodded. "I want to get out of here."

"Where's 'out'?" Stump asked.

"It's not a bad idea," Pope said. Crisp frowned at him, listening closely. "Find a quiet spot of earth," Pope continued, "build a new life. We'd have to find some women, though. I need more than you lot for company." He chuckled, but he did it alone.

"There is no 'out'," Abel said. "They weren't lying. There is nowhere to go."

"There's everywhere!" Pope said. "Anywhere but here."

Conversation bubbled around the circle, and Crisp fanned the flames, nursing his glowing ember. "I'm not necessarily saying we should run. I'm saying we need to stop doing what we've been told and think for ourselves. What is best for us, here, now?"

"What's best for us is surviving," Crow said.

"Which is also what I am saying—" Crisp attempted.

"No. Not in, not out. We find a defensive position and stay put. You said they'd come to investigate the drop zone. So let them come to us. Do what needs doing on our terms."

"That sounds dangerous. And fruitless," Crisp said.

Before he could voice another argument Duck interjected, "We have to get out of this jungle! They're going to eat us!"

Crow growled. "We can tame the jungle. At least a hectare of it. We should find the nearest high ground and just...hole up until we're done with it. Or it's a lot of hiking for nothing."

Crisp spoke louder. "Holing up and killing Outlanders is still playing their game! Still trusting they'll come for us!" He held his blue-buttoned cylinder over his head for all to see. His last words were firm, "It's out or nothing."

And he dropped his cylinder on the ground.

The conversation stopped while all took that in. I fingered my pocket, feeling the cylindrical lump. I didn't know who to trust, but I was not ready to cut that cord.

"I thought you weren't saying we should run," Crow accused him, as if the contradiction could prove his own point. The two locked horns, voices rising. The murmurs bubbled again.

Then Ivan's voice cut across the clamor. "Thirteen. What do you think?"

Men turned to me. The argument paused.

I looked at the broken machines at my feet, still touching the cylinder in my pocket. I didn't know, and I didn't want this attention. This responsibility. Thatch Patches and his *core*. Maybe they really would go wherever Happy and I went.

If the blue button was hollow metal and plastic, Crisp's words beckoned. Taj's words were tempting too. Either one could be the best or worst idea, depending on a thousand variables I had no way of knowing. This problem wasn't a Bugwall. No fixed points, nothing to untangle, no purpose taking shape.

One purpose.

I need to go back.

"The valley," I said. "We track them."

Taj gave a quiet nod. Ivan's face was inscrutable.

"Stump? Oyster?" Abel asked. They shook their heads, demurring.

Something vile knotted deep in me. I had spoken, and they had stopped. I didn't want this.

Finally, Abel spoke. "Then let's move."

"Toward the valley?" Crisp asked.

"I don't like it," Duck said.

"I don't either," Crisp said.

"It's better than here," Abel said.

Once again, something unspoken but palpable passed between Abel and Crisp. But I had spoken.

Thatch this.

"Is north where Taj says we'll find Outlanders?" Pope asked.

"We've agreed," Taj said.

"This isn't a democracy," said Crow. Everyone ignored him.

We stood. And while the argument may have stopped, I saw it had merely been shoved to the background, to be continued in quiet spaces, in twos and threes. We were not done.

Abel leaned toward Stump, saying quietly, "Can you get these piles into packs?"

Stump nodded and began to dole out instructions. As Stump passed, Crisp reached out and took his shoulder, holding him in place. He never took his eyes off Abel. "You aren't in charge."

"The jungle is in charge," Abel said. "I told you. I'm doing what needs doing."

"Is that all?"

Abel looked tired. "That's all."

Crisp still held Stump, and in his other hand was his gun. Abel had two. My whole body wound up, waiting for something to happen.

No, we were not done.

Then Crisp released his hold, saying to Stump, "These are my piles," and walked away.

As I gathered the damaged equipment, Abel squatted in front of me.

"Thanks," he said.

"For what?" I said quickly. I took a hurried sip from my water bottle and sealed it.

"Holding together?" he asked.

"Yeah," I said.

"We need survival first. Bugwall, Eyes, and Ears. Then water, food, shelter. Things like the Beacon and the Cloak can wait."

"Got it."

"I'm sorry about Patches. You aren't alone out here," he said.

I searched his face, trying to divine his purpose. I still couldn't. I nodded.

Then he moved off, and I watched as he exchanged words with other men.

The words seemed kind. But Patches had been right. Abel was just one in a line of suitors. I was in the core. Which meant they'd defer and be polite until their patience wore out, and I found a gun in my back, whispered orders in my ear. That was how this machine would work.

For now, I had a job. I did a quick survey. The Bugwall was already fixed so I searched for the Ears. Stump had taken up his post by them again, earpiece in his ear as he rummaged in his pack.

"Those good?" I asked.

"Good," he said.

Two done. But the Eyes were in pieces. Fortunately, someone with a brain had assembled the toolkit, and it held everything I needed. I started bracing the fissures with drilled holes and bits of metal. Before long, the call to pack up floated through the camp.

Jackets on. Juice on. Ears on, Bugwall off, and straps digging into my shoulders and hips.

Twelve-strong, we stood. Facing away from our landing, toward Taj's invisible valley. Kodiak near the front, his right hand unconsciously fingering the grip of his long knife. Happy in the middle, rifle held tight. I, with sweat running from my temples and between my shoulder blades. The *click, click, click* of my safety was lost beneath the rustle of wind in the branches. The trees before us stood like gate pillars, like the doors of the Hall, but no path ran through them and beyond was only the shadow of dusk.

Taj looked over the group, then turned and walked. Abel and Kodiak fell in behind him and, one by one, we followed.

*

The jungle was miserable. Hiking with a heavy pack in the humid air, I was soon loosening my collar. In the fading light the jungle didn't give much of an impression beyond long grasses brushing my legs, in the pathless gaps between trees, and dark branches filling the space above us.

We only walked about two kilometers, but when we stopped, I threw my pack to the ground, ripped off my jacket, and collapsed onto a small mound.

We made camp and someone set up a stove. Solid protein blocks floating in a pinkish sauce. It looked terrible but tasted vaguely of tomatoes and cumin. The group wasn't talkative. It was full dark when I finished, and I laid down without trying to fix the Eyes. Today had gotten all it would get from me.

Oyster bedded down next to me. "The stars. It reminds me of

that night on the hill. I tried to count the fireworks until dawn. Did I tell you that?"

He didn't say much more before we dropped off, only, "Do you ever think you're so close to a dream? Just one step away…"

– ELEVEN –

I woke up to a world that was still. The wind had blown out, leaving a breeze in its place. It gently rustled the canopy above with whispers of leaf on leaf and a dancing mottle of dawn shadow. I heard no movement in the camp, only light snores.

One figure was sitting up, his back a dark outline in the grey light. One man standing guard.

I lay there a long time. The morning quiet and the sighing high above felt like home. The air was cool and wet, clean on my skin, leaving a light coat of dew. I breathed it deep into my lungs and felt the chill spread inside of me. The dust and tang of the city was absent, but in its place was dirt and tree dander, moss and bark. It tasted green.

When the morning light pierced the leaves, the wet air ignited, making beams that lanced the space beneath the canopy until trees or branches caught them, splashing them back in spots of brilliant white. Nothing reached the ground, where I still lay low in the cool shadow.

The dull sounds of the Outlands took shape, like players tuning before an orchestra. The ripple of leaves crested into the sharp flap of wings, beating the air above in a quick staccato. There was the crunch of undergrowth as something small hurried along the ground, invisibly finding its way to a new haven.

There were a thousand gentle chirps, rising and falling in an unbroken murmur. Frogs, crickets, beetles, fliers, and all the others, but as I lay in the shadow they were simply a beautiful, soft babble welcoming me into the morning.

It was… pleasant. It was like laughter at a funeral. With closed eyes and open ears I breathed again, pulling the morning damp deep inside my lungs.

By full light I was thoroughly awake. The camp remained quiet as I ventured a few meters to take care of morning necessities.

When I returned, I approached the guard. Stump.

"Thanks for standing watch," I said, low and quiet.

"Nightmares," he said, then tilted his head to the Ears to draw me over.

"Screen's supposed to stay dark…," I said, with thoughts of a prematurely drained source.

"I remember," said Stump, even as I trailed off.

Two red dots hovered at the edge of the display.

I glanced at the dials, gauging the sensitivity and range. Big things, maybe 300 meters away.

"What are they?"

"Don't know," Stump said. "Just watching."

It could be anything. "Probably some animal?"

"Probably some animal."

I watched the dots. One moved, then stopped. "Well, holler or something."

Stump grunted.

I made my way to a ground cloth holding the metal menagerie, where we'd laid out the more essential items in case of emergency in the night. The Eyes were the only tier-one priority still broken.

I sat by them, but did not take up the pieces. Instead, I cut a strip from a canvas tarp and wrapped it around my forearm. This I fastened with sealing adhesive from my toolkit, then added a small loop with another strip of material. I took out my screwdriver and slid it into the sheath. It fit snugly but slid too easily, so I cut another strip from the tarp and glued a larger loop for the handle, coating the whole thing with a light film of adhesive to provide grip. When it was complete, I blew it dry and slid the driver in again. It held, snug.

Kodiak and Taj could have their knives. This was my domain. That done, I looked at the Eyes again.

I grabbed the propeller piece first. The structure was braced from before last evening's hike, and now in the light I turned it in my hands, inspecting my work. In another time, another place, I would have been embarrassed. The quality was makeshift, but a masterpiece for this hacked together Outlands workshop. I began working the knobs and bolts that held the unit together and made my way inside.

It was clear and clean. The propeller connected to a motor. Motor to source by a lifeline cable snaking down the tether. Simple hinges on the blades, gears to amplify the torque, and that was pretty much it. There was a separate power loop for the imaging gizmos, shunting the power line off toward a tiny city of miniature electronics. I'd have to trust those; as with the Bugwall's sonic generator, I simply lacked the tools to peer inside. The data feed down the tether looked clean.

Apart from the prop and imagers, there was nothing but a spinning wheel, like a flywheel. It was a gyro to give stability so the prop wouldn't spin the tether into a tangle. Source, pathway, purpose. Everything with purpose. The flywheel and metal shell provided strength so the prop and imaging boxes could do their work. It was simple.

It should have worked. I wished I had a voltmeter to properly test the circuits, but no one had asked me for a wish list.

I preferred the old-fashioned way anyway. I took a firm grip on the propeller unit and flipped the power switch.

Nothing happened.

I poked each wire but felt no tingle to tell me power was flowing.

With a sigh, I laid the cylinder down. It might yet be a simple job. But there was only so much I could be expected to do in the dirt with a screwdriver.

So, the base unit. It was simple work, spinning each screw out and laying them in order. The sequence was a mundane, meditative puzzle. My mind wandered as I hunted for the next fastener, mapping the people and the jungle around me, re-arranging the tangle on a flat plane. It was just another machine.

There was a burned-out spot, glaring from the middle: Patches. Something else would have to become the spinning wheel, or this machine would tangle out of control.

I thought of yesterday, a bag of ammunition, and two red somethings off in the Outlands. It was beginning already.

But it was always simple.

Source: The State sends Unforgiven to the Outlands.

Pathway: The Unforgiven kill Outlanders.

Purpose: What to call it? Restoration? That was the purpose of all this.

My hands fell still, a metal cover half removed. The loop didn't close. Killing Outlanders and going home shared no circuitry; it was not a functioning system.

So, there must be two loops to the machine, like the Eyes before me. I rearranged the map, squinting through the trees.

Source, the State sends Unforgiven out here. Pathway, we kill Outlanders, the purpose being… inscrutable. I took the screwdriver off the fastener and slipped it into the sheathe on my arm, twisting it as I thought. I could no more place a finger on the purposes of the State than dismantle the Eyes' imaging box I'd held back at the Hall.

It was pointless to probe. I shifted and worked backward on the other loop. Restoration.

If the purpose was Restoration, then the source was Conviction. Our collective conviction before a parade of Arbiters. That set this machine in motion and ensured it ran to the end. But the pathway?

I sank to deeper and darker thoughts, staring through a lattice of vines and fern branches. The chaotic greens of moss and leaf suggested patterns which never resolved to anything. I could not think of any machine or machination that turned Conviction to Restoration.

No pathway. The machine I trusted in was a plastic façade, buttons and flashing lights but no loop.

And these stray sparks and twisted traces marked the outline of only one system that made any sense. Pathway, we do what *they* want. Purpose, they do what *we* want. A barter, with two shut doors before my eyes. Behind one, the Source. What they actually wanted, what this whole machine of butchery was for. Behind the other…

Why would they do what we want once everything is done?

Crisp's words echoed. *An assumption, and a bad one.*

Back to the second loop: Conviction logically led not to 500 dead Outlanders but to 13 dead Unforgiven.

That circuit closed. Convoluted but clean. I found my hand on my pocket where the blue button was zipped into its own compartment.

Condemned, not convicted.

I descended into silence, my hands resting on the Eyes I had been fixing. I was going back. If there was a Pathway, I'd find it. If there wasn't, I'd spragging make it. State, Crisp, Ivan, Abel, and 500 Outlanders be thatched, I'd make it.

I don't know how long I sat like that, turning gears in my head, but the sky was much lighter when I was stirred by the sounds of the camp waking.

*

A few quiet risers awakened when light hit their faces. They moved, quiet and slow, and their disturbances accumulated until an unmarked threshold was breached and, all at once, the rest stirred. We shared food, water, and complaints about the bumpy ground.

Unforgiven were packing, so I sealed the Eyes, unrepaired. I moved mechanically, not yet emerged from shadowy thoughts. I watched them closely, the pieces of my machine.

Something struck me as off while I stuffed things into my pack. I checked the camp again. Then Pope called out, "We're one light! Someone's missing!"

"Did you count yourself, genius?" taunted Crow.

"I counted myself, genius," Pope said. "Who's missing?"

"Oyster," said Happy.

There was a motionless mound in a sack, still upon the spot where he'd fallen asleep behind me. I gazed at it, even as the camp wound up to a bustle, questions flying.

"He's here!" I called. "He's in his bag."

He wasn't moving at all.

I reached out a tentative hand to shake him, my muscles tensed as if reaching toward a wild animal. The camp was too loud and he was too still.

I shook him, feeling his weight under my hand, and then snatched my hand back. Nothing. I reached out again and pushed him. He rolled over and the cover fell back, revealing open, empty eyes. There was a hiss of breath and quiet curses as I snatched my hand back again.

"What in thatch happened?" Duck cried.

Happy stepped in as I scooted back, scrambling for distance. He ripped the sack open and began inspecting the body as we crowded behind him.

"No pulse," Happy announced.

It was clinical. It was the obvious. It was stark and unyielding to hear.

"The body is relatively warm," Happy continued, "but it's in the bag, so it's hard to say how long it's been." He began looking at the hands and pressing the torso, explaining at each step. As he cupped the head to pull back the eyelids he swore and pulled his hand back, shaking it in the air.

"What? What is it?" Duck asked.

Happy flicked his eyebrows at the boy, as if to say, "get this," and rolled the body up onto its side. There was a disgusting hole, or burrow, in the back of Oyster's neck.

"State's balls," someone swore. More groaned.

"What in State is that?" Duck asked again, voice several notes higher.

Happy looked more closely for a moment and then sat back on his heels, wiping his hands. He took a lecturing tone.

"My guess? *Perfossa gigans*. It's a bug. It's… pretty unpleasant really. It finds a host to feed on before laying its eggs inside. It's like a tick but larger and it kills. It's a scavenger; usually the host is already dead, but if not?" He paused. "It releases toxins to protect the eggs from scavengers. If the host is alive, the toxins travel the circulatory system and…" he shrugged.

There was wide-eyed silence around the group as we all tried not to picture it. Then Duck asked, "How big is this thing?"

"Diggers?" Happy held up his hand with his thumb and finger

entirely too far apart. The silence popped in a new explosion of curses. I ripped off my jacket, whipping it about. Others were patting down bodies, shaking out clothes, and twisting to see their backs and other hard to reach parts.

As I finished shaking out my clothes, I heard Happy chuckling. "What? What is it?" I asked.

"It's just," Happy began, then took off his glasses and wiped his eyes. "If you could all see yourselves."

"What?"

"Diggers are highly territorial. If one got Oyster, that's the only one for, oh, a hundred meters in any direction. You all can put your clothes back on."

"Well excuse me, Mr. Doctor," Pope spat at him. "We aren't all versed in the nature of *Gigaflossy*."

"Why didn't the Bugwall stop it?" Taj asked. He, Stump, and a few others stood calmly to the side, untouched by the panic visited on the lesser Unforgiven.

Happy wiped his glasses and put them back on. "That is a real question. I'm led to believe even a particularly fertile one should have holed up. We're covered in juice as well. That they both failed is…concerning?" His voice raised into a question as he looked up at me.

All remaining ten pairs of eyes turned toward me.

"What?" I asked. "I fixed it!"

"Then what is that thing doing in Oyster's neck?" Crow asked, thrusting a finger out toward the body.

"Are you saying this is my fault?" I asked.

"Does the Bugwall work?"

I looked down at the metal disc. Light on. Silently humming. There were paths inside that I couldn't see.

"Did you break it, Tinker?" he bit out.

I shoved him, his gangly body windmilling as he stumbled. Hands took hold of me, to keep me where I stood. I didn't know why they would bother. We'd murdered Patches.

"I didn't put you in the Hall, Scarecrow. I didn't bring you to the Outlands."

I shrugged the hands off and picked up the device.

"Look," I said, shoving it against his chest. "You got yourself into this. Those pilots broke it. The State gave me a box of tools, and it's on. You don't like it, blame someone else. It's on."

Crow wasn't looking at me anymore; he stared at the Bugwall in his hands. Its single light glowed in the morning. It sat inert, driving even me to doubt. But if it wasn't working now, there was nothing more I could do.

Crow gazed at his chest, silent and still as the disc in his hands. It looked small in his long, thin arms, like a giant with a dinner plate. My vision cleared. I saw a frightened man, like me.

I pressed the Bugwall into him. "It's on, Crow." He nodded. He rubbed the back of his neck, looking at the device. I hesitated but did not apologize.

"Look at this!" Taj said. He was standing by Oyster's pack and holding a tube of the juice.

"What is it?" Abel asked.

"Stupid thatcher's juice is sealed. He didn't put it on."

"Why? …" Crisp asked but didn't finish. Only Oyster knew.

"Thatcher's got two sealed tubes." Taj said, pulling another tube from the pack. He rooted deeper. "And an extra jacket. And an extra purifier."

Abel held up the jacket. "Not his size." He looked down at Oyster.

Stump sighed and walked into the trees, just outside camp. He bent down. "Tracks lead back the way we came," he said.

"Not mine?" Abel asked.

"Or Kody's. Not big enough."

Stump rose, lips pursed.

"So, what happened?" I asked.

Abel folded the jacket, laying it on the now ownerless pack. "There's only one extra jacket in the Outlands. He went back to Patches. No juice, no Bugwall."

"Why would he?" My question hung the same as Crisp's.

"Oyster chasing his pearls," Happy answered. "I told him it'd get him killed one day."

Then I understood. The extra forks, Old Man Horn, everything. *Thief.* He'd built his mountain and here it stood, beside him. A pile of scrap in the Outlands.

"Bugwall's fine, Thirteen," Abel said, looking at the body. Then he walked off and made himself busy on the other side of camp, his face inscrutable.

Two men zipped the sleeping bag closed over Oyster's head. I understood the poor thatcher. A sealed tube would have been a seed for a new fortune. An open tube would have meant life, just not the life he wanted. *One step away.* I shook my head, hoping to clear it. The morning was barely begun.

"Should we say something?"

I hadn't asked anyone in particular, but Happy was there too, wiping his hands and looking down. "Oyster," he began. He paused. "Oyster," again. "Oyster, you stupid, rutting pig's butt." And he turned and walked away.

It wouldn't do. There was no one else left, so I looked down at him, lump in a bag, and collected my thoughts. "Oyster," I began, just for myself. And for Oyster if he could hear. "May you find your house on the hill." *Not likely* I thought. It wouldn't do, either. So I added, "And may you find everything you need is already in reach." That was better.

The eleven of us pulled anything we might need out of his pack and packed up camp. The machine ground on. The Outlands would take his body.

– TWELVE –

The air grew thick as the sun rose over the canopy, turning the Outlands into a damp oven. The slick of dew was replaced by that of sweat. Stump's red dots had moved off. We walked north.

The gentle orchestra of the forest changed timbre as well. Kodiak led with a machete, the rest of us strung out behind. We placed communication devices in our ears, simply called comms, as a safety line tying us together.

Bugs and birds flew from us as we broke down branches. Primates or rodents escaped from tree to tree until they could turn and consider us from a distance.

The great tree trunks clustered like cathedral aisles, guiding us forward before opening into grand rooms, with roofs of spreading branches and knee-high shade plants carpeting the floor. Leaves were red or green, but spots of orange, white, or purple peeked where flowers grew. Everything was always in motion, ruffled by ever moving whispers, creating shifting patterns of light and shade.

But the white haze of hot, wet air hung on us. Underneath the siren song to take off my jacket, thorns stood on the branches and leaves shook serrated edges, lest we forget the dark promise of the Outlands. And the Bugwall worked slowly, needing minutes to push insects away, so small fliers harried us when we moved, juice or no. I wore my jacket and suffered the heat.

Others moved with purpose, heads perhaps full of Outlanders, battle, and the mission. I just walked, thinking of anything else. Sweat, nightfall, and a sleeping sack. As kilometers went by, I found myself next to Happy.

"Doctor," I said.

"Tinker," he responded.

Crow had meant the word as an insult. Happy intoned it as an acknowledgement. He must have been getting the carousel of suitors as well. A look passed between us, a tentative invitation that maybe we were, and would be, in this together. I relaxed, a forced smile growing genuine.

"That digger, this morning," I said, testing the water. I raised my eyebrows.

"I know," Happy said. "Nature is terrifying."

"You said they usually do…" I hesitated, trying to find vague words, "…their business on… hosts… that are already dead?"

Happy gave a guilty smile and rocked his head. "I did. I did say that. I'm not sure it's true, but I didn't want to scare people too badly."

"Ah." I digested that. "But that's my question – when I get bitten by an ant or stung by a bee, it hurts. How does the digger do that to live hosts?"

"Diggers – well, pretty much all the burrowing insects – secrete a numbing agent. Something they evolved up the chain for just that reason; it's awfully hard to feed if your host knows you're there.

Their saliva is quite remarkable: anesthetic, anticoagulant, immunosuppressant–"

I interrupted with a wave of my hands, swatting away his words. "I don't want to hear it!" Happy chuckled. "What kind of doctor did you say you were?"

"Medical."

"Not bug-ology?"

"Entomology. And no."

"Why do you know all this, then?" He seemed suspiciously expert about the wilds.

"I read about it."

"Maybe I did too," I said. "Doesn't mean I remember. Doesn't come up much day to day in the State."

"My dear Thirteen," Happy said, with an air of kind condescension, "What do you think separates us from the animals?"

It wasn't conversational. A test. Less than a hundred words had passed between us. We were both back on guard.

Even as I formed my thoughts, he pressed.

"Taxonomy, certainly. Our physiology is distinct with our soft skin and what not. We walk on two legs and grasp with our hands, but does that satisfy you?"

I noted the rhetorical flourish. I let him talk, awaiting the real question.

"For a long time they said tools," Happy continued, "but then they found an animal with tools. They said man was the only one who could learn, who could plan, who could solve problems, but each hypothesis was knocked down. As we learned more about the animals, we learned how like us they could be. So, they said ethics. But, again, we are too much alike. We both kill, we both cheat, we both nurture. Did you know a chimpanzee will lie to get a larger carrot than his brother?"

"Will it?"

"And so will a child," he said. "We all do whatever it takes to survive — when that is what's at stake. And when survival is assured, we do whatever makes us content. Ethics is dead."

"Some people sacrifice," I said.

"As do mothers in the wild. And some fathers."

"Hmf." His lecture paused, and he watched me now as we walked. Measured. Yes, I was under his microscope, and it was my turn to speak. I scrambled to reboard his train of thought.

"Are you saying we're the same?"

"Absolutely not."

It was like arguing with an encyclopedia.

Our line came to a halt, even as Happy prepared to recite another entry. Taj put his head together with Stump and the Ears. They spoke quietly, and I watched.

Pope had pulled out his dyes and held his sniping rifle under one arm to keep his hands free. He was finishing his decorations on the long barrel, a swirling pattern that wound around the metal, like wind chasing clouds.

But Taj and Abel traded urgent whispers, and my shirt, my jacket, everything began to feel tight. I began to feel how urgent this conversation was. This wasn't a job interview. This was the

Outlands and a friend in a circle of loaded guns.

What was he getting at?

Taj moved back to the front without comment, and we resumed our hike.

"They said the soul," said Happy, taking up his thought as if there were no red dots in the world. "The soul was innate and unique to man, but now there was an uproar on both sides. Some cried foul, their cat or their dog, or their ferret or their wombat had a soul. They saw affection in their pets and the concept of 'soul' is sufficiently ill-defined that that was enough. Others derided the very concept of a soul, human or otherwise. For my part, I've cut through the human body from top to bottom, and I have seen neither the evidence nor the necessity for this soul."

Happy only held half my thoughts now. I scanned the jungle around us, trying to separate leaf from shadow from monster. My ears strained to hear the approach of danger underneath the passage of Unforgiven. The exercise was a useless distraction, but it felt necessary.

"Well, the presence or absence of the soul is irrelevant," I said absently, "unless it does something." No Path without Purpose.

Happy turned his head toward me, then, grey eyes behind thick glasses. A practiced smile broke his face. "Exactly."

Somehow, I'd just been awarded a point.

He continued, "If the body-soul separation is invisible, effectless, and unobservable, is there any practical difference at all?"

Something shook a branch, high up, and leaves fell. Probably a bird. I snugged my jacket on my shoulders. "So, what do you say?"

"Tally our attempts, Thirteen, to answer. We alone ask a question, and then pursue its answer. What else on Earth is troubled by this question in the first place? It's the quest for knowledge and the ever upward climb of our species. If you learn something and then forget it, if you fail to answer a question and abandon it, you are just like the animals. Mankind must better itself. That is what makes us *us*."

So that was his point. I'd forgotten what I'd read. Like an animal.

"So, are we getting better?" I said, mostly to myself.

While my full attention turned to the jungle, I felt more than saw Happy studying me again. When I turned, he held my eyes for only a moment, then huffed and looked away. The encyclopedia fell into a deeper silence than before our first greeting.

That was something.

I was thirsty. Some water had seeped into my right boot. Maybe I'd passed his test, maybe I hadn't. Maybe I wasn't part of the upward climb of man. Still, a condescending ally was better than no ally at all.

I missed Patches.

The comm crackled to life and Stump's voice said, "Hold."

We hurried until we joined a circle around Stump and the Ears. Crisp was at his back, looking at the screen.

"What have we got?" Pope asked.

"Red dots. Two or three large bodies, maybe half a kilometer that way," Crisp gestured toward some trees. Taj looked at the screen, then clicked off his safety and began moving into the trees.

"I'm coming," Crisp said.

Taj did not comment or turn. He stopped, his back straightening. Then he began moving again, Crisp trailing in his wake.

"Give me a gun," Kodiak said as he watched them disappear.

"You're sitting it out, Kody," Abel said.

Kodiak grunted his displeasure and found a rock to sit on, facing away from us.

Duck was wide-eyed, looking from face to face for direction. The rest uneasily dispersed while Stump and Abel watched the Ears, murmuring into their comms.

Men held their rifles uncomfortably as they stared into the trees. I positioned my gun on its shoulder strap as well and tried to think fitting thoughts for the beginning of the end. But instead I thought about diggers and Oyster and our lake.

I crept back toward the Ears when I heard Abel and Stump giving instructions. I saw two red dots that must have been Taj and Crisp, and other, farther dots that were our targets. All red, the Ears couldn't tell the difference between enemy and ally like the Eyes. Stump spoke, and the two friendly dots swung wide of the target. They slowed and approached the spot where the "large bodies" glowed. I tensed, waiting for the gunshot.

The target dots abruptly shot out and away from us, sliding toward the edge of the screen. A crackle came over my comm, the signal weak at the range.

"All clear," I finally heard as Crisp's voice crystallized. "Some kind of deer or antelope thing."

"Did you bag one?" Pope retorted over the comm. "I'm already tired of warm goo."

"Some idiot forgot to bring the cooler," Crisp said. The friendly dots began moving back toward our group as Abel murmured course corrections over the channel.

I let my breath out and shared a look with Happy. "One of these days, I guess? One of these days we'll find red dots, and it'll turn ugly."

Happy blinked, refocusing on the present. "Oh, most certainly," he said, even as the pensive silence crept back over him. "We're leaving a blazed trail. Whatever finds the landing zone finds us next." And he was gone, combing through thoughts again.

"Nedder," I whispered. A hole gaped in the underbrush behind us, not unlike those great, awful doors at the Hall of Judgment. I jogged over to Abel.

I interrupted as he corrected Crisp's course. He turned, eyebrows raised.

"We need to cover our tracks. What if someone finds the landing site and tracks us?"

He looked behind us, measuring the hole as I had. But he measured with resignation, not realization. "Keep moving."

"That's it?"

"That's it," he nodded.

Smoking thatch. I left them to their navigation. I looked at the hole a last time as I snugged my pack. *One of these days.* It was like sitting on a time bomb with a masked clock.

*

I walked alone when we began moving again. I didn't want more philosophy.

The rest of the day was mud, bugs, and looking over my shoulder. I tried to leave no trail but it was a foolish endeavor with Kodiak and others taking shifts on the machete. We stopped two or three more times to chase red dots. Each time, they escaped before we could identify them. Antelope or Outlander. Happy could expound on it however he wanted but the indisputable fact remained, the difference between those two was vast, as wide as the gap between life and death.

My legs, unused to walking, were wobbly when we stopped for the night. My shoulders and waist hurt with blooming bruises from the pack. The buzzing insects, red dots, and sweat and grime had me crawling out of my skin. And each footprint and broken branch I left behind me were drops of anxiety in a rising river.

I tried to slough that off along with my pack. I took my jacket off as the Bugwall pushed the bugs away and stretched my shoulders, hoping the close claustrophobia of the day would dissipate, and squatted before my gear.

Then Ivan appeared before me and, with no preamble, demanded, "Have you changed your mind?"

"Excuse me?" I asked.

"You said track them. You said go to the valley. Have you changed your mind?"

He was shifting from foot to foot, hands nervously twitching, eyes unblinking. This was a different Ivan.

"I think we should stick together. Taj and Happy–"

"Happy isn't thinking in those terms anymore. You saw those dots on the Ears today. We don't know what they were. We're heading into the middle of the Outlands."

"We're already in the middle–"

"Bah." His voice grew hard. "Have you changed your mind, Thirteen?"

"We have our mission–"

"Smoke the mission. We have our lives. Today. I want to make sure we still have them a week from now. Nedder, what is wrong with all of you? All I'm asking you to do is keep yourself alive!"

He stepped closer. I found my hand on my sheathed screwdriver. Ivan had no loose screws, not the kind that a screwdriver might fix, but holding it brought comfort.

"I think Abel knows what he's doing," I lied. *Better Abel than Ivan.*

"Abel? You trust him? He was there first, you know. He's not one of us."

I couldn't disagree. I didn't answer.

Ivan raised himself straight and looked over my head. Some decision was made, and he squatted down to eye level, looking me in the eye.

"Let me lay this out," he said. "I won't let you get us all killed with your stupidity because you don't know what's best for you. Hear me clearly – I know what to do. You will support me and help me, help us all, when the time comes. Or I will break these machines to pieces. Everyone's death will be on your hands. It will be your fault, Thirteen. Your fault."

"But you'd also–"

"Don't test me!" Ivan spat. Suddenly he twisted his body so it came up against mine. I felt the sharp edge of his knife against my ribs.

"What are you doing?" I blurted out.

"Hush. I've tried to be reasonable. You will support me when the time comes. I'm doing this for your own good."

"What are you trying to do? We're surrounded. You'd be dead in minutes." I had no doubt he could feel my heart frantically pounding beneath my words.

"Oh yes, just like Kodiak," he purred. "I'm sure I will get a very stern talking to. I'll take my chances. Will you?"

I looked to Stump, busy with his pack, and Happy, slowly walking the perimeter of the camp. No one was watching us. I looked at Abel. If Ivan pushed the knife in, he'd be the judge of what happened.

Ivan's voice pitched somewhere between a whisper and a growl. "You keep sucking Abel's teat, and we all die anyway. I don't need to you to agree, Thirteen. I need you to understand."

Then he waited.

"I get it. I got it."

"Do not test me," he whispered, then stomped off.

With an effort, I let go of my screwdriver. My hand found the gun in the dirt beside me, and I clicked the safety off. I felt a chill that had nothing to do with the deepening evening. I'd signed my name, and I didn't know what I'd do when the contract came due.

Not support Ivan.

I'd just needed the knife out of my ribs. I thought of going to Happy but I couldn't stand his nonchalant answers to everything, and Ivan had hinted that his allegiance had shifted. Stump seemed steady, but in Abel's pocket. My best option might be standing over Ivan in the night and pulling a trigger.

I clicked the safety back off. There was no way this could go well for me now.

I heard chatter about the Bugwall and reminders to put on extra juice just in case.

I ate my dinner, looked at the broken menagerie, and got into my sleeping bag.

I thought I would fix it in the morning. I thought it could wait. But the next thing I knew, a dark figure was over me, shaking my shoulder. I blinked myself awake. It was full dark. "Up!" an urgent, hushed voice commanded me.

"What?" I mumbled. "What is it?"

"Red dots." And the dark figure moved off to the next bag.

– THIRTEEN –

Quicker than thought, I had boots and coat on and was hurrying toward a cluster around the Ears. Heated whispers came in sharp tones. My feet crunched through the foliage as I ran, the sound stark in the muted night.

The growing cluster of men was focused on the screen. Two groups of red dots, in rough lines, moving toward us. Coordinated.

I waited for the logical explanation. This was normal. I should go back to bed. Wake up tomorrow, hike through the Outlands. I stared at the screen. The whispers grew harsher. The explanation never came.

"Thirteen!"

My head whipped up. Abel loomed before me. "I need Eyes."

Eyes. The Eyes.

Son of a thatcher.

We had no Eyes.

"Thirt!" I focused on the face in front of me again. "I need Eyes, do you understand?"

"They aren't fixed," I said. It made me sick to say it. But there was no outburst, no curse. Abel studied the Ears for a moment.

"The Cloak?" someone suggested.

Abel considered, calculated. "Not yet. Give me the Ears. We have five minutes. I need Eyes, Thirt. Go!"

I jolted into motion with visions of eleven cold Unforgiven laid out with unpressed blue buttons. I grabbed my tools and the Eyes and set to work, moving with the urgency that comes with panic.

I knew the screws and latches. I had already opened it once. As I worked, the familiar motions brought calm, and the adrenaline ebbed. Someone strapped a light to my head.

Abel was barking half-whispered commands. In the daylight, Crow and Crisp and Ivan and all of them could spit their opinions and challenges, but now, in the dark, in the face of the enemy, they obeyed. Abel was the fixed point. He was the eye of the storm, and he spun them out into the trees against the approaching lines.

My fingers were flying to get inside the base unit. He sent Taj, Duck, Crow, and Stump out to meet one group of dots, and Kodiak, Crisp, Ivan, and Pope to meet the other. Pope, take Oyster's rifle, no point sniping at close range against a massed enemy. Sorry he couldn't place them more specifically; he didn't know what the terrain was or what cover was out there. He didn't know if the Outlanders would deviate in their approach. He would watch the Ears and let them know if they broke or shifted.

Every apology, every excuse, and every back-up plan twisted in my gut like a knife. Abel needed Eyes. This was on me now. There was no way we were going to die tonight. I could fix this.

I was inside. I rebuilt this in the Hall – I knew this machine. As my eyes flicked from point to point, I couldn't make sense of it. I needed to slow down. I needed to get it done.

The two teams exited our camp, and the chatter began over my comm. Had I switched it on? I must have. "Two minutes, Thirt." Abel's voice pulsed in my ear. "Two minutes to contact. Blue group, shift to your left."

Two minutes. I was looking and probing but the grid wouldn't take shape. It was too fast. I needed to slow down.

Source. There. I started with the source, the power pack. And then… I flipped the box around and looked at the projector, the piece that generated the holographic image. The hardware would be on the inside. I flipped it around, and there it was.

Yes. I had seen this before. In the Hall of the Unforgiven. In the morning.

"One minute. Yellow group, send two right to flank and listen for my mark."

No time. I don't know what I saw then but it was clear – there were the two points. They needed to be joined. I couldn't see the machine yet, but I saw the break. I cast about for metal, any loose metal, but there was nothing in the beam of my headlamp.

I looked at Abel. "I need more time."

"You have forty seconds."

"I need metal!" To no one in particular.

No response.

Happy. Happy was still here. "Happy, get over here." The doctor had stayed, safe for the aftermath. Happy rushed over on quiet feet.

"What is it?"

"I need your glasses."

Silence.

"I will fix them later. I need your glasses. Now."

Happy pulled them off and handed them to me. I ripped off one of the earpieces and handed them back as Happy gasped.

"I'll fix it! Later."

"Blue group, shift left, they've deviated. Move left, ten seconds," Abel's voice cut through. "Yellow, hole up. Wait for my mark."

"We've got a thicket in front of us." It was Taj's whisper.

"Wood or leaf?" Abel.

"Leaf."

"Wait for my mark."

My fingers trembled. Fear, excitement, nerves. I bent Happy's glasses to make a bridge between the two points. One point was secure.

"Yellow. Mark."

The night erupted, and I covered my ears. And then silence, followed by voices yelling in the night. My earpiece dissolved to a chaos of chatter, Abel's terse orders overlaid with curses as everyone started talking at once.

I ripped off my comm as a second burst of gunfire erupted on my right, followed by another one on my left. My hands were shaking.

"I need Eyes, Thirt!" Abel bellowed across the clearing. The second point was secure. The night was screaming. Happy suddenly rushed into the shadows under the trees, one hand holding his lopsided glasses to his head. I looked down at my work; the point was barely cooled, and I didn't bother closing the casing, I just held up the propeller and flipped the switch. The rotor whined to life and took off, floating up twenty or thirty meters into the air and ripping a hole through the branches above. A moment later the hologram flickered to life. It was dim but it was on. I started breathing again. I looked up, tried to call out, but Abel was already squatting by my side, hands on the dials as he shifted the view, calling a stream of orders into the comm.

The time for whispering was over. There was a staccato of gunfire breaking the night, interrupting the crashing of bushes and calling of voices. I heard voices speaking words I understood and others calling in strange sounds. And despairing cries.

I grabbed my rifle and withdrew into the shadows, squatting in silence with the weapon held tight against my chest as I stared into the dark and let the cacophony of the shattered night roll over me.

It continued. Happy dragged a body into the dim glow of our camp. I watched silently, hidden, as he laid the man down and moved around him. The body's breath came ragged, a grating wheeze both in and out, in and out.

I don't know how long it was. The night seemed to stretch, measureless and shapeless, until the rhythm of the battle slowed. The shots in the night were replaced, moment by moment, by the steady drone of Abel's voice coordinating the men and their rifles. Single shots broke the silence like dogs barking in the night – muffled punctures through the blanket of darkness, a rumor of distant trouble, and then quiet. Not like barking dogs. It was more like listening to one man beat another in an alley, in the dark hours of the morning. With every dull smack I twitched, wishing it would stop, bracing for the next.

Happy's movements slowed and the breathing quieted. He leaned down to speak to the wheezing body. Still alive.

Finally, I saw Abel reach into the air and snatch the Eyes as they fell back to earth. I heard voices, speaking words I understood, and footsteps stomping toward the camp. I heard laughter lift above the voices and a brief snatch of song.

A huge figure broke through the undergrowth, and then Kodiak stepped into the soft glow of camp. The light was dancing in his eyes, his face flushed, and his hands covered in blood. He was a man who was still alive. The blood on his hands went up his arms, and I wondered if it was his or someone else's.

Six more figures followed. That was everyone – if you counted the body on the ground. Taj glided to the Ears and squatted, pushing buttons with one hand. He did not place his weapon down. After a short moment, he lifted his voice above the others, "Clear! No warm bodies for a kilometer, maybe kilo and a half."

I watched from my shadow as backs were slapped, and laughter spread across the group. "You were a beast out there," Stump said to Kodiak.

"And you! You can fight, old man," Kodiak said, pounding his shoulder.

Then Happy passed through them with a bandage, and the laughter gave way. "How is Pope?" someone asked.

"He died, for a quarter minute or so. But he's fine now. They sent the good stuff with us. His arm may be lame for a bit, it tore through the muscle in his shoulder." He stopped and looked at where Pope lay. "It didn't hit anything important but triggered some kind of cascade through his endocrine. It happened fast."

Happy's eyes went distant again, sorting thoughts and theories.

"He died? They barely nicked him!"

"You brought him back?"

Happy refocused but didn't answer.

"He's in a swoon. I've given him something for the pain. It happened fast..." He raised his voice. "I need to see everything! Every scratch!"

They formed around him and jackets and shirts started coming off, pants rolled up.

"Come on, Doc! It's not that kind of party!" Kodiak joked, flexing a little.

Others were more somber. Happy just shook his head. "Remember, Kody. 'Everything will kill you out here.'" He moved through the group, washing wounds, wiping chemicals on, and injecting a few. He flagged some for stitches, but not before he'd seen everything once.

I could finally see the entire line. Most of them were flushed and radiant, full of life like Kodiak. Even the staid Stump had a smile as he worked out his joints. I saw the echo of Death. He had passed before them; they had walked through his shadow. But they had defied him and what remained was life, burning brighter than before.

Two of them were not so. Duck remained under the shadow. I could see his eyes staring off into the Outlands, oblivious, as Happy lifted his arms and checked his skin. Maybe death had stepped too close to him. Maybe he had become the shadow as he killed. He had not made it out alive, not as the others had.

Crisp too was silent. As I later heard from the men, he had gone fetal in the bushes, hadn't fired a shot. He now sat apart with his rifle loose on his lap, staring inward, and his jaw was set.

– FOURTEEN –

All the injuries were gashes and slices. They'd been fighting among thorns and sharp branches, but it seemed likely that the Outlanders had fought with sharpened weapons rather than guns, or even arrows. That should have been good for us, but I could not forget the rasping wheezes of Pope. They had something as potent as a bullet.

Pope was conscious now, and Abel sat by his side while Happy worked on the others. Pope was giving short answers, an occasional weak laugh. Abel put a jacket over him.

When Happy reached the end of the line for the second time, he straightened. "I think we're alright. Remember, at least half of everything here is toxic. Apparently the weapons, too. I can't just treat everyone for everything since the coffers are not endless. But if you feel anything, anything at all, come to me. Itchy, cold, hot, dizzy, dry mouth, bloody nose, numb... you get it. Find me. Quickly."

The line dispersed. People talked about what had happened, reliving a moment of the clash or teasing the other Unforgiven. Duck retired to a corner like me, while Crisp walked in small circles by himself, talking under his breath. Taj now squatted by Pope, holding the uninjured hand in both of his own and shaking his head.

As Abel walked by Stump he asked, "Joints still working, old man?" Stump countered with something about respect for elders in a grizzled voice, and another rare smile.

Then Abel walked toward me. I watched, silent, as he squatted down. "You may need to take a look at the Eyes. They were running hot at the end. I don't think they're in good shape."

I grunted an affirmative. I knew what I had done. "Why is everyone smiling?" I asked.

Abel didn't respond immediately. "You don't have to forget everything that's wrong. Just see a bit of what's right."

I watched the Unforgiven from the shadows, trying to see what he saw. Nothing looked right in the laughter.

"What else isn't working?" he asked.

"I haven't looked at the Beacon or the Cloak yet. All the cookware appears to be fine. The weapons appear to be fine. Comms appear to be fine."

Abel nodded.

"Happy's glasses." I added. "They aren't working anymore."

Abel chuckled. "There's nothing here that we don't need. If it's in your power, get it done. I can't ask you for anything you can't do, but I'm asking for everything you can."

I let out a long breath, and some of the night's tension with it. "I'll fix it."

Abel nodded. "What about you. You alright?"

I was still holding the rifle across my chest, squatting in the shadows. I was still waiting for the next gunshot. I was turning in circles, trying to make sense of senselessness. I didn't want to talk about it.

"I shouldn't be here."

"The Unforgiven don't get to choose," he said.

"I shouldn't be Unforgiven."

Abel brushed loose dirt off a rock, then dusted his hands on his pants. He sat on the rock, watching the camp.

"You don't get to choose that either."

I huffed a laugh. The twist of bitter truth. I pulled my hands off the rifle, one at a time, and laid it on the grass at my feet. It seemed unlikely I'd get another knife against my ribs, as with Ivan. I rolled back from my own squat and fully sank into the grass, letting my weight go.

"But it's always something," Abel said quietly.

"What do you mean?" I asked.

"You don't just wake up one day and find yourself in the Outlands."

There was a dark spot, oxidized metal, on my wrist. I scraped at it.

"No," I said. "You do your best, then something goes wrong. Then people turn on you. Then they abandon you. And then, *then* you wake up in the Outlands."

"So what went wrong?"

"My house burned down."

In the corner of my eye I saw a raised eyebrow. "They don't send people into the Outlands because their house burns down."

The spot would not come off. I left it; I'd need water. "Tell that to the Arbiter."

Abel laid his own rifle in the grass. The weapon was spotless, unused, but he began to take it apart and rub each piece with a grey-stained cloth. I watched the slow milling of the camp.

"What were you doing just before the house burned down?" he asked.

This was meddling. I was the tinker. Abel needed me, and I didn't need this.

"Listen," I said. "I lived by one creed. You do what's right. I tried to do right by every person, every day. And if I didn't, I fixed it. So I made mistakes, I'm human, but I did whatever I could about them. That's me. That's what I was doing before the house burned down, that's what I was doing every sprigging day until the house burned down."

Abel stopped and laid his piece down. He shook out his cloth. "I'm sorry," he said.

"For what?" I asked.

I hated that he was right. I saw Shea's form in my mind, my name at the top. He wasn't the problem; the truth was what was ugly.

"No matter how I cut it, it was an accident," I said, trying to take the edge off my voice. "But I can't stop thinking about it. I just want to go home. And put it all back together."

Abel fit two pieces together, and I watched in idle curiosity, noting the catches and seams. "Best I can," I added quietly.

He inspected the half-assembled gun before pulling it apart again. He resumed his polishing and did not comment.

"Do you think we'll go home?" I asked.

"Hard to say."

"Hard to say why? You think the State is full of thatch, or you think this place will kill us?"

"I'm more worried about the jungle. And each other."

"Worried about Crisp and Ivan?" I asked.

"I worry about everyone."

Now I raised my eyebrow, but Abel was engrossed in his work. "Not Kodiak."

"Don't write him off."

"He killed Patches." It was as simple as that.

Abel did not pause in his work, but spoke slowly, choosing his words. "I know. It was a brutal thing. But there is a spark in him; it may yet catch. Have faith in Kodiak."

"Will the process involve more killing?"

"I hope not."

There was the plan. Hoping not.

I thought of Ivan and his knife. I thought of Abel and the woman in grey. I thought of the machine, of the open circuit between the Hall of Judgment and home.

"I think we're just choosing how we die out here."

"I think you can go home," he said.

"What aren't you telling us?"

I waited. There was no answer.

I began to gather my things.

"Have hope, Thirteen."

"I'll make my own."

I left with my tools and sat before the Eyes. I'd be thatched if there were any more trouble because of me. Abel was right; they were fried in seven different ways. But I didn't care. I could fix anything.

*

Long after everyone was asleep, apart from a lone guard sitting in the solitary glow of the Ears, I was pulling the Eyes apart in the dim light of my headlamp. I pulled out the half-melted resistors and scoured away the scorch marks where the current from the unsuited metal piece had arced through the system. It had been a bad fix and almost ruined the unit. So I reduced it to a pile of bolts and wires and put it back together, tight, clean, and new. As the stars wheeled by, my hands flew, fast as sparks. Each point was made new, each anchor firm, each pathway straight.

It was not clean, as a robot would have made it, never a stray line or a wasted drop. But it was good, and it was beautiful, and it was right. I remade the Eyes with my own hands, with my own tools, manufacturing my thoughts as fast as they flew through my head. Hours later I tightened the last bolt on the casing. I didn't even turn it on to test it.

I pulled out the Cloak and gave it a look over. This one was unfamiliar, and I did turn it on. I walked in a straight line away until I saw a shimmer in the air, and I stepped past it. From the other side, I pushed my hand through the shimmering field and it disappeared in front of my eyes. The Cloak worked.

A closer inspection revealed that, though it functioned, the housing was cracked. I sealed it with adhesive, making it strong and, more importantly, waterproof again.

Before I exhausted myself, I grabbed Happy's glasses from where he slept. With heat and pliers, I reshaped the earpiece. Perfection was painstaking work, but I had broken them. It fell to me to fix them, so I repeated the process over and over until the earpiece mirrored its mate.

I felt the sand in my eyes and lump in my chest that comes when your body has passed beyond exhaustion. But I would not leave these things be, not for another day, not for another minute. I shook myself back to wakefulness. *Not yet.*

The final bit of the glasses was more difficult. In my haste to rip the earpiece off I had lost a screw. I thought of a dozen ways to fix it, but the best required more light and time than I had, so I fashioned a makeshift pin from a short piece of wire and, five minutes later, had a complete pair of glasses that would last until the next evening.

There was only one piece left – the beacon. That was the hardest, as testing it entailed obliterating it. I fought off the growing assault of sleep and pushed my way back inside.

There was no physical damage and nothing loose. I traced each circuit and divined each one's purpose. The machine took shape in my mind with clarity. Everything was in place, all interlinked.

As I resealed the beacon, I found another panel on the outside. One I hadn't noticed before. I turned the beacon inside out in my head – not maintenance access; there was nothing there.

It's never nothing. And I'm not one for loose ends. Against sleep, guns, Outlanders and Unforgiven, it could have waited. But

I spun out the screws, removing the panel to delve the secret underneath.

The compartment was small with a single red button.

This box didn't do a lot of things. Each of those things was already accounted for. There is no such thing as *just a button*. Especially not the red varietal.

I scrolled through my map of the beacon; each source, trace, and node, trying to fit this button in. I saw it immediately; two traces that fed each other and yet did not touch. I had glossed over them; the link was obvious and there was no damage. But now there was a red button standing between.

My mind stretched out, following those traces, fitting them into the machine. Source. Pathway. Purpose.

It wasn't necessary, but I opened the beacon again and flipped it around, fingers and eyes following the wires and traces, putting it all in place. I needed to be sure. Then I sat back.

Manual detonation.

This device needed no manual detonation. It was suicide.

A small voice in my head said, *every device needs a failsafe.* A deeper voice responded, *maybe this forgiveness machine, as well.*

Meeks had kept me away from this box during training, when I might have inspected it in detail.

It all murmured of secrets and hidden purpose.

What else had they wired into this machine? A traitor? An assassin? A megalomaniacal tsar?

Just a button. Perhaps a failsafe for us, perhaps a failsafe for the State. Perhaps nothing, perhaps the inconsistency that, when pulled, would unravel the whole garment. Perhaps another glimpse into this machine and how it would all end, drawing straws and then killing each other over the outcome. Perhaps nothing more than a reminder we hadn't been told everything. Perhaps they were watching me right now, hand hovering over a button of their own.

I looked up to space where the hidden satellites wheeled.

Maybe it was nothing. Maybe it was everything.

I rubbed my eyes as hard as I could. Ivan, Abel, the button – this machine was indecipherable. Real machines weren't full of lies and secrets.

I considered ripping the button out and closing the gap, but the night was too far gone. Perhaps another time. I resealed the compartment and beacon both.

The sky had not yet become bright. The air was cool and wet again, and the soft sounds of the night had returned, the violence of the battle already forgotten by the trees. I tried to shut it out, the façade that covered the death underneath.

I quickly sank into a deep, exhausted sleep. I remember dreaming. Home, and the sound of your tears in the next room. I had had that dream more and more frequently. But that night, for the first time, I dreamt I was crying too.

– FIFTEEN –

I started awake with someone shaking me again. There was a figure above me, but the sky was bright through the trees, and there was laughter.

"He's alive!" the figure shouted. Stump.

"Let me sleep."

Stump chuckled as he turned back to me. "Sorry, it was too much like yesterday. We counted, saw a lump in blankets. We thought maybe we'd lost another." He sat back on his heels. "We're getting ready."

My head thumped back to the ground as he walked away. I did not feel well. But there was nothing else for it, so I rubbed my head and struggled out of my bag.

Happy received his glasses with the promise to re-repair them, better, at the next camp. He was grateful, even though I'd been the one to break them in the first place.

Stump sat with the equipment, surveying my night's work. As we divvied and packed, I asked, "How was it last night?"

"It was dark," he said. "Being alone in the woods, at night; it frightens a man. It's worse when you know they're coming."

Stump paused to break off a branch that had caught on a corner

181

of metal, then pull out the leaves.

"Abel says we waited five minutes. Felt like more. Then he said fire and we fired. We lit a few flares, and that was that."

"It was what?"

"We fought," Stump said. The words came more quietly.

"What do they look like?"

He looked past me, shrugged. "They're men."

"They are animals!" Kodiak said from behind. He walked between, turned, and squatted before us.

"You missed it! They come with wide eyes and stabbing spears. If you don't move quickly enough, they'll skewer you." He poked me with a big finger. "Their bodies were covered with dye and scars and they came silently, not even a battle cry. Until they strike." He lowered his voice, eyes wide and excited. "Then, they scream to chill your blood. You must have heard it?"

I'd heard the voices in the night.

Kodiak took on a more somber tone. "Not the people I'd like to meet in the dark. We could have lost someone last night."

"Not while we have you, Kody," Stump said.

Kodiak nodded, still somber.

Stump stared at the ground, chewing something and nodding slowly. I noted that Kodiak still held his rifle from the skirmish. His time-out was over. Necessity had prevailed over justice faster than I'd anticipated.

"It's a bad business," Kodiak said. "But better when you're the one walking home at the end."

Then he pounded me on the back with his broad hand. "Next

time you'll fight with us!" He didn't wait for a response but moved off through the camp. I suppose he was raising morale.

I watched his back and listened to his barked laughter. Like this was all a game to him. Who could say how many more people had died at his hands last night, and it was still a game.

"He's an animal," I said.

"He's a warrior," Stump replied. "There's a place for warriors."

"Is this the place?" I asked.

"If there's anywhere for a warrior, it's Outlands."

"Explain to me the difference between a warrior and a murderer?"

Stump handed the last of the menagerie to Duck, who'd passed by, with instructions on who to give it to. Then he began to fold the ground cloth.

"It's when and where you fight," he said. "And what you destroy."

It was sufficiently vague that a philosopher could make it work. "I don't trust him with that," is all I said.

"He brought us home," Stump said, as if that settled it for him.

*

Soon we were ready for the trail. Pope was bandaged and pale, and his pack had been lightened significantly.

Before we could enter the undergrowth, Ivan's voice floated across the clearing. "Wait."

He straddled his pack, arms crossed. Though he was a head shorter than even I, he tried to fill the space.

"Here we go," Stump muttered.

"We have not decided where we are going."

"We are going to the valley," Taj said.

"No!" Ivan's word rang through the trees. "We agreed to distance ourselves from the landing site. And we agreed to discuss it later. Are we going to discuss it? Or are you a liar?"

I saw apathy, impatience, and determination painted in equal measure across the Unforgiven.

"It's a new day," Ivan pressed, "and things have changed since last night."

Crow took off his pack, along with Duck, Happy, and Pope.

Around me thumbs clicked safeties on and off, on and off. Hands rested on knife handles. Eyes flicked from face to face, measuring. And I had spoken words to Ivan that, however intended, he had taken as a promise.

I hated this place.

"So let's talk," Abel said. He unfastened each buckle on his pack, then snugged it against a tree. His eyes never really left Ivan. He sat, back against his pack, and rested his hands on each knee. Stump found a rock and sat as well, setting the Ears beside him, still listening.

I dropped my pack to the ground.

Ivan alone remained on his feet when he began to speak, using measured, rehearsed words. "Abel and Taj advised us yesterday to head toward the valley, to the heart of the Outlands, and to find the Outlanders. Last night we were attacked by these Outlanders. Pope nearly died, the rest of us as well."

He began to pace, chin high, shoulders held back. With Abel

seated, Ivan managed to stare him down. "Some might say that we are heading in an unwise direction."

"While others might say," Taj replied, looking directly at him, "that we sit idle in the place an Outlander patrol went missing."

"Don't you dare!" Ivan howled. Then, in a colder voice, "You sow fear, you would drive us until it's too late to turn back. We will move when we are moving in the right direction and not a moment before."

"Wait long enough, and we will not be moving at all," Taj sniped back.

Ivan's eyes darted, catching several other men in his glance. I looked beyond him, where a branch grew in twisted form, after years of torment. Grey fungus showed on the bark. A red bird landed upon it and cocked its head. I felt the noose tightening, around us all.

"Enough," Abel interrupted. "The facts. Two days ago, an aircraft dropped us. There is a trail leading directly to us from that site. Last night a patrol of Outlanders came to our camp. Their trail leads directly into our trail as well."

Ivan stopped his pacing.

"Whichever way we go, we will be tracked and hunted," Abel said.

"Let them come," Kodiak rumbled.

"They might not have known we were here," Ivan said. "It'll be a week before they even know their patrol is missing."

"They came in the middle of the night," said Stump. "In skirmish lines. They knew we were here."

"They came in skirmish lines," Crow echoed in a mocking voice. I kept my eye on Ivan, who withdrew a few steps, letting his seeds sprout. "Outlanders don't have satellites and biomonitors. They don't know what happened here."

"They'll come," Crisp said, stirring from his silence. He spoke the words as if to himself.

"They'll come," Stump agreed.

Duck, who had been fidgeting throughout the conversation, spoke up. "So we can wait here? We dig in, shoot them when they come, and go home?"

Home. His eyes were wide and his words too quick. I still saw the shadow on him from the night.

"How long?" Abel asked. "We have food for maybe two weeks. Ears for one. A box of bullets. We notched up thirty or forty casualties last night. We need five hundred. Are you expecting to live through fifteen more assaults?"

I quickly verified Abel's math.

"I don't know." Duck shrugged. The question hadn't been directed at him, but he bore its weight. I looked closer and saw what youthful light had been left in his eyes was fully gone. I didn't know why he was even here. I pitied him.

But Ivan smiled where he stood, watching Abel and slowly shaking his head.

"They know we are here. They will come. These are the facts," Abel said again, and held his peace.

"You aren't even trying, Abel," Ivan said. "This moment of peace here is tenuous. If we go deeper, it will only get worse. More and more trails leading to us like a spiderweb until we are tangled in a howling mass of those killers. We need to turn around."

"And starve to death?" Stump asked.

"Stop!" Ivan snapped, and, just as quickly, was back under control, calm like he hadn't lost his temper at all. "You aren't listening. Or perhaps you are listening but not thinking. We don't have to do this. Any of this!"

Duck looked at Ivan, a faint but different light returning to his eyes. Desperate hope whoring itself out to the weakest whisper of a promise. Duck and Ivan. I didn't like it. It wasn't right. Someone needed to do something about it.

Someone.

Crow nodded and smiled to himself, as if he already knew this storyline. Crisp put his fingertips in the dirt and stared into the holes he hollowed out.

Taj sat and looked at his hand. He held it steady, nudging a caterpillar from one finger to the next, toward a leaf he was trying to feed the little bug. He didn't seem to be listening, but I knew by now, he missed nothing.

"We don't need to hunt," Ivan argued. "We don't need to fight. We don't need to wait and die. We have shelter. We have food and medicine, and weapons for when those run out. Gentlemen, we can leave this place.

"We can be kings. Half a continent from the State… out here the children don't even have picture books of the things we carry. They don't even have books." He laughed.

"You make no sense," Kodiak rumbled. Ivan faltered on his

words and glanced at Kodiak.

When Kodiak didn't stir, Ivan found his thread and pressed on. "Let me spell it out for you. We don't know where exactly we are on the map."

Taj rolled his eyes but said nothing. The caterpillar made its tentative way across a bridge of his fingers.

"We head south. South takes us out, south takes us away. No matter what, we'll hit the tropic coast or the river Soneda. We follow it until we find a settlement or city."

Duck broke in hesitantly, "You think we could be kings?"

Ivan laughed. "Pope's art? Kodiak's strength? Think of what Thirteen could build for them. He'd be a god, not a king. And imagine Happy strolling through whatever poor excuse they have for a sick house. Any of us alone would astound the petty excuse for civilization we find. Just with the knowledge we gained in primary education. There are rustic settlements and cities; I've seen them on maps. We just need to reach one.

"The State has offered some paltry promise of new life, dangling a lie before us. Let's replace their lie with a truth we build ourselves. Come with me."

He held his peace as each man weighed the visions and promises.

New life, gods among mortals.

Spears and starvation, screams in the night.

Home.

My thoughts led nowhere, not for lack of effort but for lack of information. Secrets and lies. And fear.

There in front of me was Stump. He was untroubled, picking at the grass at his feet. He pulled it free, halved it, halved it again, and tossed the pieces to the wind. Again. And again.

He was waiting, unafraid.

Ivan's gaze prowled from face to face. His eyes were hungry.

"We won't make it." Duck's lament broke the silence and opened a floodgate of pent frustration.

"It's a farce anyway, what does it matter?"

"It's math, it's odds. We follow our best chance."

"There's hope."

"You can't escape the Outlands."

"They don't want us to. It doesn't mean we can't."

"Whoever we find will just be Outlander, too."

"We can do this."

And then Pope's voice rose above the rest. "I don't want to kill anyone!"

The brewing argument stilled.

Pope's face had paled again and he coughed. He tried to shrug his shoulders but winced at the pain. Stump grabbed his hand before he tried more elaborate gestures, then tightened a knot on a bandage. Pope pushed him off.

More quietly, "I don't want to kill them. This is their jungle."

Happy was shaking his head, a "no" of agreement.

Ivan smiled.

Abel cleared his throat. "They've cracked. I know it's hard. It's a sad thing. But there's no hope for them. It's fallen to us to take care of this."

Pope was indignant. "Who are you to judge? You don't know anything! This is their jungle, and we've just shown up and shot them!"

Abel looked at Pope, the weight of unsaid words giving gravity to his gaze. He held his tongue.

"What right do you have? You don't know, Abel! None of us knows. I saw them last night before they stabbed me, and they looked like men."

"They are animals," said Taj, quietly but forcefully.

"You don't know!" Pope shouted back.

"I do know," Abel said with calm certainty.

"How is killing innocents for the best?" Ivan asked, stirring the glowing embers.

"Killing innocents is never for the best, Ivan." Abel's voice became sharp, and Ivan stepped back at the force of his gaze. I watched Kodiak. He did not rouse.

He'd probably forgotten Patches by the morning after.

"You know what, exactly?" Pope asked, ignoring Ivan and Abel's sparring. "Who are you, Abel?"

Silence fell. Taj turned his head, fully engaging. The sun was beginning to shine directly through the holes in the leaves above, and the first drops of sweat were forming on my back. Abel looked at Pope for a minute, then said something inaudible and looked away.

Taj turned back to his caterpillar, and Ivan's smile grew.

Pope shook his head with a faint look of disgust. "So what right do we have?"

– SIXTEEN –

Ivan raised his voice. "Follow me! No more dying. No more killing. We will be kings!"

Abel rose. "Bullpiss."

Ivan reddened.

"Empty promises," Abel added. "And a hard road to nowhere. The only hope – only hope," he emphasized, "is to finish. We move and move quickly. We stay ahead. We plant the beacon. And some of us might go home. It's not an empty promise. It doesn't sound like much, but it's what there is."

Ivan squinted at him. "Your vision. So small," he mused loudly so everyone could hear. "We are civilized here. We can decide this in a civilized fashion. We vote. For this fool's errand, or to save yourself."

Voices rose around me again.

Democracy. Every road I could see here in the Outlands ended the same: dead, Unforgiven in the wilderness.

Stump curtailed the chatter. "I vote for the fool's errand. For the mission. I'm with Abel."

Abel followed up, "The mission."

Kodiak and Taj agreed in quick succession.

Then Crow said, "Crank the State. We run. We start our own life."

Ivan inclined his head, and Crow nodded back to him.

It came to Pope. "I don't trust the State, and it isn't our place to kill the Outlanders. I'm with Ivan." He grimaced at the words and corrected himself, "I'm for heading south."

"My position is plain," Ivan said.

Duck mumbled something, and Ivan leaned close. Duck mumbled again, and Ivan placed a hand gently on his shoulder. "He wants to be a king."

"Is that what you said?" Taj asked.

Duck nodded, never looking up from the ground.

"Crisp? What do you think of the blue button?" Ivan asked.

"I won't run."

Ivan straightened and blinked. He was still as stone. "We have discussed this," Ivan said. Calm. Quiet. Somehow terrifying.

Crisp still sat with his fingers splayed on the ground, digging tiny holes. His knuckles were white. "I'm not going to run." He lifted his hand from the ground and held it before his face. It was steady, unmoving. His eyes hardened.

"You side with Abel?" Ivan demanded.

"Thatch Abel. I'm not running."

"You need another nap in the bushes?" Crow asked. "That's all you're good for. Outlanders like your mama, tucking you in at night?"

"I will kill the Outlanders."

Ivan hesitated, staring down Crisp, who still held his hand, unshaking, before his eyes and didn't blink. Ivan began sweeping the group, pausing on each man. Counting, recalculating.

I also counted. Abel, Taj, Kodiak, Stump and Crisp. Five of eleven. Four already for Ivan. Two left.

"Thirteen?"

Ivan twisted his head in my direction. His cocky smile was gone. His hand rested by his hip, a fingertip touching the hilt of his knife.

I had wanted to not matter. But if I forced a tie, it would come to Happy. Happy who was *no longer thinking that way*. Happy who had dropped his pack at the first word. Happy who, for all our brotherhood as the Tinker and Doctor, was Spire.

It had come to me.

I scattered open this machine again, doggedly looking for the answer. After the tangled power struggle, Abel and Ivan alone remained. Two doors opening into unknown blackness.

It would be dishonest to deny I wanted what Ivan promised. A way out. A new life away from the wreckage.

But my father wouldn't have run. And I didn't trust Ivan.

Then Abel, with his secrets. He'd offered little more than a chance to die. Yet there was honesty in his bleak promise. And something hiding behind the words he'd spoken last night, something I wanted.

I didn't understand him. I didn't trust him. I didn't want to kill.

A single, whispered snatch of a laugh escaped me. Democracy: The chance to choose how we die.

I sat straight and stared back at Ivan, digging the butt of my rifle into the ground before me. I held the barrel so that my hands would not fidget.

"Abel," I said. "We go in."

Ivan's face flushed with blood. The whites shown around his eyes. With a yell, he drew his knife, tilting forward into a charge, and rushed me.

I fumbled backwards and dropped my gun, clambering for distance and raising useless hands. My heel caught and I curled into a ball, waiting for the pain.

I wondered if Happy could save me.

I heard noises and felt nothing. When I raised my head, Taj loomed over Ivan, a boot on his knife hand and a knee on his chest. One hand pressed straight fingers into Ivan's throat, the other gently coaxed his caterpillar onto a nearby leaf.

I hated this place.

I had spoken. Now Taj and Kodiak, Abel and Stump, they would hold us with their guns. Now Ivan wanted to kill me.

I began breathing hard as I felt the noose pull snug.

There's nowhere to run.

Nowhere to run.

It was too late. To change my mind, to change my words.

Then there was a hand on my shoulder and Happy was there, searching my eyes.

"Deep breath," was all he said. He took a breath along with me, and I did it again.

Crow had pressed his rifle to Crisp, who still sat, his hand before his face. It trembled now, and Crisp stared intently, all his attention fixed on it.

I looked at the light, the never-ending pattern of light and shadow spreading through the trees. It moved from moment to moment as the wind blew. I heard the sigh, and I heard the chatter of the bugs and the birds as they wandered through the jungle, rising and falling in time. I took another breath, and the cool air of the morning filled me.

Duck had his rifle pointed shakily toward Taj, who looked on calmly. Abel, Kodiak, and Stump had fanned out and had their guns trained on the renegades.

"Are you alright?" Happy asked, still peering at me.

Pope now stood before Duck, talking to him, a fast flow of words. Duck put his rifle down. Crow threw his gun to the ground and cursed Abel. Crisp let his hand fall to his lap and closed his eyes, satisfied.

I slowly breathed out, letting my body uncurl, and rubbed my eyes. "Why did we even vote?"

"Because no one here knows what they really are," Happy grumbled, pulling me to a sitting position.

"Are we done now?" I asked.

"We'll never be done," Happy said.

I rested my arms on my knees, looking at the ground between my legs. "Thanks," I said.

Stump and Abel had put up their guns, while Pope continued speaking to Duck, who was nodding. I breathed again.

"Shall I kill him?" Taj asked quietly.

A new silence settled over us. The rasping of Ivan's breath grew louder against the Outlands' murmur.

Happy took his hand from my shoulder and rose.

No, we'd never be done.

Kodiak still watched Crow, gun trained. Abel let his weapon rest in loose hands and studied the tableau on the ground, straight fingers pressed to a windpipe below wide eyes. The caterpillar inched along.

"Let him stand."

Taj disarmed Ivan and backed away. Ivan rolled onto hands and knees, then rose, coughing. Even then, he looked down his nose at the taller man.

"Is this how it will be? Will you stoop to brandishing rifles to get your way?"

"If it must be done."

"And lead us to our deaths?"

"There's only one path out of this place."

"Abel isn't the one who drew steel," Stump interjected, angry, when Abel didn't defend himself.

Ivan grimaced but withheld his retort. He took a moment to study Kodiak and Stump, both guns now trained on him. He drew himself to his full height.

"You're one of them, aren't you? You're a State lackey here to make sure we die. Why don't you just shoot us in our sleep, and you can go home?"

"That doesn't make sense," Kodiak said, but he shifted his attention off Ivan. Ivan's eyes glinted.

"Abel knows something! He was there first, you know. First at the Hall, waiting for us. He stayed back when we fought. And now he wants us to go deeper in, waste our time and our ammunition and our lives? It's what the State wants, don't you see? This is the man you want to follow?"

"He's one of us," Kodiak said.

"He is not one of us!" Ivan shouted back.

No, we would never be done.

Crisp remained seated, but now his eyes were closed. No one spoke to support Ivan, though I saw uncertainty spreading.

Ivan shook his head and turned, walking to his pack without being dismissed. "You're all spraggers. I will not respect this vote. It's lies and manipulation. It is pure idiocy. If I am right, I make a majority of one!"

No one moved to stop him.

"Give us our food, ammunition, and equipment. Give us our share and go die. Pope? Crow? Happy?"

Pope looked at Happy, who subtly shook his head. "I'm not leaving the doctor," he said.

Ivan rose from his pack now and stared down Happy. Happy stared back and said nothing. The blood drained from Ivan's face and was replaced with something cold. Still angry, still threatening, but cold as death.

"Shall I kill him?" Taj asked again.

"Peace, Taj," Abel said. The words were soft but implacable.

"There will be no peace," Taj said.

Abel did not speak again.

"I hope you aren't thinking I'll head out with no one but you and Duck," Crow said.

Ivan's shoulders finally slumped. He grabbed his rifle, resting on his pack, and threw it into the ferns at Taj's feet.

"We are not done," he said. Though his eyes swept the entire group, they rested on Happy and me.

– SEVENTEEN –

The new order was quietly enforced. Crow and Ivan were stripped of their weapons. Pope argued he'd only voted, not attacked, and was left alone. No one worried about Duck.

As we again tightened pack straps, Taj asked Abel, "Are you still committed?"

"What's this now?" Stump asked.

"We're tracking back up the Outlander trail," Kodiak said.

Crisp looked up, eyes bright.

Taj pulled a strap on his pack with a jerk, focused on his gear. "Even though it will slow us down, and whoever we find is expecting us."

"We're here to find Outlanders," Kodiak said. "We found Outlanders."

"Speed is life," Taj said, "And surprise." His arm snapped out, flinging a pebble in a quick motion. It bounced off Kodiak's face.

Kodiak rubbed his forehead.

I wondered what this meant. If the new order would crumble as quickly as the old, if it was already beginning.

There was little discussion and no vote. Abel faced us upstream, following what trail we could find.

None trusted the stability of the morning's armistice, but as long as nothing blew on it, it stood. So the waters quietly swirled in agitated currents, just below a boil.

*

We left the site where I'd settled our fate, and the Outlands swallowed us whole. It grew dark. It was the day the rain started.

Early drizzle gave way to afternoon showers. The leaves held while they could, calling a warning in a quiet tattoo above. When the big leaves finally unshouldered their burdens, it came not as raindrops but buckets.

Each man plodded along, locked alone with his thoughts, under rolling curtains of water. We bowed heads and hunched shoulders but never stopped moving.

The water soaked our hair. It seeped into our jackets and into our boots. And it soaked our souls, browning and twisting the corners, leaving ripples and stains. In the puddles, silent arguments grew and festered, corrupting remaining spaces of goodwill. Each squelched footstep was a finger pointed at the man we most condemned. Each tiny hammer stroke on our heads was an accusation renewed. We could not properly hate the rain, it shrugged us off, so we hated each other.

However, while we endured the water, there was truce with the other exiles of the Outlands. The rain hid our scent. It hid our noise, so we moved like phantoms through the undergrowth.

Chatters and shrieks rose all around in a mixture of grief and glory I could not decipher. When I lifted my head there were flappings of wings and dartings of animals. There was red and orange, yellow and green, all flashing through the trees above. I saw striped beaks and spotted feathers alongside ringed fur and bright scales.

The monkeys I had only seen in pictures huddled in groups like families, close to the tree trunks, seeking what shelter they could. Their eyes reflected the spirit of the jungle – curious, afraid, malicious. Some edged out from the rest, water dripping from fur, eyes blinking, hoping for some spark of understanding to explain this wandering caravan. Others shrieked or stared coldly, warning us that they and theirs would do whatever was necessary.

All were wet together, all waiting together. All suffering this jungle together. Nothing bit, nothing flew in my nostrils, nothing fled from me, chattering accusations and threats. I felt less alone.

Then the clouds would break, and the jungle would withdraw. The chatter and the life continued, but away. Close, all fell quiet, as if we were locked from the pulsing heartbeat behind a scab.

Nothing suffered our presence but the bugs, always testing the juice. Occasionally we would see the eyes of a large cat through the leaves. Once there was a giant snake. I couldn't see the head or tail, just folds of snake and snake and snake, twisted in a tree. We walked clear.

And always the broken branch, the smudge in the mud, reminding us this was someone else's path we trod.

The hours stretched and merged for me. Tracking was Taj's job. And Stump, who could read trees like a uniflex sheet, near-outlander that he was. Wet or dry, I was not needed – nothing was broken, nothing needed building. I could only plod, one foot at a time, each in its place until I found myself at the end of the day, on the other side of the next rain.

My thoughts always returned to my workbench, hidden in the foundation of my Spire. They turned to the rooms of my childhood, open windows gathering the wind off the lake. They turned to home, of the way it was before it all fell apart.

*

In the slow hours of the day, I also untangled the new order. Behind me lay Ivan, weaponless, turning slow thoughts of his own. Before me, the men with guns. With secrets and schisms of their own. And, somewhere in the distance, beyond the next tree, the next hill, Outlanders.

I found Duck. He walked, wet and silent, like the others.

"Hey, kid," I said.

He looked up at me, up from the mud. A rapid, jerky motion. He said nothing but watched me.

I think it was the first thing I'd said to him.

"Would it be alright if I walk with you for a while?" I asked.

The kid kept watching me. He did not nod or shake. It took me a moment to place the look in his eyes: pleading.

I fell into step beside him.

Immediately, there was a shadow at my shoulder, and I found Crow looking straight at me like a predator. Pope was by his side.

"Gentlemen?" I asked.

"Mind if we walk with you?" Crow asked, with uncharacteristic civility.

Like Duck, I did not respond, and they fell into step as well.

Duck's small frame grew hunched.

Crow opened without art. "You aren't a soldier. You aren't Spire. Why do you want to shoot people and go back?"

"Who's asking?" I asked. "You or Ivan?"

"Don't be a cranker about this, Thirteen. We've got to stick together."

I closed my eyes and turned my face toward the sun, peeking out behind the heavy clouds. Crow took on a conciliatory tone. "I'm not crazy about Ivan either. Doesn't mean he can't be right about something."

Crow spoke on. He believed we had a chance. Ivan had his wrinkles, but Abel was a liar. My voice might matter against their guns. On and on.

It was structured, logical. Deadly. By the end, I couldn't even see the lie, but I knew it was there. Logic is a fine thing. But logic and lies weave together into a terrible shroud whose only purpose is covering the dead.

For every word I put forth, he had ten counters. But that did not make him right. He did not stop until Stump wormed his way next to us and interrupted the debate with his silence. Crow looked perplexed, then drifted off, taking Duck with him.

"Thanks," I said, watching the kid retreat with his keepers.

"What for?" Stump asked and kept walking.

And then I was alone.

It felt deeper, now, than the simple absence of Unforgiven near me. I looked after Stump but he was already beyond Kodiak, and I didn't want to cross that space. Of all the others, there was only the doctor.

Ivan had hinted that Happy had changed sides. But Happy had not moved this morning. Yesterday, at least, we'd had some sort of brotherhood.

I dropped back to find him.

He acknowledged me as I fell into step. "Why didn't you go with Ivan?" I asked.

"Why would I go anywhere with Ivan?" he said, an artificial flatness masking his thoughts.

"He said you would. You dropped your pack this morning like you were one of them."

Happy smiled a small smile, as if remembering an old joke. "Ah, you noticed. Did he come to you, too?"

"He cornered me," I said. "Did he threaten you?"

"No," said Happy. "I told him I agreed with him. Little thatcher. Skew his calculations, force his hand early, whatever his game was." Happy gave a grim laugh. "But you snookered him, too. What did he tell you?"

"He said he would kill me. Kill us all."

That silenced Happy. He chewed slowly, something from his pack, while we walked.

"I believe him," I added.

Unless we struck first… Taj's words echoed in my head.

"Maybe the bugger will just up and go?" I suggested.

"He's not going to kill you, and he's not going to go," Happy said.

"Kill us all, not just me," I corrected.

"No, he's not. Look at me, Thirteen – If I told you this was it, I'm not walking any farther today, would you leave me behind? No. I could make the entire group stop or go at my whim. Because I'm the doctor. You're the tinker. They didn't come to you because you're a vote. They came because you're the prize."

I knew this. But that was before.

"You don't kill the prize. Ivan needs you," Happy concluded.

"Everything's already fixed. He can just steal it and go."

"That's awfully short-sighted. Let's hope he's smarter than that."

"And what odds would you put on that?" I asked.

Happy *hmpfed* and retreated to his silent chewing again. I sighed, trying to loosen my neck, my jaw, everything that was locked into solid knots. "I wish they'd just fight it out. I'm not sure it even makes a difference who wins."

"Oh, they'll fight it out. But never forget, you're stuck in it. Abel wants you. Ivan wants you."

"And they want you too?" I asked.

Happy nodded beside me.

"Well, be careful."

"You too."

We drifted apart but stayed close enough that neither of us looked "alone." Pope was singing snatches of songs ahead of us. Since he'd been pierced, he was waxing on about his new status as war hero. But when he asked, "Come now, who else has been shot before?" Four hands raised.

He was not impressed. He was, it turned out, the only one who had been shot with an arrow. His strength was returning beautifully, and he was sure it was only a matter of time before he was carrying us, rather than leaning on a different shoulder each half hour. Happy kept him drinking, said it would help with the blood loss, and that got Pope talking about wine. And from there, to women. Because, as Pope stated, it goes without even stating – no wine can be fully enjoyed without the presence of a beautiful woman.

He told us there was a Senorita in Viento Nuevo that would make him forget his pain, if only he could make it once more to Viento Nuevo. There was a Belle in Old Massa who could make sure he never felt pain again. A Lily from the South Spires who would sing music so sweetly it broke his heart, until he was deep in the arms of sleep. On and on the list went, always with the refrain - if only he could be there once more.

I don't know if he was entertaining us or if he truly believed it; with Pope it was likely a measure of both. He painted himself the tragic hero and the lost love of half the State for the better part of the hour, until Abel offered to not punch him in the arm in exchange for shutting up. It ended with Abel chasing Pope into the bushes. They returned, laughing, after a moment, and Pope talked on as Ivan glared.

I watched. Now Pope and Abel. The waters swirled.

*

The night after the vote, I devoted hours to watching for dark figures over me. The sleeping bag was soft, enough to keep out bugs and what little cold there was. It would do nothing for a knife or a bullet. Or even a boot.

Abel and Kodiak. Ivan and Crow. Stump seemed to be holding fast. The others… I didn't know where they stood. I didn't know where I stood. The battle lines were faint on the ground, shifting and dissolving in the whispers and rain. Tomorrow they would shift again.

And around us, like a ring of tree-shadows, the secrets and the State. The Program. The red button and its reminder: *We haven't told you everything.*

I could almost forget the Outlanders. Wide eyes and stabbing spears, scars and screams. It seemed madness, all the effort and anxiety I was pouring into surviving until we found them. Every door held monsters.

Madness and hope. *Hope.* The primal instinct that drives you to scrape your fingers raw, scrabbling at an immovable stone in the search for light.

I held my vigil as long as I could. All I got for my trouble was darker rings under my eyes.

*

In the morning, Unforgiven clustered by tribe. Abel and Kodiak. Ivan and Crow.

I attached myself to Stump when we set out. He moved quietly, eyes scanning and gun in front, his grey head barely bobbing as he glided through the ferns.

We walked in silence under the ever-changing tapestry of leafwork for an hour, and he never left my side. He seemed so steady, so certain.

He seemed what I was not.

"There's another button on the beacon," I said, eventually.

"What's it do?" Stump asked.

"Can you think of a reason for local detonation?"

I watched him closely. Nothing moved on his face, and he never broke stride.

"Failsafe?"

It was the correct answer. It didn't put me at ease. "If you were the one building, would you put a local detonator on a bomb?"

Stump pulled a stalk off a low hanging branch, inspected it, and put the end in his mouth to chew. I awaited his collapse, but he kept walking. He'd grown up under thatch, after all.

"I would not," he said.

"So I'm wondering why it's there. If it's even what they said," I pressed. "What if it isn't a beacon at all, just a glorified toaster with an on-switch? So we'd get on a rotorcraft without a fight?"

Stump removed his leafstalk and spit on the ground, then resumed chewing.

"Crisp was right, they don't need us to do this. They could survey with rotorcraft and light the place up from an office somewhere."

"Or it's a failsafe," Stump muttered.

"Nothing makes sense," I said. I was either stupid, or something wasn't as it seemed.

"If there's a second way to set it off," I continued, "why not a third? Maybe they're watching and will just blow us all up together when they've punished us enough? Or if we break from their plan? Maybe that's another reason not to run with Ivan."

"Too convoluted," he said.

"Convoluted like abandoning us in the Outlands and ordering us to kill people in exchange for our lives?" I asked.

Stump grimaced. It was the first real reaction I'd seen from him. "Kind of like that," he conceded.

It did sound far-fetched. But the secret still niggled. And secrets rarely travelled alone.

"Why are you even for the mission?" I asked abruptly. "You seemed pretty upset earlier about killing them."

"I don't like it. But this is the road. Walk it."

"Hmph."

"Hmph," Stump agreed.

We passed a plant that looked the same as Stump's. I broke off a branch and inspected the end where the sap oozed. Stump snatched it from my hand and threw it on the ground, never breaking stride.

We walked in silence again.

"It doesn't matter," I said, after a time. "Ivan'll kill me before we get that far anyway."

"We've got your back," Stump said.

I was the one following, and I looked at the back of his pack as he led the way. My own back felt exposed. "What, no 'don't worry, it won't come to that?'"

"It may," Stump said.

"Nedder. You think he'll really try? Happy thinks he's too important. Me too." Though I hadn't fully believed Happy, I'd still chosen to find his words reassuring. I'd take anything.

Stump stepped aside to catch his breath, and I stopped with him.

"You know what drives a man like Ivan?" Stump asked, peering into my eyes. They looked big, behind his glasses. Deep. And tired.

"He's crazy?"

"Did you note when he lost control yesterday?"

I revisited the scene, still vivid in my mind. It had been sudden.

"When I said no."

Stump nodded. A few men passed us, then Stump leaned in. "Don't assume you know how far he'll go to take his little throne, or what he'll do when he can't get it."

I grimaced. It wasn't assuring at all.

"But we've got your back," Stump repeated.

Abel approached the two of us and caught Stump's eye. I moved off and walked ahead, following someone else's pack, before the two started to speak.

And so I ended up still alone, still wondering which leaf Stump had eaten earlier. I didn't dare pull another twig.

*

No one tried to kill me that night. I saw no Outlanders, not even a hint of their passing. When Stump took over tracking the next day, Taj fell back.

The man made me uneasy. He was a killer. More controlled than Kodiak, but that somehow made him less predictable. Stump had suggested he, too, had my back.

I took a deep breath and approached him.

"I never thanked you for stopping Ivan," I said.

Taj grunted.

"I don't know what might have happened."

Taj grunted again but then, eyes constantly searching the undergrowth, he spoke a soft reply. "It is the job of great men to stand against the idiocy of small men."

I laughed. Grandiose words for a simple insult. "Though I think everyone would assume they are one of the great men."

Taj stopped scanning the trees and shadows and fixed me with an inscrutable look, and then returned to his vigil. He neither laughed nor grunted. "And you, too, would say you are a great man?"

I had no clever retort. I mumbled something about what everyone else might say being more important, and Taj grunted another affirmative.

"Are you an assassin?"

The hint of a smile creased Taj's eyes. "I never used that word myself."

"Is that how you ended up out here, then?"

"I killed the wrong man."

I puffed a laugh. "I saw you in training. I can't imagine you missing."

He wheeled on me, voice still low but finger raised, quiet words jarred with his flashing eyes. "I took the wrong contract. I do not miss, and I do not make mistakes. Understand. I know you think that you are special and everyone here needs you and wants to know what you think about everything. I do not need you."

I fixated on his finger, remembering it pressed to Ivan's neck.

He exhaled, a puff, what might have been a tightly reined laugh, and withdrew it.

His pack nearly knocked me off my feet when he spun, to press ahead and search for broken twigs. I stood until Crisp, walking past, shoved me on the shoulder and got me moving again.

*

I felt the hole left by Patches. Days rolled from light to darkness, and still I had no place here, tinker or no. We were not heroes and villains, only Unforgiven. Abel, surrounded by unstable killers. Ivan by greedy manipulators.

The morning sun drew up yesterday's downpour, thickening the air into grey haze. I withdrew into it, though the solitude offered no more protection than my sleeping bag.

Taj continued to grumble, to point out each footprint and broken leaf as signs of recent passage. Then we found two rodents, skinned and affixed to the trees with sharp wooden spikes, like the posts of a great gate.

Crisp eyed them quietly, hands on his rifle. Kodiak now had two rifles, one slung on a shoulder and the other held loosely as he looked through the gate to the jungle beyond.

"They know," Taj said. Abel studied the slaughtered animals and showed nothing. The trees were still wet where blood had flowed.

Then Abel began to walk, following the trail between.

– EIGHTEEN –

The shadows lengthened, the angled sunlight making dusty shafts that cut across every open aisle in the trees. Nothing had fundamentally changed. The signs on ground and branch still appeared, nearly invisible to nearly all of us. The Outlands still pulsed and rustled just a way off. The Ears emitted no beeps. But the gate the Outlanders had left us now lay in our wake.

We walked slowly and stopped early. Men were hesitant to unpack and kept rifles close at hand. Ivan and Crow were placed in the middle of camp and told to sit still.

Before sleep, sitting among the camp lights and stoves, I took Happy's glasses again. I had broken them. I had not yet made good on my promise to perfect them.

As quiet snores rose, I opened my box of tools on a clean corner of the ground cloth. I began to heat and mold a small piece of metal, forming a better hinge piece, and my jaw unknotted. I worked with an iron and pliers. It was mundane work, slow and satisfying.

I niggled at it until the earpiece held firm and swung smoothly, giving the slightest resistance. Satisfied, I left the glasses on the ground cloth, with the other equipment, to await the morning.

Before I lay down to sleep, I noticed something moving at the edge of the camp, a figure shifting in the dim light. I placed my hand on my screwdriver and crept forward, curious and afraid.

The outline of Stump took shape. I released the screwdriver and, rising up, let out the breath I was holding.

He was whispering in the dark, "Please forgive me."

"Please forgive me."

"Please forgive me."

As I listened, the cadence only slowed, never stopped. His dim figure continued to rock and shift in the shadow. I left him alone with whatever memories held him, creeping back to my bag as he continued to whisper to the dark, until all I could hear was the chirping of night bugs.

*

A crack of thunder yanked me awake. The sky was light, but dim, and the rain crashed upon us mere seconds later. The world dissolved to lightning, squawks, and running men. Everywhere, hands stuffed things into packs, arms snaked into jackets.

I ripped the ground cloth over the menagerie, laid out and ready in case of emergency. Everything was waterproof, but the protective action was instinct.

I shoved my feet into my boots, socks already wet, and rammed my sleeping sack into its waterproof carrier, then dashed off. Water and mud were getting everywhere.

The rain slowed and stopped just as we finished securing the camp. We looked at the sky and cursed. Our frenzy dissipated, like a rolling river emptied into a lake.

A stove was lit. The sunrise broke through as our thunderhead drifted on. Someone pulled back my ground cloth and parceled out the equipment. I changed my socks and tied the wet ones to my pack. They would get at least a little drier than they were now.

Back at the menagerie, the Eyes and the Bugwall were left for me. My toolkit had been tossed into the mud under a bush and fallen open. I collected and counted my screwdrivers, wiping each one, drying it, and putting it back in place until I heard a tentative voice behind me.

"Thirteen?"

It was Happy, squinting at me.

"Your glasses!" I said, grasping the unspoken question. "Your glasses," I repeated, turning to the rumpled, twisted ground cloth. I'd left them there.

Worry stalked the edge of Happy's voice. "There's a problem."

"No, they're right here." I knew about where I'd put them. I pulled the cloth taut, exposing the folds.

They weren't there.

I shook the cloth out to be sure, then rolled it up quickly.

"There's a problem," Happy said again, with growing certainty.

"It's fine." I searched the ground, starting where I'd found my tools.

His voice grew soft. "I don't have another pair, Thirteen."

"My toolbox got tossed to the bushes. Your glasses must have, too. They're here."

I raised my voice. "Anyone seen Happy's glasses?"

Those nearby shook their heads. "Wait here," I said.

215

To one side, Ivan and Crow argued under their breath. Duck fidgeted uncomfortably, hands twisting in aimless activity. Pope stood with Kodiak, quietly commenting to each other as they kept an eye on the argument.

Ivan hissed and waved me away. Pope apologized. None had the glasses.

Taj's eyes flicked to me when I approached him and Abel.

"We're wandering with a train of children," he said, ignoring me.

"Don't blame them. They haven't done this before," Abel said.

"Maybe if we'd gone the easy way, but you insisted on tracking. If it was the few of us, no problem. But it's them."

I didn't like the way he said *them*. He'd made clear when we spoke that I was *them*.

"They're trying to get home, Taj."

"They're going to get us killed. That's what happens when you rely on children."

Abel sighed and searched the trees for words. It seemed this wasn't the first they'd discussed this.

"I have listened until now," Taj pressed in Abel's silence. "If it comes down to them or me, do not be uncertain of my choice."

He brushed by me, nodded to Crisp, and the two began arranging their packs for the day's hunt. I watched them confer, Abel and the glasses temporarily forgotten.

Ivan was batting Duck on the head and speaking angry words. Kodiak now stood alone, gun across his chest and blood still under his fingernails. Pope, pale but smiling. Happy, nearly blind, Taj roughly packing his bag, and Abel, arms crossed and still.

The Outlands were grinding us down.

"What is it, Thirteen?"

Abel's eyes were more tired than before. "Happy's glasses," I said. "We can't find them."

"How did he lose them?" he asked but became distracted. "Taj! Crisp! Wait!"

The two men ignored him, disappearing into the trees, following the trail I couldn't see. Ivan and Crow rose to follow.

"Wait!" I called. "We have to find Happy's glasses!"

Ivan gave me a look that said, *what have you done now?*

Crow said, "I don't need glasses."

"Did you take them," I said.

Crow had given all the answer he would give. They continued walking before Taj slunk out of sight.

Abel curled his fingers into a fist, even as the Unforgiven slipped between and out of his control. "Stump." The old man came over. "They're either here or in a pack," he said as he spun Stump and studied the Ears on his back. "There's nothing nearby. Take fifteen minutes and then follow. Kodiak, hang back with them."

"You aren't walking alone with those guys," Kodiak said.

"I can find the path," Stump added.

"Fine," Abel said.

So he, Kodiak, and Pope disappeared into the trees as well. Then Stump, Happy, and I were alone.

*

"Catch me up," Stump said.

"How bad is it?" he asked Happy when I'd run through the repair, the ground cloth, and the rain.

Happy held his hand a half meter from his face. "I can see about here. I can probably read; I can treat the men. Can't see the Outlands at all."

Stump adjusted the glasses on his own face. "Well, they aren't nowhere."

"I'm sorry," I said. "I'll find them."

Stump was already down, forcing the greenery aside and trawling the soil. I joined him in the ferns.

It was useless covering our tracks, so we ripped plants out by their roots, exposing the earth. We looked close to where I'd slept, then in the unlikely places. We did not speak apart from when Stump called out, "ten minutes," and then, "five."

Happy crawled on the ground, too, feeling his way through the dirt.

At fourteen minutes, we'd circled out farther than the glasses could possibly have been. We unfolded and refolded the ground cloth twice and went through our bags.

"I don't like it, but those empty woods may not be empty anymore. We can't stay," Stump said.

I rolled off my hands and knees to sit. "Well, they aren't nowhere, and they aren't here. They must have been rolled or folded up, someone doesn't even know they have them."

"Are you *sure* they aren't here?" Happy asked.

Stump and I traded a look. The silence was oppressive.

"I'm sure we won't find them if we haven't already," Stump said.

I lifted Happy's pack onto his back. "I'm sorry."

I picked up the Bugwall to stuff in my own pack but paused.

"What is it?" Happy asked.

"It's hot." I sat back down, slid my screwdriver from its sheath, and quickly spun out the screws.

"We need to go," Stump urged from behind. He still watched the jungle, breathing quietly through his nose so he could hear each sound coming out of the trees.

"Just wait," I said.

Someone had opened the device. Signs were everywhere. Most notably, a wire had been twisted into place, bypassing the componentry to feed directly back into the source. It shorted the circuit, draining power at an alarming rate.

It was both better and worse than I thought. Fixing it took moments. But the break itself was sabotage.

"Any guesses on who might break the Bugwall?" I asked as I sealed it, glancing toward Happy.

"We didn't put Ivan on watch last night, did we?" Happy asked.

"Duck took watch after me," Stump said.

"I told you," I said to Happy. "He said he'd kill us all."

"What's this, now?" Stump asked. I sometimes mistook his posture for apathy, but that was not the case. He was engaged, the way a stone was engaged with rain beating down on it.

We told him about Happy's clever double-cross and my clumsy one.

"Could Ivan do this?" Stump asked.

"He watched me repair it the first day," I said. "I don't know."

"So, he thinks we'll bed down one night and the juice will wear off?" Happy asked.

I stared at the Bugwall. "He said he'd do anything."

"Little tsar," Stump said.

I closed the machine up, already cooling.

"We'll tell Abel and Taj," I said.

"No. Pretend you haven't noticed," Stump said. "It will be a day or two before Ivan knows his plan didn't work, and those will be days he doesn't try anything else. Short of killing him, it's the best way to keep him out of trouble."

It was blunt. It was practical.

"And when he catches on?"

"A lot may happen between now and then."

A lot could happen before lunch.

"Yeah," I said. "Well, good thing we stayed behind." A chuckle escaped Happy before despondency took him again.

Stump and I shouldered our packs, but Happy still faced the clearing we'd camped in. "You're sure they aren't here?"

"We'll find them tonight," I said.

"We've been here too long," Stump said, scanning the trees once again.

– NINETEEN –

The Outlanders had something planned. We were scattered, disorganized. Vulnerable. They hadn't planned a dawn rainstorm. They hadn't planned misplacing Happy's glasses. But they'd planned something, and here we were like ripe fruit drying in the morning sun.

Stump led us down the Unforgiven trail. Happy walked behind him. There was nothing and no one behind me.

Hopefully, whatever they'd planned was later. Farther.

The Unforgiven black of our Hall-issued uniforms was mottled into natural camouflage by the Outland's scars. Tears and scuffs, mud on our hands and knees. The ground began sloping uphill, and the dirt grew dry and hard. We found a skylight in the canopy, where a fallen tree had ripped down branches, and I saw a ridge in the distance making one arm of a shallow valley.

It was the fourth day since our fight. Four days of no votes and no Outlanders, just pervasive reminders that all was not well. Just slowly swirling water.

The tree trunks grew thicker and the undergrowth thinned. I asked Happy if he thought the change might be due to water runoff or even the small change in altitude. His response was inaudible.

The weight of the extra minutes in camp pressed on each of us. Stump paused periodically, raising a hand to silence us. He would kneel and close his eyes, slowly rotating his head as if his ears were ancient radar dishes. When satisfied, he would rise and resume an aggressive pace.

Taj said the bloody gateway meant Outlanders waiting ahead. He said there was no war party chasing from behind. Either he was right or it would be my dying scream that sounded the alarm.

I glanced behind for the hundredth time.

The more I thought about it, the stronger it grew: the weight of presence at my shoulder, grasping hands and thumping feet pounding through the jungle. I tried not to look. A minute, maybe two would go by. Then I would jerk my head around, scanning the trees. Nothing. Every few minutes, nothing.

I did not want to fight. I did not want any of this.

Abel had said they needed killing. That made no sense, but they said he was a good man. And he knew something.

They had tried to kill us in the night.

Or maybe they knew why we were here. Maybe they only defended themselves.

500 deaths could not make me clean.

Ivan was not finished with us.

It all muddled my head. I wanted to know what I should do. I still expected what was right to happen to me in the end, somehow. What I did not yet understand was that right and wrong had little to do with it anymore.

This was the Outlands: Eventually, a man would stand before

me and try to kill me. And I, to preserve my life, would try to kill him. One of us would die, and the process would cycle anew, at another time, in another place. The only question that mattered was, when I saw him before me, with two eyes, two ears, ten fingers, and snarling teeth, what would I do? Would I pull the trigger and live? Would I refuse?

Why this happened did not matter. Whether it should or should not happen did not matter.

Some will tell you that the Outlands have a way of changing a man, but they are liars. The Outlands only scrape you raw and show you who you always were.

The Outlands scraped at me, layer by layer, but I did not yet know what lay inside. I had not yet been tested. I'd huddled in the shadows while the warriors returned, bloody and triumphant.

So I wrestled with thoughts of two eyes and ten fingers, myself in a mirror. I tried to think instead of animal screams in the night, of the terrifying stories I'd heard. Of those who had not just gone rustic in the wilderness but had gone feral. Those were cold thoughts that would keep me alive when the time came.

And I turned to look behind. Nothing.

*

Before the sun was fully overhead, we stumbled on the rest of the men taking lunch. In silence, I sat and took the proffered food while Happy wandered to ask after his glasses. He was still blind when he returned, leaning close to make sure it was me.

"No one wants to unpack. Everyone is sure they'll turn up when we stop tonight."

I grunted. We ate.

After the meal, Stump, Happy, and I fell to the rear again. While tracking wasn't quick, neither was guiding a blind man through undergrowth. Kodiak fell back with us.

When I felt the itch between my shoulder blades and looked, he caught my eye. He smiled a big, laughing grin, though nothing about the day was funny.

He said, "I feel it, too. How long can you wait without looking?"

"Five minutes," I lied.

"Try to go six," he said. "I'm going to go an hour." He glanced up at the sun through the leaves, as if marking its position.

"Have we seen anything this morning?" I asked.

"All morning. Out at range, moving with us. Won't be long, won't be long."

I looked over my shoulder again, and he barked a laugh. It sounded friendly, if you could sound friendly with blood on your hands.

To ignore the itch at my back, I looked sideways instead. I watched him move, copying his grip on his rifle and the way he put his feet down, making so little noise. As I shadowed him, it began to feel natural, and the weapon felt lighter in my hands.

"I've always been a big man," he said abruptly.

I did not know why he spoke or what he intended by it. I walked until the silence grew tiresome for him again.

"I can do whatever I want. Do you understand?"

He went on, as if talking to himself.

"Imagine; *anything you want.* Most people live in a small world, small as the reach of their arms. Life plays out, and no one pays any attention. This is what Abel says."

His tone wasn't as arrogant as his words.

"When I was young," he said, "a boy had a hydrogen engine that fit in his pocket. I took it. They told me that was bad."

"It was," I said.

"When I was older, I saw three men around a woman. She looked unhappy. They started grabbing her. I left them on the ground and walked her home."

He glared into the tree-shadows, as if looking for those men again.

"They told me that was good," he concluded.

I nodded. Kodiak glanced at the sun, and I wondered if he could really tell time that way.

"What do I do if I can do anything?"

While he rambled, I imagined the sound of running feet behind. I thought of Kodiak's words, "won't be long," said as if a shipment were coming into the Spire dock. I did not know why he was talking to me.

"Look, you…Kodiak." I replaced several words I was thinking with his name. "You talk like this strength is a burden. Don't make yourself a victim."

"To you it is simple?" Kodiak asked.

"Don't take things. Don't…" I couldn't say "kill." Not to his face. "Just do good."

Maybe he was trying to talk about Patches.

"How?" Kodiak asked.

"How what?"

"How do you *just do good*?"

"I…" I said, sputtering as I tried to put words to the obvious. "You do what's right. When you fail, when things go wrong, you fix it. It's as simple as that."

"No."

I began to turn to look behind me, but Kodiak's hand shot up to catch my arm. I set my jaw and looked ahead.

"*You* don't choose!" he pressed. "You want something, but you can't take it. Because you are weak. Or afraid. Later you call it restraint. *Conscience*. You call yourself 'good.' But you didn't choose."

I rolled my eyes and tugged my arm free. He growled, leaning close.

"When you have to choose, everything inside of you comes out. And everything goes wrong."

I shook my head as I fixated on the trees and packs straight ahead of me. I saw, now, what this was, and it was pathetic. Kodiak trying to put reason on all the death on his hands. He couldn't because there was none. He was a little more than a beast, and that was the whole of it.

"And look at everything you've broken," I said.

He glared. I took a step away, out of arm's reach, but returned his glare.

"I'm not like you, Kodiak."

I braced for the word, or the fist, that would fly back at me. But

226

he softened.

"No, I don't think we are the same. But I think it is for different reasons than you think."

What had been an argument had somehow turned to condescension. As if he held the answers. No delusion he pulled from the mud at his own feet could help me find my own way.

I liked it better when he was angry.

"Is this also what Abel says?" I asked gruffly.

He was already back to watching the trees. We walked once more in silence, and I wondered if it would rain.

"I've always been a big man," he said again, and it made little more sense than when he'd first broken the silence.

"Gift or burden… So much has happened. So much… It's never been a gift. I want to know what it's for."

"What do you mean, what it's for?" I asked.

"I don't know yet. Abel's been asking."

I didn't have the energy for this. Kodiak wasn't my job. Life would roll on, *this machine* would roll on, and eventually grind it out of him. He was a beast, the price would come due one way or another, and he'd have his answer. He didn't need me any more than I needed him.

Some motion caught his eye behind us. He looked for a moment, then with a grimace looked at the sun.

"Nedder, twenty-five minutes? I can do better than that." And we kept walking. I found I walked a little farther from him, but not too far.

*

We came around a clump of underbrush to find the Unforgiven in an uneasy huddle. Rifles snapped up, then lowered more slowly. Most continued to watch the trees, uneasy, as we approached.

"What's wrong?" Stump asked.

"The trail splits," Abel said, not looking up.

"How did they split?" Stump asked.

"The real trail goes that way," Taj gestured in roughly the direction we'd been moving. "But they doubled back and trampled a larger trail going this way," now gesturing in a new direction.

"I see," Stump said.

I didn't see. Though even I could see the larger trail left by the second group. It was a mess of torn vegetation, like our own.

"Meaning what?" I asked.

Taj sighed. "Meaning, *they* went this way," gesturing in the first direction, "but they want *us* to go this way," gesturing in the second direction.

"I still don't see what the thatchers are after," Crow said, but it was hint enough for me to solve the puzzle.

"Ambush," I said to Crow. Taj gave me a sarcastic look as if to say, *Welcome to the conversation.*

It seemed a clumsy trap, but they didn't know what we were capable of.

"Wait, ambush?" Ivan spluttered. "Is that what you all are debating? You can't be thinking we'll walk into this, Abel. Are you thinking we'll walk into this?"

Abel's eyes were pinched. "It keeps us in control. We know where the trap is. If we don't follow the decoy trail, though, they'll follow. Likely be caught between two groups."

Taj looked condescendingly at Ivan. "But don't be troubled by this. We knew what would happen as soon as we tracked them." He spared a sideways glance at Abel, who still studied the ground. It seemed Taj had enough sarcasm for all of us today.

Abel measured the lengthening shadows and took off his pack. "And if they've already chosen the time and place, they won't bother us here tonight."

Taj tossed a gun to Ivan, and another to Crow. They both checked immediately and found them unloaded.

"I need bullets."

"Tomorrow," Taj said.

There was no way a few days had cooled his vendetta, though I hoped the looming battle would hold his focus for the time. Then maybe we could take the guns away again.

Ivan studied the empty hole in his rifle, then threw it to the ground.

"No! I won't be caught between two packs of savages, and neither will I walk into their jaws. Why are we doing any of this?"

Stump unslung his pack and quietly pressed off the safety on his rifle. No one moved or interrupted.

"It's your fight, not mine!" Ivan walked to a lone backpack and began rooting through it. "If I have to go alone, I will. I'm not dying for you!"

"I don't think we vote today," Kodiak murmured beside me as his hands tightened on his rifle.

"Don't." I said.

"Don't what?" Kodiak gave me a dark look. "This is how it begins. Can you tell me what the right choice will be?" He studied me.

I looked away.

"What are you doing?" Abel asked.

"We," Ivan hesitated as he looked in another bag and then at the growing bundle in his arm, "are taking our share and leaving you to your little *adventure*." He moved on to another pack.

Everyone was watching him, rifles in hand. There was no way he would be able to leave.

"Who is 'we'?" Abel asked.

"Anyone who is tired of you." Ivan stopped at this and gave Abel a direct stare, even as Crow and Duck stepped closer to him. I watched Taj and Crisp, but they didn't move.

"Your share is with us." Abel said.

Kodiak's hands moved on the weapon, and I heard his breathing pick up. "There's a time for everything," he said quietly. I stepped behind him.

"So there's three of us," Ivan said, thinking to himself. "And eight of you," now giving a pointed look at Pope, who stayed by Happy. "We will take *our share*, and you will be rid of us."

He was staring at the pack I still wore. His eyes looked off into the distance for a moment, whispering to himself, and then he stepped toward me.

"We'll just see what's in that pack, now," he said to himself, but then Kodiak was there. He planted a huge palm on Ivan's chest. Ivan looked up, frozen and wide-eyed, for a drawn out second, as if only just noticing the man. Kodiak, almost lazily, stepped forward and drove Ivan to the ground, saying, "Like hell, we will."

And all hell did break loose. Duck dove for the supplies that toppled from Ivan's arms while Crow threw himself at Crisp and Happy, empty gun swinging like a club. Briefly, all became a whirling mass of arms and legs, kicking, scrabbling, shouting like a troop of monkeys. A body crashed into me, and I stumbled under the weight of my pack, falling to the ground.

Before I could roll to my feet, it was over. I lifted my head and saw everyone, standing, sitting, lying on the ground, brushing dirt off of legs and sleeves. Pope and Happy stood back from the melee. Abel also stood over them, arms crossed.

"Mercy, Lord," Stump said.

Had I heard a shot? I tried to replay my memory of the frantic minute, but there was nothing. And then I saw it. Crow, knife rising from his chest, staring up at the blue sky through the trees. I got to my feet and looked closer; I didn't want to but I couldn't look away. I never could look away.

My eyes first leapt to Kodiak, but he was on his feet, watching Ivan. Clean hands. Who had snapped?

We never knew. But like everything else, I wondered if it mattered anymore.

– TWENTY –

Deep in the night, I walked in circles in the darkness. The Outlanders would not know about the Ears, Taj had explained, and we had to keep up appearances.

They were expecting us to follow the false trail. They were expecting us to be worried about attacks in the night. So we patrolled, two at a time. A third man sat back with the Ears, the actual guard. Ivan retained his weapon but slept under a faint camp light, in sight of the real guard.

In my comm, the Ears man reported dots, sitting just outside our patrol routes. They would show up for a short while, then drift away.

My eyes adjusted in the dark, but not enough to pierce the night under the canopy. I had never understood what darkness was, living near the spires of the State. There, night was lit by a thousand tiny lights, a mass of circuitry binding our civilization together and standing watch in an endless dusk. Here was palpable shadow like a pool of ink. Here was night and all its hidden predators.

Abel and Taj said these Outlanders wanted the battle to happen elsewhere. It was the disciplined, logical plan. Abel and Taj did not say the Outlanders were disciplined and logical.

It seemed to me a fine plan to pick us off, one by one. A tenth claimed with every spear. I gripped my rifle, trying ever harder to pierce the darkness. Hoping the Ears man would tell me if a red dot grew impatient and drifted into my path.

Before we'd set camp, we'd scoured every backpack, pulled each item into the fading daylight. There were no glasses.

Ivan and Duck had been nearly strip-searched, but they came up clean. It didn't surprise me. Ivan already had an outlet for his malice; his little plan with the Bugwall.

I hadn't known what to do; I hadn't known what to say. We couldn't scour yesterday's bushes again. *It was an accident*, I kept telling myself. An accident. That was the only pole I had to stave off the lump in my chest. It didn't work then, as it hadn't worked before.

Happy tended to Pope's wound, with his face held close to the other man's arm. When he thought no one was looking, despair crossed his face. When I stood beside him, looking blankly into the branches, and said "I'm sorry," he waved me away.

Little was said about Crow. Someone moved the body and covered him with branches. There were no accusations and no trial. But if you listened closely, you could hear new whispers from the roiling water.

Kodiak had squatted by me as I'd laid out gear on the ground cloth for the night.

"He won't get you," he said. I assumed he was talking about Ivan. I hadn't thanked him then. I still didn't now but nodded without looking up.

"It's the only time I feel alive," he said, apparently unsatisfied with how we'd left things before.

I thought of him tossing the drill sergeant to the ground, knocking out a cluster of men around a harassed woman, stepping in front of me to stop Ivan in his tracks. I remembered him flushed with the radiance of life some dark hour after midnight, having survived our little battle. I also saw him striding up to Patches's unprotected back, chest heaving and knife drawn.

"But it ends up wrong," he added, as if reading my thoughts.

I continued my work.

"I'm supposed to use it," he said. "Sometimes it goes all wrong, but I'm not supposed to sit quiet." He waited a moment, then rose and walked away. There was a pathetic echo of an apology in his words. But if he really wanted to say it, he could say it.

Kodiak wasn't my job. I had my own thing to set right.

I'd called Duck over. Told him I needed help. He'd handed me screwdrivers as I took something apart, pretending it needed fixing.

It didn't, but maybe he did.

His eyes lit up a bit. I'd told him what things were, and he asked a few questions. He understood. If I'd had him in Abbey, I think I could have made something of him.

So I'd sent him to bed, with plans for an ephemeral *tomorrow* that might not come, and took a few hours of restless sleep before pretending to patrol the jungle. Now I made noise with every step to be sure I didn't trip over an Outlander, that I didn't force the issue between us. Like a beggar shaking a coin tin in a corridor, I repeated over and over that they had chosen the time and the place.

It wasn't here. It wasn't now.

After two hours I crawled back to my sleeping bag. I found no rest in dreams, only endless chase and struggle against a stream of half imagined monsters.

When I woke with heart pounding, the sky was already beginning to glow with light. I felt I hadn't slept at all. I lay there counting the fading stars to reset my mind. They shone softly, a bright, still counterpoint against the yielding darkness, and eventually my breath calmed and my heart slowed.

*

The sun rose with grim, red visage.

Today I will fight. Numbness spread at the thought. What would come would come.

The early light spilled through a growing rustle, the others also awake early. I slipped out of my bag and started packing the menagerie, still numb, until a hand fell on my wrist. I looked up at Crisp, fully dressed and geared up.

"Keep it out. We need it today," he said, and moved off. I began instead separating survival gear from tactical.

Around me rose the click and clatter of weapons being checked. Nothing needed checking. It wasn't so much preparation as keeping busy. All needed something to do.

All except Abel, who stood alone, looking into the trees. He was singing, a low song with words I could not hear. It lilted, never drifting far from its cadence, like a lullaby. He stood, oblivious to us, and I wondered what inward thought he cradled. The battle ahead, or the home behind.

He'd fallen silent by the time we finished our work, both the necessary and the nervous. He turned abruptly, sharp and focused, and called us together.

"Close," he said. "Everyone close. Stump, is anyone watching?"

Stump, on the Ears, shook his head. "No one."

"Good. Lay it out, Taj."

Taj drew on the ground with a stick. "About a kilometer that way," he said, drawing the decoy trail, "I found a small ravine. It's the correct place for ambush."

I stared at the man, casually drawing his map on the ground. He'd either gone out in the night, blind, or gone out in the morning when the breaking sun could reveal him. Both were madness. It was Taj's way.

"There is a small hill, here," he drew a circle, "and across from it, a larger hill, steep, forming a ridge. The ravine runs between. They are at least a little clever, as they have chosen good ground and are trying to lead us there like a row of ducklings." His brow furrowed, waiting for Duck to register the insult. Duck didn't. Taj continued.

"If they are only a little clever, they will be here and here," he said, marking two X's on the hill and the ridge, with a larger X on the ridge. "If they are a little more clever, they will also have people here," he marked several O's around the area, "in case we were to decide not to go through the pass and find the trail on the other side.

"If they are planning for contingencies, these stragglers will run like bunnies, tempting us into the ravine. If there's enough of them, they may have entire squads spread out–"

"Spread out is better, right?" Crisp said.

Taj looked up, annoyed. "No. Your gun fires in one direction. So, we prefer to have our targets in one direction. Regardless, I don't think they are more clever. I found them here," he tapped the X marks, "and here. If I am wrong, the Ears will tell us."

I squinted at the map, concerned. Of course the "great man" would never over-assume another's cleverness. If he was wrong, we'd be surrounded. I didn't put much stock in his confidence, though I did have confidence in the Ears.

"They will first attack from this side," Taj pointed to the small X on the hill, "and when our backs are turned, the true attack will come down from the ridge," pointing to the large X. "It is the standard plan. It is a good plan. Our job is simple. We take the hill and trade places," he concluded, drawing arrows between the ambush route and the small hill.

Taj sat back, relishing our confusion. He understood, we did not, and that was how he liked it. I would not be the one to give him the satisfaction of asking.

"Why?" Pope asked, for all of us.

Taj smiled. "The larger force," he began, tapping the larger X, "will attack blind at the beginning. First, they will kill their own for us. And once they enter the ravine, they'll be in one direction, all of them, which is how our guns work." He looked again at Crisp. "And everyone knows it is easier to hit targets from higher ground – less to get in the way of a bullet. Simple tactics."

Nodding heads. Scratching chins.

Ivan was keeping his peace. *Good*, I thought. *He knows when to shut up and do what he's told*. It was pleasantly out of character. Uncomfortably out of character. I looked more closely, but he was only inspecting the map with a creased brow.

"Tell them what they need to do, Taj," Abel said.

"Someone will go up front."

"I'll go," Crisp said without hesitation.

Taj studied the ground, then nodded to himself. "Crisp, you will take Ivan and Duck. I hesitate to use the word, but you are the bait that will draw them into the ravine."

"Bait?" Duck asked, voice tight.

"Do not worry. It is more dangerous for the one who goes second." Taj re-focused on his drawing. "They will be hiding and unable to see you clearly. When you reach here," he drew a line in the dirt, in the first part of the ravine, "you will fire up the hill. Draw the attack. You don't need targets; just make them believe they are spotted. Then, before they can charge or aim, you run like crazy. Run through the ravine, circle back and climb the hill. You'll meet us there; we will have your flank."

Taj stopped here to check on his bait. Ivan and Crisp silently studied the sketched map. Duck's eyes were fixed on Ivan.

"Their weapons are most effective at short range," Taj explained. "Spears for stabbing, arrows that can't pierce underbrush. Keep up your pace and they won't stick you." Without waiting for any kind of consent, he continued. "Kody and I will circle behind the hill, to ensure no stragglers come at you. No stray arrows. It's the two of us because we stand the best chance of slipping through undetected. This all depends on them not realizing we're springing the trap.

"Stump and Pope, you are with Abel. As soon as Crisp and his team stop firing, you will rush to the top of the hill and clear off any straggling Outlanders. Kody and I will push from the other side, of course. Crisp, Ivan, Duck - once you start running, stop firing. Don't fire again until you see us. You'd be firing at us while we take the hill, got that?"

Again, I looked at Ivan. Gun in hand, thoughts masked. He only studied the map.

Ivan had to know now was a bad time. If he took his revenge, he'd be slaughtered by Outlanders within an hour. He had to know.

Crisp rose, still studying the map. Taj continued looking at them until they both met his eye and nodded. No firing.

"And Abel, make sure the hill is cleared well or Crisp will meet resistance. That would be… a problem."

Abel nodded. "Don't worry," he said to Crisp.

"Happy, you're as good as blind. Your job is after the battle, not in it. Follow Abel up the hill and sit tight. Thirteen, you're with Happy."

"What?" I'd been dreading this, but I hadn't expected to be benched. "But there are only ten of us!"

"You carry the Eyes. You follow Abel up the hill, you loft those things, you talk to us. You talk to Crisp, to me, and to Abel. Everyone else, mouth shut. Abel says you know how to work the Eyes? Can you do this?"

"I can direct you," I said.

"You don't know skirmish tactics," Taj said.

"Who does?" I asked.

"You don't," he said, matching my tone. "I'll ask the questions. Just tell us what you see."

I glowered as he went over the important points again. Who does what, when, what not to do, and especially when not to shoot. In its most basic form, we were drawing them off the hill, circling behind to meet at the top, and then waiting for the Outlanders to gather in the ravine.

"After they chase the bait," Taj was concluding, "they'll try to retake the hill here," drawing where Crisp would run up, "and here," a line up the middle where their rear would be closest to the summit. "They'll be joined by the rest of their little army. We'll push down into them with heavy fire. Pope, you're still weak. You stay on top with Thirteen and Happy. With these weapons, seven of us will be enough."

I was one of the few heads not nodding. "And what about those Outlander stragglers you mentioned? What if they're out there after all?" It all felt too clean and orderly, nothing like the battle we had known the first time.

Taj scratched out the O's with his stick. "They won't be."

That is how we left it.

*

It all took five minutes. Taj scraped out his diagrams from the dirt, and we formed into a column.

Taj handed a magazine to Ivan himself. "There are a hundred

Outlanders not half a kilo from here. Use this on us, and there will be no one to save you from them. Here are 20 bullets. I will listen. If you try to save one, I will kill you."

Ivan met Taj's eyes, face completely blank.

Crisp, Ivan, and Duck took the front. Duck's gaze was unfocused, like when he wandered the shadows after our first skirmish. Behind them were Abel, Stump, and Pope, ready to cut left and charge the hill once the trap was sprung. Happy followed closely, wearing the Ears on his back, and I walked just behind, keeping an eye on it. Ten days. We were using the screen too much, but I wouldn't be the one to turn it off, not now. My rifle was on my back, the Eyes in hand, ready to loft. I held them with white knuckles, indignant, grateful, terrified. Behind me were Kodiak and Taj, ready to slink off as we approached the ravine.

Our comms let out a constant, dull hiss, laying a foundation under our silence. The oblivious jungle sang on, unaware that Crisp in front and Kodiak in the back, and all between were wondering if we would be dead in an hour. I saw a flash of red, feathers in the sunlight. A butterfly landed on the Ears.

Both hills were stained red, as Taj had said they would be. Red dots with no space between. They had crouched there on their hills, waiting through the night. Now they sat in the sun and weathered the dread as we did. Except we had guns.

I asked myself what we were doing for the hundredth time. For the hundredth time, I didn't know. I hooked the propeller back on the Eyes. I twisted the screwdriver in its sheath: clockwise, clockwise, clockwise.

In the gaps between trees, I saw the ridge poking through, tilting the horizon. It wasn't overly large. Large enough to put a man with a spear above me. I heard Kodiak's breathing behind me, deep, even, loud. I looked at the ridge again, and wished I was on top rather than below.

Something throbbed in my chest, and the vein in my neck began to pulse. I could feel it in my boots and the tips of my fingers pressed against the screwdriver. I was nauseous. We had not eaten breakfast.

I knew what was happening; my body was trying to survive. Clear the stomach so I would be lighter. Oxygenate the muscles in anticipation of anaerobic stress. Pool the blood in my abdomen so that extremities would not bleed. I knew what was happening, but it felt like death. It was prehistoric, feral, the instincts programmed by millennia upon millennia of death and mistakes. I felt savage; I'd felt it before but never this intensely. And every time before, it was a misfire of evolution, a programmed response to some minor snag of civilized life. This was who we really were. This was what we'd evolved for. To kill and, by killing, to live. I wanted to fight and flee and scream.

Clockwise, clockwise.

The ridge was closer still, visible through the trees even where they were thick. Taj's voice broke the hiss on our comms, a hushed whisper. "We're gone." I felt the air move behind me and, looking back, saw no one.

Up again. Closer again. There had been no other dots, no stragglers or contingency plans for the Outlanders. Taj had been right, and I hoped he continued to be right, because I worried we were the ones who might not be clever enough.

But we had the Ears, and guns. State help us. I shook my head, not the State. Never the State. *Something* help us.

The red blotches began to surge, the edges swaying. They knew we were here. I took the Eyes again and held them tightly.

Suddenly, another voice broke the silence over the comms.

"You chose this," it said. "This is your fight, not ours."

Ivan, I realized, as I looked up and saw him and Duck sprinting away toward the ravine.

– TWENTY ONE –

The descent into chaos was immediate. Taj's voice cut over the comm with a whispered curse, asking what had happened. The blob on the small hill began boiling down toward us, catching the motion in the ravine. The blob on the ridge did not move, too high up to know what was happening, I hoped. Or perhaps waiting for a signal.

"Thatch you Ivan, you oil sucking, inbred, rustic humping..." Crisp ran on in a constant torrent, as he chased them and began firing shots up the hill, trying to salvage the plan.

Too late.

Abel shouted after him to fall back, but Crisp was already gone. The second one through. The more dangerous place. Underneath this ran an urgent whisper, Stump trying to communicate the status to Taj and Kodiak.

I stood. My job was to follow Abel. Abel was not moving. I watched the Ears in horror as the patch of red flowed toward us.

"Double time, let's move," said Abel, breaking up the chatter. He began running up the hill, angled toward the ravine, perhaps to intercept the small army descending on Crisp.

"Crisp, you better run like a gazelle, those spragging thatchers sprang this mousetrap and you're in it!" he shouted, and I couldn't tell if it was curse or encouragement.

"I've got this," Crisp shouted back. We couldn't see him anymore. "State's balls, so many!"

"Keep firing! Kody and Taj can't be on the hill yet." I watched the Ears, but it was all red churning about.

"Thirteen!" I startled out of my jog. "I need Eyes! Loft it! Talk to Crisp!"

"We aren't–" The plan.

"Loft it! Pope, stay here." And they were gone.

I sent the Eyes up and waited for the picture. More shots were sounding, and the shouting of battle had begun. I glanced at the Ears and saw the blotch from the ridge coming down. *Nedder, nedder, nedder.* They must have started when the shooting began.

I leapt on the Eyes when the picture came up and dialed it in. Crisp…Crisp was running like a thatcher, chased by ten or fifteen Outlanders. Kodiak and Taj were near the crest now, but some Outlanders had hunkered down on top and weren't running. I saw what Abel had done, by running a slant on the hill he'd made the third point of a triangle, giving all three teams clear lines of fire. I watched the dots in horror, Abel chasing the Outlanders chasing Crisp, Taj and Kodiak trying to cautiously hurry to secure the hill.

"Talk to me, Thirteen," Abel called out.

I was the only one seeing all this.

"I told you he's useless," said Taj's voice.

"Shut up." No time. "Taj, you've got three hostiles directly in front of you, twenty meters, and you need to clear them out for Crisp, now! Crisp, shoot at whoever is closest. You won't hit us."

Kodiak and Taj began moving more quickly, but not fast enough.

"Damn you, Crisp, run! They're right–" and then his blue figure blinked out. It just disappeared.

"What is it, Thirteen?"

It filtered in, seeming to take forever as a moment passed, then another. Taj and Abel linked up at the crest of the hill, forming a front to receive and defend a Crisp who simply wasn't there anymore. The hostiles in the hologram began winking out as they drew near to the four remaining squad members, spears and arrows against a solid front of real weaponry, and the hill was ours. It was done quickly.

"Talk to me Thirteen." It was Abel again.

"Crisp disappeared. I lost him."

"Leave it. What's going on now?" he asked, urgently.

Leave it. I looked again.

"Larger group in the ravine. Can't count, maybe forty or fifty."

"Our left or right?"

"Maybe ten to your left. Rest to the right..." I trailed off. We were well separated from the other four Unforgiven now.

"They're coming!" I shouted.

"Calm down," someone said.

"They're coming right at us!" I reached for my gun.

"Calm down," again. "At you-us or at us-us?"

"The three of us!" I said, watching the trees. It had been fifteen or so in the image. They were coming.

The last thing I registered was a voice in my ear, barely heard,

"I'm coming." My head was wagging left and right, looking for movement. My gun, the safety was on. I switched it off. I quickly checked the magazine, the routine clicks and clatter the others had done before.

"What's happening?" Happy asked. He knew; he could hear everything. But he couldn't see, and he couldn't fight. He asked again. It was all he could do.

"They're coming," I said.

"I'm coming," again the voice in my ear.

Pope began to move toward the trees. "Come back!" I shouted but he shook his head as he stopped a way in front of us. He fired a shot, two, then a burst. An arrow came through the undergrowth, and I saw him go down. I shouted for him.

"What happened?" Happy shouted, frantic.

"Pope!" I shouted, sending a spray of bullets into the woods. Shadows flickered through the light, mottling the darkness under the thicker trees.

I heard it again, urgent, "I am coming," but I couldn't listen. I could see them.

Pope was still moving; they were close to him. I fired again, and I found a target An Outlander standing out from the trees collapsed, the skin and bone and life pierced, flowing out of him, the blood and his cry rushing into the air around me. Two arms, two legs, bare skin, but a face unlike mine. I breathed rapidly, now hearing only the thud of my pulse in my ears. Other Outlanders stood, confused for a moment. They stopped to look cautiously at their fallen comrade, not comprehending what had struck him.

More emerged. I fired again, a branch erupting into splinters, the leaves of a bush ripping as my shot went wide. Still more of them, now howling and leaning forward to run. Happy opened fire beside me, literally shooting blindly into the trees.

"I'm coming," again in my ear. I ripped the comm off, silencing the voice.

I fired again and again, wild, unaimed shots. I had killed a man. I was horrified. I wanted desperately to do it again, even as the bile rose in my throat, and my skin crawled where it touched the weapon in my hand. I needed to kill, but I could not. Wild eyes and tormented fingers sent my shots wide. I could see them now, white eyes and open mouths, the dirty nails on their fingers where the jungle dirt had wormed its way in. Tanned skin, ridged teeth, and pounding feet.

Then I heard a roar and a rush behind me. The Outlanders dropped at my feet; one, then another, then another. Something crashed into me, and I was knocked to the ground. In front of me I saw a foot plant into the soil, pushing up a great mound as it dug in. Above it was a twisting shape, striking like a snake, rooted like a tree, gun held like a club as it sliced the air with an angry rush. I saw an Outlander lifted into the air and cast back crumpled to the ground. Another leapt, but quick hands snatched the howling figure from the air and swung the body to the side; the gun dropped in the soil. Spears were like twigs, snatched as they thrusted and broken asunder. Everything was howls and grunts, and then it faded into thumping. The Outlanders were running away.

Kodiak did not hesitate. He dropped to a knee and picked up

the rifle, and with a steady rhythm dropped the running figures one by one, each in turn. I buried my head in shame. The frantic fear ebbed.

I felt a heavy hand on my shoulder, a long steady press, and then it was still. He pushed me back into the earth, and I felt my breath slow and my pulse recover. One breath. Another. Another. Kodiak's weight shifted as he scanned the clearing. Nothing moved. And then the hand was gone, and Kodiak ran into the trees, following the running shapes.

Happy spoke into the eerie calm left behind, "Where is Pope?" I looked around, remembering his fall, and he was still there. I pointed, and Happy scrambled to the correct body, speaking softly and inspecting him.

I wiped my nose and eyes. My whole head felt swollen. There were bodies everywhere; shot, broken, and crumpled. In the morning, in the quiet huddle, I'd felt slighted to be relegated. But I'd failed. The three of us should already be dead, our figures blanked from the map like they'd never existed.

I stared around me, dazed, until I saw my discarded comm. I had a job to do, too. I hooked it on my ear and turned back to the Eyes. I first made sure the bodies all around us were dark. There were three blue figures. One, still, for Pope.

I dialed the scope out and saw the four friendlies steadily advancing, coordinated in a skirmish line, mopping up what was left. This is what Taj had wanted, all of us sweeping together, facing a grouped enemy as a killing wall. I fed them numbers and directions to make sure nothing slipped out of the net.

Some of them got away anyway. I watched on the Ears as the farther dots escaped, slipping off the edge. Every escaping dot was a loose end we'd pay for later.

But for now, we were victorious. I buried my face in my hands and shut my eyes as tightly as I could.

– TWENTY TWO –

When the four skirmishers reached the edge of contact, when the comms started crackling, I called them back. I brought the Eyes down and went to see if Happy needed any help. Pope's leg was injured but fixable, the wound cleaned, stitched, and detoxed. Happy patched up each of the ways it could kill him. Still, he wouldn't walk well. That could kill him good as anything else, just slower.

Duck and Ivan had disappeared completely. No dots.

I wandered toward Crisp, or toward the place where his light had gone out. He was there, lying alone, abandoned; the battle had moved on from where he fell. Arrows had brought him down, bright feathers on shafts made of smooth jungle wood. Crude pieces of rustic technology. Enough to kill a man.

Our small army of four had stood indomitable, a killing wall that had mopped up sixty Outlanders, but they'd each had each other, on the right and left. Crisp had been alone.

The trap was already closing when Crisp ran. If he had stopped, he would have been overwhelmed. Maybe that's what happened. Maybe he saw the Outlanders still at the top of the hill and turned to fight. I didn't know, I couldn't read the jungle like Taj or Stump.

I hadn't liked Crisp, but he had died well, whatever that really meant. I pulled out the arrows and dragged him to a dip in the ground, where I covered him with branches. He'd been our bait, clearing the hill so the rest of us could get behind. Maybe it was what he would have wanted, standing alone in the ultimate test, to see what he was really made of.

Skin and bone, blood and breath, just like the rest of us. I stacked a pile of rocks at his feet and left him for the Outlands.

*

Ivan.

He weighed on me as I returned. Were we seven now, or nine? Was this the end, or was this the beginning of something more maddening than before?

I found Kodiak before a stony Taj, at the site where I'd launched the Eyes. The argument was not about Ivan.

"No," he growled. "Why bait?"

"Earlier, you understood. Earlier you agreed." Taj appeared diffident, as always. But he stood on the balls of his feet, his weight in perfect balance.

"You said it would work. It didn't. Crisp died. Why did you need bait?"

"We needed to be on the hill. We needed them off the hill. It was the best way."

"Yesterday you said 'only way'."

"Only sensible way," Taj rejoined.

"It was neither."

Now that I'd seen what four of us could do to fifty or sixty of them, I sided with Kodiak. Four of us with guns. But maybe the plan had been good. Maybe it was wholly Ivan's fault.

Abel emerged from the undergrowth, not alone. Before him was a figure, nearly naked.

"What's that?" I yelped.

The others followed my finger, cast at the stooped man now in our midst. His head was completely hairless, and as near as I could tell, so was his entire body. He was scarred and burned in grotesque patterns, like a white tattoo, lines and craters woven together to turn his skin into some kind of hide. The mangled lace spread over his shoulders and across his chest, even up onto his skull. I could almost believe he wasn't human. Red blood followed the ridges of his scars, where it flowed out of two or three wounds.

The last thing I registered were the canvas strips woven around his hands, arms, mouth, and eyes. A prisoner.

"What in the Spires are we doing with an Outlander?" I demanded, overriding my first question.

"I'm hoping to learn something," Abel said.

"Learn what?" I asked, but Abel, impatient, focused on Taj and Kodiak.

"Well, we got him," Stump said to me, quietly. He reached in and clicked on the safety on my rifle; I hadn't even realized I was still carrying the thing. "And now we got him, we can't just execute him."

"Isn't that what we're doing here?" I asked.

"It's different once the fighting is done, Thirteen. Are you going to pull the trigger?"

No, I wasn't. I spread my fingers wide, my hand spasming outward, trying to get the feel of the trigger off it.

Abel had quickly taken over the argument and was trying to put it to bed. "Things went wrong, Kody. We had one shot, and it went wrong. You live with it."

"What kind of thatcher goes into a gunfight without a contingency?" Kodiak fired back, not taking his eyes off Taj.

"Is that for me or for Taj?" Abel asked. He spoke calmly, but there was anger buried in his voice as well.

Kodiak didn't answer.

"Crisp was no one's fault, and everyone's fault."

"Ivan's fault," Taj said.

"We should have swept wide," Kodiak said, biting out the words. "We didn't need bait."

Now Taj raised his voice. "There's no control sweeping wide! If we charged the hill, we might have cleared it, or we might have been caught between them. Maybe we'd all be alive now. Maybe we'd all be dead."

The Outlander stood straight as a rod now. His head didn't turn; he only listened. Kodiak's nostrils flared with deep breaths, but he did not speak. He did not move to strike Taj.

"Abel is right," Taj pressed. "Who are you going to blame? Me? Yourself?"

Who to blame?

My thoughts returned to Ivan. He'd been the brick that fell, pulling the whole wall apart. But I had found the Bugwall. I'd known the malice in Ivan's thoughts. I had warned no one. Crisp was dead.

Who to blame?

"It's done," Abel said, raising his voice as well. "It's past. Right now our problem is Ivan."

I felt Stump relax beside me. Kodiak's eyes widened, as if only now remembering Ivan.

"Yes," said Stump. "He'll be looting our backpacks."

"He'll be lost," Taj replied.

"Well, we've got to get the packs," Stump said. "We've got nothing to lose by hurrying."

"He won't find them," Taj said. "If we want Ivan, we'll have to track him."

"Perhaps we should allow for a contingency?" Kodiak said. Taj's eyes lit with fire.

"I'll take Pope and Happy, and this one, up on the ridge," Abel said. "Can you all handle the gear?"

"I am going to collect Ivan," Taj said. He raised his chin, looking Abel in the eye.

Abel paused, measuring Taj.

"I can handle the gear," Kodiak said.

"Fine," Abel conceded. "You three, grab the gear. Taj – bring Ivan back."

"He may…resist."

"Bring him back."

Taj gave Abel a long look, then turned to the ravine and began walking.

"Do you need the Ears?" I called after.

"I have ears, little man," Taj called back, and disappeared.

"What's eating him?" I asked Stump.

"Oh, you know Taj," Stump replied.

"No, I really don't."

Stump shrugged.

*

Kodiak, Stump, and I trekked back the way we'd come. The sun was past noon. "We fought all morning?" I asked.

"Wasn't much fighting past the first ten minutes," Stump said. "But we've been busy all morning, yes. Ugly business."

I nodded, still seeing the bodies where we'd sent the Eyes up. Some of them mine. It was an ugly business.

I'd be one of those bodies if not for Kodiak. I watched him as he watched the space between the trees. I should have been grateful. I should have said it out loud. I couldn't.

Kodiak, with all his questions, with his *what's it for* and on and on, had had his violence justified by the universe once again. I couldn't be part of that, I couldn't say it.

I could only keep waiting for life to slap him in the face and confront him with what, and who, he really was.

"What will we do with that Outlander, then?" I asked instead.

Kodiak grunted, displeased as well.

"Maybe we're just stuck with him," Stump said. "Or maybe we'll leave him behind and let fate do its work. Maybe we can communicate and find out something about numbers or directions. Maybe there's 500 Outlanders he doesn't like somewhere, and he'll be our guide."

"There's that," I said. "But did you see him? How do you make someone like that talk? Did you see his skin?"

"I saw his skin," Stump said.

Both were only half listening, heads swiveling and eyes scanning the trees. I didn't bother them any further and walked quietly in their wake.

We found the packs as we had left them, unmolested apart from ants scurrying over the muddied canvas. Nine bags. Kodiak took three, Stump and I took two. We left Ivan's and Duck's bags for a second trip. If they found them now, they could have them.

*

We rejoined the other three, and the Outlander, without incident. The top of the ridge was a sunlit spread of grass, sparsely planted with few trees and no bushes, trampled flat from the milling Outlander camp. The sun shone brightly, still close to its zenith.

There was no sign of Taj or the two renegades. There had been no gunshots either. Taj had a comm; I had to assume he'd let us know if their trail doubled back and there was the risk of attack.

Ivan could be so foolish.

Kodiak headed off alone to retrieve the final packs, unconcerned with the danger. Abel had the Outlander lying on his stomach, and as I watched, he twisted the man's arm around, inspecting the fingertips. Happy looked on from a short distance, though it was far enough he couldn't see anything without his glasses. Pope lay on the ground, shading his face, watching the clouds.

"It doesn't look like an interrogation," I said, drawing near to

Stump. "What is he doing?"

Stump slowly shook his head, his brow drawn down. He didn't take his eyes off the unfolding scene.

"Someone should ask him," I said.

Stump only watched in silence. He scratched his cheek and the growing grey stubble against the grip of his rifle barrel. It looked like a long-practiced habit. An unsettled habit.

"I never know what's going on. Why start now?" I said, and left him there. Things were as they were.

We'd have to re-sort the gear again, now for the fourth time. It was something to do.

I rooted through the packs until I found Crisp's. As I was piling his belongings, three figures stumbled into the clearing. Ivan, pushed from behind, regained his balance a few steps in. His cheek was swollen and bleeding. His hands were empty. Duck stood behind Taj's shoulder, silent and small. Taj glared at Abel, face stony. One of the three rifles he now carried pointed unwavering at the back of Ivan's head.

Abel rose, a boot planted between the Outlander's shoulders.

Ivan still stood, frozen, with one foot in front of the other, in mid-step. We looked at each other across the open ground.

"Where's Crisp?" Ivan finally asked, rising.

"Dead," Abel said.

Ivan digested this, eyes following Taj, who had begun to walk in a slow circle to stand with the rest of us.

There was now nothing between Ivan and the tree line. "What if he runs?" I asked.

"What if he runs," Taj echoed softly. Ivan heard, and quieted his nervous feet, eyes never leaving the tip of Taj's rifle.

"Kodiak?" he asked.

"He's fine," Abel said.

"We were going to come back," Ivan said.

"Why?" Abel asked.

"I…" Ivan said and faltered.

"What did you expect to find?" Abel pressed.

"I expected to find all of you," Ivan said, finding his story. "With your weapons, I never expected you to have any trouble. We were only making a point. An important point."

"We had some trouble," Abel said. "What was your point?"

I could almost hear the lies running through Ivan's head one by one as he discarded them. Whatever he had hoped to accomplish this morning, he'd lost his last hold over his Unforgiven. Crow dead, Crisp dead, Taj angry, Pope annoyed. He'd played a dangerous game poorly.

"If you'd just listened, we wouldn't have resorted to these measures!"

"Listened when?" Taj interrupted. "When you told us to run aimlessly through the jungle? When you told us to go live like rustics? When you told us to turn on each other and make you king? When you told us to vote and you lost?"

"King?" Ivan cried. "Who said king? How could I compete with King Taj and King Abel? State forbid I tread upon your mighty train!"

"Stop!" Abel barked. "Come. Sit. We will deal with this. It

would have gone better with you if you'd kept running."

Ivan remained where he was, eyes rapidly flicking from man to man. Calculating, planning. Abel walked to where Pope still lay, rifle in hand. Stump moved to our Outlander, but the beast made no move to get up. He only lay with head twisted, staring at Ivan, then Abel, then back again, measuring the two.

Ivan still did not move, watching us and counting, recounting. But there were six of us and one of him. Duck, as always, managed to make himself not count. Finally, Ivan hung his head and began walking, muttering under his breath, "The State, then the Hall, then this lot, an unbroken chain of tyrants."

There was a crash in the bushes behind us. Rifles came up. I spun, then looked down, finding the safety on my rifle, afraid the second it took might be the second I needed.

Kodiak burst into the clearing, face twisted in rage and eyes fixed on Ivan. Those who didn't get out of his way quickly enough were shoved aside as he passed. Ivan was putting his hands up to ward off the attack when Kodiak reached him. His hand rose and fell like a sledgehammer, driving clean through the space where Ivan's head had been. The little man crumpled to the ground.

And then Kodiak was on him, arm rising and falling, again and again. Some instinct of humanity gripped me, and I leapt at the big man. I don't know why I would move to save Ivan, but I wasn't alone. We dove in and each, in turn, were tossed aside, our cries swallowed in Kodiak's grim silence, our small hands met and cast off by his giant ones. Again and again Kodiak's arm rose and fell until I was sure nothing could be left of Ivan.

Then Abel lunged in. He did not try to grab or tackle Kodiak as we had. He took a long stride, planted his foot and, with the other swung full back, drove a boot square in Kodiak's ribs. Kodiak barely lurched at the impact but did grunt loudly. And he stopped.

His wild eyes fixed on Abel. There was no question, only a flat stare.

"Not like this, Kody."

The flatness dissolved. He released Ivan and grabbed Abel, standing and lifting him in the air with a growl. "This is what it's for!"

Abel cried out as his feet left the ground. "Not like this, Kodiak! Not like this!" Kodiak's growl grew, and he surged forward, driving Abel into a tree.

"He betrayed us! He lied to us!" Kodiak yelled, driving Abel into the trunk again and again to punctuate each sentence.

"Stop!" Abel protested. Kodiak did not.

"People are dead! This is exactly what it's for! He deserves it! He deserves everything!"

I cringed at the sight. All of us together weren't enough to stop Kodiak. Unless we used knives or guns.

"It's over, Kody," Abel managed to gasp out. "It's already done." He was fighting to keep his head from bouncing off the tree with each impact, but he could only do so much, and the blows were taking their toll.

"He's dead! You can't save Crisp like this!" His voice broke on the words. I lifted my rifle.

But Kodiak stopped. He looked at Abel, considering. Then he

turned and looked at us, his eyes finding Ivan lying motionless on the ground. He studied the scene for a long moment, and then he bowed his head, blowing out an enormous breath. Abel was still suspended against the tree.

Finally, he said, "I'm so angry."

"I am too." Abel spoke gently, looking down at the top of the big man's head.

"What am I supposed to do?" Kodiak asked, still looking down.

"Rest. You saved who you could."

"And just ignore it?" Kodiak's eyes flashed, looking back at Abel on the tree. "He deserves to die! There are consequences, Abel! He deserves to die!"

"So do you," Abel said.

Kodiak worked his jaw silently. "I'm changing. He won't."

"Maybe so," Abel responded. "Put me down, Kodiak."

Kodiak looked surprised, only then realizing he still held Abel up in the air. He stepped back, sliding Abel to the ground and letting him go. He took a long look at Ivan, who was feebly moving and coughing on the ground, while Happy looked on dispassionately.

"I don't understand yet. I'm sorry. Justice and anger, and selfishness, and fighting, and talking, and power, and everything you say. I'm sorry." He spoke to the rest of us without looking up. "I'm sorry."

He grabbed two rifles and disappeared behind bouncing branches without a further word, leaving as abruptly as he had appeared.

– TWENTY THREE –

Men lay scattered as if a tornado had passed through, the debris of Kodiak's passion. Abel sank to the ground and held his head. Happy hurried to him, but Abel sent him to Ivan with a wordless gesture. The last branches were still bouncing where Kodiak had left.

At a fundamental level, I agreed with Kodiak. Ivan wasn't worth this. There was no reason to stop Taj, or Kodiak, or anyone from killing him. One more body for the jungle, and we could move on.

Yet I also felt grim satisfaction seeing Kodiak chastised and broken. Maybe today was the day he'd see himself. There was no insight that could pull his murder and his futile violence into focus.

There was no answer. Only regret unto death.

But something else niggled at me, something real and immediate. Taj, Ivan, and Duck should not have surprised us. I wrested my thoughts back to the clearing.

We'd meant to check the Ears every few minutes, making sure no one entered our corner of the jungle unannounced. Either we'd failed in our vigilance, or we had a larger problem.

I suspected the larger problem. We should have at least heard the blips of Kodiak fetching the packs. I hadn't noticed the silence, and it was unforgivable.

The check didn't take long. Stump approached, catching the mood of my furtive work. I could tell by his face that he'd put it together, too. "What's the prognosis?" he asked.

"We're going deaf."

"Cute," Stump said. I hoped it would make it easier to hear. It wasn't.

"Source?" Stump asked.

"Source," I confirmed. "They told us we had ten days. How many has it been?"

"Eight or so?" Stump guessed.

I did a mental count. "Seven," I said. "Those rustic cranking spraggers."

"Is it dead?"

"Not quite. Range is way down." Liars or incompetent. Or maybe we'd used the screen too much. Memories of night sentinels outlined in the glow of the Ears flashed in my mind; they should have been listening, not watching.

Maybe they hadn't recharged it after the training with Meeks.

"But if you power it down and wait a little bit, it'll give you a burst of activity."

"Ivan again?" Stump asked. We both studied him, sitting against a tree now, alone, coughing weakly. I was surprised to see that there was still a man beneath the blood and bruises.

"I don't think so," I said. "This thing isn't a Bugwall."

Stump hemmed, doing his own mental tally of the fighting and recon we'd needed since arriving, pushing the range out.

"What now?"

"Save it for emergencies," I said. "If we can figure out in advance when it's an emergency. Thatch it, what are we supposed to do?"

"Well, first, we tell everyone we're deaf," said Stump.

I looked at the Ears, hoping for inspiration. It offered none. I looked at Stump, but he nodded back at me. I was the tinker.

Taj had reached Abel ahead of me. He was squatting and speaking softly.

"You listen to me now."

Abel grunted.

"You know Kodiak's right."

"I do," Abel said, still rubbing the back of his head.

"They are different. Kodiak has hot blood. Ivan betrayed us in cold blood, and he'll do it again."

"I know," Abel said, rubbing his head more vigorously.

"So Ivan needs to die."

Abel did not immediately reply. "Patience."

"We have enough problems, Abel, that you don't make another. The solution is simple. Why protect Ivan?"

Abel's face hardened. "I'm protecting all of us. Everyone, Taj, not Ivan."

"Protecting." Taj forced a laugh. "Ivan is the one who will stick a knife in your back."

"I won't let Kodiak execute him. And not you. Not now."

"I'll take care of it."

"Patience."

"Patience can be lethal in the wilderness." Taj flicked his fingers out, as if to wash his hands of it and cast it on Abel. "I'll give you until sundown."

Taj rose and left, sparing a glare for me as he passed. He stopped by the Outlander and began to sharpen a stick with his large knife, while both I and the Outlander watched in fascination.

"Thirteen. Bad news?" Abel asked. His head rested against the tree now, looking at me.

"Yeah," I said, leaving the Outlander to Taj. "How did you know?"

"Outlands," Abel said.

My huffed laugh was hollow. "The Ears are nearly out of power," I said. Others heard.

Ivan bowed his head at the edge of the clearing. Happy put his face in his hands. The rest doggedly looked on.

"What is 'nearly'?" Abel asked.

"We probably have five minutes out of every hour. Sources can be odd like that. That will last us another day or two. Or three. I can't say."

Abel nodded. "Very well."

"Very well?" Happy cried out. "What do you mean very well? How is this very well?"

"We've faced the Outlanders twice, once at night. They'll be more cautious now," Abel said, with patient logic. "They aren't likely to descend on us when we're moving. Even if we check once an hour, they won't hit us without warning. Even today we didn't need Ears to see them coming."

Happy could not see the worry on Abel's face, but I could.

"Nights, though. Can we do one minute every fifteen at night?" Abel asked me, quietly.

I shrugged. "Do what we have to and see where it gets us."

"Better," Abel said.

Taj had remained quiet during the exchange. Now there was a dull thud as he struck the Outlander across the face with the back of his hand.

A few stood, but no one moved to intervene.

Without a word Taj struck the man across the face again in grim silence. Then Taj stepped on his chest, pushing him to the ground, and leaned close. "Why don't you all die?" he yelled.

The man barely reacted. When Taj removed his foot, he pulled himself straight, hands still bound at his back. Then he watched Taj with stoic curiosity, flat eyes set in a scarred face, as if he were observing a scene that only vaguely interested him.

It wasn't human. My skin crawled, and I stared, spellbound, with a fascination that the Outlander was unable to muster for his own plight. Taj pulled his arm back again but paused in the face of the inhuman stare.

Then the man lifted his chin and said to Taj, "Come."

The vowel was wrong, the cadence off, but the word was clear.

Taj twisted in a sudden motion, grabbing the stick from the ground. He struck the Outlander with all his strength; once, twice, and a backswing, sending the man's head rocking.

The scarred man finally reacted. He closed his eyes and took a deep breath, slowly bringing his head back to level and arching his back. He was stretching. When he opened his eyes again, he looked directly at Taj. Only now he was interested, now he looked on Taj with a new intensity, one of anticipation.

Anticipating what? I hated to think. Taj himself was finally unnerved, the stick falling from his hand, so that Abel did not need to stop him. He just said quietly, "No more, Taj." And Taj nodded.

"They speak English," I whispered.

"They do," Abel said.

"Did you know this? Why aren't we talking to him?"

"They aren't interested in talking," Abel said. "You won't learn anything."

Stump began binding the man's eyes again, and Happy began rooting around in his pack, face buried deep.

I was still hearing that word, "come," when the Outlander whipped his head back into Stump, knocking him off his feet, and leapt at Taj. His eyes were again covered but his arms had somehow come free. He tackled Taj from behind, sending the two of them tumbling to the ground.

Taj spun around so quickly his shape blurred, rolling with the Outlander and regaining one of his feet. But the scarred man held him fast, clutching his ear and grabbing at his face, emitting a strained, inhuman whine. The Outlander surged forward, striking Taj's face with his own, wrapping his legs around Taj and dragging him to the ground again. The two rolled, rattled breath punctuated by grunts, as Taj tried to subdue his adversary. The Outlander scrabbled and clutched like an animal, clawing as if to pull Taj's skin from his body.

It was only the space of seconds before another figure flew in, diving on the two before rolling away. The Outlander faltered. He released Taj, to balance on his hands and knees. Then he quivered again and rolled onto his side in the grass.

Happy rose from the ground, standing where he had rolled clear. Walking to the Outlander, he nudged the figure with his foot and nodded to himself.

"Sedative," he announced. "About five doses. I can still tell Outlander from Unforgiven." He bent over and with a moment's groping, pulled a syringe free.

Taj also rose but he was looking at the doctor, not the figure on the ground. His face was inscrutable. "I will tell you if I need help," he bit out. Then he retreated to a corner of the camp, again making himself busy with whatever he could find in his pack.

"You're welcome," Happy said quietly.

The rest of us traded glances. We bound the Outlander, more carefully than before, and left him sleeping where he had fallen.

*

The passing rains fell on us as the hours of the afternoon crept by. The bound Outlander remained unconscious in our midst, slumped in his bonds.

The eight remaining kept to ourselves, pulling leaves off of branches, unpacking and repacking. Abel took each piece of his gear, disassembled it, polished it, and laid it out in neat rows.

Taj watched Abel as the shadows lengthened. It was not yet sundown.

Kodiak would return. There would come another argument. Perhaps another death. Taj would serve the practical, the expedient. Stump, the necessary.

Abel was a mystery, his actions unpredictable. He was forcing a status quo fewer and fewer of the Unforgiven could stomach.

Ivan fit into none of it.

The system eluded me; order eluded me. I returned to the fixed points. *We do what they want; they do what we want.*

And the unwelcome whisper beneath that thought: *We are dying, and they have no cause to bring us back.*

The doors before me were closed, silent.

Happy sat by himself staring into the foliage at nothing, which was all he could see. When he spoke, his voice was broken. "Abel?" he asked. "They speak English. What is going on?"

Abel looked up at Happy, across the clearing, a pained look in his eyes. Happy still stared to the trees.

"You said they needed killing, Abel. Why?" His voice neared a whisper. "I don't understand."

"I don't understand," he repeated. The words pained him.

Abel rose and walked to him. Happy tilted his head, listening to the approach. Pope turned to watch, and I wandered close with Stump. Taj continued stripping branches with his knife, alone and ignoring us. Duck watched from a distance, and Ivan stared only at the ground.

Abel sat heavily beside the doctor and stared into the distance with him.

"They're cracked," he said. Stump nodded, but the rest of us looked on, expecting more.

"I don't understand."

"Their hearts are cracked."

"We're broken. We're broken, too," Happy said.

Abel smiled, looking down at the earth between his feet, reaching down a hand to run a finger through the dust and leaves as he nodded.

"We killed today. You fought because you had to. Because you have been condemned and ordered to this. Because you are trapped. When the fighting was done, you stopped."

I looked to Ivan, wincing as he shifted his weight. I looked to Taj, running his knife along wood and stone. It was true, and it wasn't.

"They cannot stomach peace," Abel continued. "They choose suffering when there is no need to kill. It needs to come to an end. For their sake as much as anything else. For the sake of those who will be born to them, and those not yet taken."

I was not comfortable with this. No one spoke.

"What happens out here cannot happen," Abel said. Firm. And sad.

"Are they men, then, or monsters?" I asked from behind the two of them.

"And what are we?" Stump muttered under his breath.

Abel looked up at us steadily before answering. "Somewhere between the two. We're all somewhere between."

"I can't do this anymore," Happy said. "You say this, you say all this. How do you know? Why does he speak English? What is happening out here?"

Abel drew on the ground again while Happy caught his breath. "You know the State wants to be here, in the jungle. Resources and all that. Not a popular topic since the Cataclysm, but the world doesn't change as much as people want."

Again, no one spoke.

"The Outlands are not a hospitable place," he began again. "The State engineered people to survive here. Gave them resilience against the poisons, diseases, and weather. Thick skin, thin blood, that sort of thing."

I looked at the Outlander in our midst, and his lace of scars. They were not accidents of the jungle, they were deliberately placed.

"The bodies, at least, performed as planned."

Still, no one spoke.

"Maybe it was the treatment, side-effects, unintended consequences, all that. I never thought so. I think they strengthened the body but neglected the mind, and it was too much. The Outlands are a brutal place. Full of death. When the weather tipped and the Cataclysm rolled around the world, there was so much death. It was natural selection on a brutal scale. Only the meanest survived and got meaner. Living out here, away from the technocracies…I think death became a way of life, and they… they just broke."

I stared at our prisoner. What terrors lived inside his head?

"How do you know all this?" Pope asked.

"My Grandfather. He made them."

– TWENTY FOUR –

"Who are you?" Taj spoke softly, approaching across the clearing.

"I am the forgotten man. I am the Unforgiven."

"We're all Unforgiven," he said.

"If we get back," Abel said, tiredness stretching his words, "you will go home. I will not. They will send me here again and again. Until I die."

"Explain," Taj said. He held a knife and a carefully sharpened stick. His hands were restless.

Abel measured him from where he sat on the ground. This was where he usually fell silent. He looked at the bound Outlander, gazing for a long time. And he spoke.

"You are criminals. Murderers, assassins, rapists, thieves…" I couldn't tell if he was listing us in order or simply listing crimes. I fought an instinct to look at my feet.

"I am something else," he said. "I am of the State. I was trained by my father to fix this."

"Fix what?" Taj asked.

"The Outlanders. It was my life to find a remedy. But it's been decades. Memory and patience grew short. Then came pressure for a new experiment.

"Hints became requests became demands, and then threats. But I knew better than anyone what had gone wrong. There is no better way. Once was enough. I wouldn't give them what they wanted."

Abel was looking at the Outlander, not at us.

"They crafted a narrative again, the same narrative, that we had the technology to create a race of super-humans that would thrive in the Outlands, that we could settle them and claim them for the State. Like none of it had ever happened. The Elite were listening. Wheels began to move.

"I prepared a narrative of my own, the forgotten truth. What the past generations had done, with all the questions that still had no answer after 63 years. I tried to contact the Hall of Speakers, so the story would be recorded, and known by all. The State had surrounded me. Instead of the Speakers, I handed it straight to them. My paper disappeared. And I disappeared."

The tip of Taj's stick moved in slow circles, pointed toward the ground.

"And now I am here to resolve their problem any way I like: destroy the Outlanders or die."

"You are State?" Pope asked. Abel nodded.

"Then what are you doing out here?"

Abel shook his head and looked down. The question was answered, it was just hard to believe.

"How many times have you been here?" Happy asked.

"Nine," Abel said. "Maybe ten. I forget sometimes."

"Nine times," Happy said to himself. "And you're some kind

of geneticist?"

Taj burst forward suddenly and stood directly over Abel. "So it's you!" he shouted. "You are the reason we are out here. You spragging son of a rutting rustic! You are the reason I am out here!"

Abel leapt to his feet, his face centimeters from Taj's flushed visage, but spoke softly. "You murder people for money, Taj. You are the reason you are out here." The words, quiet, were inexorable.

Taj's chest heaved. His arms were tense, ready to move. Ready for something. He was always ready. He did not back away.

"I will go home, Abel, I will not die because of you, nor any worthless Unforgiven here."

Taj turned to leave, but Abel said "You are responsible, Taj. You know that, don't you?"

Taj turned back and spat on Abel's foot. "I'm not one of your Outlanders, State-man. Stop trying to fix me."

He stalked away, making himself busy on the other end of camp. Abel watched him, the rest of us forgotten, until Stump drew him back. "What's happened to the program now?"

Taj cleaned his knife and set to cutting branches again, overexaggerating a turn to put his back to us. Finally, Abel turned away, and he sat with us again. "I don't know if they're moving forward or not. I do know now, there is no cure for what the Outlanders have become."

"You mean you didn't find it," Happy said.

Abel looked at a spot on the ground near Happy, his face unreadable. "What the Outlanders have become cannot be undone. All we can do is end it."

He drew on the ground again. "State's heart wasn't in it anyway. Finding a solution, administering it, on and on… expensive, dangerous, difficult. Why go through all that for ten thousand cracked Outlanders?"

"Ten thousand," Happy whispered.

"If they didn't want the Outlands for themselves, they'd probably just leave it and pretend it never happened. As it is, they just want them dead."

"So why don't they do the destroying?" Pope asked. "What are we doing here? Do they hate you that badly?"

"Doesn't matter," Stump said. "We're here."

"It matters to me," Pope said. We looked at Abel again, as his shoulders gently rose, gently fell. With an open hand he rubbed out the lines he had made in the dirt, a shapeless thing.

"Do you know?" Happy asked.

"Do you want to know the politics of the State? Or do you want to know what your life is worth to them?"

"I know what my life is worth. Why are we here?"

"Treaties. Closed door agreements. New Silica, The Amazon, all the proximate Technocracies are watching. You know the doctrine since the Cataclysm – *what you have is enough*. Though I think motives are more likely 'don't take what we may want.' Anyway, no land grabs, no State business, no official insertions. Inserting the Outlanders. Inserting the Unforgiven… these things are small. Unnoticeable. Easy to lie away or disavow."

"But they could send soldiers to do this," Pope complained.

"They would have to tell the soldiers what they were doing.

And they would have to tell the soldiers' families why they died. Us, though…"

I unzipped my pocket and pulled out the stick with the blue button. The sunlight shown through the button, turning it translucent.

"And if the Amazon caught them, it'd be harder to explain what trained soldiers were doing in the wilderness."

"The satellite will not be small or unnoticeable," Happy said.

"For whatever reason, it's a risk they are willing to take."

"Do they come for us, then?" I asked. "Does anyone go home?"

"They come," Abel said. He didn't meet my eye, though.

We sat in silence for a time. It was as if a curtain had been pulled back, I was looking through the same window but the lines were clearer, and everything looked different.

"Sometimes I wish," Abel said, "I could have done something bigger with my life. Solve it. I wanted to rebuild it. But maybe this is it; end this before new generations are born into it. End with as much compassion as I can what would otherwise end in torment and anguish. Maybe this is it."

"What happened to the other teams?" I asked.

"The first trip's quota was fifty. Then eighty, a hundred. We'd be home already if you'd come on one of those trips. As I said, though, as much as they want the Outlanders cleared out, they grow tired of me coming back. It's harder each time."

"Is the beacon real?" I asked, thinking of the local detonator and Meeks's coyness in the hall.

"They started the beacons two trips ago. This is the third beacon."

So it worked. Probably. Except for the variable about them wanting Abel dead. This still might be the trip they sent him out with a toaster instead of a bomb to be sure they were rid of him. Of all of us.

"Why didn't you tell us this?" Happy asked. "You let us parade around, you let us vote on Ivan, and all the while you knew everything? Why did you do this?"

Abel dug his fingertips into the soil, eyes focused far beyond. He did not speak for some time. We waited.

"The first time, I told them, as soon as we were briefed. They took the other Unforgiven into the courtyard and made me watch as they shot them.

"So I waited. The second time I waited until we landed. I tried to tell them. They blamed me. We fought. One third of the team was dead before sundown." He cast a dead leaf away from him. The air quickly smothered its flight and pulled it to earth.

"Smoking thatch," Pope mumbled.

"I've been…cautious…since then."

"There's always a Taj," Stump said.

"There's always a Taj," Abel echoed. "But our Taj is more practical than some."

No one spoke, each pondering, digesting. Asking if this changed anything. As much as I craved these answers, the why behind each what, it meant nothing. Things remained what they were.

"Did you have family?" Stump asked quietly.

Abel ran his thumb against his finger in a slow movement, almost a caress. He did not look up or speak.

"Where did you learn to fight?" Stump asked, replacing the question.

"I told you, I've been here before. You learn or you don't go home."

"So why aren't you cracked yet?" Pope asked.

"This place is getting into my bones. I'm breaking every day..." The leaves shook in the wind, reflecting the sunlight back to us in sparkles. Abel did not continue his thought.

"What about you?" he asked, abruptly present again. "Where did you learn to fight? You said you grew up Outside?"

"Me?" Stump asked. "Almost Outside, but not quite. Out past the Communes, in the outskirts. Far enough to be outside the reach of notice or law."

"What was it like?"

"The Families look out for themselves out there. Nothing matters but Family, blood or adopted, it's all the same. You're in the Family or you aren't. Best friends and worst enemies of my life. And every few years another war."

"And then what? What brought you out here?" Abel prompted.

Stump frowned, choosing his word. "I'm a thief."

"Thief?" I asked. "I can't see it." I couldn't see him as anything – not a thief, not a child warrior in a Family militia. I could only see him planting his feet and letting the world wash over him. Stump knew his way around, but he didn't belong out here, not the way

Taj and Ivan and Kodiak did.

"It's complicated," Stump replied.

"We've got time," Pope said.

Stump puffed his cheeks, then removed and polished his glasses. "Well, I worked the trainyard. I'm not State, not like you Abel, but I still worked for them. I was out there for years, decades really. Every day, all I could think about was how little my people had, everything they ever needed and couldn't get. Everyone who was killed in the Outskirts fighting over food and land and pride. And every day I saw all the… the stuff. Flowing in day after day. I made sure some of it got lost."

"A noble vigilante!" Pope exclaimed, his face breaking into a wide smile. He had been somber, subdued since the second injury. Some mix of pain and worry clouding over his usual mischief. His outburst was refreshing. "Steal from the rich!"

Stump looked down, hiding a small smile. It was gone when he looked up. "Don't paint me noble. I made money on the side. Still, in the balance of help or hurt, I think I was on the right side. But I did wrong; I knew this might happen, and here I am. Just got to get it over with."

"And you, family?" Abel asked.

"Years ago."

"What happened?"

"Life," Stump said. His face went cold. No one pressed.

"Well, what about you, Pope?" Happy asked.

"You first," he said.

His voice was playful, even with a laugh. But something hidden in the words caught me. A tension. I'd never heard Pope demur the floor before.

Happy shrugged. "I'm a doctor, you all know that."

"Yes, we know, but what'd you do?" Pope said. Still acting, still trying to keep Happy talking. The others focused on the doctor, unconcerned, but I saw Pope, truly Pope, for the first time. Behind the swagger and grace… A broken man hiding on a stage.

Happy reached up as if to clean his glasses, but there was nothing there. He wiped his hands on his shirt instead.

"Hideous experiments against humanity?" Stump suggested, waggling his fingers.

"Look," Happy began, flustered. "People look at doctors and sees a homogenous field. Intelligent. The same training, the same information and treatments. All rich. They hand out awards as if charisma were the only differentiator, because medicine is deterministic science.

"But it isn't. Those who have been truly sick know. There are skilled doctors and inept. Timid and courageous, those with instincts and… Well, there are doctors that can save you and doctors that will kill you."

"So what happened, Doc?" Stump prodded. His earlier teasing had mellowed to monotone. I, too, wondered if he'd hit too close to the mark.

Happy released an exasperated sigh. "Yes. I was tired of being surrounded by timid, ineffective doctors."

"So you killed them!" Pope interrupted. There was a tightness still around his eyes.

"Hush," Stump said, laying a hand on Pope's shoulder.

Happy looked at him, irritated. "I am a doctor. I did nothing of the sort."

"What went wrong?" Abel asked, more gently.

"I had a colleague, Doctor Munrow. An unintelligent, cowardly man who stumbled on a treatment for *ossicardia*, or what you call Stoning. I had been studying it as well, but Munrow stumbled on the right question at the right time. He was too stupid, or too timid, to see it. I told him to press forward but he wanted to wait, to research, to test, on and on and on with no end."

Happy was knocking the knuckles of his right hand on the ground. It was the closest I'd ever seen him to a fidget. This time no one prompted him.

"So I stole his research and began administering treatment to patients," he concluded.

"That sounds... hasty," Stump said. "Did it work?"

"Yes, it worked," Happy snapped. "52.9% of them improved."

"52.9%" Stump repeated.

"The others were too sick," Happy replied opaquely.

None of us responded.

"Yes. The problem is, *ossicardia* has a 54% survival rate. I'm so tired of explaining this." His voice began to rise. "Never mind that just one more survivor would have made 58.8! Never mind that my sample were hideously sick, with a baseline near zero, not 54%! I treated those well beyond the help of cowards like Dr. Munrow!"

He quieted. Abel studied the fingertips of his open hands, heavy with thought but silent.

"Zero. Fifty-two point nine. Fifty-four. One life. Fifty-eight point eight. Do not try to explain mathematics to the Arbiters," Happy concluded.

Abel huffed, an echo of his own shadows slipping into the daylight.

"You think you saved those patients?" Stump asked. There was no judgment in his voice.

Happy rubbed his face, looking into the distance again. "I think they were going to die anyway. They just died faster. I'm tired of explaining this. I'm so tired. The treatment can work. If you understand the disease and understand the treatment, it's so obvious."

"But did they know you were experimenting on them? The patients?" Abel asked.

Happy deflated. "The first ones, but when it started working, I just administered treatment. Too many people I might have saved were saying no. Timid. And they died anyway. Sooner or later, what difference was it? The only difference is life."

"The families didn't know? That's not...not right." I said.

Happy looked in my direction. "That's what they said at the Hall of Judgment. And the families, they said that I killed their loved ones. I, not Stoning."

"And what do you think?" Abel asked.

"I was so certain," he said, the last of his bluster gone. "52.9%. What could I have missed?" He was no longer looking at us; he wasn't even talking to us anymore.

"I... I don't know."

He sat there, hollow. I understood. Inside, the tower of his life was coming down, stone by stone. It had been falling from the moment he'd stopping binding it together by stubborn will.

But we were men. We sat quietly and watched it happen, each alone.

Stump turned to Pope. "He went. Now it's you. What's your story, Pope?"

Pope glared back at Stump. His face grew cold. I could not see the shame anymore.

Stump waited.

"I was an artist. And then I did something I regret."

It was the shortest explanation of Pope's life.

"The end."

Stump shrugged, "It's alright."

So the doctor, the artist, and the scientist turned to me, the janitor. The stories were so similar, tangled and woven together.

I did something I regret.

I'm so tired of explaining this.

I knew this might happen.

Here I am.

Words, my own familiar phrases, took shape in my head. What stories I had told.

What stories had I told myself?

For the first time, I felt suspicion about what those words might be: truth, curated to deceive.

The Unforgiven looked to the Unforgiven. To listen, to judge. What if they were wrong?

What if they were right?

My heart began to hammer. I opened my mouth, unsure what to say, where to begin.

"I just want to go home."

Silence descended on all of us. It was heavy, and it fit like a shroud.

– TWENTY FIVE –

Taj, unconcerned with the words passing between us, raised his voice across the clearing. "The sun is setting, Abel."

We stirred.

Ivan rose on unsteady feet before anyone could answer. He cleared his throat. "No. Don't speak, Abel. I'm going to leave. I'd like food and weapons."

His voice faltered.

Abel rose. He approached Ivan, leaving us behind. "Why did you come back?" he asked, as he had before.

"It doesn't matter. It was a mistake."

"Why didn't you ask before?" Abel asked.

"I did!" Ivan spat. "And you killed Crow. What was I supposed to do next? I'm asking again, I'd like food and weapons."

"You demanded and threatened. Then you betrayed us, and Crisp got killed."

Ivan stared with hatred, but he made no response. He was a supplicant. It burned him to his very heart.

"There is nothing out there," Abel said.

"What's here? You? Taj? Just let me go. I know you want it. I know you want me dead. Let me go."

"I want you to stay."

Ivan shook his head, disgusted.

"You'll die out there."

"So let me die! Let me go and die! We're all dead anyway. You know it, and I know it. Let me go and be done with it."

A shadow of uncertainty crossed Abel's brow. "I've been through the Outlands before, Ivan."

Ivan only glared.

"Is there no hope for you?"

"You've won," Ivan hissed. "Give me what I ask and let me go."

Abel's gaze passed over Taj and then lingered on me. His head shook, and he released a deep breath.

"You can take food. We are low on ammunition. Taj, what can we spare?"

Taj mulled, weighing the truth against his contempt. "Two magazines."

"I suppose you'll hold onto the Eyes? The Ears? The Bugwall? Will you give me anything else?"

"If you want the rest, stay."

Ivan's stare leveled out, his small victory straightening his back. He studied Taj. "No. No, I don't think I will."

Imperious eyes shone from swollen cheeks. The poor man could barely stand, yet he mustered all his strength and presence.

"Give me my gun and two clips."

"Magazines," Taj said, quietly.

"We'll be heading in this direction," Abel said, gesturing, "if you change your mind."

Ivan smirked. "And we'll be heading this direction. Come, Duck."

Duck startled and looked up.

There was an outcry. I leapt to my feet, and Stump beside me. Stump hurried over to their little group, muttering, until Abel stopped him with a hand.

"You don't have to go with him, Duck," Abel said.

"Duck!" Ivan barked louder, the twinkle of the old tsar now shining. "Come!"

The boy sat where he was, shoulders hunched, eyes on his master. Fingers plucked at his bootlace.

I approached, more slowly than Stump, and squatted by the boy. I'd only spent a few minutes with him. Not enough for him to listen. "Duck," I said.

I had to try.

I should have started earlier.

There was a loud thump as Taj dumped a pile of rations at Ivan's feet, then kicked me aside and dropped a second at Duck's. With a jerk of his head, he shooed the boy to the jungle. Stump grabbed Taj's shoulder, trying to spin him around. Taj merely bared his teeth, then returned to his gear.

"He can't protect you, Duck," Abel said, squatting down in my place.

Duck looked at his allotment of food. He looked at Ivan, above him, then at Abel. His fingers balled into a fist. He did not move. He did not speak.

"I don't know what he's promised you," Abel said. "He can't give it to you."

"They are liars, Duck," Ivan crooned. "They will get themselves home over your broken body. They don't care for you."

The boy's brows knit.

"Come." Ivan shoved him with a foot, spilling him toward the supplies. Duck rolled to his knees and began filling his and Ivan's packs with the meager bounty.

Abel locked eyes with Ivan, and Ivan smiled.

Afternoons flashed before my own eyes, each hour I'd spent campaigning my allies or lamenting my lot, while the boy walked alone. Too little, too late.

Duck shouldered his pack and took a few steps into the jungle.

"You'll die out there!" I shouted.

He stopped and gave a last look from the shadows but he did not come back.

"Look at all of you," Ivan said, stepping between us and Duck. "When I see you in hell, I'll tell you how I died in my sleep, many years and many kilometers from here. You can tell me how your little crusade worked out. You! You can't see it, can you?

"Abel, with your self-righteous 'I'm going to help everyone and furrow my eyebrows and speak in a firm voice' act. Help us. Save us. How is that working out? How about Crow? And Crisp? And Oyster and Patches? How is that working out? 'Ivan, I want you to stay.' Well I've got places to be, Abel, and it isn't following your butthole into your grave.

"And the rest of you! You aren't better than me. I don't know how you made it this far. I'm not talking about this jungle. I'm talking about whatever you called a life for all your sorry years. You aren't better than me. If you have to die to learn that, so be it.

"Pope?" Ivan spit on the ground. Then he turned, as gracefully as he could in his battered state and hobbled into the undergrowth past the smaller boy, again saying "Come, Duck."

*

There was an uneasy silence among those left behind. As the man and the boy disappeared, a voice spoke out of nowhere, "Want me to bring back the Duck?"

Kodiak emerged from the dusk. No longer the battering ram. He looked to Abel. Abel watched the bushes where the two figures had disappeared.

"Yes."

As Kodiak tried to pass, Abel gripped his jacket at the shoulder, knuckles white, holding him fast.

"What are you doing?" Kodiak asked.

"I don't know. I don't know, Kodiak."

Kodiak studied his jacket, balled up in Abel's fist. He did not try to break free.

"I don't know," Abel said again, his face pained. Abruptly, he released Kodiak, grabbed a rock, and hurled it into the trees.

"If he wanted to stay, he would have stayed," Taj said.

Abel growled out wordless anger.

"That isn't true," I said. "He's just a kid."

"So should I get the Duck?" Kodiak asked again.

I wanted to say yes. Kodiak could have him back in moments.

We looked at each other, leaderless.

"We stay here tonight," Abel said, stalking to his pack.

"You're just letting him go?" I demanded.

"We stay here tonight," Abel said again, harsher. "He'll have every chance to come back."

"That's all?" Kodiak asked.

"He can come back," Abel said more quietly. Telling himself there was hope.

"If you say so," Kodiak said, though he kept looking at the jungle.

Stump was still watching the trees where they had left.

"Go," I said.

Stump gave a small shake, echoing Abel in the end. "He chose."

Still, a force in my chest drew me toward the trees, but my feet did not follow. I was a janitor.

This was Kodiak's job. I waited for him to move.

Instead, Stump asked him, "Where have you been?"

Kodiak stirred and looked at the old man. "I've been thinking."

"About killing Ivan?" Pope asked.

"About not killing Ivan."

"Meaning?" Pope pressed.

"Making sense of it."

"There is no sense to be made of it," Taj said, glaring at Abel through a drawn brow.

"No. I think I understand now." At this point, he pulled himself up straight, as if delivering a presentation before a classroom. "I pledge," he said, "to use my strength, and my size, only when someone without my strength needs my help. Or my size," he added as an afterthought.

He looked so serious that I tried not to splutter, but I failed. A staccato of laughter spread through the group.

"You pledge?" I asked. This was not the broken man, the red-rimmed eyes I'd expected. Only a bear parading flimsier and flimsier delusions. "You can't be serious."

"I am serious," Kodiak said, dropping the pledgers act. "You were right, it *is* a gift. But it's not for me. Do you understand?"

"No!" I shouted.

"Peace, Thirteen," Abel said.

Peace.

"*This is what it's for?* Go get Duck!" I shouted.

"Abel says…" Kodiak said, glancing at the man.

"Abel says! You pledge! What right do you have?" I shouted, walking up to him, standing in arms reach, as I had sworn I'd never do. "Don't you realize what you are?"

"Yes," Kodiak said, too simply. It enraged me.

"It means nothing!" I yelled. "Even if your pledge meant anything, even if you kept it, which you can't, it would still mean nothing! You can't come up on this hill talking like a seven-year-old and make everything normal!" I emphasized each word, "You – are – a – murderer!"

Kodiak hung his head, but the show of contrition fueled me. Sorry didn't fix anything.

"This is what you've been thinking about? You're an idiot!" I shouted, and I struck him as hard as I could across the face.

It hurt like thatch, but I was satisfied to see his head rock from the blow. When he turned back, his eyes met mine. They were not angry; they were pleading.

I looked back, angry, frustrated. As futile as Kodiak's gesture was, so was my outburst. I could not hurt him. I could not fix anything either. There, in each other's eyes, we both saw it.

"I'm sorry I killed Patches," Kodiak said. "I wish I could take it back. That and so much else."

I had to look away. "Is that supposed to fix all this?" I felt tears coming. Not for Patches. For what? I pushed them away.

"No," Kodiak said. Simple. Unadorned. "But it's all I have. We aren't meant to die Unforgiven."

My hand burned, my eyes burned. A deep hollow space opened inside me. "What choice do we have?"

– TWENTY SIX –

What choice do we have?

The question hung from the night as we quieted in the growing dark. What choice? How to die. Who to die with. The program could not give me back my life. It could not fix us or what lay behind us. It was a room of shadows and thorns, walls closed by twisted branches.

No, I had not given up the search. Yes, I would fight and fix and scream my defiance until the Outlands came for me, too. But it wasn't because I had a way out, I now understood. It was just my nature.

We aren't meant to die unforgiven.

I could not believe that the idiot Kodiak had an answer. Yet I had seen his eyes.

The campsite shrank in the dusk, the trees blocking the sunlight long before the sky stopped glowing. We were scattered, small mounds of men and backpacks like anthills around the clearing. We checked the Ears four times in an hour, the night standard. People talked. We all stayed clear of the Outlander, both concerned and relieved that he remained asleep where Happy had injected him. He was a problem that would keep for tomorrow. The perpetual cleaning and repacking filled the empty hours.

We were seven: Abel and Kodiak, Taj, Happy, Stump, Pope, and myself. The question still felt open, though, with an unconscious Outlander in our midst and, somewhere, Ivan and Duck wandering in the dark. Still, seven. I remained one of the living.

*

In the early hours after midnight I sat up with Abel. Watch had become a more serious affair, two men at all times. One minute of illumination, the Ears listening and piercing the dark, followed by fourteen minutes of moonlit blackness. The first few minutes were bearable; after that, imagination took hold.

"You alright?" Abel asked, after a cycle of the Ears.

I shook my head, though he couldn't see it.

"What have you been telling Kodiak?" I whispered.

"Telling Kodiak about what?"

"About all this, about what we're doing out here."

"You mean hunting Outlanders?" Abel asked, his voice clear in the cool air.

"No. I guess you don't think about it. You got under someone's collar, they sent you out here with the hope you'll die. And they've dangled the carrot in front of you that you just might solve the problem first, and your argument with them will disappear. Right? You know why you're here and what you need to do."

"Not much of a carrot," Abel said, "But generally true."

"What am I doing out here?"

"Paying your debt to society. That's what they say, right?"

"No," I said. The questions that had dogged me since the first day began coming out. "Listen. I'm out here because... never mind because. An accident, a tragic accident. But they decide it's my fault. They decide I'm Unforgiven. So far, so rational, right? Then they decide to fly me State knows how far to this jungle, I kill 500 cracked experiments, and they bring me home. At this point, the State says, 'Great, you aren't Unforgiven anymore. Everything is fine. You can go home.'"

Abel laughed in the dark.

"And then I go home. To where it all happened. And everyone says, 'Hello there. Looks like you're Forgiven now. Thanks for killing those Outlanders and nearly dying in the process. Everything is good now.'"

Abel chuckled quietly. "Or would they say, 'Is that supposed to fix all this?'"

My own words. I felt the blood rising in my neck, but it was fair.

"Ever heard of good, old-fashioned punishment?" Abel asked.

"It fixes nothing."

I looked up to where the moon should be, hidden behind tall branches. Its light reflected through the sky where the stars poked through.

"This is too convoluted, too contrived to be punishment, anyway. This is something else."

"What is it you want?" Abel asked.

He was ever patient. In the space that followed his question, I listened to the night, the rustles and chirps that had become so familiar. I felt the dirt under my heels and squeezed my fingertips in the damp soil. The words that came had eluded me until that moment.

"If one person, just one person would say, 'It wasn't your fault. You aren't a bad person.'"

Abel waited.

"And underneath that, it wouldn't matter so much if I could just fix it."

"Why not?"

"Because then I could say it to myself."

Abel chose his words before speaking. "What if it can't be fixed?"

"Everything can be fixed," I said. If it couldn't, what recourse would we ever have? What else held this fragile world together if we couldn't patch it up when it inevitably fell apart?

I just had to survive. Get home. Get to work.

"Tell me what happened," said Abel.

"I told you. I burned down my house. It was an accident."

The faint camp lights reflected off his eyes, and I said nothing more, hoarding my secrecy as if it could assure me safe passage.

But Abel waited. I had to speak and be judged again. Again and again, until it was fixed.

I sighed and began. I hated the way they looked at me when it was done.

"We were arguing."

"Who?"

"I was arguing. With my wife. We always argued. Well, we

hadn't always, but it started one day. And it got worse. Weeks, months, years, it just got worse. So that day could have been any day.

"We were in the kitchen. And she started to cry. I made her cry," I amended. Usually I started with the flames, abridging all before, until it was safe and sanitized. Now, in the long night, details I had forgotten trickled back.

"I don't remember her ever crying. That night I made her cry. And the book fell into the fire."

"You don't have conductors?"

"You really are Spire. We ask for them but don't get them out in the communes. Methane tanks. 'Clean enough,' they say. So yes, fire."

"Sorry," Abel said gently. "But start over. I don't know what you're saying."

I sighed. "She was cooking. I came home and asked what she was doing. She didn't answer."

I still felt the frustration. I felt the will to lash out, and the blanket of inaction holding me still. Fear, Kodiak had said. Maybe so.

"My mother had a book of recipes. It's all I have of hers. Had. It was the photo album of my childhood; so many memories pass through it. When I think of my family, I think of the kitchen she ruled. It was my mother's domain, her kingdom. She was always there. Feeding us, watching out for us, sometimes the only one in the world who was on your side. She'd wave her spoons around like batons, wild gestures when she told her stories, sharp swipes when she was angry."

"You really loved your mother?" Abel asked.

"She really loved me. I could have loved her better. But that's the sort of thing a child doesn't learn until it's too late."

I lifted my hands out of the dirt and rubbed off the loose dirt. My fingers were filthy. It would rain tomorrow.

"My wife found the book and was making me something from it. But I didn't know. And she didn't answer."

Abel grunted while the scene played again in my mind.

"She didn't answer. I got so angry, so fast. I tried to force past her to see. I don't know if she wanted to surprise me or if she was already regretting her gift, the moment I turned cold. I don't know. She kept her back to me, pushing me out. I pushed. And then my mother's book was in the fire. Her head was twisted, looking up at me. I was focused on her. We didn't see."

The jungle sounds bespoke movement and activity in every direction, nocturnal explorers navigating the blessed safety of shadow, while we remained still.

"I don't know how long it was until we got sick of sparring and separated. Long enough, it was half blackened and shrinking in the flames. I saw it first and went numb. She snatched it and threw it into the sink.

"It was reflex. But it was done in moments. The thick paper, the blackened edges… it all fanned out in the soap and water. Each evening, each meal, the voice of my mother, bleeding across the pages. Gone."

"I'm sorry," Abel said.

I was rubbing my temples, as I always saw Abel doing. "It was all a mistake. A careless mistake. But I felt it, I felt it in here. And she didn't say sorry."

Abel hesitated. "What did you do?"

He could not see the dark look I gave him in the shadows. His words bent under the weight of the suggestion – that I'd turned into some sort of monster. It was a tired shadow that had attached to me from the moment the Wardens came to collect me.

"We'd been arguing for years," I said, side-stepping. "Just...nothings that are suddenly everything, the distractions that hide the ugliness you can't seem to uncover. But not once in all those fights did I feel like she understood me.

"Maybe it was the same for her. But I'd tried talking. I'd tried not talking. I'd tried giving it time, tried intermediaries. But I could see it behind her eyes. I could feel it when she launched into me one more night. I could hear it in the words she never said; she didn't see.

"Here I was again. It wasn't the carelessness. It wasn't the loss. Not just that. It was how she didn't say sorry. It was how, instead, she attacked me."

"And yet," Abel said in the space that followed, "she was making that recipe for you."

I knew it was true, part of the truth. There, months later in the jungle. I could already see it hours later when the air cleared, but even then, it had been too late.

"What did you do?" he asked again.

I turned my head to his shadow, speaking at his feet.

"It's the part I'm ashamed of. But it isn't why they sent me here."

I waited for Abel's comment, but he didn't offer it.

"I said whatever I could think of. To hurt her. She took it, like stone. Like she didn't care. I kept waiting for a crack, something to tell me that she felt it too. Felt the way I did. It never came.

"At some point, I demanded to know "if we were just burning things now." I threw a towel off onto the stove. But there in her eyes, she didn't understand.

"The towel meant nothing. I took her hat from the table by the door and threw that in as well. She told me to stop, that I was out of control. I knew what I was doing.

"Her face was still stone, stone and disdain. Then I saw the picture above the sink; her and her mother cooking. She's a child, standing on a stool. Her mother is behind her, guiding her hands in a bowl. I don't know what they were making. It was what I needed. I took it from the wall and held it over the still lit stove, keeping her away."

For an instant, I found myself back at the Hall of Judgment, the hidden chirps of the Outlands like the murmur of response that had always followed my words. I had become the monster because this was the night that everything had gone wrong.

My voice grew softer as I admitted, "I wanted her back. She's the one I needed. I wanted her to stop hurting me. Nothing else had worked."

Most people wanted to say something at this point. Abel did not.

"So there we stood, the picture and the flames, I looking at her and she looking at me. And I finally saw it, there in her eyes. My pain, my fear, mirrored. She understood."

The jungle played its part, murmuring and chattering on, the tide of judgment rebounding through the trees around me.

"It was the worst moment of my life."

Layer by layer, the real world fell away. First, Abel and the Outlands. The memories of the Hall. All that was left was myself and those eyes. I could still see them, reflecting at me across the kitchen, a moment in time indelibly etched onto me. That was my work that night.

I'm so sorry.

"Anyway." I swallowed against the dryness that had formed in my throat and shook my hands out. The dirt and leaves kept getting on them as I fidgeted. "She made a grab for the picture. I shoved her away. I still meant to go through with it. But I shoved her into a shelf. It fell from the wall, and the jar of cooking oil broke on the corner of the stove. Oil, coating the stove, the hose to the tank, and the gas tank in the corner of the kitchen."

"Thatch," Abel breathed.

"For the second time we pulled away and stopped fighting. Again, she was first to move, but she just threw towels on the spreading flames, trying to smother it. I knew it wouldn't work.

"I grabbed her. She fought me. There was no time."

I held a fist under my nose, feeling the knuckles brush my skin, one by one. The memories were more vivid in the dark.

"Did you leave her?" Abel asked.

"I hit her. With everything I had, in the jaw. She went limp, and I put her on my shoulders and ran."

I paused.

"You argued and burned your house down. That doesn't get a person sent to the Outlands."

I closed my eyes. "Her mother. And eight others. Nine people died in my fire."

In the darkness, I saw Abel lean back against a tree.

– TWENTY SEVEN –

"Winter Joseph Odel."

"Callie Joan Mendes."

"Who are they?" Abel asked.

"Children."

It was a while before Abel spoke. "How did the fire spread?"

"The houses are built like mirror images," I said, the blueprint now indelible in my mind. "It's a stupid design. There, in the back corner, four kitchens come together. Four gas tanks and thin walls.

"So I carried her out. Got her away and laid her on the grass under a tree. And I went back, shouting the whole way. Her mother lived in the next dwelling." Abel leaned in, catching my quiet voice. "I was so close, so close I felt the heat when the first tank blew. Flames came out the window. Then three more. I was still standing there when the building fell. Six of the eight residences caved in."

"And that's why you're Unforgiven."

"No!" I said, too loudly. I waited for the light snoring around us to stabilize.

"I told you. Accidents upon accidents. If she'd been more careful, if I'd been less angry, if she'd spoken rather than grabbing for the picture… Nedder, if she'd just answered my question when first I walked in the door, if if if."

Perhaps it had been too much to hope for, that Abel might be the one to understand. "A matter of seconds or centimeters in any direction and everything would have ended differently."

The light was dim, but I could still make out the furrow in Abel's brow.

"Don't think me callous. I care, believe me, I care. I think about them every thatched day and night. How we balanced on that point... My wife, and those parents and families, lost far more than I did. And I pushed it the way it fell.

"But I, *I* didn't balance us all up there in the first place! Blame the State for keeping their conductors. Blame the builders for putting a bomb in our house to save time and money." My voice grew again. I reined it in. "It could have been anyone, any day. It was just waiting for me or her, or anyone, to set a foot wrong. To have a bad day. And come down.

"Did you hear what the Speakers said? Did it reach inside the Hall? 'He beat his wife and blew up a city block.' 'He murdered his in-law but his wife got away.' It's not true.

"Don't think me callous," I murmured, the old exhaustion consuming the frustration. "They're two different things, tragedy and evil. I was angry. Angry isn't murder."

Abel sniffed in the darkness.

"Just a chain of accidents. Some mine." I could taste the bitterness on my voice. "And that - unintended, unforeseeable consequences – is why I'm Unforgiven. So they throw me in the jungle to die. Does it make any sense? Can you explain it to me?"

"I thought the resources in these Outlands weren't worth running experiments on humans, and someone saw fit to throw me in the jungle to die. Can you explain that to me?"

It was my turn to sniff in the darkness. "Yeah," I said. "Yeah. But you opposed the wrong person. It's revenge, cause and effect."

"Unfair, but logical. Yeah," Abel said. "Would you rather have that, or fair and illogical?"

"Fair," I responded without thinking.

"Well, then. Do you deserve to be here?"

"No," I said without thinking.

Abel shifted himself up onto a rock, facing me. "What do you want me to say?"

It wasn't your fault.

I'd already told him. He could say it if he wanted. I turned my attention back to the dirt, digging little holes with my fingers.

"It's fine," I said. "Sometimes I don't believe it either. You could say it, and there'd still be this…thing…weighing on me."

"What *thing?*" Abel frowned and turned to the Ears. He lifted them onto his knees and cycled them on. For sixty seconds his face was illuminated by the faint running lights as he swept the area, listening. He cycled them off and placed the metal box on the ground.

He snorted quietly, as if dismissing a cadre of unwanted thoughts. "You know what your problem is?"

I wanted to know, and I didn't. Not from him, not now. He didn't understand.

"You want to fix it," he said. "So this *thing,* this weight goes away. So that everything is better."

"Not everything," I said, pushing back. "I'm not that naïve. I just want to move on knowing I've done right by those I hurt. Because now it feels like I'm dressed in someone else's skin, the skin of a killer."

I thought of the Outlander I'd shot in the morning.

Abel's head twitched. A subtle shake, then a bigger one. "Doesn't work that way," he said. "Fixing won't solve your problem."

"Fixing is solving," I said.

"Life isn't a machine, Thirteen. It grows and erodes. It fractures and scars. You don't *fix* a tree that falls down."

"Those are metaphors; doesn't mean it's how the world works."

Abel tilted his head so that a shadow covered his face. "Your wife will never be whole."

His words were quiet. So is a fist cutting the air toward your face. He might as well have risen to his feet and driven his boot into my stomach.

I squeezed my eyes shut, covered them with my hands, though it barely made it any darker. The night of the Outlands already blocked out everything beyond our dimly lit camp.

I knew he was right. I'd always known it, but I couldn't give in to it. Letting those words in was giving up. That's what I thought.

"You can't rest until it's done, and it can't be done. That's your problem. You're trapped."

"So what then?" My voice grew to a growl of frustration. "I

had one shot to get everything right? What can you do? Give me all my life lessons right now, and I'll take them. I'll get everything right. If that's what it's going to take–"

"It's–" Abel interrupted, then stopped. "How do I say this? Doing good doesn't make you good."

I shook my head where I sat.

"I'm not saying it isn't of worth. It isn't the point, and it isn't enough."

"A good person does good. What else does it mean?"

Abel let out a small laugh. It wasn't his life that was gasping on the ground here. I uncovered my eyes.

"Have it your way, and there's no good man. No one's ever passed the test, Thirteen."

"I used to," I grumbled. "Close enough."

Abel's laugh dried up, and he shook his head. "When? Right up to the moment the house burned? Or did it go wrong when you grabbed the picture? Or when you walked through the door that evening?"

"I don't know Abel, maybe somewhere in there."

Abel grabbed my collar and yanked me toward him until we were locked, eye to eye. Then he thought better of it and let me go, shaking his hand out. I watched him warily.

"I'd ask who started the argument, but what's the point? Life isn't moments you can take and weigh. Label and swap out until they make sense. One of your machines.

"These arguments flow like rivers. Uncountable droplets running together until it's flowing, and it's going where it wants."

"Metaphors," I said. "It's fine. So you can send me to the jungle and murder me for my droplets, not the river. Well, they do whatever they want. They *shouldn't.*"

I raised a hand as Abel tried to interject.

"Yes, I know, I'm not perfect. I'm not so blind as that. But, I put good water in the stream. When the bad water comes, I stop it or take it back."

"How do you take droplets from a river?"

"Metaphor, Abel. It's a metaphor."

"So take your words from your wife's ears."

I wanted to shove him. But the problem wasn't that he was being difficult. The problem was he was right.

I rested my head back in my hands.

"What's your point, Abel? Just make it."

Abel considered me before answering. "Can't you see the futility of it? You tell me in one breath that you have to do right, and in the very next you tell me you have no control."

"Scrub your own smoke, right? I did my best. What more is there?"

"Your best..." Abel mused. "Wife in tears, mother gone, home gone. Two children, you said. And you in the jungle. Somewhere between four and six of us dead, too. Add that to the pile – maybe your best could have done something about that. This is all there is? This is as good as it gets?"

"I'm not the only factor."

"Your life is in ruins."

"Stop." My head bowed as his words rolled over me. "Your

point."

"This didn't start with the fire, and it won't end with the beacon. No one is good, not even one. You haven't solved the problem of human existence with the insight 'try really hard.' I promise you, you can't even fix yourself."

I did not believe him yet. But neither could I escape his words.

"I need to stretch," I said, and stood up.

"Thirteen," Abel said. "Until you let go, you'll be stuck. Like a... no, that's another metaphor."

I did not walk away. I stood, half turned. I felt so tired.

"You'll be right here."

Still I stood, silent, half turned, but I stayed.

Abel sighed. "Life is so much more than parceling out blame and scrubbing your own smoke."

"It used to be."

"It is."

"Abel," I said, and stopped. My mind was not blank, it was loud and tangled and broken. "Maybe this jungle is better. What would I do with another chance?"

I could see Abel in the dark. His head was down, his hands moving slowly. He tilted his head for a moment, at a sound, but it did not repeat. I waited for him, growing more and more certain of my words. Maybe it was better this way.

"You're still trying, Thirteen," he said. "Dying won't fix it. Or balance it."

"So I'm out here," I said, frustration focusing my words again. "Maybe you're right. Right about everything. I've cranked up my life, I've cranked everyone else's lives, what do I do now?"

"Everything you still have," Abel said. "What's it for?"

"I don't know anymore."

"Think on it," Abel said.

– TWENTY EIGHT –

Duck did not return by morning. Abel's gaze strayed to the trees frequently while we shoved our camp back into our packs.

Crisp, Ivan, Scarecrow – The voices of dissent had disappeared. There was little discussion before we returned to our heading before the ambush, following the real trail.

The first red rays of the sun had found the Outlander still lying where he had fallen. The body merely lurched and settled back to earth, with an exhalation of dust, when Taj kicked him. Two fingers along the neck confirmed it.

Happy had rushed over for the rudimentary autopsy, his face centimeters away. He worked quickly before sitting back on his heels, face twisted in disgust.

"Not another," he said.

"What went wrong?" Abel asked.

"The sedative must have been lethal. You said you changed their physiology?" He wiped his hand down his face, tugging his eyes wide on the way, before adding, "I guess?" His gaze was distant, staring straight through the body.

"What is the base pH level of the Outlanders now? Did you alter blood proteins?"

I'd strayed while Happy peppered Abel with questions. Abel had only mumbled answers to the half-heard interrogation. Only Happy obsessed over the mistake.

I would not have been content executing him, nor releasing him, nor tugging him along in bondage waiting for him to escape. For my part, it was the best outcome.

I dwelled instead on the lattice of burns and scars, wondering if they were a mark of pride or shame. If he'd been afraid or insane.

That eerie gaze of anticipation stayed with me. Desiring what? Every possible answer shook me. Abel was right, the man had been cracked. The world he had provided a window into, it was not a place anyone should live.

Abel sang to himself, a mournful song with mumbled words, as he led the way out of camp. We hitched our packs and headed down the hill, picking our way around bodies as we descended.

*

I led Happy across the uneven ground. He walked in relative silence, dutifully holding onto my pack and following directions when a rock or tree root sprawled into our path.

The sun rose higher, and the air thickened. "How are you doing?" I asked.

"Outlands," he said.

I unconsciously stepped over a gnarled root, without comment. A step later, Happy yelped and tumbled to the ground.

"Nedder," I said, as way of apology. "That's on me."

I extended a hand to help him up, but he didn't try to rise. He had rolled over and sat there, elbows on knees, face and hands covered with dirt and loam, staring at a spot between his feet. There was nothing there but dirt.

"Come on, Happy. We've got to keep up," I coaxed.

Happy shook his head. "I'm lost."

"I don't know where we are either. Taj knows." I reached my hand out again.

"Oh. Outlands. Yes." He grasped my hand, and I pulled him up.

"Wait, what are you talking about?" I asked. "Is this about the Outlander?" He found his footing. I hesitated a moment, but, when he remained still, staring at nothing, I reached out and brushed some of the bark off his face. He didn't seem to notice.

His eyes searched the trees. "I'm blind, Thirteen."

Sorry about your glasses flashed through my mind. "There isn't much to see," I said instead. "It's the same trees, same undergrowth. I think you're actually better off not seeing the Outlanders," I joked. "Ugly thatchers."

Happy didn't laugh. "It's interesting, Thirteen – you start seeing things." He turned and began walking without my guidance.

"What do you mean?"

He stopped. "Things I'd forgotten. They began floating up, a few here and there, but it's getting faster, brighter. My life, Thirteen, my life…I'm so lost."

I stepped around and in front of him so I could look into his eyes. His words were scattered, but I had a sense of their center. He looked through me, eyes flicking back and forth as if tracking something in the trees behind. His lips moved.

"Stay with me," I said.

He tried to focus, then stared through me again.

"My mother told me I was the brightest boy."

"Doesn't surprise me," I said cautiously.

"My father too. And my academy mentor – said I was the brightest pupil that had come through his office. Friends looked up to me, came to me for help. Professors held me up as the example."

He pushed past me and began walking unguided again. I hurried to catch up and grabbed his elbow as we walked, turning him back to the trail. "That doesn't sound so bad. Better than what my father told me." I hazarded a glance at his face. It was impenetrable.

"Do you know what happened?" he asked, rounding on me.

"What?"

His eyes finally found the range, and he focused on my face. "I believed them."

He snorted, as if clearing foul air from his lungs, and walked off. I heard him muttering under his breath, "Couldn't see until I was blind."

I caught up again, although he was heading in the right direction now.

The sun was getting higher and the direct light came through the leaves. I held a branch as I passed, and he strode through.

"What are you talking about?" Looking over my shoulder, I saw his eyes light up for a moment, the familiar twinkle. But he quashed it quickly, his eyes darkening to their former gloom.

"I'm sorry," he said. "I'm obfuscating to demonstrate how

much I know. Again." He grimaced quickly, so quickly I almost missed it. "Let me be plain," he began, thinking about his words.

"I know I'm intelligent. I won't say that with pride, though I always did before."

"That's fine," I said. "I figured it out quickly."

"I make sure of that, don't I?" Happy snapped, though his anger wasn't at me. He let out a sigh and stared into the invisible distance.

"Well, yes," I said, before I lost him again. "But it's fair. You're a thinker."

Happy waved me off with a weak arm flap. "I was invincible." His voice picked up intensity. "Nothing was out of my reach. Nothing I couldn't solve, nothing I couldn't answer, no person I couldn't surpass. I believed them," he said, his voice losing its edge. "Smart enough to believe they might be right. But not smart enough to see they were wrong."

It was like a spinning motor, and all I could get were glimpses of what lay inside as gaps in the metal flew past. I knew he was hurting.

We walked while the sparse whispers of air found a way through the jungle to rustle the leaves and cool the sweat from our skin.

"I am not smart enough," he finally said to himself.

"For what?"

"For the Outlander last night, for one."

"That was an accident."

"Yes," Happy paused. "It was. Another mistake. I couldn't

316

have known how the sedative would affect his system. It isn't a dangerous compound. But I didn't even think about it," he said, biting the words. "What is worse than not knowing something?

I knew this one. It was easier when it was a broken pump than a lost patient. "Being so sure that you stop asking questions," I answered.

"Yes," he said. "That."

"It was just an Outlander–"

"Eight people, Thirteen. Dead because I believed I knew."

He stopped, and I didn't urge him back to the trail. There would be time to catch up.

"How many alive because of you?" I asked.

"How many alive," he echoed. "Yes. Some are alive, too. Why don't I think of them?"

He paused, considering. "It was never about them. It was about me. Always me...I am the problem."

I didn't have much reason to like Happy, if you'd asked me for one. Yet I did. We'd been in this together. I was lost, looking at him hurting like this. This was far past a simple "no, you're not."

"It's just since my eyes have opened that I understand," Happy continued, as I still searched for words. "I really don't know if I should be killing the Outlanders or letting them kill me. I don't know if I deserve to be here or not. I don't know what I did to those patients."

"Dying won't fix it. Or balance it," I said, Abel's words floating back to the surface.

"And yet it might be necessary," Happy added quietly.

That thought settled on us.

"I wanted it to be true. I wanted to scrape the stars from the sky and hang them in my library. So I believed it when they told me, whispered to myself that it was them speaking, but it was always me. 'You're the brightest boy...'"

"I've made a right mess of everything, too."

"Is the truth hard for everyone, or just us? Us Unforgiven out here?" Happy asked. He looked at me, and I swear he could see me clearly.

"The truth is hard," I said. I looked in the direction the others had disappeared. I couldn't hear them anymore, but the machete trail was clear. There would be time.

"So we make it up," I said. "We make something up and hide inside it."

"It can't stand forever," he said.

His eyes were unfocused again. I wished I could stare into nothing, like him, and stop seeing this endless prison.

"What do we do when it falls?" I asked.

"What do we do when it falls..." he echoed back. And he shook his head. "I don't know what I'll do if I go back home."

"My hope is, nothing that leads back here."

"But it's all we know," Happy said, his brief spark burning out. His quiet voice mingled into the soft breeze. "It leads straight to us, like this spragging trail behind us. It'll catch up to us."

"You were already smart," I said. "Now you're smarter. You'll do better."

"Don't you see yet?" he nearly whispered. "I will never be smart

318

enough. I have nothing to build, nothing to build on."

I looked at him helplessly as he studied his empty, dirty hands.

"You're my friend," I said. It was the only thing I could think of.

He smiled weakly, patted me on the shoulder in that awkward, too hard double slap a man does when he doesn't know what to say. Then he nodded and looked away.

I meant it. I gave him a double slap of my own. Then I took his hand and lifted it, guiding it to a loop on my pack.

"Big root," I said, stepping over as I turned.

"Big root," he echoed behind me. And we made our way again down the broken path.

*

At midday we came upon the others sitting on a small pile of rocks with blue sky overhead. The food was still being distributed. Twice an hour on the Ears, there had been some blips, but nothing suspicious enough to investigate. Taj and Stump had been out front, and both had seen other trails. Some rather worn, crisscrossing our own. We were officially in Outlander territory.

I found myself running my thumb over the blue button as I listened to the chatter. I thought I wasn't as lost as Happy, but maybe I was. I'd lost some bluster and pride but hadn't yet gotten to the heart of the machine. It would take more than 500 Outlanders to get me home, really home.

Unbidden, an image of my own body, burned and scarred, flashed through my head.

More immediate, I remembered Abel's question to Taj: How

much ammunition can we spare? What if Taj had told the truth? Two magazines wasn't enough. Not if we were found. In my own pack I still had six, but I hadn't done much shooting. Everyone else had.

The conversations fastidiously skirted these worries – continue on, be careful, be quiet, Pope, how is your leg, on and on. As if we hadn't learned time and time again that plans were worthless.

Then Unforgiven began to fall silent. All were looking into the trees, back the way we'd come. I stopped chewing and heard the noises too, faint but growing.

Men stood up, rifles in hand. No word was spoken as we spread out and crouched among our rocks.

The noises grew closers, stopping periodically. Perhaps the bill for our machete-hacked trail had finally come due.

Several guns came up, and Taj waved them down, gesturing with the Silent that he held in his hands. I'd forgotten about it. I lowered my rifle. It sounded to me like only one thing coming, man or animal or monster, but what did I know?

In a last crescendo, the thing crashed through the bushes into our clearing.

Ivan, packless, breathless, nearly collapsed when he saw us, blood flowing from lacerations on his face where the jungle had torn him.

"Oh, thank God!" he gasped.

"Didn't think you were a believer," Stump said. He hadn't lowered his rifle.

"Shut up!" Ivan coughed out between breaths.

"What are you doing back–" Taj began, but Ivan cut him off again.

"Shut up!"

"What is it?" Stump asked, his tone shifting.

"They're coming!" Ivan rasped as he got back to his feet and began trotting past us and out the far side of the clearing.

"Stump!" Abel barked, but Stump was already cycling the Ears on. All around us, packs were slung over shoulders and food was stuffed away.

"What have we got, Stump?" Abel demanded.

"Where is Duck?" Kodiak asked.

"They got Duck," Ivan panted over his shoulder. "They got him."

"We're surrounded," Stump said. "There's a web, moving quickly, spread out in this direction." His gesture took in nearly 180 degrees. "Abel?"

"Bad ground," Taj said. "We need a hill, sight lines."

"We have the Eyes," Abel said.

"They have our guns!" Ivan wailed.

We stared at Ivan, recalculating.

"Eyes of the State," Pope cursed.

"They're coming!" Ivan cried and disappeared again into the trees.

– TWENTY NINE –

"Run."

Abel spoke the word, but we jumped as if a pistol went off. We disappeared into the undergrowth, snapping twigs and breaking branches, leaving a trail ten meters wide. A howl sounded behind. It was taken up on several sides. The hounds had flushed their prey.

Taj passed Ivan, sparing enough breath to say, "Good thing I only gave you two magazines. We'll have what, 10 bullet holes each?"

I, too, spared a glance as I passed, wondering how he had stumbled upon us. An elaborate betrayal? No, a second glance, his terror was real.

Bait? Perhaps these Outlanders were a little more clever. Or a little more *something*. They could have found us without Ivan's help more easily than with.

A plaintive cry came, off to our left.

"That wasn't Outlander!" Stump said.

"Happy!" I shouted, my stomach turning. "Who's got Happy?"

We slowed. I counted. Six plus Ivan.

"Happy!" I shouted again, veering toward the voice.

There were wild splutters. Our names, and cries for help.

Beneath it all, the treble and waver of a man who is terrified and alone.

And howls.

"Happy!" Kodiak added his voice to my own, running by my side.

"We're losing ground," Taj shouted, somewhere behind. But foliage crashed and broke behind me. The Unforgiven were following me.

"We're coming," I said, a quiet promise.

There was a yelp of pain.

Abel spoke urgently into the comm. There was no response. The branches and creepers entangled me, forcing me to slow even as I tried to push faster.

Kodiak growled, "He's bringing them straight to him."

"And we are running straight to them!" Taj bit out, now at my heels.

The howls came closer together. Louder, nearer.

"Come on, Happy, come to us," I whispered.

The straps on my pack ripped tight, and I flew upward, off my feet. I landed on my back, rolling across the ground. Taj stood above me. "Stop this!"

Kodiak slid to a stop as well, already meters ahead.

"This?"

"Abel! Thirteen! Kodiak!" Happy's voice still sounded, now growing farther again.

I tried to climb to my feet. Taj stepped on my shoulder.

"Here!" I shouted, uselessly wrestling with his boot. "Slow

down!"

"Leave him. We go," Taj said.

Kodiak rushed back, eyes flashing. But he did not help me, did not move against Taj.

"It is him or all of us." Taj said. He was not even breathing hard.

More howls came from ahead. And Happy's cries still carried, ever farther away.

"Then go," Kodiak said suddenly. He pushed Taj off me with one hand and lifted me to my feet with the other. "Go."

He pushed me forward.

"Happy!" I bellowed, pulling my voice from as deep inside as I could, and took off, leaving Taj behind. I expected a knife to fly into my neck. None came.

"Thirteen?" Happy cried. He'd heard me.

"Happy!" I shouted again. "We're coming!"

"Where are you?" he called back. I laughed out loud.

The howls changed in pitch. I did not know what that meant.

"Stay put!" Kodiak shouted.

"Where are you?" Happy shouted back, the panic rising. "I can't see you!"

"Stay where you are!" I shouted.

"I wish he would just shut up," Kodiak said, now beside me again, pushing branches aside as he ran.

"Abel! Thirteen! Where are you?" Happy's voice grew nearer but it had risen several keys. There was another yelp of pain. "I can hear them! I can hear them!"

Kodiak swore and unslung his rifle.

"I can't see!"

We could hear branches breaking now; he was trying to run again. He'd get injured, if he was even closing the distance between us.

"Just sit tight!" I shouted. "You son of a thatcher," I added.

The howls stopped.

Happy's voice grew closer.

Passing under a branch I straightened to charge on but found nothing under my foot. I pitched forward into a sudden hole, until a hand grabbed the neck of my jacket and pulled me back.

"Careful," Kodiak said.

I swore.

A steep, shallow gorge lay across our path, with a stagnant stream at the bottom. It had run parallel to our own flight, but now lay between us and Happy.

"Help! I can hear them!" Happy shouted. I looked at the far trees.

"He's coming," Kodiak said. Happy's panic still tore at me while I listened, now helpless.

"Stop, Happy! Stop!"

I heard the Unforgiven as they emerged around me, but I only had ears for Happy as his words struck and fell to the ground, collecting at my feet in a lifeless pile.

Oh God, Oh God, I can hear them. Help me.

We have to get him across!

I can't see. Help me.

Happy! Slow down! You have to slow down!

I can hear them. Oh God.

We have to get across! Now!

Help me.

There was nothing I could do. Happy tore out of the bushes, hands and forearms laced with ribbons of blood from the untamed jungle. He was running wild, looking over his shoulder. His cry turned wordless as his foot found the chasm and his body pitched forward. His head snapped around, eyes wide with terror, uncomprehending. As he reached out his hands to catch himself, grasping for anything but finding nothing, his blind eyes fixed on me. On whatever smudge I was that stood out from the trees.

Our eyes met for a moment too brief to hold onto, too brief to say *it will be all right* or *I'm sorry* or even *I'm here.*

Maybe the last. Maybe it was enough to say the last.

And then he was gone.

*

Around me, rifles came up, the click of safeties, whispers over the comms. No one else appeared across the gorge. Softer rustles, entirely unlike Happy's rampage, murmured in the empty space. They were there, I could feel it in the air, sense their weight in the shadows, but they had learned enough not to show themselves.

All of this registered somewhere in the periphery for me. I only had eyes for the gorge. There at the bottom, damming the torpid stream, was his body. The gorge was shallow, but still too deep.

Stay put.

Slow down.

I'm coming.

I'm here. I'm here. I'm here.

Kodiak pulled me back into the shadows. Only my body. My mind still ran wild. As if there was still something to do. As if this had not yet happened.

We had to stop him. We had to get him across.

"We have to go."

Abel looked at me, his hand grasping my shoulder, his eyes piercing my own. Everyone else was backing away, deeper into the shadows.

"Now."

– THIRTY –

I nodded but did not move. Abel turned me, then began a dogtrot, following the edge of the gorge.

I followed. He relayed directions to Taj, who had fallen back with Pope and his wounded leg during our sprint. Or perhaps just fallen back and found Pope.

We soon left the gorge, leveraging the obstruction to gain distance from the hunters. We left Happy behind. In his way, he had saved us by leading the Outlanders to the wrong side.

The burn in my legs fought for my attention, against the afterimage of Happy's eyes and flailing hands now burned into my own eyes.

Hours passed, and my ragged breath and aching legs won out; the haze of the gorge replaced by the haze of the trot, of pushing, of surviving. Taj spread us out, saying that seven faint trails would be harder to follow than one clear one. I tried to jump from root to root and stone to stone, but I soon tired. When weaving around branches became a burden, I ran straight through them. Even the featherlight screwdriver on my arm became too heavy, and I jammed it into my pack.

The only break was a brief stop every hour to turn on the Ears.

Someone would look, say, "They're still coming," and we'd be off again.

With each stop, this new reality came into sharper focus. We were running without destination. We would run until they hunted us down or we collapsed. Maybe with a hill or a river we could make a stand. There were only trees and jungle.

Some men picked up stones and branches, hurling them to the sides, hoping to set false marks and trails. Not enough to lead the Outlanders astray, but enough to buy a minute while they assessed the distraction. Taj also sent a few bullets whispering from the Silent, hoping to tear off leaves and break branches even farther astray. I didn't bother. They were rustics. Despite all they had forgotten, they could track.

We ate on the run and drank sparingly, unwilling to stop and refill. That too couldn't last forever. Hours went by, still trotting, still weaving when I remembered and cursing myself when my foot hit soft mud and left a print.

Still wondering, *Why didn't I grab Happy?*

I couldn't go back.

Some things can't be fixed.

Burn thatch, Abel.

When dusk began to fall, anxiety billowed into panic. We couldn't trot through the night. Could they track at night? Could we stop? Would they stop? Did we fight now? In the darkness, we'd have an advantage with the Eyes. But it would only take seven bullets to end this. Why hadn't the State given us armor?

Because that isn't the purpose.

They probably didn't expect us to give our guns to the Outlanders.

You want to fix this? Die. Eye for eye, life for life.

It fixes nothing.

When we stopped again to check the Ears, Pope collapsed. Kodiak had been nearly carrying him the last few hours, anyway. Abel asked how we were doing, but nobody bothered to answer. Taj and Kodiak looked fine. The rest of us were glazed over, no longer out of breath but no life left in us. The numbness helped, after Ivan, after the Outlanders, and after Happy. Abel saw it, sparing an extra glance for Pope.

"Thoughts?" Abel asked, as he and Stump looked at the Ears. Taj stepped over to look as well.

"We can keep running," he said. "I think we have more food and water than they do, they may have to slow down first."

"Not likely," Stump said. Taj bounced his head side to side, agreeing.

"Loft the Eyes," Pope said, mumbling into the ground where he lay face down. "Let's shoot the buggers."

"We'll take casualties," Abel said, not looking away from the Ears.

"We'll win," Pope said.

"But we'll take casualties."

"Can we take a right angle and flank them as they go by? Would that work?" Kodiak asked. I laid down on my face like Pope. It was the longest we'd stopped since the gorge. It felt good, though I was worried I would not be able to get up again.

"The first volley will work," Taj answered Kodiak. "We'll surprise them, but they're fanned out too far," he gestured across the screen on the Ears. "When they turn, they'll envelop us… we'd have to make a hard dash." He looked at Pope.

We have to leave him, I heard Taj's voice again.

No, I thought. *Not again. No one else. There is already too much we cannot fix.*

Stump and Abel were shaking their heads.

"Shut it off, Stump," Abel said. "How far ahead are we?"

"Looks about fifteen minutes," Stump said. The old man showed nothing, so I had no idea what his legs actually felt like. He must have been tired, too, but he was stalwart.

"Let's go," Abel said.

"What are we doing?" Taj asked, dragging Ivan to his feet by the back of his jacket and giving him a starting push. I pushed myself back onto my feet without knowing how I got there.

"A hill, anything. We need ground. Or an idea. We can't keep this up all night."

Yes, I thought. *Not all night.* Just a bit farther.

*

In twenty minutes Abel stumbled upon both ground and his idea. We emerged from the trees into a large clearing. It was at least a hectare, nearly as large as the clearing we'd been dumped in a week before.

"Thirteen. How's the cloak?" Abel asked as I caught up.

"Cloak's fine," I said, putting my hands on my knees and bending over. I froze. What had been in Happy's pack? Ivan's pack and Duck's pack too. *Spragging burnt cranking…* "Kodiak's got it," I panted.

We had the cloak. What had we lost? Another gun, and more than two magazines.

"Kody!" Abel ordered, "Give the Cloak to Thirteen. Unforgiven!" Eyes, some bright, some lifeless, snapped to him. "Ten more minutes! Spread out, run to the other side, head fifty meters or so into the undergrowth, and come back. Criss-cross as you go, confuse the trails but make them plain. Every which way. Then meet us in the middle. Thirteen, Pope, you're with me."

The Cloak was in my hands. I didn't really hear Abel, but I followed his pack when it started moving again.

In ten minutes, it was done. The hectare had soft, wet dirt and long grass, above the knee, and it took the trails well. Standing, I could see them going in all directions. I hoped it looked just as chaotic in the jungle on the other side. We gathered together, piled our gear, and I powered up the Cloak.

Only the slightest shimmer revealed that a barrier was there, otherwise nothing changed. If not for the trials I'd run it through, I would have felt completely exposed. But I knew that, from the outside, we had disappeared, homogenous grass projecting in our place.

We waited, rifles held in tight hands. Finally, Stump asked, "Are we going to fire when they get close? We can probably get a bunch in the first volley, once they're in the open. Go from there?"

"No," Abel said quietly. "We are going to hide in plain sight and let them pass us by."

"What if they don't pass us by?" Kodiak asked.

"Shoot like hell and hope we make it," Abel said.

No one spoke any further. We all faced the wall of trees, waiting for the Outlanders.

– THIRTY ONE –

In the fading dusk, an Outlander trotted out from the eaves of the trees, slowing to a stop. One by one, more figures trotted into view. There were fewer than we'd handled at the ambush, but there was an air of unpredictability about them now. They'd learned.

One, then two came into view holding rifles in place of the usual sticks. These two had on headdresses of a sort, animal skin and tusk. I could not see the scars underneath in the dark distance, but I knew they were there.

They were perhaps forty in all. Half that, and we would have attacked, but forty left too many loose ends. The light was fading quickly. Despite the Cloak, I held my breath, waiting for the howl. They walked around stooped and inspecting the grass, some beginning to gesticulate. Stragglers continued to arrive, more than forty now, but I did not see any more rifles. Maybe they hadn't looted Happy.

They began to move again before night fully fell. Most spread out to circle the outside of our hectare, but a handful began stalking slowly across the open grass, perhaps the sacrifice in case we had set a trap. One of them was heading straight for us.

"Abel?" a strained whisper came, tense in the dim light.

Abel looked to Taj and gestured; Taj swung the heavy rifle up over his shoulder and pulled out the Silent. With another gesture, Abel sent Kodiak creeping to the shimmering wall of our little dome. Kodiak bobbed his head and wove as he crept forward, trying to gauge the subtle ripple and forced perspective of the Cloak and find the edge. Taj threw a questioning glance at Abel who passed it onto Kodiak, who raised his open hand toward Taj before turning to face the Outlander.

This took moments. The man was halfway to our position. I held my breath and felt the silence descend around me like a snowdrift. One breath, one cough, could be all that stood between us and the other side. The man drew closer.

I felt my pulse pounding and realized my safety was on. I did not dare click it off, but I covered it with my finger, ready. The Outlander was only five steps from Kodiak, still moving slowly, looking straight through us. Kodiak stood still, hand raised, and Taj watched with the Silent.

The Outlander stopped, sniffing the air and sliding his head from side to side, as Kodiak had. He took a hesitant step, and I pushed down on the safety, cringing at the muffled click that only I could hear. I was ready. Ready for him to call out, ready for his eyes to go wide with sudden realization. He was looking straight at Kodiak, not two meters from him, but still he wove and hesitated.

Another step, another head bob. Crouch. Another step. Suddenly, Kodiak's hand dropped, and a fierce hiss cut the air. The bullet flew true, striking the Outlander directly above the eyes, even as Kodiak reached out a hand like lightning, snatching the now limp form and yanking it inside our invisible dome.

We sat perfectly still, afraid to even look around. Slowly, heads began to turn left and right, watching for any signs of alarm. There were none. The rest of the Outlanders continued stalking across the open ground.

Soon the hectare was clear again. We began to whisper, hesitant at first but gaining courage with each minute. The first words were the obvious, "How long will the Cloak last?"

"They told me twelve hours, cumulative. I wouldn't trust it past ten," I hedged, remembering the Ears.

"One night and change," someone translated.

"Two nights, if we can find a way out of this early," someone added.

"What do we do next?" It was the second obvious question, and I had no idea. My best thought was to wait and hope they went away. At least if we made it to daybreak, they would have to convince themselves we weren't in the field.

"I need a gun," Ivan whispered. I only now remembered he was there. No one reacted.

"What? We are literally surrounded by Outlanders! Has it gone this far?"

Stump was first to move, pulling one of the extra rifles from a pack, but I stopped him.

"I don't trust him," I whispered loud enough for all to hear.

Stump stopped but did not put the rifle back. "None of us do. But he's a gun in the fight."

"He is no longer one of us," Taj said.

"He isn't stupid, Taj," Stump said. "An Outlander body is a puzzle for them. An Unforgiven body will put them right back on our trail, double quick. It would be suicide to harm us before we're out."

"*I'm* not stupid, Stump. It's the only reason his body isn't wedged in some tree roots at the edge of this clearing. I don't need him to get out, I certainly don't need him armed–"

"He is suicidal," I interrupted.

Stump nodded slowly, and finally put the rifle back in the bag.

Abel watched this, face blank. "What do you two know?" he asked.

"He sabotaged the Bugwall. Shorted it to drain the battery. If I hadn't found him out, we might all have diggers in our heads now."

"That's ridiculous!" Ivan said, his voice rising dangerously loud. His cheeks flushed in anger, his eyes white in panic.

He hadn't known. Known we'd known. Stump had been right to keep it quiet. Ivan had still been calculating on the Bugwall all this time, and some of his insanity finally made sense. Some of it.

He was quickly hushed, and blustered in a whisper, "Why would I do that? I don't even know how to do that!"

"I saw it too," Stump said. "There'd been tampering."

"And Ivan watched me repair it when we landed."

Ivan did not respond immediately. Only his eyes moved as he surveyed the group, flashing from face to face. When they lit on me, he said, "Thirteen, I believe you're the only one who could…" He trailed off, deciding not to squander the last of his credibility finishing the sentence.

"Then there's the ambush and Crisp. Almost Pope, Happy, and myself as well." I ticked off bodies on my fingers in the dusk. "And now he comes running, leading an army of Outlanders straight to us."

"What?" Ivan nearly exploded before he was hushed again and spluttered out, "You think I'm with them?"

Ivan was looking scared at the others rather than staring death at me, this time.

"No," Abel said at last.

"No," Kodiak agreed.

"This remains his fault," Pope countered. "Maybe he's not in league with the rustics, but he is the one who left us. He is the one who stumbled upon the Outlanders; he is the one who brought them to us. Ivan, how did you lose your gun but keep your life and your pack?"

Ivan was lost for words. I could neither figure out how he could have struck a deal with them, nor how this could have happened innocently. Little about Ivan ever made sense to me.

Thinking for a moment, Pope added, "Maybe they don't know the rest of us are here? Can we tie him to a tree and leave him as an offering?"

Ivan was making more noises of protest but had become too afraid to respond.

Abel said, "They know we are all together now. They saw the trail, they found Happy."

"Pope's point, though" Taj said. "Fault or no, Ivan is going to get us killed."

Stump had already put the gun away. Now he cinched the sack with a firm yank, as if to settle it all.

"I don't trust him," I reiterated. "I just want him unarmed."

"Please," Ivan said. "I want to go home. Without a weapon, I'm just a target."

"Just home?" Pope challenged. "What about revenge? I thought you wanted that, too. Familiar? I seem to recall some things you said before leaving? Yes? No?"

"Abel," Ivan tried. "Please. Let me help you. I can fight."

"I think," Abel began, but stopped, reassessing. "No," he said. "No rifle. And no peace offerings. Let's see how this unfolds for the time being."

Ivan began talking to himself. He might make a grab for a rifle later, for now his hands were empty. I still remembered what Stump had said about Ivan, *he'll make trouble if he can't find any*. Well, we already had trouble. Maybe his idle hands would keep to themselves.

"Anything else for the committee?" Pope asked. There was an edge to his voice.

"Rest," Abel said. "Where are the snipers?"

They'd been useless in the close underbrush, but now, maybe not so useless. Pope procured one. "Who has the other?" Taj asked.

In the silence, we confirmed the answer, *Happy*.

"What kind of sight we got?" Kodiak asked.

"Night vision," Taj replied.

"What? I can see in the dark with this?" Pope held the rifle, with its ridiculous painted barrel, to his eye and swung it around.

"They didn't show you?" Taj asked, walking over and doing something on the sight. Pope held it up again, whispering "*Incroyable…*"

"Taj," Abel said. "Wait for full dark. They will probably spread out to canvas the area. Thin out to sleep. See if you can pick off any lone stragglers on this side of the field," gesturing away from where we had entered. "I don't want anyone to see them fall, just to find the bodies."

"Won't they hear us?" I asked.

"It isn't silent, but it's quiet," Taj answered.

"Alright. Eat, rest. Let's see how this develops," Abel said again. "Stretch."

Before we could settle in, Pope spoke again, the edge in his voice sharper. "Abel?"

In the dark, I saw Abel's form, standing perfectly still after he turned back to Pope. His hand went to his head and down again, then he squatted next to Pope.

"How are you doing?"

Pope whispered something I couldn't hear, so I crawled over on my tired legs. I was worried about him. When I got there I saw he had pulled his pants off and underneath it, the leg wound was bloody and oozing.

We gathered around and looked in the faint light. The hours and hours of trotting had not been kind, straining the bandages and re-tearing the barely healed tissue. It looked bad.

Happy. I looked up at Pope, at the worry on his brow, and realized what this meant.

"Who knows anything about medicine?" Abel asked. Kodiak squatted down and began probing the wound but his answer was about the same as all of ours, *only a little.*

"You're a biologist or something, right?" Pope asked Abel.

"Who has the medical kit?" Abel asked, though we already knew the answer. Miraculously, Stump pulled a small satchel out of his pack, and Pope stretched out a hand, showing someone where to look in his.

"Happy thought it was too risky to have it all in one place," Stump said. Here was our lifeline: two small satchels of medical supplies, beyond the first aid we all carried.

"Do you remember what he used?" Kodiak asked Pope.

"He cleaned, with this," Pope said as he rooted something out of the bag. "Then he did something for the bleeding, bandaged it, and injected it for infection."

"Do you know what he injected it with?" Kodiak asked.

"It was a clear liquid," Pope said.

Abel looked at the small set of remaining vials with incomprehensible labels and shook his head. "None of these are what I'd look for."

Kodiak got to work cleaning the wound and wiping away the extra fluids while Pope gritted his teeth. Stump and Taj returned their attention to the trees, watching the Outlanders weave in and out of the shadows along our trails. None crossed the open hectare anymore.

Abel squatted down, looking levelly at Pope. "Anything we do now could be the wrong choice, Pope. It's yours to make. We can let it be and hope it heals, or we can pick one at random. Or we can just inject you with everything we have. I know these four vials, they are irrelevant. The rest are possibilities."

Pope tilted his head back, still gritting his teeth through Kodiak's work. "I understand," he said, and then said no more.

When Kodiak finished bandaging the wound, he urged, "Pope, what do you want to do?"

"Lady luck," Pope said, a wry smile lurking underneath the painful edge and shadow in his voice. "I will place myself in her loving hands. There is none I trust more. Bring me the vials."

There was a ceremony to it. At Pope's instruction, we set out the vials, turned the labels away, and shuffled them around. He then kissed his fingers, tugged his earlobe, and spoke to the sky. Finally, he closed his eyes, let his hand drift lazily back and forth until his fingers brushed a vial. "This one," he said, picking it up. Kodiak injected him, and we all watched as he quickly fell asleep.

Kodiak checked his breathing. "He's fine," he said. "It's all normal. I think we're all right." Of course, there shouldn't have been anything lethal in the vials; there was just some magic to it, and we all thought anything could happen.

We let him sleep. Taj took up watch with the sniper, and the rest of us stretched and laid out to sleep.

Stump sat near me. "I can't believe we lost track of him."

I couldn't sit up. I shut my eyes against the stars; they shone too brightly.

"What happened?"

"Panic," Stump said. "We should have grabbed him. But it's

done now."

Should. It seemed an increasingly impotent word. Happy should have still been here. Maybe we should already be dead. *Should* had no bearing at all on what *was.*

I ran. I left Happy behind. This is my best.

"He was an arrogant prick," Taj said.

I propped myself up on my elbow to look in Taj's direction. "He was a wise man."

"Worthless," Taj replied. "Worthless when you are dead."

I didn't want to have another argument. While the Outlanders circled, I laid down and slipped into dreamless sleep.

– THIRTY TWO –

The stars twinkled through the Cloak, the rippling barrier causing them to quiver like leaves in a gentle wind. I woke only once, seeing Taj and the barrel of the sniper in the moonlight. There were gentle sounds of sleep. One man sat upright, dark in the night, and I heard the gentle lullaby on Abel's voice again. Taj faced away, but I knew he was listening too.

I closed my eyes and let the words drift past, light and air and green things stirring in the spring and falling in the autumn, the life of summer and slumber of winter as the song wheeled on and back on itself.

The next time I awoke, it was to the now familiar shaking of the shoulder. I was no longer startled by a dark figure looming over me.

The first thing I noted was the stars - it was still dark. The second thing was my body, screaming in pain when I sat up. Every muscle was tight, and my head ached from dehydration. I began to move and stretch in silent agony, knowing we might start running again.

Around me, men were going through the same throes. Pope was moving about and looked pale, though it might have been the moonlight. He worked out his leg with special gingerness as he got loose like the rest of us. He looked all right.

The dead Outlander body startled me. Of course I had been there when we collected it, but from everything the night before, that was the one item that had escaped my memory. He lay there crumpled, a twin to the other Outlander we captured. Rough, scarred skin and blank, wicked eyes in the dim light.

"What's our status?" Stump asked.

"We have an opportunity," Abel said. My heart leapt. *Safety*, the thought had seemed unrecoverable.

"Taj has been methodically sniping on this end of the field," Abel said. "Professional work. They had been spread out, patrolling the area one-by-one. He got about four of them, and then as others find the bodies, he's bagging them too. Six or seven more. Anyway, the bodies are now gathering attention, and they're spooked. With their numbers thinned and their attention focused to the north, we can slip out the south side. We'll retrace our own trail if we can, so we'll be harder to track."

"They'll look closely," Taj said.

"Then they'll move slowly," Abel replied.

"The south won't be empty," Stump said.

"Outlands," Abel said simply.

"Outlands," Stump conceded.

No one had further objection, which was to say no one had a better idea, and none was eager to wait for sunrise. We put on our packs, ready to move.

"Can I have a rifle now?" Ivan asked again, the only whisper in the group. This time, with the threat of a fight so close to hand, several heads nodded.

"Just keep him in front where we can see him," Kodiak said.

Abel dug in a pack and pulled out a knife, holding it handle first to Ivan. "No need for guns now," he said, as Ivan snatched the weapon from his hand.

Taj continued to scan the edge of the trees with the scope. "I see three. Two, one went back in. He's back now, with others. Five or six. Six."

We waited.

"There's another set, five more."

Finally, the number climbed to twenty. When those twenty got curious and began to cautiously look around, spreading out, it was as good as it would get. There was a delicate balance, waiting until enough of them were concentrated away from our path out, but leaving before they began spreading again.

We took everything but the body, trying to straighten the flattened grass, which was futile. Perhaps enough to fool them in the dark, but once the sun rose, they would know we had been there. Four of us moved inside the Cloak's dome while Taj, Kodiak, and Abel spread out like shadows, hoping to confuse the visible trail. I could barely see them and couldn't hear them at all. At the edge of the trees, everyone knelt.

Abel was among us again. "Time for the Ears's last hurrah," he whispered. Obediently, Stump unslung the box and powered it up. The screen was dim, but more than sufficient in the darkness. There were red dots, but few and far between.

"If we run the Ears hard at this point, they aren't likely to come on again," I cautioned. Abel nodded.

"Comms on," he ordered. "Taj, you're the first line with the Silent, but don't shoot unless you have to. I want no trace. Kodiak, take the sniper, it's the next quietest thing we have. Not unless we absolutely need it," he said. Kodiak's big head nodded.

"Everyone else – knives only. Walk slow, walk silent, leave no trace. Be ghosts."

I must have missed that table during training. I cinched my pack and rifle tight, and felt for my knife before recalling it, still buried at the bottom of my pack.

"Thirteen," Abel said, as I uncinched my pack and opened it to begin rooting. "Carry the Cloak, we may need it." Gratefully I took the machine back in my hands and prepared once again to move. "Gentlemen, get ready to be back in the real world."

Though I couldn't see anything to say the Cloak was gone, I felt its absence like cold wind.

There was no word, no signal, but we were off, fanning out through the trees like shadows in the night. I could see nothing, but I followed the faint rustlings of the men around me and the whispered words in my ear. We would suddenly stop, all dropping low, and wait. I could not know how close we were or what was happening, but there was never any urgency in Stump's commands. He nudged us left, nudged us right, hold, hurry, back, quiet.

The adrenaline worked its way through the fire in my legs. I squatted and knelt, I spun around the fragile bushes, and dashed forward on light feet when the ground was good.

All the while, the inky shadow under the trees took on a certain weight. I felt the eyes on me, sensed the heartbeat of the Outlanders watching us. But they never materialized. Fifteen minutes passed, and then thirty, silent zigzagging through the night. I wondered how many Outlanders there could be, how far we had come.

The pauses became shorter the farther we went. Finally, the order came, "Circle up."

"The Ears are good and gone," Stump said. "I haven't been able to get a spark out of it for five minutes. But last I saw, we were clear. Thirteen, do you need this box for anything?"

"I might be able to plug it into the source on another box, not sure."

"I'll stow it then. Abel?"

"We're going to continue in this direction for a while. No way to know if we're doubling back on our own trail, but at this point it's unlikely. Still, we know the general direction, and if they see marks going this way, there's a chance they'll discount the trail. They came this way too. Be careful with your boots, though. If you see a patch of soft ground, leave a mark walking the other way."

"Right," Stump said. "Really turn and walk the other way, it's no use walking backwards."

"But no matter what we do, they'll find us eventually."

Grim thought. Still, I would run.

*

Dawn found us after an hour or two. Thankfully, my legs were loosening up rather than wearing down. We'd found some water and stopped to refill everything. Yesterday, speed had meant survival. Today, it was silence and care. Our spirits rose with the sun until, as it fully crested the horizon, a howl floated across the distance behind us.

We remained dispersed, still hoping the many small trails would be fainter than one clear one. When the trees opened up and the ground was hard, we trotted. The rest of the time, we snuck. I stared at the ground, fully devoted to delicate steps, gently slipping by the foliage.

Kodiak was now carrying Pope's pack, though Pope appeared to be walking all right. Pale, but all right.

By midmorning, a faint cackling of birds had replaced the last, faint howls As the cackles grew louder, we began to see them through gaps in the trees. Great birds, ascending and descending in circles ahead of us. We paused to watch.

The birds sang like death; discordant and clashing as they chased each other into and out of the sky. I thought of Happy, but we couldn't have come so far yet. It was still morning.

"Should we go around?" Pope asked.

"I want to see," Taj said.

"I don't," Ivan said.

"I don't either," said Abel, "But whatever it is might give us another trail to double over."

The birds suddenly spewed up in a great, flapping maelstrom, like a volcano of screaming meat and feathers, before settling back down toward the trees.

We marched on.

In a few minutes more, we entered a small clearing. The birds flapped away as we were assaulted by a new smell. At the center of the clearing stood a metal scaffold, maybe fifteen meters high. It tapered to a blunt point and had great arms, or wings, outstretched near the top. It was bent and rusted, a relic from before the Cataclysm.

And Duck hung from one of the wings.

There was a mixture of gasps and curses when we saw the body. Ivan turned and retched on the ground.

His clothes hung in rags from his body. They had mangled the poor boy almost beyond recognition. His hands, more than everything else, hung broken at the end of arms that swayed like willow branches in the wind. Even with my eyes closed tight, I could still see it all before me.

It was mid-morning. So this had been done yesterday, amidst the race to catch us.

"Holy skies and pits and the seven spires and all the thatching crankers in the burnt world!" Pope suddenly exclaimed. "What is going on out here?"

"I told you," Abel said with a heavy voice. "And it needs to be ended."

"What did they do? Do you see this?" Pope was still in shock. I was still in shock, my eyes returning again and again to the hands, pleading at the end of the limp arms. I felt nauseous, my senses and sensibility utterly overwhelmed as Duck swung in the breeze.

Before it had been squirrels. These were what we ran from.

"There isn't much bleeding," Abel said. "If he was alive at all, it wasn't for long."

"Which way does the trail go?" Stump asked. His voice broke and, even as he spoke, he did not look away. None of us did.

"Can't we get him down?" Ivan asked, his voice hoarse.

"No," several voices said at once. "No trace," Abel finished, but his voice wavered as well. Kodiak unslung a rifle and threw it to Ivan. It landed in the dirt, where Ivan stared at it, unmoving.

Abel and Taj looked questioningly at Kodiak.

"No one goes unarmed," Kodiak said.

Abel nodded after a moment, though Taj shook his head.

The corners of my horror began to lick away, to curl back, as fury burned the edges. I had been wracked with guilt over pulling the trigger, ashamed at my relief when the sedated captive didn't wake up. I had wondered who we were to come into their Outlands and kill. And all along, this.

Who were the State? They built this; they let it endure. Thirteen untrained criminals sent to put an end to it. The condemned to judge the condemned. Maybe they didn't know, maybe they didn't care. Maybe it was just convenient. Maybe this was the point.

"We'll kill the spragging rustics," I said.

Abel turned and began a slow walk back toward the trees. He said, "I'm sorry," as he passed near.

"Sorry why?" I asked.

"We all die out here, even if we make it out. I'm just sorry when it happens."

I didn't understand then. But something burned me from the inside. I wanted to kill.

"Which way?" I asked.

"Yes, can we leave?" Pope gasped. Ivan still stared, his new rifle hanging loosely from a single hand. The other four were cold and distant.

As we left, the cackling birds closed in behind us, working through the day to erase what lay behind.

– THIRTY THREE –

The rains came again that afternoon, a blessed gift to hide our trail and slow pursuit. We moved quickly while the water erased our passage and then rested, until the muddy ground firmed against prints. We counted magazines and counted losses. No more Ears. Low on medicine. Low on bullets. Low on men. Perhaps half a night of invisibility. It was a war of attrition, and we were eroding.

But the loss of mouths to feed ensured food and water. The Bugwall would run for weeks, the Eyes were strong, and there was always the beacon. The beacon with its hidden button and perhaps the hidden purposes of the State. We still had those.

We did not find a clearing for nightfall. We had no Ears, and the Eyes could not patrol the night. They would attract attention anyway. That left us with one tool, the sniper scope, but the close vegetation and narrow field of view rendered its night vision nothing more than a novelty. So we made camp with no lights, huddling down like wild animals, trusting in the shelter of darkness and leaves.

There was no sign the Outlanders had picked up our trail yet, though there was also no doubt that it was only a matter of time. But for now, time appeared to be on our side, and we needed rest.

I took my turn holding the Silent and sitting blind while the others slept.

*

I had never before sat alone in the dark, true dark. I knew we were invisible, and now saw clearly we could not be tracked at night in the shadows beneath the canopy. I could guess the odds of Outlanders, or anything else, stumbling on us by chance. Favorable.

Yet I was afraid. Of the dark, of things in the dark. In the ever-shifting patterns of the insect chirps, my ears discerned a thousand telltales of hunting cats and stalking Outlanders. In the inky blackness beneath the canopy, I saw the deeper black of bodies moving from shadow to shadow.

I imagined Kodiak, sitting cross-legged and straight-backed. *I bet you I can go 20 minutes.* Minute by minute, I snapped the sniper scope to my eye to inspect the shadows.

I despised my fear and the hallucinations. My thoughts turned inward to escape that dark hole in the jungle, coming to rest before the small flame, which had lit before Duck's broken body. The flame flickered to the hillside where I had first pulled the trigger, dragging forth the horror I had felt in that moment and changing it into something new. Too, it found me crouched in the shadows after I hacked the Eyes and took ahold of my disgust. All became rage, and in that rage was power. And absolution. I would kill them.

For Patches, for Happy, for Duck. The Outlanders stood between me and my home and all the labor left undone – though Abel named it useless; still it was my labor to endure. I would kill them for that as well.

Again in my mind's eye I pulled the trigger, again the first Outlander fell before me. I felt nothing.

Someone began to snore. I poked at the body, agitating it back to silence, and returned to my small flame, feeding it against the cold and the dark, ensuring it lasted to daybreak.

When my hour was done, I passed the two weapons to Kodiak and quietly fell asleep.

*

Hours later I jolted awake at a thump and a clatter. A dim light bobbed through our midst. It was sneaking. As my eyes focused in the dark, the bobbing light revealed Taj's profile, then Abel joined him, and someone else. I jumped up, grabbing my own weapon and tried to silently make my way to them.

"…something by the gear," Taj was whispering as I drew near.

"Which way did it go?" Abel asked, matching Taj's hush.

"Down," Taj said with a hint of pride. He had turned on one small light, pointing it at the ground, as we converged on the source of the noise.

Slowly, the light shielded by his body and hands, Taj turned the dim glow forward.

And there was Ivan.

His chest was wet, a single hole torn through his jacket, and his body curved and humped around the menagerie machines that had arrested his fall. His eyes reflected the dim light that was shone on him as he stared, unblinking, into the sky.

He was already dead.

"Ivan?" Pope asked.

"Ivan," Stump confirmed.

I leapt forward. "What was he doing in the gear?" Threats and promises, all the foiled plans flashed through my mind in an instant. He'd been too amenable of late. He'd just learned the Bugwall wasn't frying on schedule. The man would not rest until we were kneeling or dead, and he'd stopped insisting we kneel.

"What did he take? What did he break?" I asked, becoming frantic. I knelt by him and began to search. What was near to his hands? Was anything turned over? What was missing? What was broken? I looked underneath him and counted the pieces again and again.

"Relax," Taj said, a little more loudly than before. "He wasn't here for more than a moment. If he'd been up to anything I would have seen it."

"Why did you shoot?" Stump asked. The hardness in his voice sparked my own wariness. Taj still held the Silent in two hands.

"I didn't know what it was." The words slipped out easily.

"But you said you would have seen if he'd been up to anything," Stump said.

After the slightest pause, Taj said, "Seeing what something is is different than knowing how long it has been here."

"You could see well enough to find his heart," I said, matching Stump's tone.

"…A lucky shot," Taj said, with a dismissive shrug.

Abel stood over the body, looking down. I could not see his expression in the dark, but his shoulders were curved with weariness.

"It was an accident," Taj insisted, hand pressed against his chest.

I did not grieve Ivan, but I feared Taj's little tribunal, knowing where I stood in his view. We had lost more Unforgiven to infighting than to the mission; we had no margin for this.

"Who did you think it was?" I asked more forcefully than before.

"I thought it was a threat," Taj said, staring me down.

"So you flash it with the light, or look at it with the scope!" Stump said in a whispered shout. "What if I'd been going for a piss?"

I held my peace. I knew exactly what Taj had meant.

"Did you execute Ivan?" Abel asked.

There was in implacable quiet in Abel's voice. Taj grew wary, shifting his grip on the weapon in the space before he answered.

"I believe I told you," Taj said, each word carefully placed, "patience can be lethal out here."

Abel did not reply, still looking down on the body. He was fighting for footing in the rubble between the Outlands and the Unforgiven.

"Don't shoot anyone else. You are a capable man, figure it out."

Taj spat. Abel turned to me. "Thirteen, do we have another problem?"

I crouched among the equipment again, methodically this time. All was accounted for, all was close to where I'd left it, so I searched the body, emptying the pockets.

My hand froze on a sealed pocket over his chest.

"What is it?" Stump asked when I stiffened.

I felt all eyes on me and closed my own. I needed a moment alone, as my fingertips twitched across the fabric, feeling the shape.

Tearing the flap on his pocket open, I reached reluctant fingers in, knowing what awaited. I drew out the pair of glasses and held them in Taj's light.

"We strip searched him," Stump said. His voice was flat.

"We did."

The light caught the steel rims as my hand shook, reflecting off the curved metal in little points like stars, but so much nearer, and so small.

"Spragger," Stump whispered.

The small flame I had been nursing billowed into fire, cauterizing my soul into something hard and unfeeling.

I squeezed Happy's glasses in my hand, dropping the bent metal to the ground. Then, lifting my arm up to the sky, I curled my fingers and hurled myself down like thunder, striking Ivan's dead body across the face. I raised my arm again, my chest pulsing with a scream that had been building since they dragged me through the doors of Judgment. A firm hand grasped my wrist and held me fast.

"It's too late, Thirteen," Abel's steady voice said.

I pulled my arm free with a jerk and looked at the lifeless shell sprawled on the ground.

"It's always been too late, hasn't it?"

Taj laughed.

*

I did not sleep further that night. Dawn broke dimly, the clouds still heavy from yesterday's rain. Perhaps it would rain again, and that thought should have lightened my spirit. But I noted this as if through cotton stuffed in my head.

Others managed the guns and gear, though there was no managing the body. "No trace" was thrown wistfully out the window. Happy's bent frame was in my chest pocket. I found a pack on my back, and when they said to move, I stood up and followed. One foot before the other.

The first hour was slow, moving only a kilometer. We covered every footstep and avoided every plant, so when they inevitably found the camp, they would have trouble finding the trail again.

Then we began in earnest. The morning wore away as we covered the distance, quickly but carefully. Rains came and went as they always had, and I trundled on mechanically.

Then there came soft noises in the jungle to our left. Whispers, rustles, snaps. My eyes went wide.

The branches parted, and people emerged not five meters from me.

I did not see their skin, smooth and scarless. I did not see their eyes, alight with life and terrified. I did not see the children.

The cold fire flared up, and my eyes squeezed into slits. I yelled a wordless yell as I brought my rifle to bear, and my hand tightened around the trigger. The sharp report screamed like the angry primates in the trees, bellowing the jungle into silence and sending birds up a plume into the air.

A man fell dead before me.

– THIRTY FOUR –

There were shouts. Then hands, pulling at my weapon, pulling at me. As my vision cleared, the shouts resolved into voices and words, some flying at me and others at these people. Then, for a brief moment, everything fell silent as a howling voice drifted across the jungle, faint and far away.

Another rose like an echo, farther and fainter. Then a third and a fourth, from other directions.

"Thirteen!" Taj shouted. "What in thatch was that?"

"Hey! Hey," Kodiak was repeating slowly, approaching the people with open hands, trying to make calming gestures. It was impossible; they were terrified, huddling in an ever-tighter ball of twined arms.

"These aren't cracked," Abel muttered to himself.

Stump grabbed my head and twisted my face toward his. "Snap out of it, kid," he ordered. Then he slapped me. My eyes were twisting back toward the man lying on the ground, and I closed them. When I opened them, there was Stump.

"They aren't cracked," I muttered, echoing Abel.

"You realize you just told everyone within several kilometers where we are?" Taj demanded.

"Who are they?" said Pope. "And what are they doing here?"

"I shot him."

"Hey. Don't be afraid. It's all right now."

"It was an accident."

"They will come straight here."

"Is he dead?" I asked.

And it was silent again.

A woman broke free from the huddle and slipped deftly around Kodiak, though he made no move to stop her. She knelt by the man and rolled him onto his back, dissolving into wailing tears. I looked up, but no children followed her. Thankfully, no more children. Even so, I felt sick.

Abel had begun speaking, a stream of words that I knew if I listened closely, but there was a lilt and accent to them that made it sound foreign. The eyes of these people turned toward him. They clung to each other less tightly.

Abel fell silent, and their eyes wandered again. None of them spoke or moved to us; there were only the now gentle sobs of the woman over her man. Stump let go of me, and I watched her cry. Her back jerked sporadically with her sudden breaths, but the man underneath her was perfectly still. Her hair fell and hid his glassy eyes from me.

Another howl drifted through the air; new direction, but still far off.

"What have I done?"

"I almost shot, myself," Stump said softly to me. "It could have been any of us."

"That doesn't fix it," I said.

Stump let it be.

"What did you say to them?" Taj demanded of Abel.

"I told them we thought they were the cracked ones, that we are sorry, that we will not hurt them further. I tried. The vocabulary is narrowing each generation."

"That's great. Let's go," Taj said. Another howl came lightly on the wind, emphasizing his words.

"We can't just leave them," Pope said.

After a pause, Kodiak said, "No. We won't."

"I'm sorry, I didn't know you were acquainted. Who are these people to you?" Taj asked.

Kodiak was unmoved. "These are the people we just shot and brought the Outlanders down on."

"No," Taj corrected. "These are the people Thirteen just shot and brought the Outlanders down on. If he wants to stay behind and make it up to them, it's on his head. The rest of us don't need to be here."

"Taj," Abel interrupted.

"What."

The word fell like a glove thrown to the ground.

"Stop talking. For a minute. We'll go when we're done here."

Taj looked furious, and for a moment the only sounds were the quiet sobs from the woman again. I stepped forward and squatted down, placing my hand on her back. It was the hand that had killed him, but even so I felt her go quiet, some of the grief draining out of her.

"Minutes," Taj conceded over my head. "Longer and I leave."

Abel was already trying to speak to the huddled people again. He held out a hand and an older man stepped out of the huddle and placed his hand in Abel's. Abel turned it over, running his eyes and fingers up the length of the man's arm. Gently, ever so gently, he reached up to the man's face and placed his fingers around the eye, spreading it and looking at the white. Finally, he stepped back, and the man stood there bewildered.

"What are you doing?" Stump asked.

"They're Outlanders," Abel said. "They're ours. But they aren't cracked."

"What do you mean?" Kodiak pressed him.

"They're still whole, not like the cracked ones we've been fighting. This changes things. This changes everything. We need to tell them."

"Tell who?" Stump asked.

"They're sound... tell the State," Abel muttered, but his eyes were flicking back and forth, his thoughts a thousand kilometers away, opening old boxes in the attic of his mind.

My eyes drifted to the dead man's hand, lying where it had fallen to the earth when the woman rolled him over. Thick skin, callused, but smooth. I had done this.

A howl sounded again. I could not tell if it was closer.

"Abel!" Stump barked. "What now?"

"I don't think I can run," Pope said. When I looked at him, the paleness was more pronounced, and he leaned against a tree. "Don't leave me..."

"Then it's time," Abel said. My blood chilled.

He looked at Pope, and then looked at me and the bereaved woman before shaking his head. He looked into the trees but, unsatisfied, squatted to the ground and beckoned the whole Outlanders.

An older woman with a child strapped to her back squatted down next to him as he drew a circle. After lilting words and hand gestures, she agreed that the circle was where we were. He drew arrows and spoke. When he mocked a howl, she understood and contorted her face into a mask, eyes wide and tongue out, drawing her nails across her forearm. Abel nodded.

"Defals," she said, and in the accent I heard her name for the cracked ones. Devils. Or the devil's.

Abel drew an arc on the ground, away from the defals and their arrows, and asked "Is there a hill?"

"Heel?" she asked, rounding the word out.

"Hill," Abel repeated, mounding some dirt in his hands, then gesturing at the horizon.

The woman said "mont." Abel echoed the word and nodded.

Solemnly, she flattened his little mound.

Even as my heart sank, she shifted her position and created two new mounds, one small, and a larger one closer to our circle.

"That's it!" Abel exclaimed, jumping to his feet. "Which way?" he asked, the accent forgotten in his excitement. The woman raised an arm with a finger half extended, tilting her head to sight along its length into the jungle.

"Pope," Abel said. "Just a little way. Not all day like before. Can you do that?"

Pope nodded. He would run until he couldn't.

"What about them?" Stump asked, indicating the new Outlanders.

"Fite?" the woman asked, looking at Abel without blinking.

"Yes," Abel said.

"Victer?" she asked, twisting her head, dropping her chin, and looking at Abel through her eyebrows.

"Yes," Abel said again. He hefted his gun, though the gesture was doubtless lost on her.

She put her hands on the straps that carried the child behind her. The other Outlanders had released each other and now clustered, facing the direction of the hill, shifting from foot to foot and tightening whatever loads they were carrying.

"It looks like they're coming," Abel said.

"Wonderful," Taj said already ahead of us and waiting. "Children, Abel! I'm so glad we've met your family."

"Let's go," Abel said, and took up the familiar dogtrot into the trees.

"I won't die for them," Taj said as Abel passed.

"Then save your own life, and let them stand behind you," Abel said.

One by one, people filed after him. I rose to my feet, but the woman was still there, staying with her fallen man. She was no longer weeping, but had sat back on the ground, gazing where he lay.

Almost everyone had disappeared into the trees. "We have to

go," I said. She did not look up; I wasn't sure she even understood the words.

"Woman, we have to go," I said more urgently. It was just us now. Still, she sat there, as the running feet dwindled into silence, as more howls carried on the wind past our meeting place. I could not leave her.

I stepped over to stand by her and reached a hand down. Startled, she turned her head to look up at me. "I'm sorry," I said. "We have to go."

Tentatively, she took my hand, and I pulled her to her feet. When she stood, she left her hand in mine, the skin thick and tough. She peered into my eyes, and I knew she recognized me, the one. I was too ashamed to look away.

She was young, but in her eyes, I saw a storm of anger and grief and compassion. Daughter of the Outlands, born into death and bereaved, she peered at me with compassion. Then I did look away.

She let go and ran into the trees.

My legs had grown strong with the passing days. I followed, chasing our companions into the jungle, following the direction the woman had pointed.

– THIRTY FIVE –

Abel had set a pace that Pope could keep, and it did not take long to catch up.

"No, we don't know what happened," Abel was saying as I drew level. "What we know is that they turned into homicidal monsters. We recovered a few and couldn't determine if it was biological or psychological. All we determined was that we can't put them back together."

"So you don't know why these whole ones turned out different from the howlers?" Kodiak asked.

"No one knows about the whole ones at all, and no."

"Are they going to crack?" Kodiak persisted.

"I don't know."

"What are we going to do about them?" he asked again.

"I haven't figured it out yet!"

"I have another question," Taj joined in. "Remember that time when we killed one of them? What if, once the Howlers are dealt with, they stab us in the back?"

"So you don't want to give them the extra guns, to help out?" Kodiak asked Taj.

"No, no I do not want to help the Outlanders kill me, no."

"I think you're a little paranoid," Stump said.

"I think I'm a little alive," Taj parried. "Call it what you want."

"Good to see some contingency planning," I said. Taj did not reply, not with words, but our eyes met.

I had made a terrible mistake.

"Save it for the Outlanders, all of you," Abel said.

"For the Howlers," Kodiak corrected.

"For the Howlers," Abel agreed.

*

The hill was decently tall, perhaps thirty meters, and not too rocky. Decently steep, as well, with trees scattered over its face. I wondered what forces had put it there, abruptly rising from nothing.

I thought of Happy.

We had run twenty minutes. Pope sagged to the ground. "To the top, Pope," Abel ordered. Wordlessly, Pope rose, using all four limbs to push off the ground, and began trotting. Three steps later, Kodiak hoisted him fully onto a shoulder, and we followed.

At the summit, Abel deployed us. "Packs off. Thirteen, set up the Eyes and give Pope the tour. You have fifteen minutes. Stump, get the ammunition, all of it, and divide it as you see fit. Taj, scout the hill for their lines of ascent. I want to know where they will come up fastest and where we're likely to be surprised. Kody, take a weapon and explain to these Outlanders what it does. I don't want them wandering in front of us."

"I'll have to fire," Kodiak said.

"This is our ground. We're committed. They're coming either

way."

He looked at the sun, as if to gauge time again, and shook his head. "When you're done, find Taj and start digging where he tells you. All of you, when you're done, start digging. Except you, Pope. Rest. You made it."

Abel himself wandered off and stood, head leaning against a tree. The cracked Outlanders had stopped howling, which probably meant they had found the trail. I sat down with Pope and lofted the Eyes.

Pope's brow was furrowed, and he was breathing heavily through his nose, periodically taking what appeared to be painful swallows.

"You're pale," I said.

"I hurt." A deep breath. "Show me."

He looked ready to collapse, but a hardness in his eye told me he wouldn't.

"Maybe you should switch vials," I said. "You looked better when Happy was taking care of you."

"I felt better, too," Pope said. "But that was also before I ran a marathon on this star-crossed leg. Listen," he said, and he smiled. "Luck is my lady now. You stick with your lady, even when she does you wrong."

"Has that ever worked for you before?"

His brow unfurrowed long enough to rise to a dramatic quirk. "I've never tried it."

I laughed despite myself. "This is medicine, not love. We're trying a different vial tonight. I don't care what you say."

He grew serious again. "And if it doesn't play nice with what's already in me?"

"Ask your mistress," I told him. "It's in her hands."

He didn't argue, and we turned to the Eyes. I showed him once how it worked, then had him do it, just as Meeks had taught us a week ago, a lifetime ago. Pope learned quickly, so I shared the extra tricks I'd collected, first from watching Abel on that first night and then from my own foray into mission control.

"Be brief, be definite, be clear," I told him. "You are the Eyes, you make the decision. We are your hands. Don't forget how blind the rest of us are. Tell us where to go."

Pope nodded.

"Brief, definite, clear."

"I am nothing if not that."

I looked at him, waiting for the smile, for the laugh at his own words, but his eyes were hard again.

Abel was pacing back and forth through us now, head turned in the direction we had come. I stood and went to get a shovel while Pope dialed the Eyes out to their maximum range. From the top of the hill we could see a decent way but not far enough, not like the Ears. We'd only have a minute or two of warning. Moreover, the new Outlanders weren't color coded like the rest of us. If the Howlers got in, Pope would be as blind as the rest of us.

I switched on my comm. "I'm digging, Taj. Where do you want me?"

*

I dug for another fifteen minutes. The Outlanders were late.

By the time I threw the shovel down, the battle plan was set. One slope was especially steep; it could be climbed, but not quickly. Taj had clambered down to confirm the Eyes could see him, then we had set our backs to it and dug out earthworks every ten meters around the rest of the summit.

Kodiak and Abel took up middle bunkers while Stump and I took the wings. Taj would float where needed. With only five shooters, we'd have to scramble.

Even so, I did not miss Ivan.

Taj made clear I was the weak point, and he planned on backing me up. I swallowed my indignation. I still remembered firing my weapon, not three days before, with devastating effect on the foliage while Pope, Happy, and I were nearly killed.

Stump found seventeen magazines; three each with two for Pope, or resupply. I still didn't know how many bullets I had. Stump said three magazines made sixty.

The others agreed it would be enough. The math was three bullets per hostile. Fine for them. I was thinking in multiples of ten: six rounds for the trees, two for grazing hits, and one or two lucky shots. After five or six Outlanders, I'd be overrun.

Our Outlanders gathered near Pope at the summit, Wholers to face the Howlers. They held crafted wooden weapons of their own. Perhaps they knew, better than us, how to deal with the Howlers. Perhaps I could summon them with the right shout when my rifle started clicking.

Easier to swallow my pride and call Taj.

The weak point.

I rolled onto my back in my shallow bunker and focused on my breathing. The sun was hot, and the overhead branches were thin on the hilltop. The heat had dried the ground but made the air thick with stolen moisture. The birds and other semi-intelligent life had fallen silent, watching us in curiosity or anger. Only the insects marched on, dutifully sorting the crumbled earth I had dug up. My screwdriver was back in its place on my arm.

I thought of Duck, nursing the cold fury again. The men, the monsters coming to my hill deserved death. I would give it to them. That was my labor; that was the penance given me for my failures.

I studied the insects again, in their mindless scurry, while the great matters of life were sorted around them. Soon they would madly scatter, just like the birds and monkeys and weasel-things that knew trouble and fear.

I would bring death.

"Here they come," Pope's voice crackled into my ear.

THIRTY SIX

The cold fire almost quenched as my soul chilled, but it held.

"How many?" someone asked.

"A lot. They're still entering the viewer thing here."

I waited and watched the trees, though Pope's voice would tell me long before there was anything to see.

Finally, Pope spoke again, now urgent. "Kodiak, you're on point. They're coming straight at you in a mass."

"Got it," Taj and Kodiak's voices said as one.

After a minute, gunfire erupted off to my right. I stared at my trees while the staccato needled at my ears, needling my soul.

There were no voices but the guns', no screams or calls or howls. My mind painted vivid images of Taj and Kodiak, sighting down their barrels and sending metal into the living wave crashing at them. Men were dying not a hundred meters from me.

But the jungle around me was still. I continued scanning the undergrowth.

When the gunfire stopped, Abel's voice came over the channel. "Report."

"Lot of Howlers," Taj said. "But they slipped into cover and ran down the hill before we could do much damage. Notch five, maybe ten."

"Fall back, Taj. Pope?"

"They're massing again, but…" he trailed off. "Kodiak, shift left a bunker. You're still on point, but it looks like they're spreading some wings up toward Abel and Stump as well. Abel, you're good where you are. Stump, you may need to shift left as well."

Keep it crisp, Pope, I thought.

"How thick are the wings?" Taj asked.

"Sparse. Go to Kodiak. Here they come."

I squinted at my trees, trying to see through the leaves and branches. No matter how many times I relaxed my fingers, I found them slick and white-knuckled where they clung to the gun.

The gunfire began again, closer. It was rhythmic and methodical, professional. A third rifle joined the chorus and pulsed with the others.

Then a shadow moved between two trees. Not darting, but stalking.

I fell still, even my breath stopping. Only my eyes moved, while inside a maelstrom of fear and rage and shame twisted my gut.

The shadow again.

It took shape: an Outlander, a Howler, walking wide enough that he'd drifted into my path. He held a strung bow in his hands, an arrow nocked. Two spears hung at his back in some kind of leather harness. His head was bald, and even from a distance, I could tell that there was no hair anywhere on his chest or arms. The lattice of scars ran from his waist to the top of his head. His dark eyes scanned the bushes, his face flat and expressionless. He walked carefully, gliding smoothly like a jungle predator.

The adrenaline seeped into my veins, and my heart began to pump wildly, but I breathed low and slow. "I've got one," I whispered.

"Get him off Abel."

I sighted along my rifle. I no longer heard the guns firing. I no longer felt the twisting inside. I was a veteran. I was death. I felt my knee in the earth, holding me still. I waited for my breath, watching the man in front of the muzzle. Then I fired.

The shot went wide, my hands jerking the rifle as I pulled the trigger.

I cursed.

The Outlander turned, startled. My second shot found him before he could respond, and he fell.

"Thirt! Another!" Pope's voice warned.

I saw him, low as he rushed me. I stood and sighted, this time unthinking. I released a burst, then a second. Six bullets.

The man rose as he got closer. *Wait.*

He grew larger, he grew closer.

I fired a third burst, and he fell.

I stood exposed when it was over, staring at the body on the ground. Nine bullets, eleven for the pair.

Eleven for the pair.

Elsewhere the firing slowed and then stopped, silence returning to the jungle.

"Are we done?" I asked hesitantly.

"No," Kodiak's voice came back. "They ran back down the hill again."

"Count?" Abel asked.

"Fifteen-ish all together."

"Three over here," Stump's voice reported.

"Five here," Abel added.

"I got two." I wasn't hiding behind the rest of the Unforgiven this time.

"Puppy speaks," Taj said.

"Ammo?" Abel asked, speaking over Taj.

"Finished a mag," Kodiak said.

"Still on number one," Taj chimed in.

"Barely started," Stump said.

"…I fired eleven bullets." *Rounds,* I imagined Taj's voice correcting me, but it didn't matter now.

"Fine," Abel said. "Pope, can you give us a headcount yet?"

"That's five," Pope mumbled, thinking out loud. "So that's about ten, twenty. So that and that… There're seventy or eighty down there, by my estimate," he returned to his speaking voice.

"Seventy or eighty *more*?" Kodiak asked.

"Yes. I'm the Eyes, right? Seventy or eighty."

"Cranking Howlers," Taj muttered.

"We can take them," Abel said.

But we could all do the math. There would be no maneuvering the enemy and spraying them with bullets this time. No catching them in a volley in the dark.

I wiped my hands on my pants, my wet palms betraying me. Nine bullets in my gun. I laid on my belly in the hole I'd dug, pulled out the magazine, clipped it back in, flicked on the safety and flicked it back off. Trying to keep my attention off the paper-thin barrier between us and whatever lay on the other side.

"What are they doing, Pope?" Abel asked.

"Spreading out," Pope said. "If I were a betting man, and I am, I would say they are going to come at us from all sides."

"I'm going to Thirteen," Taj announced, and I surged with both gratitude and indignation.

"No! To Stump. He's got over half the spraggers in front of him, everywhere else, they're thin. What on Earth are they doing?"

"I can guess," Kodiak muttered.

"Are they moving? The massed group?" Abel asked.

"No," Pope said quickly. "Hanging back, as a matter of fact."

"Hoping we can't see them," Abel said. "Be ready, everyone. This is it. The small groups will come first. Once we're pinned, the rest will come hard. They won't melt back this time. Taj, stay with Stump. You two will be overrun."

No one spoke.

"Everyone else, you're on your own."

I swallowed. It felt unnatural. The muscles clenched and caught. I tried to breathe deeply, bowing my head.

This is it.

"Or the big group could come first?" Kodiak asked. "To draw us together and abandon the wings?"

"Not if they're hanging back."

I wasn't listening anymore. The trees stood out brightly in the sun, the colors and shadows stark. The leaves flickered as the air moved, the only life left on the hill.

Eleven for the pair.

This is it.

Be ready.

The preposterousness of it struck me as I looked out over my earthworks. I was not ready. I reached for my fury. It slipped against my fingertips.

"Why are they trying to kill us?" Pope asked, babbling over the silence.

Fury at Ivan, fury at the State, fury at these Outlanders.

"We're on their land, they're cracked, we keep killing them, pick one," Stump said.

My flame flickered to life, and my breathing stabilized. I swallowed easily. My heart still pounded in my ears, but otherwise, I stilled. My gun was steady, and my knuckles lost their white.

"Cut the chatter."

I will do this labor.

"And why are we killing them?" Pope asked.

"Forgiveness program," Stump said curtly.

"And why–" Pope cut off abruptly. "They're coming."

I will be death.

– THIRTY SEVEN –

I laid with my head poking over my mound, moving nothing but my eyes. Behind the barrier, I reached to loosen the next magazine.

"Watch to your left, Thirteen. Kodiak, you'll see them on your left, too. Abel, the ones coming right at you will get there first. Nedder, they're really spread out."

"Distance?" Kodiak asked.

"Close." As if on cue, I saw a shadow move between my trees. A shadow, and then stillness.

"Don't let anyone through," Abel ordered.

No shots had been fired. I wanted a target.

Another shadow, flashing from a tree, this time directly in front of me. Too fast. I didn't shift my aim; movement was danger.

Then a shot sounded. Abel or Kodiak, by the direction. I squinted to pierce the undergrowth. I needed a target.

"Thirteen! Why aren't you shooting?" Pope demanded.

"I can't see them!" I whispered.

"But they're on top of you!"

"Where?"

"You've got three – Kodiak!" And he disappeared, guiding Kodiak in another fight elsewhere on the hill.

379

I watched, my nostrils flaring and filling with dust. I felt the itch on my shoulder blades as more shots reported.

Why wasn't I shooting?

I imagined the Outlander standing behind me, driving a piece of sharpened wood through me, dying Unforgiven in the Outlands.

I dared not turn my eyes from the trees before me. Discipline and stillness. I breathed silently.

An Outlander rose from a bush, meters away, not looking at me, and stalked forward. The thinnest screen of branches spread between us.

Even as I shifted my rifle and squeezed the trigger, even as the man fell dead to the Earth, Pope's excited voice filled my ear, "Stump! Here they come!"

A flurry of movement broke to my left, and I turned to see another figure straighten up, startled. I fired a burst, then a second.

The jungle erupted into an almost constant chatter of gunfire away behind me. I heard Stump and Taj shouting in the comm and could not make out the words.

A third figure dashed away from me, into the trees, and I pulled the trigger until the gun stopped firing. I yanked out the magazine and jammed in the ready replacement, cursing at the gun's clicks.

As my eyes flicked up, a shaft of wood flew and stuck in the dirt in front of me. I fired a burst into the trees and collapsed into my hole.

Two more magazines is forty bullets.

I'm forty bullets away from being strung up for the birds.

"Pope!" I called. "I need Eyes!"

"We've got climbers! I've got to clear them!" Pope shouted back.

"Stay!" Abel commanded. "Send the Wholers."

"Well, I won't be here in five minutes unless they get the little squirrels with their pokey sticks."

"Let's talk in three minutes," Abel said and went silent.

Far to my back the fierce gunfire continued, and I could hear shouting even without the comm. Sporadic but persistent shots were echoing closer, Abel and Kodiak. My woods were silent again.

They knew where I was. The silence was terrifying.

I sent a few wild shots into the trees and slipped from my hole, trying to sneak to another bunker before the next arrow came.

As I rolled into the next hole, a man broke cover only a few meters away, spear raised over his head, eyes wide, mouth held stubbornly shut. I raised the gun and shot him, close enough that I wasted no bullets.

"You holding, Thirteen?" It was Kodiak.

They only yell after they're on top of you.

"I'm holding."

"Keep holding," he said. "Pope?"

"Good," Pope shot back. "I sent the Wholers and their sticks to the top of the cliff. We are Howler free."

"We're almost to knifework here!" Stump shouted over us all. "We can't hold."

Howls arose over the din of battle, from where Taj and Stump were making their stand.

"Get your gun, Pope!" Stump shouted. "We're coming!"

Echoing howls rose in a ring around the hill, and the bushes before me came to life. Men sprang forward all at once, rushing me, but not enough. I rose to my feet, bellowing my rage, and pulled my fingers into a fist.

By the time the gun clicked, seven men lay dead.

The gunfire behind me was replaced with a growing roar of voices.

Seven bodies, twitching on the ground in front of me.

"Kodiak! Flank!" Abel's voice. "Hit the mob from the side as they rush in!"

"My targets—" Kodiak said.

"They're mine! You get the main force. Thirteen, get ready to turn and flank *my* Outlanders after I flank Kodiak's."

As I heard a new purr of gunfire and Kodiak's voice raised in a roar, I slid in my last magazine. Twenty bullets strong. I was standing, exposed, the last dregs of my salvation clenched in my hands, ready.

Cold fury. Rising death. This could not make me clean.

"Thirteen! Do you hear me? I will flank Kody's Outlanders as they pass," Abel barked. "Do you understand? You need to do the same when my targets rush in!"

I had enough ammunition for maybe four more.

No, Abel's Outlanders would rush the camp, and I would be *salient*. That was a term I remembered from the briefing tables in the Hall of the Unforgiven. It meant exposed. It meant dying.

"I understand," I said.

An arrow flew at me. Useless, deflected by leaves and branches.

I sent a bullet back toward its source and was rewarded with screaming. I wanted to vomit.

The roar of voices from behind me continued. Wholers, Howlers, and Unforgiven striving in the final dance. I considered turning my back and running, hoping that I and my twenty bullets could find a safe haven, but safety was a phantom, as it had always been.

"Now!" Abel's voice commanded, even as a man emerged from the trees and rushed at me. He held a javelin high, having learned well the danger of loosing a useless arrow.

"Now, Thirteen!"

I turned, not fast enough, and shot. The bullet hit his arm, knocking the javelin askew so that its point passed me by as he crashed into me. We rolled to the ground, losing javelin, gun, and comm in the fall.

He was on me again before I could find and grab a weapon. His hot breath washed over my neck as he grabbed at my hair. With the convulsive agility of a terrified man, I scrabbled at the strong hand that clawed at me, batting away the weak and bloody arm. I felt for his face, his eyes, for anything. I found nothing, but my fingers twisted into skin, into cloth, into everything they touched, and I pushed against him, against the ground beneath me, and with a mighty convulsion found myself on my feet, the Outlander thrown to the ground.

I stood, feet wide, fingers hooked, and glared at the Outlander. He rolled to his feet, bleeding wildly, and let out a high yell.

I did not dive for my gun. There was no gun, there was no

jungle. Only a trembling sheet that billowed between me and the beyond. I ran at the man, grabbed his head, and drove it into a tree.

His spit sprayed over me. I felt scars against my palms. I felt blood running down my sleeve where it flowed off of him. Wild fingers dug into my neck, into my ribs, and I bellowed, throwing wild fists toward him, catching bone and tree and flesh.

Something heavy struck my stomach, and I lost all breath. I stumbled backward, unable to breathe, and he pounced on me again, hands wrapping around my neck, shaking, bleeding, squeezing.

I felt screaming in me, panic, instinct, will, darkness. I scrabbled again, scrabbled for anything but found nothing. My fingers found his open mouth, and I pulled his jaw, fingers slick, twisting his head as he grunted. I hooked his cheek and pulled with all my might but he arched away in a splutter of spit. I swung desperately at his ribs, but he did not let go. He swallowed the pain and held onto me, the sweat shaking from him as we strove.

Wildly, I swung at his exposed ribs once, twice, then I snatched the screwdriver from its place on my forearm and drove it into his side.

I held it there. *Clockwise, clockwise…* His hands weakened on my throat. His mouth twisted up into a grin as his hands grew limp, and still I held the screwdriver in place. His breath began to rattle. My face contorted as I forced him onto his back, rising to my knees.

There he lay, in the shape of a man.

My gun lay next to him. I grabbed for it, fingers fumbling over the barrel and then clenching tight, seizing the weapon as I scrambled away, kicking across the dirt until I found my feet. Nothing moved but his eyes, wide and white, tracking my crooked steps, and his chest, slowly undulating with rattling breath.

I was panting, one hand dangling my rifle by its warm barrel and the other on my head. I couldn't look away. I stumbled backwards, backwards, trying to escape the dying man.

Something hard jabbed my back.

I don't know what I saw first. The scarred skin. The leather and tusk headdress. Our gun, pointed at me.

My own still hung from its barrel, at my side. I looked at the meter between us, farther than my arms could reach. I looked at his barrel, the ring of silver at its end open like a gate to the darkness within.

I looked at the man, his face blank, and he looked back at me. Nothing moved but his eyelids, blinking to measure the seconds. I smelled the jungle a last time. I listened to the wind, still blowing below the rifles' crackling, through the chaos of shockwaves bouncing through the trees.

His mouth twitched into an open-mouthed grin.

With an abrupt yell, he shook the rifle. My body convulsed. For one instant there was surrender, there was peace.

There was no pain.

In confusion, I stared at him. He leapt in the air and shook the gun again with a violent yell, but there was no crack of a bullet.

I tilted my head, raised the rifle to my hands, and shot him where he stood.

Twenty bullets.

I scrambled to grab his gun, yanking the ammunition free and slipping it into my jacket. As I flipped the spare gun onto my shoulder, I unconsciously tried to thumb the safety on, but it did not budge.

I held it to my face. The safety. *Safety*. I wanted to laugh. I couldn't.

My legs buckled and I sank to the ground, legs crossed, two guns in my lap, with too many bodies for the holes I had dug.

*

Had they come again, then, they could have killed me. But they did not.

The next thing I heard was the familiar voices of the Unforgiven. Someone stepped behind me and slipped the comm back onto my ear.

"…so there are all these Outlanders, where are the women?"

"Maybe they don't have women," Stump said.

"It's an army, thatcher," Taj said.

"There's the last one," Pope said.

"I found him," Abel said. He stood over the Outlander I had stabbed.

Stump squatted in front me and wiped something off my face. "Alright?"

"I'm holding," I said. There was blood on his shoulder, and I stared at it as I spoke. I continued to stare at the place it had been after he stood up.

"Still holding," Kodiak echoed, scanning the trees.

The four gunmen were rumpled but well. Taj held the silent,

and Stump had traded his rifle for the sniper.

"Is he alive?" Taj asked.

"He's lit up," Pope responded in our ears.

Abel flipped his gun onto his back and squatted next to the last Outlander. The rattle grew louder as the man became agitated. I could see the whites of his eyes again. He raised a hand, fingers grasping, toward Abel's eyes, but Abel deflected it effortlessly.

He looked down at the Outlander. I briefly thought of a father sitting over a fevered child, knowing there is nothing to do but watch. It had been an ugly business, as Stump had said. Maybe they needed killing, and maybe I did too. The Outlands claim us all.

Abel's eyes were sad as he reached out a hand and took the screwdriver. With sadness but no hesitation, he grasped the handle and yanked it out. The man let out a great gasp followed by a rattling breath and began fighting to stand up. Abel stepped away and let the man writhe around until he finally found his hands and knees. We watched as the man began to crawl, wobbly at first, but quickly settling on a direction. Once the crawl became determined, Abel walked up to him and pressed him to the ground with a boot. "I'm sorry," he said softly, then raised his rifle and ended it.

"Gentlemen," he said, turning to us. "We have our bearing."

– THIRTY EIGHT –

Early the next morning, we found lazy columns of smoke rising into the sky. Cresting a ridge, we looked down onto rudimentary huts and tents in the bowl between small hills. Houses rose from the ruined corners of old, cinderblock walls. In places, the flat, black stone roads we'd sometimes found stretched in straight lines, while in other places, worn dirt paths divided the dwellings. There were people moving through the space. A settlement.

No more Ivan. No digger bugs. No Outlanders hunting us. Six men, beyond hope, watched the curling smoke with the same unspoken thought: *Our quota*.

I might have laughed if laughter had not been burnt out of me at the hill.

We had been hunting or been hunted for days, and the fight had seeped into my very bones as if life had never been anything else. Then, between one moment and the next, the Eyes had whirred down into silence atop the tall hill, and there was no one left to fight.

I could not settle into the peace. It seemed, every moment since, that all would descend back to chaos. Like water collecting at the tip of a faucet, molecule after molecule, while the child in the next room lies awake in the dark, waiting for the drip.

Looking at the curling smoke that morning, I saw the wave cresting, I saw the droplet grow heavy. My fingers tightened around the blue button still carried upon my thigh and held fast.

*

We had not lingered long at the hill after the battle. The Wholers had no desire to follow us into the cracked lands, and we said farewell as best we could. They had fought well and held the center. Two had died. Many more were wounded, but their very bodies had been crafted into medical kits by the State's geneticists. They needed nothing for the toxins and infections with which the jungle and the Howler arrows assailed them.

Pope had looked on with jealous, mournful eyes.

The others had counted and sorted the equipment while I stared at the dirt. Abel found me and held out my screwdriver in an open hand, wiped clean.

"He would have killed you," Abel said when I didn't move.

"I wanted to kill him," I said.

Abel had looked at the tool in his hand and offered no reply.

I'd taken the screwdriver, and he'd returned to the others. There was blood in the cracks, darkening each flaw in the metal, and trapped where the shaft met the handle. It was not the tool I had loved. I dropped it to the earth and left it.

The sheath remained on my arm, empty when the hill shrank behind us, an unmarked mound in the Outlands. We were left with one magazine for each man. So, we each carried one rifle, loaded with everything we had, hoping the time for shooting was past.

The jungle revived as the kilometers slipped by. Birds again flapped and squawked the daylight away. The rare monkey again peered at us, and one inched out to sit on a bare branch and watch our passage, eating a long, green fruit. The flowers filled the shadows with color and spread their perfume. I began to remember there was more than death in this jungle. As there had been more than silence and thunder in our house. Life was always there; it was always there. But I had no part in it. There was blood under my fingernails.

The tang of smoke the next morning had been the first sign. Then the lazy clouds rising into the sky, and then we had found the settlement.

We surveyed the layout, and Abel led us down close, following established paths where we could and leaping carefully from stone to root to stone where we could not. We kept a sharp ear out for approaching Outlanders. We heard none.

Taj found a hiding place, a small hill. It wasn't more than four meters tall but had steep, cliff-like sides. The top was flat like a shelf, about the size of a small house. In the rear another cliff rose, finally turning into a ridge running away into the Outlands. High enough that we couldn't be seen from below, small enough that no curious Outlander would feel the need to climb it. It was the perfect spot.

At first, we took turns lying on our bellies and peering over the edge, but as the day wore on and the rare Outlander passed by without giving our shelf a second thought, we began to rest.

Pope lay flat and barely stirred. The prior day had drained whatever was left in him. We had given him a different vial in the night, hoping it might nurse him back to health. Again, he had chosen his medicine by chance and providence, letting a bottle present itself.

We had hidden our concern at the angry red lines snaking out from the wound. "Bad infection," Kodiak had said quietly, when he fell asleep. But he did not know what to do about it anymore than the rest of us. We could only hope the second vial worked.

What Pope needed was the blue button and an aircraft. It was a race against time, and we were nearly there. We could get our quota. He slept through the morning, dreaming the same dream as the rest of us.

*

We watched the slow milling of the settlement below through the morning. Thinking through an impossible *how*. Abel found me in those quiet hours, when the frustration, the lack of epiphany, drove him to break from the puzzle.

"Tell me about her," he said.

"Why?" I asked.

"I want to know why it all matters to you."

"Mpf," I grunted. It had mattered. Had. I wasn't sure it mattered anymore. I eyed the empty sheath on my arm.

"How did you meet?" he pressed.

"My crew. We were talking about bread. I don't know why. Simmon told me I needed to try real bread, that whatever I was describing was just hot, spongey grain. Not bread."

I hadn't thought about it in a long time. The thread glowed in the shadows. I followed it and smiled.

"There was a bakery in the Lake district. I smelled it most days. Went out of my way that day, passed it walking home. I didn't want to deal with Simmon again in the morning.

"There she was. Covered in flour."

"Is there a lot of bread in this story?" Abel asked. Like me, he was tired of cubes in sauce. I nodded, and he grimaced.

"As I walked in, she lifted this bag the size of a pig. I asked her if she needed help. She gave me one of those looks, those looks women teach each other in the secret halls of silent combat, to tell me, to make sure I knew, I was extraneous. She hoisted it onto her shoulder. Her arms, elbow to wrist, were ribbed with muscles like mine.

"What do you want?" she asked, holding it there.

"I… bread."

"You bread?" she asked, softness coming over her face when I stuttered.

"I want bread."

"What kind of bread?"

I was at a loss. Simmon hadn't told me there were kinds of bread.

"Real bread?" I hazarded. That was all he'd given me.

But she laughed. "That's the nicest thing a customer has said this week. This year."

"Thank you," I said. I don't know why. She was beautiful. Flour fell from her hair as she finally flipped the bag to the ground with a twist of her back.

"You're welcome," she said, and looked me in the eye.

It was the first time I saw her smile.

I walked the long way home most days, then. I bought a loaf a week; what I could afford. Rye, sourdough, seedbread, even corn. Simmon had been right. One day it was dusk, and one of her streetlights was out. I looked at it, that dark spot above her wall, like the coming of dawn.

"Bread?" she asked when I entered.

"Your light is out."

"Heh," she laughed, "that and my mixer." She rubbed her arm below the elbow. "What you going to do, right?"

She stopped her rubbing, noting the glint in my eye.

"I can fix it."

She leveled a look at me. Long years of suspicion, nurtured by raw deals and hidden costs. The communes aren't the wilds, but they are not a kind place. People have never handled desperation well.

"Not for bread, I'm assuming."

"No," I said. "I want cake."

I remember the way she squinted at me then, measuring, weighing. I don't know what questions she asked in that moment, but when they were answered, she said, "Sunday."

"Sunday," I agreed.

"What happened?" Abel asked.

"I showed up at sunrise with my tools. I left after sunset knowing I'd marry her."

"How was the cake?"

I smiled but did not answer. I think the cake was indescribable, but all I properly remember is the kiss.

*

By noon, the sun shone brightly, bathing the Outlands in white, dusty light. Abel set out food, and we gathered to eat.

Pope rose and joined us. "Well, we found a settlement," he said. "I believe that was step one."

There was a breath of silence as we each looked around our small circle, at the six men left. Pope's weak laugh dwindled to nothing.

"And now we plant the beacon," Abel said, "which means getting in. Then we trigger the satellite. Desolation and blue buttons."

The week we'd survived had been even simpler to describe: "Find an Outlander settlement." Living that week had nearly destroyed us.

I again counted each man in turn. Taj, the arrogant assassin with all the skill we could need. Stump, the stalwart soldier, the unbreachable wall at your back. Kodiak, the mountain, the force of nature. Pope, the flowery philosopher who would keep our eyes open and our spirits fresh. And Abel, the good man. He had fought for us since the beginning. This was the group that would bring us home, Forgiven.

"Anyone feel…off…about lighting that beacon now that we're here?" Stump asked. "I mean, I know what we've seen. I saw it too. But, I'm just asking… Anyone else off about the brand of Forgiveness that comes out of that?"

"No," Taj said.

"Yes," I said.

"It's a terrible thing to be the hand that holds the knife," Abel said. "The task has fallen to us. You will ask for the rest of your life if you did right."

"It doesn't sit right," Stump persisted.

Kodiak stayed silent, chewing his growing beard. Heads turned toward the settlement and the small groups we could see, punctuated by scuffles and squabbles.

"And everyone is intently looking at what?" Pope finally asked.

"Looking for a place where the beacon will be both central," Abel said, "and also concealed. Then we figure how to get there." Everyone kept looking.

"We have no plan," Pope grumbled. "I don't know why I imagined we had a plan."

"I keep looking at that big structure," Kodiak said.

"Me too," Taj said.

"Too busy," Abel said, still scanning the settlement.

"You've been looking for hours now," Kodiak said, turning to him. "If there's anything else, you would have seen it by now."

"But it's in the center of the densest cluster of huts."

"Good coverage."

"But almost impossible to plant and hide," Abel countered. "I assume you're thinking about the roof?"

"The roof," Taj and Kodiak both echoed.

"Risky," Abel said.

"What about the other structure there?" Stump asked, pointing to something poking out among the roofs and touching the trees at the edge of the settlement. "Got a high roof, too."

"It's not central. We need to hit the whole cluster." Abel's voice trailed off again. "Too dangerous to stomp half a hornets' nest."

"Definitely too far off center," Taj said. "We've got to target that meeting house or whatever it is. I'll get the beacon in."

More than one eyebrow raised.

"Send me at night," Taj insisted. "We've got the comms. You can watch with the scope and guide me."

"A lot of the path is hidden from here," Abel said.

"And it's coming on full moon," Kodiak added. "I don't like it. We only get one shot."

"I've never needed more."

"If you're taken, with the beacon, we don't go home." Kodiak raised his voice.

"You think I can't do it?"

"I'd give you two out of three," Abel said. A vein pulsed on Taj's forehead. "Which means one in three you die, and we're stranded. I'm not done thinking."

"Could we bury it?" Stump mused. "Away from town center, but close enough for coverage?"

"The hole would have to be perfectly filled," Kodiak said.

"And there's concrete all over," I said, finally having something to add.

"We'd still have to get in," Kodiak said. "And digging's slow... slower than throwing it on that roof, anyway," he said, finishing his thought.

"Could we draw *them* to *it?*" Pope asked. "What if we dressed it up? Like, an idol? They'd be scared to touch it and anger the gods.

If they take thirty minutes working up their nerve, they'd have front row seats."

Abel's eyes flicked here to there across the settlement, subtly shaking his head.

"Seriously?" Taj asked. "You take that seriously?"

"It's an idea," Abel said. "But I'd rather have you run it in."

Taj grunted, mollified.

"If only we could go over," I said.

"What are you thinking?" Abel asked.

They waited. "No," I said, after a moment. "Nothing worth voicing. It's just that it's right there. We can see it. If only we could fly or something."

"What do you think?" Abel asked Taj and Kodiak.

"Think about what?" I asked.

"Can we go over?" Abel asked again.

Taj looked at the huts. "It's not even an idea. We have no wire, and nowhere down there to anchor it."

"Roof to roof?" Abel pressed. "Is there a path?" He alternatingly tapped two fingers on his cheek, counting out huts with his eyes.

"What did you do before?" Pope asked.

Abel didn't answer until he finished counting, shaking his head. He still studied the settlement as he spoke.

"We haven't always had the beacon. They keep changing the game, upping the quota. But once… once it was small enough that we could leave it in the trees. Once it was a new moon, and we got lucky. The other time… the cost was high."

I stared at the huts with him, with thoughts of leaping onto that broad roof. The space between felt so small. We were so close. So close to home.

"What if we lured them out of the settlement?" Pope asked, and Taj and Kodiak began kicking the idea around.

"The Eyes fly..."

Only after Abel's head snapped to me did I realize I'd spoken out loud.

"And they can lift the beacon?" Abel asked.

Now Taj laughed.

"Yeah," I said dismissively. "But I don't know what I'm saying. There's no steering. Unless..."

Expressions grew curious. "Unless what?"

I stared at the huts now, the men forgotten. I stared at the space between. I'd found a thread, and I rapidly followed it through the maze, doubling back at every dead end, marking the turns, working the theory, solving each exception.

I could do this.

"Well?" someone asked as my eyes came back into focus.

"It'll work," I said.

– THIRTY NINE –

"What will work?" Taj asked, inspecting his fingers and flicking something off absentmindedly. Pope still looked at me without blinking.

"I can fly the beacon."

"Explain," Abel said.

"Well, the Eyes are made to loft straight up," I said, holding my arm vertical. "If we attach a weight – or attach the beacon so the balance is off center, the whole rig tilts." I placed my fist against my forearm and tilted, to demonstrate. "It's like if you hung it with rope, but by the corner. Then the rotor will pull it forward in addition to up, like that rotorcraft that brought us here."

"At this distance, it would be impossible to launch it straight," Stump said. "And how do you land?"

"The thing is stabilized by a gyro; it sits in place and spins. Normally it just spins there so the rotor doesn't twist the cable. I can't explain this here, but if you tilt the gyro left or right it would torque and turn the whole rig. It's one of those physics things. As for landing, we only need a way to drop the power. That would slow the rotor."

"Yes?" Stump asked, new intensity strengthening his voice.

Taj turned and strode to his pack, noisily filling his pockets.

"We've got five spare comms now. I'll need four of them to get distinct signals inside and control everything... I'll use the tether's winch to tilt the gyro and can wire one into the main power. I think it will work."

Taj returned and poked me hard in the ribs with the barrel of the silent. "Not bad." He looked to the other men. Abel turned his back on the settlement, nodding at me.

Taj's breath picked up, growing audible a moment before his voice rose. "Me sneaking it in in the dead of night is too risky, but this is the plan?"

"Calm down, Taj," Abel said.

"Don't 'calm down' me," Taj threatened. "I've had enough of you thatchers and your warped theories of how the world works."

Abel spoke back as if Taj wasn't pointing a rifle at my vital organs. "I understand everything he's saying. If he can build it," and here Abel paused to look at me, "it would work. And if he can't build it, our options, including you, remain open."

I nodded slowly, inching to the side. Taj's gun did not track with me. "The comms will be ruined. The Beacon and Eyes can be restored."

"No!" Taj interrupted, as loudly as our hideout would allow. "A part of me is convinced you are all joking, because there is no other way we are having this conversation. We have everything we need, right here." He pointed violently at the ground between his feet. "We do not need him. I cannot understand why you would place your lives in his tinker's hands when I am right here?"

Looks passed back and forth between all of us. Quiet nods exchanged. No one spoke.

"I will not place my life in his hands!"

"You need to calm down," Abel said again.

"I am the best you have. I will not stand here and be told I am not good enough. So you all, stay and pleasure yourselves however little boys do around here. I am going to scout, not be seen, not be caught, and come back with a real plan. Good day."

He walked to the edge before coming back to jab a finger under my chin. It brushed my windpipe. "Do not break my beacon. If you thatch this up, I will crank you so far you'll run into next week." Then he turned and leapt off the edge of the camp's shelf.

Abel looked to Kodiak and nodded after Taj. The big man took a rifle and followed.

"Well. Glad that's finally out in the open," Pope said, shaking his head.

"What's in the open?" I asked.

"Taj gets all hot and bothered around you. He'll feel better now."

Stump glanced at my stricken face and chuckled. "Ah, don't let him get to you. He's just jealous."

"Jealous?"

"You know, a man like Taj, thinks he can do everything. Then you come and do things he can't understand."

"He thinks I'm going to get him killed."

"Nah," Stump said. "When you get to be my age, you've seen men like Taj a thousand times. As if all-encompassing sufficiency is

401

some altar to worship at." Stump sat with his back to a tree and looked at me, unperturbed. "That man can do things I've never even heard of, and it's not enough for him."

"No, I think he wants to kill me."

Stump laughed with a small smile. "He can't win if you're dead. He ain't Ivan. I told you, don't let him get to you."

Stump's words made little difference. Taj had gotten under my skin days before, and he wasn't leaving any time soon.

I was done talking about Taj. I looked around our small base, drafting a quick inventory of what I'd need and where it was. I ended up staring at the beacon. The beacon.

"Abel. Can we talk?"

He continued to watch the Outlanders move about their settlement. "What is it?"

"You've done this before?"

He nodded, noting my tone and giving me cautious attention.

"So tell me about the red button."

"What button?"

His face showed more confusion than guile. It seemed genuine. That was good, or bad. All it meant was if there was a lie, he wasn't part of it.

"The one that triggers the beacon while you're standing next to it," I said.

Abel's brow drew down. He didn't answer, but quickly moved to the menagerie and began running his hands over the beacon, searching. "Why didn't you tell me before?"

"I didn't trust you."

Abel lifted the beacon and turned it over onto his knees. "Do you? Now?" he asked.

I watched his every move, every brush of his fingertips. They passed over the hidden compartment. He didn't know.

"I follow you," I said carefully.

Abel paused, though he did not turn his head. He heard what I had said, and what I had not.

Three more passes and he found it. He rotated the beacon on the ground, with the small compartment cover facing the sky, looking closely, searching for a catch on the small door.

He looked up. "I don't know what to tell you. This beacon looks the same as the others."

I passed him a flathead and he pried the door off.

"If you're right, it's probably a failsafe, right? What's got you so agitated?"

I scrubbed my hands through my still-shorn hair. He sounded the same as Stump. I had to pause to make sure I wasn't the crazy one.

"You don't put failsafes onto bombs!" I blurted. "What's got me so agitated is what if that's not a beacon! And I don't know who is in on the secret and what they want from us!"

"They want us to kill Outlanders," Abel said. He was gazing at the button now, as well.

"You said they're tired of you coming home," I said. "So maybe it's just some toaster with an on/off switch that they handed us, so we'd get on the aircraft?"

"It has always worked before," Abel said. His voice was thicker now, my doubts taking root. "We landed; we planted the beacons. We burned the jungle, and they came. We just never found your little compartment before."

Did I trust Abel now? Enough. Enough, now. He was one of us.

No one spoke. Pope looked at his leg, I watched Abel, and Abel studied the beacon. It sat between us, like a live and dangerous thing.

"Well, I'm about to torch our comms," I said. "Rip up the eyes. Send that thing we need where we can't get it back. I just want us to know what's going on before I do something... before I get anyone else killed."

"They want them dead," Abel said, his voice finding bedrock. "Maybe they don't come. Maybe they don't come this time, but they'd still send the fire."

"Yeah," I said. "That at least makes sense."

"Got to be a failsafe," Stump said.

"Send it," Abel said.

"Do you want me to disconnect the button?" I asked.

Abel closed the little door.

"No, leave it. And open it when we send it out. Who knows? If it's a failsafe... if it doesn't reach the roof, maybe the Howlers will push the button when they find it."

"Fine," I said.

"Yes. Everything's fine," Pope said.

*

I set to work. Pope went back to sleep while Stump and Abel

watched the settlement. I opened the toolbox and spread my instruments. I grabbed a crosshead driver and held it in my hand. The handle was solid, the balance good. I slid the tool into the sheath in my sleeve.

I gathered all I needed – four comms, the Eyes, the Beacon, and the Cloak. I set a driver to the first screw, and in the space of a moment I was away from the jungle.

It came more quickly this time. The familiar wiring, the cold, clean angles of the casing. Screws and circuits, hinges and clamps, even the faint smell of damp metal diffusing through the air.

Home.

Layer by layer, I could see more with my eyes closed than with them open; I was no longer a lost, condemned man. I was a spark, treading pathways too small for the eye, exploring cavernous rooms where the roadways joined. Then, with its secrets laid bare, I became the puppeteer, the weaver, the sculptor, tugging and chiseling, molding the great machine to my will.

The Eyes. I needed the Eyes. I twisted the rotor free, and it too gave up its secrets. The winches that wound the tether became mine, and I grafted them into the stabilizing gyro like a gardener dreaming of spring. The tree would grow, it must grow, and yield its fruit. The graft, the splice, ever so delicate and yet strong like it was birthed from that joint.

I pulled the source from the Cloak, and the familiar tingle of contained power teased my fingertips. The few hours of visual camouflage remaining were meaningless; that technology devoured wattage. The rotary motor was one of the simplest, oldest engines.

This source would run strong; it would burn bright as long as we called on it. I quickly fitted it to its new insulator to stop the trace leakage of energy.

Then the comms. They were so small, so delicate, like ducklings pulled from the nest. I was scared to breathe, scared even to move, so I sat motionless as my fingers worked. Too small for my eyes, I moved fingertips to where I knew each piece would be as I lifted the wires and traces, spliced on new material so that they might grow like the climbers and creepers all around us, reaching into new nooks and anchoring themselves to new purpose.

Hours passed as I forged my machine. In everything, there was only one blemish; a grey, metal cube that stood in my way. Nothing more than a grey box, cables in, cables out, serving its purpose. It could serve it still, but not where it was. I lovingly lifted it, scraping away the solder and adhesive that secured it to the wall and made way for new paths. I found a new spot for it, in a nest of wires, and laid it gently to rest in the cablework.

*

When all was sealed, the tools gathered, Abel asked me again, "Will it work?"

"It will fly."

They all looked at the new machine, nodding, questions of detonation still darkening the corners of thought.

"When can we do this?" Pope asked.

Abel looked at the sky. "Dawn or dusk. Dusk comes next, but we need to wait for Kody and Taj. When they return."

Abel and Stump continued to watch while we waited,

exchanging ideas and obstacles, noting the patterns of their daily life.

They beckoned me over when the children gathered to entertain themselves. Once they formed a circle, and two boys beat each other until one stopped moving. A second time, they gathered around a small animal, one of the squirrel-weasel things. When they left, the animal was gone, and the ground was stained. I told them not to call me again.

In the space of the day, we grew cautiously comfortable, hidden on our shelf. I sat with Pope while daylight faded, watching the settlement and the sky and the wind on the leaves as we awaited the flight of the beacon. We leaned against a large, smooth tree that grew from our hideout.

In the setting sun, Kodiak and Taj came tramping back, walking comfortably along a well-worn trail. They'd announced their approach over the comms. As they pulled themselves up onto the table, Taj retained the same, forced nonchalance as when he'd left us. Kodiak looked grave.

"What news from the outside?" Stump asked.

"We have a problem–" Kodiak said.

"There is no problem," Taj interrupted.

We looked from one to the other. Taj let out a theatrical sigh. "The other large structure? The one near the tree line? It is a cage full of Wholers."

"We can't torch this place," Kodiak said.

– FORTY –

The argument began, whispers sharpened like knives to cut the air.

"We can," Taj said. "Our task is to destroy Outlanders, yes? They are all Outlanders, as Abel has determined."

"We have to let them out," Kodiak said.

"Aren't you supposed to be criminals? Why did the State incarcerate me with this nest of humanitarians?"

"We have to let them out," Kodiak said again.

"And I will," Taj replied.

"You want to burn them," Stump said.

"And you want to go home, yes?" Taj asked.

Neither Stump nor Kodiak answered. Abel stood aside like Pope and me, listening.

"So I put the beacon in the trees near the settlement. We let them out. The Howlers go to get them. When they come back, the others come to greet them, and they all gather around the cage, inside the radius…it's the quota. We go home."

"But you torch the whole ones," said Kodiak, dogged.

"Them or us. We go home."

"No," Abel spoke.

Taj pivoted. "Give me a reason, Abel."

"One you would care about? You assume they will actually catch the whole ones. And you assume they will come back on the same path."

Taj lifted his lip at Abel. A sneer, or a snarl. "Coward. The beacon will be in the trees, I can collect it if I must. Still two out of three, Abel? Come, give me my odds."

"Pope is sick, Taj," Stump said. "Escape, hunting…how long until they come back into your kill zone? Pope doesn't have long."

"What works is quicker than what doesn't, however long it takes."

"And what if they kill the escaping prisoners rather than haul them back?" Stump persisted.

Taj looked down onto Stump, rising to his full height to cast a shadow on the old man. His face darkened. "You of all people know what this is, thatcher. They are livestock. You don't kill your livestock."

"We save them," Kodiak said.

"For what?" Taj bit out. "They are nothing. They are lambs for slaughter. Abel, you yourself said it needs to end."

"Not for the whole ones. Not now." Abel's voice was hoarse.

"I ask again, give me one good reason. What would you have us do instead?"

"We fly the beacon, then open the cage. Torch the settlement before the Outlanders can react. There will be minutes while the wholers run, before the others give chase. We only need seconds. It is quicker and we have more control over the situation."

"And saves your pet Outlanders."

"Yes, it spares them."

Taj squared to Abel, drawing nose to nose. "And will you collect the beacon if you fail? Even if you fly it in there, your timing is questionable. When your choices are torching an empty settlement or waiting until they drag back your Wholers, you will be right where you started. Or stragglers, Abel! And we have no more bullets. Let me open the cage."

"After we plant the beacon."

"No!"

No middle ground remained between them. The argument would be long, and my voice meant nothing to Taj. When Pope tugged my shoulder, I turned with him, and we retreated to the large tree, facing away from the four men and their fierce whispers.

The part of me that yearned to listen, to finish this quickly and bluntly, was the same part that was ready to die. I would stand with Stump and Abel, and even Kodiak.

Pope and I quietly watched the light change, the blue sky fading to a dull grey before lighting up in red and purple and pink, until the black luminescence of night claimed the embers of the day.

"Do you think I will dance again?" Pope asked.

"Yeah. Sure."

"It has been so long. So long since I felt the soft thrum filling the night, held a woman in my arms and breathed the same air in time with her. Felt the movement of her body as we step, two as one. The band plays. It is a moment, and it is gone. Lost forever, perhaps. But it was there." He took a deep breath. "It has been so long. I wonder if I will ever dance again."

"We'll be home soon. You haven't lost your legs."

"No, I haven't lost my legs." He looked at them, one limp on the ground. "But I have lost so much. Wasted. That was a beautiful sunset."

"It was."

"Ahh, what do you know about beauty, Tinker?" Pope lifted his chin and rested his head on the tree, closing his eyes.

I shrugged. "It speaks?"

"No," Pope said. I could tell from his tone I had not been meant to answer. "True, yet not the truth. You do not capture it. Did you see that sunset?"

I nodded.

"It was unlike anything you could imagine. You could try a thousand times and not create that one. It spoke to you in a language you do not know, and you understood every word. You heard it in your soul. It wound around memories you had forgotten. All of you heard it in an instant, and even now it is too much to remember. It will soon be gone."

Pope breathed deeply while the dim stars emerged. "It is vast. You could stare into it every day and every day fall deeper. You can hold but a piece of it at a time, and once you set it down..." He opened his hand, as if releasing his thought to the wind. "Like a whisper into the dark."

I chuckled. I could not match him word for word, and I didn't care to. Pope was being Pope, and it enraptured me.

"Vast and small. Sometimes it is the fall of a petal or the toss of her hair and, in that moment, everything contracts to a point."

A quickness took his voice, rushing to get everything out. "In that moment, balancing on that point, the world disappears, and you are alone in the expanse. You are left with one, incompressible mote. And the moment is gone."

He blew across his fingertips, then sighed and let his hand fall. It lay there, weak and limp, and Pope stared at it.

"This is beauty, Thirteen."

"I wish I saw it like you do," I said, as the first stars grew bright and new, dim lights emerged to fill the spaces between.

He peered at me then, looking for something, but did not find it. He smiled. "It is perfect. What is perfect cannot be changed. It must not. It is pure from edge to edge, a singular thing tucked away in some corner of creation."

"Perfect beauty," I said.

"It sounds so mundane on your lips," he sighed. "Do you know what I'm talking about?"

"No," I confessed with a crooked smile.

Pope leaned back against our tree again and puffed a breath through his lips as the drone of the discussion behind us wove into the night air. "Are you ever lost in wonder?"

"When I build."

"Tell me."

I told him about the world that unfolded before me when I built and fixed and tinkered, how the real and possible blended into one as new machines formed. I told him about the rushing river, answers tumbling into obstacles only to scatter and reform on a new path, an inexorable push until they found still water below. I told him about soft fingertips as they nurtured a fragile vision into being.

I paused when I feared I would bore him to death. However, he sat straight and watched me with a smile, the starlight reflecting off his eye with a mischievous twinkle.

"You are a strange one, Thirteen. But you do understand."

"Understand what?" I asked.

"Your work is beautiful," Pope said.

"My machines?"

"Maybe. Maybe they are."

His words flickered like the stars above.

"Look," Pope said.

His face was turned to the sky. We had so rarely had as cloudless a night as we did now. I gazed into the soft lights of the night sky. It was a better explanation than any that Pope had offered.

The crickets and beetles had taken over as the birds fell asleep. Their soft hum pulsed the night. Pope began to hum and click with their rhythm, adding his music to their own. When he fell silent, I felt him deflate as he had before, but the music played on. My gaze moved from star to star, trying to find the patterns in light.

"Every woman was made beautiful," he said.

The words, soft, broke over the flow of light and sound that washed the night. "What do you mean?"

"I know," he said, and it sounded like an apology. "It is often gone before the end. It erodes, it is broken, or taken. But every one was made beautiful. They always carry that spark."

I wondered what was driving his wandering thoughts.

"I've always known it. The perfect world has been right in front of me, and I never saw it." He was no longer talking to me, just speaking his thoughts to the night sky. "Everything wasted. What was I thinking? What was I thinking when I took her? She was beautiful."

I waited.

"I broke it. Destroyed her, for nothing. I was the one to shatter the beauty. All the others, cast aside when I grew tired. How could I grow tired? Any one of them could have filled a lifetime. I was chasing…"

He trailed off. "What was I chasing? All those nights, chasing a toxic haze, chasing the next 'yes', chasing tarnished mirrors of the world I wanted. Tearing down God's tapestries. Wilder, quicker, painless. Worthless. And always the stars were just over my head."

"But you see it now."

"What have I done, Thirteen? I've chiseled the beautiful lines off of everything good. What do I do now?"

I rubbed a hand through my hair. I didn't know; this wasn't the sort of thing that you could fix. "Start again?"

"It's not enough."

"No, it's not," I said. All the doors were closed, there was no road out of this jungle. Nothing was enough.

The stars continued to wheel by as minutes slipped into hours. We both sat enraptured by the ever-shifting night as moon-dappled shadows wandered over the ground, and new constellations wheeled into view.

As I drifted into sleep, Pope whispered, "There is something beautiful out there."

Dreams overtook me as Pope kept his watch. The moon waded through the starry expanse, the invisible distance belying its madcap race through the cosmos. Stars, galaxies, and towering nebulae all burned in the dark, throwing back the vacuum with violent brilliance. And all the light in the universe gathered at two singular points, one man's eyes, resting beneath a tree on Earth. Beneath his fingers, the blades of grass strove against the dirt, moving millimeters as the hours ticked by, waiting for the wet dew of the morning. Through the night, through my sleep, I heard Pope's even breathing as he waited.

It had grown cold when his hand clamped down fervently on my wrist. I jumped, startled awake. Pope's eyes were wide, staring at the lightening sky.

"Look!" His voice throbbed and yearned and, wide eyed, I searched but saw nothing. I looked to him, then followed his gaze to the sky, more grey than blue as the few clouds caught the light of the sun rising behind us.

"Do you see it?" He was begging me, his voice rasping. "Do you see it?"

I looked and, for the briefest moment, my heart leapt. Something.

Pope's breath caught and then, more slowly, his hand fell loose. Looking at him in the dim light, I saw the angry red lines of infection spreading above his collar, well past his heart. But his eyes remained open as the dawn gave way to day.

– FORTY ONE –

The unfinished sunrise grew hollow. But it retained a majesty, nonetheless: Pope's epitaph, quickly dissolving into white daylight. I could not stay at the tree, so I retreated among the deeper shadows where the rest still slept. I sat until they woke.

Stump, then Abel and Kodiak rose one by one and asked me morning pleasantries. I nodded at Pope's tree. One by one, they stood over him, returning in determined silence.

"Did you see the infection?" Kodiak asked. We nodded mutely.

"All he needed was a doctor," I said. "Tonight, maybe tomorrow. He could have been fine."

"Chalk up another for Ivan," Stump grumbled. My hand went to my pocket, feeling the frame of the broken glasses I still kept.

"No," I said, "Not for Ivan." They looked at me with curiosity. "Pope found what he was searching for."

"What was it?" Stump asked.

I couldn't say. Beauty, regret, absolution, goodness. "An answer."

"I could use one of those," Stump said, an expression on his face I had not seen before.

"Nedder," someone voiced the thought.

All too often it came to that, all of us together, each alone. We didn't dare move Pope to the jungle, and there was nowhere to bury him. We sealed him in his sleeping bag and left him under his tree.

"Wake Taj," Abel said.

But Taj wasn't there. Two backpacks were in his sack, making the lump of a man.

"Thatch!" Abel cursed, as he turned to the menagerie. The Silent was gone. As was the modified beacon.

"Stump! When did he leave?"

"He handed off the watch to me. He must have organized while we slept and then snuck away after. I…I'm sorry."

"Thatch," Abel said again, quieter, colder. "Not your fault. Unless you were sitting on him, you couldn't have known. Not Taj."

He fixed his comm to his ear. The rest of us did likewise. Taj's voice crackled back after a short pause, hushed.

"Where's the beacon, Taj?" Abel asked.

"It is safe. In a tree. Forgive me for being terse."

"What are you doing?" Abel asked.

"I am by the cage."

"We know what he's doing," Kodiak said.

I felt the growing wish that I had listened to the conversation last night.

"This is an unnecessary risk–" Abel began, but Taj cut him off in a fierce whisper.

"I lure the Outlanders, we push the button, and we put this farce of a Forgiveness program behind us. It's that simple."

"It's not that simple."

"It is! Why you would risk my life – or any of your own lives – to save a handful of savages is so far beyond me that I suspect *beyond* is not the right word at all! So please, let me take care of this."

"Come back, Taj," Abel said.

There was only white noise. Taj was a practical man, in ways I found increasingly frightening.

"Taj? Do you hear me?" Abel asked.

"My issue with you," Taj said, "is never my ability to hear you."

"Come back, Taj. We have a plan."

Again there was no response. I looked from face to face, but they were staring at the ground, hands on hips, thoughts fixed on the man away in the jungle.

"Taj?"

"I will not complicate the simple. I will not delay getting Pope home while we untangle a knot none of us tied."

"Pope's dead," Abel said.

There was a short pause. "Forget Pope, then. The rest stands. I still may need some of you, so you may follow after me. But I will not follow you any further."

"Taj, come back."

"I note the objection; your hands are clean. Just be ready when the window opens. Maybe you can catch them on the way out? Maybe a few of your pets will be far enough away? There will be time to blame me later."

"Taj!" Abel pleaded. Kodiak's face was growing more and more frightening.

"Hush," Taj breathed. "I am working."

Stump shook his head and wandered away.

"This is an unnecessary risk," Abel repeated. "You are alone, and this is their ground."

"Risk? I have watched for hours. No one knows I'm here. But I know their patrol system, at least one every half hour. And the last one left fifteen minutes ago. That should be a sufficient but not over-sufficient head start. Yes?"

"We won't trigger the beacon if you do this," Abel said.

"I will."

"Where's the beacon? What if you get caught?"

"I told you, Abel. No one knows I am here. There is no guard."

Abel rubbed the bridge of his nose, eyes closed. "And what about monkeys?"

Taj snorted. "Even now? The scientist? The monkeys are not important, Abel. No one cares about the monkeys."

Abel stiffened. "Wait! Yes? How large? Are they orange?"

"Hush," Taj said. "It is time."

"Wait!" Abel called again.

And then there was screeching, caught faintly in each of our earpieces.

Taj cursed.

"It's an alarm!" Abel cried. "Get out of there!"

"Alright. It was important." Taj spoke through clenched teeth now. "Come on, you spraggers."

"Thatch, more monkey Outlanders," Abel bit out to no one.

Kodiak looked to us, then off into the trees, helpless.

The screeching continued, and now voices. We could see

movement in the camp, streaming toward the cage.

An alarm system? Again, these Outlanders seemed a little more clever.

Kodiak still looked into the trees, now his jaw worked, and his hands opened and clenched.

"Get clear, Taj!" Abel shouted.

We heard faint shouts and crashing branches through our earpieces. Then there was a wretched grunt over the comm, followed by heavy breathing.

"Spraggers, spraggers, spraggers," Taj was repeating under his breath, punctuating something. He might have been swinging fists or firing silent bullets. All I heard were curses and breathing.

"Get clear, damn you!" Abel shouted again.

There was a strangled cry, and then the noises stopped. No one moved. We strained on our earpieces.

"Taj?"

"No, Abel. Damn you."

There was another sharp grunt, and we heard nothing more.

"Taj? Taj! Get clear!" Abel waited for a response. We all waited.

There were faint voices, then rustling.

A new voice crackled over the comm then. It spoke in unfamiliar, rhythmic syllables, droning on in an unbroken chant. It was loud and distorted, as if the speaker was holding the piece against his lips. We stood in our circle, dumbfounded, as the voice continued, rising, falling, barely pausing for breath as it pounded on beat by beat. The deep voice swelled; I was unable to pull myself away or even rip the comm from my ear. The sounds were strange and foreign to me, but I understood them, beckoning toward death, toward darkness. It rolled on, and I heard it repeating, louder and higher than before, even as the discord of other voices joined in the background.

The singular voice faded, and the atonal chant continued. My breath came quickly, and my heart raced. It sped up, and then the many became one voice, the sounds repeating in precise dissonance like one great mouth.

No one moved, the great voice rooting our feet and shutting our lips. Then Stump snatched off his comm, frantic fingers fumbling at his ear as he wrestled with the hook. He threw it to the ground, eyes fixed on it. The spell broken, I quickly pulled mine off, as well. Kodiak did likewise. Abel slowly reached up and switched off his own with a grim visage.

In the new silence, a quieter rhythm replaced the chant: quick, soft bursts of breath. Stump had raised his hands, still shaking, back to his head, and now he stood, sobbing.

I watched. I did not know what to do. It grew, until Stump crumpled, sitting on the ground, grey head in callused hands, each now laced with a single strand of tears.

Abel knelt before him, hands on his shoulders, forehead resting on Stump's head.

"Old man," he said, speaking only the two words. Stump reached up a wet, wavering hand and found the back of Abel's head. There the two of them remained, while Stump's exhausted strength poured out.

How my heart broke.

"It's too much. It's too much," he repeated, again and again.

"I know," Abel always said.

"I haven't killed since I was a boy. It's death, death every day." His breath grew sharp again. "Did you see what they did to that boy? I can't do it anymore."

"It's alright," Abel said.

"I can't hold it out anymore."

"Then don't."

The tears grew again. Names began to fall between the breaths.

Seth. Evan. Jonathan. Clara. Hanna. Larch. Jacob. Connor. Violet.

The list went on. I did not know who these lost names were. They carried grief, each one.

Patches. Oyster. Crow. Crisp.

I have never known what to do. I sat on the ground behind him and rested my back against his, my long even breaths counterpoint to his spasms. He leaned into me as I looked into the trees, listening to each ragged breath, punctuating each name.

Happy. Duck. Ivan. Pope. Taj.

I felt his hands brush my head as he laced them behind his own. "Oh, Elsie," was the last he managed, before the tears took his words away again.

Kodiak scanned the trees, though his eyes were unfocused. He saw nothing. I closed my own, feeling Stump's ribs press and retreat, as his grief poured out. Abel remained before him.

It was some time before he quieted, the breaths coming with more regularity as they slowed. Stump growled out a last word,

"Enough."

The shell remained on him, but I could feel the warmth through my back, could feel the man underneath.

"Enough," he said again. "I'm too old for this."

Abel's voice comforted. "No one is old enough for this. But you're strong enough."

Stump had leaned forward. Despite the heat of the Outlands, my back felt cold.

"Strong? Strong like a rock, right? That's what they said." He laughed, chopped and bitter. "Dead like a rock. I'm sand, sifted. Running out. There's something wrong with me."

He coughed. Kodiak cleared his throat.

"It's wrong with all of us," Abel said.

I felt Stump raise his head, behind me. "You don't know." He slumped; I caught his weight as he leaned against me again. "Strong, dead. I've run so far. Forgot how to feel. But I still do, I feel everything. I can't…"

"Don't do it alone," Abel said, when Stump didn't continue.

"I don't want to be alone anymore. But I don't know how to do this."

Abel's voice dropped into the ground, like the trees rising around us. "You are on this ground, and you are still standing. Pain, regret, grief… tears. They do not make you weak."

For a time, no one spoke. Stump shifted behind me. Something with fur and four legs took a few hesitant steps toward our supplies before turning and disappearing.

"Adam, they do not make you weak."

423

Stump curled in on himself, growing soft at my back. It was cold again. Over my shoulder, the two of them sat, Abel's sleeve gripped in one of Stump's hands.

"How do you know my name?" Stump said.

"I've been here a long time, old man."

Stump grunted, still gruff but softening at the edges. Only Abel and I were close enough to hear him whisper, "Elsie, I'm so sorry. I miss you so."

There we stayed. None knew the way forward from that moment.

*

When something shifted down in the basin, Kodiak said, "They're up to something."

"Help me up," Stump said, and Abel rose, pulling Stump behind him.

"*Old man...*" Stump muttered as he rose. "*I've* been here a long time."

I remained where I was, still dwelling on his last whisper. There was no response to those words. Whatever scars laced Stump's life, there were no words to salve his loss. A haunted sorrow still flitted at the corner of his eye.

Kodiak lifted the binoculars to his face.

I did not need them. I saw what they were doing, and I didn't want to see it closer.

They dragged Taj's body into an open area and lit a fire.

"Yep. He had the Silent with him. It's right there." Kodiak lowered the binoculars.

"Do you see the beacon?" Abel asked.

Kodiak scanned the crowd again.

"No."

"Well, there's that," Abel said.

We stood in a row and watched as the flames licked up the pile of kindling, insatiable, until they obscured all they devoured. "I supposed they'll be looking for us now," Stump. The featureless certainty had returned to his voice, though wet lines still divided the dirt on his cheeks.

"I suppose so," Abel echoed.

I looked at each man in turn. Three of them, and me. Four of thirteen.

"Abel, is it always like this?" I asked.

Memories flickered across his face before Abel hung his head. He nodded at the ground. "It's always like this."

– FORTY TWO –

We needed the beacon. The beacon was a machine. I was the tinker. It was mine to find.

I obsessed over it, searching for revelation. It would be useless to wander, eyes to the sky, hoping to catch a glimpse of metal. Useless and suicide, now that Taj had ratcheted up the Outlanders' patrols.

The others left me alone. Their silence was restless, and I knew they obsessed with the same thoughts. They waited and looked to me. And I walked in circles, sifting the menagerie part by part, looking to some unknown muse for an answer, for an overlooked tool and salvation from this place.

When I rolled out a corner of the ground cloth and opened my toolkit, the others drew together, shoulder to shoulder, and watched from across the camp. They spoke to each other, not to me.

They quickly rose when I approached, half an hour later.

"Ever heard of the game warmer, colder?" I asked.

They nodded.

"Let's hope Taj left the beacon on. If he did, the comms wired inside will be on; they're part of the new navigation system. These," I gestured at two of our last three comms in my hand, "now spit out static based on how close they are to another signal."

"Will the two interfere with each other?" Stump asked.

"No. Nothing's coming out of these anymore. Both just listen."

Heads nodded. Eyes lit with hope.

"I strung some resistors together, the result should be exponential feedback. So as you get close, the change in volume will be more extreme. Should help."

"Tonight?" Kodiak asked, looking to Abel.

"Find it now," Abel said. "We fly at dusk. I want out of here."

Kodiak nodded, and he and Stump moved to their packs, where the needed gear was already laid out.

"But be smart. Come back if the neighborhood is too busy."

Five minutes later, Kodiak and Stump were gone.

*

The plan settled into its new bed, flowing down the shifting course carved by erosion and dead Unforgiven. Kodiak and Stump would follow my static and recover the beacon. We'd fly it at dusk, when there was light enough to guide it but less to reveal it. In the morning, we'd let the Wholers out and torch the Howlers before they could chase.

And we'd press our blue buttons.

Simple was still revealing all its ugliness. Hope rusted over. Nine already left behind. Four remained, becoming we knew not what. Going we knew not where.

Abel and I waited.

The Outlanders now crawling through the jungle were sparse and moved slowly. It was a big, tangled place. There were no

427

moments of real danger for us on the table, and the other two did not return in retreat.

I began to unpack Pope's gear, adding it to piles that grew as the conviction set in: for better or worse, this was our last camp.

"Keeping busy?" Abel said. It wasn't a question.

"Taking care of things," I said.

"They don't need taking care of."

I stopped and straightened. "What's it to you?"

"I need you grounded."

Pope's spare socks dangled from my hand, dirty and damp. "Abel…"

"I'm sorry," he interrupted, waving a hand. "I'll leave you alone."

But I dropped the socks, letting them roll to the dirt. "No. It's just I don't want to think. I'm so tired of it. I think about them, over and over: Pope. Duck. Happy. Patches." Abel slowly nodded. "I think about her."

"No one comes here without…that." He settled on the vague word. There wasn't a better one. I sank to the grass.

"I shot people. I know, I know," I stopped him before he could interrupt. "I know what they are, and it helps. But not enough." I was smoothing my brow, trying to erase whatever weight had caught Abel's eye. "It's getting easier. Every day it's easier, and it frightens me. I've made friends and buried them without learning their names. Abel, I punched a dead man in the face. I don't understand what's happening to me."

"All paths through this place are twisted," Abel said.

"Twisting."

"I don't know what I am." I pressed, his words dim in my ears like the unending murmur of the jungle bugs. "I thought I was a victim. Now I think I'm a monster. I can't feel out normal anymore, I can't feel out right. What's happening to me?"

Abel shrugged. "You're unravelling."

Unraveling. Unraveled. Like yarn through a maze, but I fled from the exit. Hoping to find something deeper in the dark.

"What happens when we go back?" I asked.

Abel rocked where he sat, then reached for his rifle.

"Two children are still dead. Your mother-in-law is still dead. The rest, too. Your home is still blackened ground. Your wife is still estranged."

Abel began to disassemble the weapon, as I'd seen him do each day. He always cleaned the pieces in the same order.

I looked into the branches, as I had done each day. There was nothing else here. The jungle was all the same. Roots laying the pattern for this maze, tall grass and short brush between. Smooth bark rising from it, catching the dappled light.

"I can't go back," I finally said. "I'm not being forgiven, or fixed out here. Nothing is getting fixed. Home is gone, and I've become something I hate."

Abel separated the barrel from the main body of his weapon, carefully laying it on a cloth. "Or are you just understanding who you've always been?"

I didn't know which was true.

"I stabbed a man with a screwdriver," I said. "He was trying to kill me. I would do it again…"

"I let Duck go," Abel said softly.

"Ivan made his choices. Duck made his."

"And I made mine," Abel finished.

"And I made mine," I said as well, even softer. I was thinking about red flames and black night. Here, the lazy smoke still rose from the settlement. Death rising like the flood until the Earth was free of us.

"Was there ever a right choice? I thought everything had a purpose. System, design, broken or whole, the design was there, and I could figure it out. Make it work. I just had to…"

Had to make it work.

"Can you fit it all together?" Abel had pulled his magazine apart and spread the bullets. He now peered at me, waiting for an answer. Hoping for an answer.

I put my hands over my face and sifted the broken pieces. Duck needed a friend, I needed Happy's glasses, Pope needed Happy, on and on.

"It's all chaos."

Abel closed his eyes and squeezed them for a moment, then returned to his bullets, arranging them in two neat rows.

I heard, in my words, Kodiak's lament. You act, sometimes it goes wrong, and you hope the consequences don't matter. I owed him an apology.

"Chaos and death," I said, "Running off my fingertips every time I reach out. Abel, what am I?"

"We're the men we've always been. It just comes to the surface here."

I picked up my gun from where it lay, close by, looking for the catches and clips. I had never cleaned it. It was just another machine. It was something I could understand. "Yeah. This is me."

It felt right. Right enough.

Abel now stared into the trees, lost in thoughts of his own. Looking back, looking forward, I could not tell.

"So what do we do, men like us?" I asked.

"We keep pushing," Abel said.

"Pushing what?" I asked. "I pushed. I gave my best and thought things would turn out right." They didn't; they hadn't.

I'd pulled my gun to three pieces. I set them down. "Pushing what," I muttered again.

When Abel moved, it was to grab a single bullet. He slid it into the magazine where it clicked into place. He grabbed another. "Who are you?"

He selected another bullet, fourth from the top of his row, and slid it above the first. He waited.

"I'm Thirteen."

"That isn't even your name."

"No, it isn't."

"What are you, Thirteen?"

The barrel of my gun was back in my hand. I was studying the threads where it screwed into the next piece. "I'm a janitor," I said.

"You're a tinker," Abel said. "What else?"

"I don't know, I fix things. I build things. I…" *What else?* "Everyone here seems to want to tell me their story. I don't know why."

"It's because they can feel you sifting the pieces, trying to put them together. You're a fighter, and you fight for them. You try to heal them."

"I've never been called a healer," I said.

"Fixer, healer. But you're a stubborn thatcher, too." The words didn't hurt, not the way Abel said them. "Why did your wife fall in love with you?"

"I don't know," I said. "Everything and nothing. Isn't that how it always is? We would talk through the night. We liked who we were around each other. At least, we used to. I… I wanted to be there for everything that happened to her and happened near her. I wanted to see who she would become. Maybe she felt the same."

"And everything you are, everything you're becoming —what's it for?"

"That's what you asked Kodiak."

"He asked me," Abel said.

"Yeah, he asked me, too."

"So, what did you tell him?" Abel asked.

I had told him to do good. We'd failed. He'd been right.

"I don't know. Maybe just what you say. For building. Fixing. Maybe I'm for healing."

Abel clicked the last bullet into his magazine. He nodded. "So keep pushing."

"Pushing what?" I bit out the words this time. I would have yelled them if our survival wasn't balanced on fragile silence. "I pushed. It wasn't enough! I pushed until there was nothing left of me. I pushed every day, and you know what came of it!"

"Yes. You built a self-righteous mountain and tried to plant your stone on top. Stubborn thatcher."

This time, I seethed. But my temper was chained, like the Earth pulling the sea back to its bed. Two children dead. Mother-in-law dead. The rest, too. Home, bare ground. Wife estranged. And my fingerprints on Patches, Happy, Duck, Pope…

No argument left to me could whisper away the broken glass behind.

So there we sat, stubborn men on the grass, like two black stones in our jackets. I thought again of Kodiak, walking through the trees alone, thinking blunt thoughts until he came back a changed man. I thought of Happy, face-first in the soil, seeing who he wanted to become. I thought of my father.

"Damn it, Abel. What's it for?"

Abel squinted into the wind, and as he did, he smiled. It was the first smile I'd seen in days. "It's not for you."

The picture shifted. And I saw Abel again, for the first time.

A good man.

I was not.

*

Abel assembled the rest of his rifle in silence. I had not cleaned mine, but I began fitting the pieces together to mirror his.

"I suppose it doesn't matter what it's for. Who it's for." I finally said. Dead in the Outlands. It swallowed all else. "There's so little left."

"So little? Is Kodiak more man than Duck because he's

strong?" Abel asked quietly. "Happy than Oyster because he's smart? Taj than Crisp because he could kill?"

"No…" I said.

"Every man is given strength. Arm, head, heart… ideas, passion, friends, scars. It takes a thousand shapes, but it's there.

"So lay it down. Take the gifts, take your pride, your dignity, your self. Lay it down."

The words brought me back where I had started, back even further to when Abel had tried to tell me it was all futile, and I had refused. Seeking some glorious purpose, some noble answer.

He wiped his blackened fingers on an already dirty cloth. "So little. It's not what strength you are given, or in what measure. It's only what you do with it."

"What if it's not enough?" I asked.

Abel shrugged. "One day, you'll die. But before that day, maybe you find you are stronger than you knew."

None of this was easy. I began to overlay this thought with my life, with all I had done. The pictures overlapped poorly, and my memories looked frail through the lens.

"What if I fail?" The words escaped.

"You will," Abel said simply.

I rubbed my soiled fingers on the grass.

"It's not enough."

"It's not enough," he echoed.

The sun came slanting across our table, casting tree shadows across us. Before us the settlement still lay, small huts standing over long shadows. Smoke and blood.

"Then we just push until we die, Unforgiven?"

Abel's head moved, a small shake, but then held still. He looked at me sideways and chose his words. "You don't think you can be forgiven." His smile now mixed with a sadness. The same compassion I'd seen on the woman I'd bereaved. I slowly shook my head.

"We aren't meant to die unforgiven," he said.

"Nothing's enough," I repeated.

"It doesn't' need *enough*; it doesn't need you at all, Tinker. This is something you can't fix. That doesn't mean it can't be."

"Who can?" I asked.

"Who will?" he answered.

Who will. Who can.

It's all chaos. The thought answered. And I felt myself whipped away by the maelstrom, one of the ants running through our gunfight. Kicked into the air or crushed under a thick callused foot.

"I can't do this."

"Have hope," he said gently.

I nodded and stood, picking up Pope's socks again and carrying them to the growing pile of unneeded gear.

*

Kodiak and Stump returned unexpectedly. I'd kept my comm off, to minimize interference, and Abel had received few updates.

White teeth showed through dirty beards with an excitement and triumph I could not feel.

"Thirteen, you're a genius," Kodiak said, thumping my back and leaving a bruise. "Anyone ever tell you that?"

"Not recently," I said.

Stump carefully laid his backpack on the ground, then pulled out the Beacon, laying it in its place among the menagerie. We said little more about the matter.

– FORTY THREE –

Shadows lengthened as hours passed, until the air began to cool. Dusk was a welcome sight for the restless and anxious. The thought was never spoken, but all knew if this didn't work, we'd have to sacrifice the Wholers. If we could complete the mission at all.

Kodiak was the spotter. We sent him into the jungle with a pair of knives. It wasn't the time for shooting, and the silent was gone. While he stalked, I showed the other two how to use my device.

I took the three comms I'd set aside in a row, all facing the same direction. "I wired the comms into the controls.

"Left," I handed one to Stump.

"Right," I handed another to Abel.

"And forward," I hooked the last one on my ear.

"So how does this work?" Stump asked, eyeing the comm in his hand.

"When you talk, the signal becomes current–"

"No," Stump interrupted. "How does it work?"

"Well," I fumbled. "I connected the receiver so that, when it receives that current, the stabilizing gyro will tilt–"

"No! What do I do?" Stump asked, the edge of a smile on his face. He was laughing at me.

437

"Oh," I said. "You speak into the comm. Or sing, hum, whatever. And the unit will turn left."

"Clever," Abel said. He looked at me levelly.

I looked away. I was the tinker. Maybe this would work, maybe some Wholers would live. Maybe this was pushing.

"It's just electronics and physics," I said, grabbing the tether I'd tied to the main unit and powering on the beacon.

"I'll be the motor," I said, and then hummed into my comm. It was a long, low note punctuated with quick breaths. The rotor spun to life.

The unit lifted into the air. I'd rigged off-center, so the rotor pulling up and the Earth pulling down torqued it forward, and it began to float toward the settlement.

I pointed to Stump, and he tentatively hummed into his comm. The beacon rotated left, stopping a heartbeat after he did.

"Come back," Abel said, and the beacon twitched to the right at his voice.

I lowered the volume of my hum and reeled the tether back in.

"Alright. Let's do it," Stump said.

We practiced, trying to land on rocks or bare spots of dirt, while Kodiak found his position. Abel and Stump took to it immediately. I had a harder time; there was no way to hover or reverse so I had to judge the distance and drop it down in one smooth line. That's what Kodiak was for, to triangulate and let me know when to drop.

If we missed, we could circle around again. Possibly.

However, the roof we were targeting was enormous, at least a hundred square meters, and there was no fear of the beacon running out of power. The danger was rather being spotted, or one of us passing out from prolonged singing. Even so, I shut it down once we'd practiced. No sense pushing the boundary of the Cloak's old source. We suited up, comms to Kodiak in one ear and the control comms in the other.

"Let us know when you're in position, Kody. Daylight is fading," Abel urged.

"Need another minute or two. They're still poking around out here, looking for more of Taj. Believe me, I don't want to wander back through this place in the dark."

"Full moon," Abel reminded him. "That's why we're doing this in the first place."

"Spragging moon!" Kodiak lamented.

It was fine. He could want it both ways.

"Alright," Kodiak spoke again a few minutes later.

"Clear view from the edge of the trees to our target?" I asked.

"It is."

"Alright. I want you to give me numbers. One hundred percent is the tree line. Zero is the building. Tell me when I cross the hundred line, then read me every ten from fifty down to zero, got it?"

"Got it," Kodiak said.

"If you're unable to speak safely," Stump added, "Tap it out on the comm. Five, four, three, two, one, and one last one for zero. We only have one shot at this."

"Yeah," Kodiak said.

I reached down to power on the flying beacon. My heart began

439

to race.

Abel gripped my shoulder. "Is the second button uncovered?"

"It isn't."

I pulled the new screwdriver from its place on my arm, quickly spinning the screw out and opening the compartment.

"Thirty minutes before the satellite is on us?"

"So they say. Maybe sooner," Abel said. "We do what we have to. Is the beacon on?"

"Yes, it's on. I disconnected all the lights."

Abel looked at the unit for a long second. I knew every wire of that thing, where it had started and where I had put it. Everything connected. It was on, just silent and dark. It was on. "Alright," Abel said.

He and Stump stepped into position to my left and right.

I began to hum.

*

I hadn't anticipated the biggest danger to the entire enterprise. Most of the flight was me humming. Abel and Stump had little to say, only course corrections. The result was them watching me, moaning like a fevered idiot, for minute after minute.

Abel tried not to. But he chuckled, and the beacon veered right. Stump grunted disapproval, pulling it back into line, but then laughed himself.

Abel pulled it back.

The two of them continued to reprimand each other, both silently and aloud, as the beacon twitched left and right. I tried to tell them to shut it up, between hums and breaths, and ended up laughing. The beacon jiggled up and down, the rotor speed fluctuating along with me. Kodiak cursed.

"Is something wrong?" he demanded.

Able and Stump were bound to silence. "Nooooooooo," I sang out at a steady pitch, as Abel and Stump covered their comms to keep their choked laughter off the channel.

"Hundred," Kodiak said. "You all need to lock it down."

We did our best.

I was running out of breath maintaining the beacon's flight. I'd kept the center of balance close to vertical so it would fly slow, and it took nearly five minutes to cross the few hundred meters from us to the building. Kodiak whispered the rest of the distance markers to us.

By the time Kodiak's relieved voice whispered "touch down", daylight was nearly gone. It was all Stump and Abel could do to switch off their comms before they collapsed into the choking laughter that comes from holding it back too long.

It spilled from me too, like water, like light. The shadows recoiled at the betrayal – of the Wholers in their cage, of the dead Unforgiven, of those behind in the State, of the fire saved for tomorrow. Yet it came.

Tears ran down my cheeks. The three of us were bound together in that moment, strung between grief and mirth, death and peace, in a sacred moment between tragedies. Light that could be covered but not quenched burst forth and the shadows fled. We choked and laughed, begging each other to be quiet, and still the tears came.

When at last I could breathe again, I lifted myself from the ground and looked up in the last light. The beacon still rested on the big hut, two-thirds of the way to the roof's peak.

Simple.

*

It was another hour before Kodiak reappeared. As he climbed up to the shelf, he shook his head and broke into a wide grin. He'd been listening to us the entire time, first moaning like a dirge choir and then laughing like children.

"You all are amateurs; you know that?"

I nodded enthusiastically. "Glad you're back."

The four of us sat in a moonlit circle that night; we feasted on protein cubes floating in rehydrated sauce and toasted with water. Our thoughts and words passed from the mundane to the serious and back again, weaving trails through our pasts and futures, though we rarely lit on the present. My thoughts did flick periodically to the trigger. We could set it off right now and end all this... but we had decided.

When we each drifted off to sleep, the dreams took me again. I found myself in the kitchen, surrounded by the old house and roaring flames. My eyes, however, were caught by the other set of eyes looking back at me. There was no blame or anger in them, only fear. And sadness.

I grabbed the hand that was held out to me and held it tight, running. But when I got outside, my hand was empty; there were only flames and the sound of broken timber falling to the ground.

– FORTY FOUR –

Morning dawned bright and clear. It would be a dry day. We moved around the camp with the restless activity that preceded battle. But there would be no battle today. We had only six magazines of ammunition and four men to fire it. Even with perfect aim that wouldn't account for one in five of the Outlanders.

"You realize this would be easy with the Silent and a pair of Eyes or Ears?" Stump did not look up from the rifles he was checking and re-checking.

"It's no concern. I'll go." Kodiak replied.

"Alone?" Stump asked, looking up.

"I can find my way. It only takes one to open the door." Kodiak looked intently at Stump, his feet planted on the ground.

"No," Stump sighed after a moment's hesitation. "No, two pairs of eyes. Two pairs of hands. We'll do this last thing together."

Kodiak peered at Stump, reluctant. But he saw the sense in it. He nodded.

"You all remember what to do?" Abel interjected.

"I remember," Kodiak said, waving Abel away with a hand.

"You'll watch for the monkeys," said Abel, dropping his voice. "The orange ones."

Kodiak lifted a bag. "One can of food for every three monkeys. Enough to feed them, but little enough that they will fight among themselves. I know what to do."

"The Outlanders arrived quickly," Abel pressed. "Taj missed something."

"We have two pairs of eyes," Kodiak said with a laugh. "Just let me do this and come back."

"There's no rush. We can wait all day," I said. "We're hidden up here. We can do it tomorrow or the next day. Understand?"

"Of course," said Kodiak more somberly.

"Just don't rush anything."

Kodiak reached out his big hand and shoved my head playfully. He wore a crooked grin, but when our eyes met, there was something more serious there. I remembered the last things I said to him the last time we had spoken, really spoken.

You are a murderer.

We aren't meant to die Unforgiven.

We said no more now. A handshake, a grip on the shoulder, and a nod of the head. Abel said "God speed" and Stump and Kodiak disappeared over the edge, four rifles, four knives, five magazines, and one pair of binoculars to their names.

We waited. I fingered the beacon's trigger unit in my hand, the piece that would call down desolation from the heavens. Abel watched through the binoculars.

"It's quiet down there," Abel mumbled. "Going to be hot today. Maybe they'll lie low."

"I doubt it," I answered. They didn't seem put off by pain or discomfort.

Abel handed me the binoculars, but I didn't want them. There was nothing to see. "No, you're right," said Abel. "Maybe. It's just quiet."

"Do you think they're gone? Out hunting again?"

Abel didn't answer. "Kodiak, Stump," he spoke into the comm. "We're worried the settlement may have emptied out. Don't do anything until we've confirmed targets."

"I hear you," Stump's voice came back. "You keep watching. We'll keep moving."

"Maybe we should wait?" I asked Abel. "They might be all stirred up after yesterday. Extra vigilant."

"Might be," Abel mumbled, scanning with the binoculars again. "Might not be. I don't want to leave those people in the cage or leave that beacon on the roof any longer than we have to."

I turned the trigger in my hand, sliding the unit back and forth across my palm. I didn't want to wait either.

In another twenty minutes, the comm crackled in my ear again. "We're here. About fifty meters from the cage. No trouble, no monkeys."

"Statc's balls," Abel cursed. "The good news is there's nothing going on. No alarm. The bad news is there's nothing going on. If they're all in their little huts, now is perfect. If not... I don't know what to tell you."

"There is no rush," Kodiak's voice came over calmly.

"No, no rush."

"Want to fire off a round?" Kodiak suggested. "See if the

445

hornets come swarming?"

"It'd take all day to get them back in the hive," Abel said. "What I wouldn't give for those Ears."

"And the Silent," Stump added again.

"Well, I'm counting while we wait," Abel concluded. "Onesies, twosies, moving in and out. Mostly women."

"Monkeys," Stump said, after some time had passed.

"Thatch," Abel said.

"Thirteen of them," Kodiak said.

"So, four cans," Stump concluded. "I'll get them ready, just let us know, Abel."

And we waited.

We didn't have to wait much longer. Abel announced, with relief, "There they are."

"Yeah, something's going on," Stump said, anxious. "What is it?"

"Sit tight. There's a whole mess of them coming out of the big building. One, two hundred maybe. Nedder, they were right under the beacon."

"Any coming this way?" Kodiak's patient voice overrode them.

"No, but they're lingering. Now there's a fight," Abel added.

"Is it a good distraction? Do it now?" Stump asked.

"Sit tight. It's all too close to you. It'll clear out. Drown it, that's a big fight."

"We can hear it," said Stump. To me it was just a mass of bodies quietly roiling in the distance.

"Is it too much to hope that we'll get credit for their hard work?" Abel asked.

"Don't worry," said Kodiak. "There will be enough."

It felt like half an hour until it finally quieted down. We kept our chatter to a minimum, not wanting to tempt the two below to speak idly. Eventually the Outlanders lost interest or became incapacitated. As the fight broke up, there weren't as many bodies on the ground as I expected.

The attention in the settlement coalesced again, this time at a new pyre being constructed in the same place as the day before. A few individuals dragged still bodies from the meeting hall. Stump and Kodiak saw it as well, all four of us beginning to mutter observations to each other. The crowd moved away from the cage. We all felt it; this was the window we'd been watching for. I began to fidget.

Abel made the call. "Stump, Kody; open the cans. They're gathered over in town center. Loud, distracted. Unless you see something or someone I don't, this is it."

"No patrols," Stump responded.

"Get the door open and run. We'll make sure they don't follow. Run as far as you need, we'll be here when you get back."

"You don't need to keep explaining," Kodiak said. "We will run."

"I just worry," Abel said quietly enough that only I could hear. I worried too.

The monkeys began to chatter, but not like the screeches of the day before. The sounds faded in my ear. I could almost see the two men slinking through the shadows beneath the trees. Kodiak, the mysteriously silent mass moving from tree to tree. Death on two feet, coming to whoever was unlucky enough to find him. And Stump who, despite his confessions of the day before, remained the fixed point. No force on Earth could stop the inexorable plod of his feet, one after the other. These were the two men who were descending on the Outlanders, who would unbar the door. Yet I knew, even as I watched Abel fidget with the binoculars, that I was doing the same with the trigger.

"Come on, guys," I said to myself. The Outlanders remained fixated on the flames, and now I could hear the quiet roar of hundreds of voices.

All of those voices, though, and the thousand voices of the jungle, were as nothing, as thin as paper, when a sharp breath whispered into our ears.

"Nedder!" Kodiak swore.

"Kody! You all right?" Abel and I spoke over each other.

"They've got some kind of lock here, metal. Don't know where the rustics found it. I can't break it."

"Nedder," Abel said. "What can you do?"

"Give me your knife. Give me a minute."

There was grunting and the sound of wood rubbing wood, and clanking metal.

"There's a child," Stump's voice came.

The noises stopped.

"What's he doing?" Kodiak asked.

"He's watching," Stump said.

We whipped our binoculars to our eyes. Stump and Kodiak

were obscured, behind one of the nearer roofs. There in the space between two buildings we saw a child. Short, naked, motionless, facing the cage.

"Kill him," Abel whispered, though there was no need for silence.

"I can see that," Kodiak said to Stump. "What's he doing?"

"He's just staring," Stump said again.

"Kill him!" Abel said, louder.

"Watch him. I'm getting this door open." The sounds resumed.

"It's a child, Abel," said Stump.

"In five minutes he's gone with the settlement. He's already dead, Stump. Save the others."

"I can't!"

I watched. The child still did not move. He didn't do anything.

"It's him or you!" Abel shouted back.

"Get out of here! Stop staring! Go on!"

"Kill him, Stump!"

The child tilted forward, rushing, and disappeared behind the roof.

There was a sickening grunt.

"Stump! Kody!"

"Oh, cranking…" Kodiak said. Stump's breathing came loud and labored in our ears. There were broken sounds of brutality. Then a strangled howl, over the comm. It was more like a squeal. We couldn't hear it with our unaided ears at the shelf. Hopefully they didn't hear it at the pyre, either.

"Kody, what happened?"

"Everyone, shut up."

Stump did not speak to fill the unexplained silence.

I stared at the roofs through the binoculars. Abel turned to the bonfire.

Then came Kodiak's voice, exhortations to move and a milieu of urgent whispers, voices we didn't know and words we barely recognized.

"He's in," Abel said.

"Where's Stump?" I asked.

As if in response, Stump rasped, "Go, Kody, go."

I felt, more than saw, Abel shake his head beside me. He now frantically scanned with the binoculars.

Stump. I was still hearing that first sharp grunt. We were almost home.

"Kody, it's going to get busy in a few moments. There's a handful headed your way and more will follow."

"Come on!" Kodiak's voice shouted. "Move!"

"Can't move," Stump rasped, but Kodiak was talking to the Wholers in the cage.

"I can't, Kodiak. I can't." Stump sounded delirious.

"I'll get Stump out." Kodiak's voice remained calm.

He would do it, and it would be done.

"What happened?" I asked. It wasn't the time, but I couldn't stand it.

"Kid's dead. I killed him. Little runt rushed Stump, and Stump just stood there... took it in the gut. Just stood there and watched."

"Get out of there, Kodiak," Abel said. "It's too late. Get

Stump."

"Not yet," said Kodiak, as his words were replaced with a murmur of confused voices and exclamations, paired with a stream of quiet but direct commands. Kodiak was still inside, pushing them out.

"Come on, come on, come on," Abel was muttering to himself. I now watched the edge of the crowd around the pyre peeling off toward the cage, five became a dozen became a hundred.

"Hang on, Stump," I urged. "Kodiak's coming back for you."

"Elsie!" Stump wailed. "I couldn't do it. It's my fault! I'm sorry. Stupid, stupid, I'm sorry." His voice turned plaintive again. "Come back. You said you'd come back if I would only ask. Please! Come back!"

"Hang on, Stump," I said. "Kodiak?"

"I'm coming, I'm coming!" Kodiak said, now shouting as if his voice could carry the distance to us. "Nedder, there's a lot of them. I'm clear! I'm coming!"

"You aren't clear!" Abel yelled into the comm, fear and frustration breaking down into anger. "You need at least two hundred meters, thatcher. Get Stump and get clear now!"

"I'm going, I'm going," Kodiak murmured as his breathing grew labored.

I watched from our viewpoint above. Kodiak was at the cage, Outlanders were already close and running. I did the math, my mind pulling all the bodies forward in time. There was no "clear" anymore. By the time Kodiak was clear, they would be as well. And nearly every Outlander was streaming from the fire toward Kodiak and Stump.

"The Wholers aren't going to make it," Kodiak puffed, reaching the same conclusion.

"No. Abort, Kodiak. Just get Stump and get out of there."

"Come on! Run! Run!" Kodiak wasn't listening to us.

"Kodiak!" I shouted. "Get Stump!"

"I've got Stump!" Kodiak shouted back, annoyed.

"Leave them, then!"

"No!"

I worked my jaw in silence, listening.

Stump carried on, a broken stream of confession and lament. He couldn't hear us any longer.

"I've got him." Kodiak's breathing was growing faster.

The settlement was almost empty. Abel spoke again, now in a calm but commanding voice. "Kodiak, they're leaving. They've left the settlement. We tried, but it didn't work. Get clear. Bring Stump."

Kodiak took a long, labored breath. He'd stopped running.

"Do you understand, Kody?"

"No!" said Kodiak.

"We tried. We did what we could. They are going to catch the Wholers and take them back."

"No."

"Kodiak, what are you doing? Come and regroup."

There was silence.

"Stump," Kodiak said gently, "You're bleeding. I can't stop it. It will come quickly. And quietly. Don't fight it. I'm sorry, old man."

Stump's lament trailed off. "Go," he said.

"Come back," Abel said.

"No. I'm going to take care of this."

"Kodiak!" Abel shouted.

"You told me, Abel," Kodiak's voice was like a slow river. "This is what it's for."

Then the jungle in the distance erupted with gunfire. A low growl rose to a roar in our comms.

"You stupid thatcher!" Abel shouted, wiping sudden tears off his cheeks.

Bullets chattered across the morning. There would be one hundred, and then silence. But still the man roared. I had seen him; I had seen the earth plowed up by the edge of his foot as he braced against the very ground. I had felt the weight of his hands, like mallets, as he patted me on trembling shoulders. His rumbling laugh shook the air; his roar broke it to pieces. I knew even now the jungle groaned at his approach, no more able to stand against his onslaught than the dappling shafts of light barring his way. I knew that the dust, disturbed by his earlier steps, now broke before him as he ran in its face, swirling and eddying in the morning air, the twisting testament to his passage. And, just so, I knew the Outlanders broke before him. I could see it all, though it was masked by distance and trees, and I heard the gunshots heralding his approach, one by one. Over the gunshots, I heard his roar.

Before us, at the edge of the settlement, the surge of Outlanders collapsed into a mass, their momentum arrested. Even as they milled uneasily, slivers of motion began pushing through, away from the trees, fighting through the ball of confused bodies. The slivers eroded the stationary walls, and the Outlanders began streaming away from the jungle like schooling fish.

"Come back, get clear," Abel said hoarsely, but it was futile. There was no turning back. The guns fell silent, and then we saw him. He streaked from the trees into the settlement, black in his uniform like the angel of death, long knives flashing. Those too slow or too brave to flee fell at his passing with barely a touch. And still he roared, the unending challenge bellowing from his lungs, inciting the Outlanders to terror.

His was the heart of a mountain. The heart of a warrior. Yet it was only one heart, and their broken hearts were many. "It's done, Kodiak, turn back!" Abel was shouting now, but how could he hear? The very air shook around him. As we watched, the wings of the Outlanders slowed and turned. Death strode among them, but he was alone. Their jaws began to close.

Kodiak rushed on, and where he met them, bodies flew, cast into the air like chaff to the wind. They descended on him, pressing him in beside a building, and I thought it was the end. The hut shook and broke instead, the big man bursting free through the opposite wall as the roof collapsed. And still he roared.

"What can we do?" I asked. Abel shook his head.

"Push the button." It was Kodiak.

"Kody!" Abel shouted immediately. "Get out of there!"

"I can't."

As we watched, another group of Outlanders broke and fled, Kodiak giving chase.

"It was enough." Abel said. There was nothing else to say. We watched as two masses of Outlanders charged. Kodiak stopped running. Rifles gone, knives gone, head high, feet planted. "It is well," Kodiak said, and I heard a broad smile behind his voice.

The bravest of them died first, meeting Kodiak where he stood. The cowards behind them piled on until he disappeared, pressed down under the mass of bodies. I turned away as the big man went down.

It wasn't right. It's just what happened.

Abel and I stood in silence for the denouement. The pile grew, then shrunk, until a small mound was left and nothing moved. Those who had survived backed away. You could no longer see Kodiak, but the silence and stillness of the settlement marked his resting place with resentful reverence. Even now, much of the settlement was milling in fear against the trees opposite the huts; in fear of the man they had already killed.

The silence was thick, as if no voice were permitted to speak his name again. Abel held the binoculars limply against his side. His voice was hoarse. "Push the button."

– FORTY FIVE –

I held it before me. There was nothing else to do. Vengeance, penance, justice, whatever it was, it was time to light up the jungle. Squinting my eyes against whatever might come, I pushed the button, hard, and held it.

A second went by, then another. When it stretched to five, with my voice shaking, I asked, "How long does it take?"

Abel snatched the trigger from my hand. "Seconds." He also held the button down and swore. "No, no, no," he began to mutter.

"Give me that," I ordered as I snatched it back. "I knew he was rooting around the gear! I knew he wanted us all dead! I knew – I should have known…" I threw the now useless trigger against the ground.

"They gave us a toaster!" Abel said, not hearing me.

"Ivan!" I spat the name. Even in death, he would reach out to kill us.

"Ivan what?" Abel asked sharply.

"Kodiak, Stump, Pope, everything. All for nothing. Everything for nothing because of that cranking son of a thatcher!"

"Ivan?" Abel voiced. "Wait. The trigger or the beacon? Is the beacon working?"

"His little spragging vendetta, and he's going to pull us all down from the grave, for nothing!"

"Thirteen!" Abel grabbed the collar of my jacket and yanked me off my feet.

My eyes snapped up from my tirade.

"Does the beacon still work?"

I looked past him, searching the tree branches. I had done the work. I had done the work after Taj killed Ivan. I had never opened the trigger, but I knew every millimeter of the beacon. If it ever worked, it still worked.

"Yes."

Before I could speak again, he asked, "And you left the button open?"

Words dried in my mouth.

"Don't," I said.

"You aren't sure?" asked Abel.

"No, I'm sure," I stammered. "The beacon is fine, but… no!"

"The Wholers are free, and the Howlers are confused. The door is open." He grabbed the last rifle.

"Give me time!" I cried out, scrambling to my feet. "I can fix it! Give me a little time!" I cast about for my tools, why weren't they here with me? It would only take a moment.

"This is the time," said Abel, grasping my shoulder.

"We can't!" I protested.

"I can," Abel said.

"I…" I stammered again. "I can't."

"Go back, Thirteen," he spoke inexorably. "Push."

"You don't need to do this."

His hands flashed out and grabbed me by the collar again, pulling me close. I could see the morning light shining through his irises and feel the warmth of his breath. I smelled the long days of jungle on his skin.

"Listen, understand, Thirteen. It's freely given."

We remained there for a moment. "What is?"

He held my eyes, breathed out. Then he was gone. He leapt from the table and disappeared into the jungle.

I fumbled for the sniper rifle. When I held it to my eye, I could not see through silent tears. Cursing, I wiped the water free and held the weapon up to my shoulder again.

"I won't let them get you," I promised to myself.

"They won't," Abel said, still listening through the comm.

The Outlanders still milled; such was the terror of Kodiak's passing. In a minute, I caught sight of Abel through the thinning trees and, ahead of him, a lone Outlander. I squeezed the trigger and watched the bullet pass clean through his neck, the man falling impotently to the ground. Abel ran on.

Another stepped into his way, and I sighted and fired again. Too quickly this time. And this time the wood of a hut exploded into splinters beyond Abel's head. He stumbled. I hurled the rifle into the bushes and grabbed the binoculars, ashamed. Abel ran on.

Few saw his coming. Startled, they fell to Abel's hands as he shot through their midst, the arrow to Kodiak's boulder. The hands of a scientist debased to ripping out the rot in this jungle. The hands of a son, a husband, and a father emptied of all they had held in life and given death in exchange. They were the hands of a good man.

He drew ever closer to the beacon. The rifle was cast aside and the silver of knives flashed in his hands. Those ahead were cut down, those behind ran to pull him down. Wild arrows and clumsy spears leapt out, thrown from running feet. They did not understand this man who did not fight. Most slowed and stopped, content for him to return to the jungle from whence he came. And Abel ran on.

Then he was at the great building. His labored breathing was the only answer to my stream of exhortations. With a mighty leap he grabbed low hanging branches that protruded from the roof. He pulled himself up. I shouted in dismay even as the Outlanders drew near and fired again, this time an arrow appearing in his leg, then another in his side. He did not stop.

I willed him upward, onward as he climbed the roof with agonized leaps and lunges, drawing ever nearer to the silver beacon we had planted.

Too late, too late, I recalled the object of his mad dash; his victory would end in flames. "Abel!" I yelled, my hands knotted into my hair. With a final lunge, his hand stretched out and found the beacon where it rested.

The world hung in the balance for a breath. All went silent as I felt the jungle around me exhale softly.

Then white fire flashed down from heaven, and the very Earth was ripped open.

– FORTY SIX –

There was grass in my mouth. "Abel!" I called. I choked on dirt.

"Abel!" I called again. "Stump! Kody!"

Nothing.

"Abel?"

I heard nothing. No static, no white noise. I could feel the weight of a comm on my ear. I tried to take hold of it. I couldn't move my arm.

There was still grass in my mouth. I spat, and spat again, uselessly. I tried my arm again, growing frantic. Something held it.

With a great heave I pulled and the world spun.

I spun?

Light flooded my eyes. My hand came free. Shapes came into focus, tree branches.

"Stump?"

I spat, and the grass now fell away. I fumbled at my ear again and found it bare, the ghost of a comm only a nervous illusion.

My skin felt burnt. My heart raced and my breath came in loud rags through my throat. I fumbled at stray thoughts, trying to find and piece together a blueprint of the present.

I was on the ground.

I was alone.

Gingerly, I rolled again and pressed myself up to all fours. The world still spun, but I braced and waited until it passed. I rose to my knees and looked.

The jungle was changed.

Black and grey, luminous red and orange where fires danced. There was a great bowl. At the edges, the trunks of splintered trees stood at disparate heights, like the bones of fingers worn of flesh. Those quickly grew shorter, and sparser, until they disappeared in a broad lake of ash.

Dispirited flames burned slowly. Distant patches of green held back the smoldering wall, though a great cloud of smoke rose inside the cauldron, tendrils weaving together to block out the blue of sky and even the sun.

Thoughts fell, clumsy, as if guided by numb fingers. There had been buildings, roads, kitchens, and people down there. There had been Stump, Kodiak, Taj, and Abel.

Ivan.

My thoughts turned black, black as the center of the deadland before me. I howled, though the sound held little of the terror of an Outlander. It was pitiful, as was my fist driven into the ground, as was my tumble onto my face as I lost my balance. It was all the rage I had left.

Even if Stump had silenced the child, even if he and Kodiak and the Wholers had gotten away without alarm...

Ivan had reached beyond his grasp, then beyond all reason. Now he had reached beyond the grave to pull us down.

He'd hooked Abel. I'd slipped away. Now I remained, left to pull the curtain back from his sin and arbitrate his fate.

I was the Arbiter now.

I rose to my hands and knees again and crawled, the world spinning more slowly now, to my toolbox. It was rolled onto its side. I clutched it to my chest and tottered across the grass until I found the trigger resting against the earth.

I collapsed and breathed until the world stilled beneath me.

I was the Arbiter now. Ivan must be judged.

My fingers felt thick, and trembled, as I twirled each screw. The bar cracked open, two halves of a shell. I gently lifted a metal plate, searching for the cut wires and scraped electronics that would uphold my case and condemn him this final time.

But icy hands closed on my throat. The trigger was untouched. And there, nestled among the perfect, machine-crimped wiring was a grey box. A cube whose twin I had seen before.

A cube I had pried free from the beacon. I, not Ivan.

There I sat, Arbiter, silent and still. Nothing moved. Nothing changed.

I always imagined horror to be a loud and wild place. But no, horror is lonely, stifling. Light is gone, hope is gone, the candle snuffed. The worst has already happened, and all you can do is sit beneath and endure the weight that crushes you.

It was so plain, now. The twin cubes a transmitter and receiver, and only that. So, the casing they were attached to served as a modified antenna. I had separated the cube from the beacon's case. I had not broken the beacon, no. It still had its purpose; it still did that purpose. For maybe three meters.

I had dismantled the antenna.

The finger of the Arbiter turned and again found me. The name Unforgiven again pressed upon my shoulders.

It was me.

A thousand times I saw again the moment when I pulled the grey box free. The muscles in my arm twitched with the memory.

I can't fix this.

Abel was already incinerated. The antenna was already broken and beyond reach. Pope's infection had already passed his heart, Happy's glasses were already broken in my pocket, Duck was already taken by Outlanders, and Patches already lay in the long grass.

What if I fail?

I heard Abel's voice again. *I will.*

Further back, the house was already burnt to the ground, her mother already lost.

Further back, the tears were already on her face. My words already spoken, blood already drawn, the dark scars already latticed across her memory.

Further back. I looked out at the destroyed earth again, and the blackened edges blurred through the smoke until I could believe it stretched on forever. It should have stretched on forever; the trees were a lie, and the grass was a lie. The truth was the death that walked through the jungle; the truth was scorched earth and burnt skin.

"I killed you."

Shattered memories coalesced into their grisly mosaic. The flight, the storm, a knife to the neck. Shots in the night and bodies in the daylight. White eyes, scarred skin, a hanging boy, despair and rage and shame.

"Abel."

I no longer called out to him. I merely spoke his name. It was done.

"Oh, Abel. I should have gone."

Should.

I threw half the transmitter into the trees. I hated that word. Everything was wrong. I held my head between my hands and pushed.

*

I don't know how long I sat like that, trying to press the light from my eyes.

The blue button brooded, inert, in a pocket at my thigh. In a moment of boldness or stupidity, I shouted a challenge and a curse out into the trees, but there was nothing, not even an echo. I listened until I believed the jungle was empty. It was empty, truly. There was no rustle, no chirp, no song. Even the wind had stopped. I was alone.

There was no task left for me to earn my place among the living. No sacrifice left to die redeemed. I felt the proper thing was to lie there until the Outlands took me, the proper capstone. But there was no point to it.

I searched my other pockets, anything to avoid the cylinder and its blue button. I found Happy's glasses at my breast. With two fingers I drew them out, gently. I swung the right earpiece back and forth, back and forth. It was smooth, just the slightest friction to give it substance and keep it in place. I had done good work.

The smoke and cinders blurred and warped through the lenses. The glasses made sense, but they were not for me. As I looked at the great, ashen bowl through them, I saw a tree. A great log, rather, stripped of all branches and green, driven upright into the ground. It alone stood in the middle of the desolation. Everything looked different. It may have been the support of the meeting hall we had targeted.

"If I didn't understand what you were saying then... I do now," I said to the glasses. To Happy. "I killed Abel."

He had never worn them after I fixed them. I looked at the earpieces, worrying at the one I'd mended to move the bend a fraction closer to the lenses, just like it's opposing twin.

"Close enough. I killed you, too. I should have fixed the Eyes when I had the chance. I could have. I never should have needed your glasses. So I never should have lost them. Maybe you'd still be here. Maybe you just would have died somewhere else. I don't know."

The bile rose at the thought of Ivan. But let the dead tend to themselves. There was trouble enough left for me.

"What do we do, Happy? I built a mountain. It couldn't stand; it couldn't stand forever. And now it has come down..." The jungle had resolved, as ever, into a closed door. The doors and Halls behind me were closed as well. The empty corner of a rotting jungle was left to me.

"I wanted to fix it. Fix everything. But it was never about them. It was about me. It was all for me but it's not for me. That's what Abel said.

"So, nothing is fixed. Nothing can be fixed."

Abel said it could.

"What do we do, Happy?"

The great log, standing from the ash, gleamed in the sun between passing clouds of smoke. The certainty grew, that was the hall, that was where Abel was burned from the Earth. He wasn't there, but I wanted to talk to him. It drew me – ever so gently, like a whisper. Nothing held me now to this hill, so I drifted, again and again, back to the log.

"I can't go home, Happy. I have no right. Blue buttons or no, the program is a lie. I can't go home. I'll go out to that tree. Pope found an answer. Maybe there's one for me, too."

*

The dizziness was gone. I rose to my feet and placed the glasses onto a rock, open and facing the sun.

Feeling like a thief, I rooted through the equipment. I took my pack and put what I wanted inside. It was little. I grabbed all the bug juice, thinking of Oyster and his new life. A little food and a water purifier, which I wouldn't need. The toolbox, a knife and the clothes I was wearing.

A final inventory revealed nothing else, nothing that I wanted or needed. But I saw Pope's black bag, nestled back among the trees. I went to him and sat at his feet.

"It's time to go home. Doctors could be here in a couple of

hours."

I turned my head. It felt disrespectful to stare. "I'd like to say 'we did it.' But it's just me now."

Pope held his peace.

"So the plan now would be to push the button, right? The plan is never simple. Even this."

I took time to pick the right words. Pope would have.

"I understand now. She was enough, like you said. More than enough. It was all enough. And I tore it down, like you did.

"What did you see?"

There was ash settling on my hands and sleeve. I brushed it, and it took to the air in a swirling cloud.

"You watched the sky. What did you see?"

Pope said nothing. He was now an inarticulate lump in a sleeping bag, only a pair of foot-bumps sticking up. I looked up through the branches as Pope had the night he sat there. Then there were stars and the soft breath of the jungle air. The crickets chirped, and the predators stalked through the shadows. All I saw was blue, and below it, ash.

Whatever Pope had learned, it wasn't here anymore.

I tried again. "You kept asking us, what right did we have? To come here and kill. None. I saw enough; they deserved what they got. But not from us, not from us. We aren't better than them. I'm not.

"And now I'm supposed to go home. What right do I have? She sent me out here."

A breath of wind passed through, and the smoke clouds

hurried. Faint flowers rode on the wind, and then the breeze stopped.

"I want to know what you saw."

Pope still lay wordless.

I walked through the camp until I found three flowers. Each was purple, one a slightly darker shade, one with a touch of red. I placed them on his forehead, his belly, and between his shins.

"Well, I'm going." The tree drew me still, but now the mapless shadows of the jungle did too. Pope did not ask, and I didn't need to explain. "Goodbye."

Back by the pile of everything I didn't need, I cinched down the straps on my pack and hooked a comm onto my ear. The motions were familiar by now. I touched the screwdriver on my forearm. It was familiar as well. Comforting in its utility. A tap on my thigh verified the blue button was still inside its pocket. And with a last look, I climbed down from the table.

*

I stood at the base of our hidden table. To my right lay the scorched earth and the vanished settlement. The other way lay the jungle; shadowy, silent, intact. I turned left.

There, the trees still stood in their haphazard semblance of order, making halls and trails twisting beneath the roof of leaves. I hated them, but they were familiar. I needed no trail anymore, following their curves deeper inside.

With each step, the cylinder pulled tight in its pocket at my thigh, insistent and unquiet. As if to say, "Where are you running? You know what comes next…"

I have to go back.

The promise I'd made when I thought I could return, innocent.

They don't want you back.

They had the right of it.

"I'm going away," I said, and pushed deeper.

There is nowhere to go.

There's everywhere! Anywhere but here. I'll head south and cross the river Soneda...

That was Ivan's voice.

My steps slowed. I raised a hand and leaned against a tree, heedless of what I might be touching. This was Ivan's solution to the thatched mess we'd landed in.

"I am not Ivan," I said aloud.

The jungle did not care, brooding like the button at my thigh. Watching me. Weighing me.

I would not be Ivan. Maybe I could be Stump. Maybe I could endure.

I searched the sky and found the haze – not behind me as I'd expected but over my right shoulder. My aimless wandering had merely led me in a circle around the ashen basin.

I turned.

"Stump," I said, clinging to the thought lest Ivan take up residence again. Stray thoughts, as I walked, whispered that he might hear me. That Kodiak had laid him outside the radius and that he had not bled out onto the ferns and weeds, and his comm still crackled on his ear.

"You never did tell me about your family. Who was Elsie?"

The smoke was clearing. The fires must have been dying, and stray breezes driving the clouds out through the Outlands. The jungle around me was still green.

"And you. Why didn't you go back?" I asked, quietly.

I pushed aside bushes to force my way through a thicket. It felt dangerous after so many days watching each footstep and dodging every branch. Beyond the thicket was a small clearing.

"Probably because you were wrong," I concluded.

Stump was not here. Stump was not anywhere, not anywhere I could find him. I picked up a stone and carried it to the middle of the clearing and placed it down, then looked for more.

"Did it always bother you?" I asked as I worked. "What I really want to know is how many years was it? How did you stand under it?" With a stone in each hand, I made my way back to the first and set them down, side by side.

"You stood straight, Stump." There were more stones under the trees. "But here's the problem. I don't want to run. I can't go home. So maybe I've got to stand, like you. But I'm not like you. I don't know if I can carry it."

The pile grew, stone by stone. "I know what you'd say, now that you've finished. You'd say it's not worth it. You'd say go home."

Stump had sunk to the ground, collapsing in like a mined tower. Was that the first time? Was that the moment the balance tipped, a thousand moments in a lifetime falling like grains of sand until one instant, the mass shifts? The moment it took him.

"But what then? Yeah, you never figured that one out either.

So here we are."

I found a great stone just under the trees and picked it up with both hands, shuffling back to the middle where I placed it on top. The pile held. It didn't even reach my waist, but it would stand.

I stood over the cairn, searching for final words. "Does it break you fast or slow? How long will it last?"

It was no great mystery. *Until the end.*

I knew Stump would nod and look away. I knew there would be a glimmer of pain in his eye that would remain invisible in his face, his posture, his words. I knew he would understand.

"Well," I said, casting around the clearing. The stones were gathered, the branches cleared. "You made it, Stump. You did well. Maybe Elsie would have been proud. I think she would understand."

I unhooked the comm and, leaving it on, placed it on top of the large stone.

"...Maybe Elsie would understand." I stood above the small cairn for a long moment.

"I don't want to go back."

I wished he were there.

"Good-bye."

*

A few dozen meters beyond the clearing the foliage ended in a sharp line, where green and brown turned to black. Wisps of smoke still rose, even a few spots glowed red where embers mulled, unquenched. With the slightest pause, I grabbed the straps of my pack and stepped out, feeling the dark ground soft underfoot.

At first, a few stumps still rose, to my shoulder, then to my knees, then not at all. In some places, the corners of walls still stood, no higher than a footstep, marking the small outlines of houses.

At first, there were bodies, then bones, then nothing.

I saw something rising from the flat earth and began walking, then trotting. It was a pile of bones, skeletons burnt bare by the satellite. They were massed in a pile, and as I drew near, I saw in the middle bones larger than the rest.

Here lay Kodiak.

With a cry I waded in and began pulling off the small Outlander bones, casting them away. They were dry and clean to the touch. A femur, an ulna, ribs upon ribs, until the ground around him was clear.

He lay there, prostrate, arms raised beside his head.

"Oh, Kodiak," I moaned, and sank to the earth with my hands on my head. "What have we done?"

What wonders and terrors that frame had wrought. I contemplated him there, fingers, toes, and skull softly nestled in the ash.

"What have we done?" I asked again. "How many did you kill, Kodiak? Do you even know? I've lost count. I'm not sure which lives go on my scale."

He looked at rest, his teeth grinning into the dust. The lives he saved might have included Abel's, but for me. He had given his own. "Was it enough?"

No, that was the same broken question. It did not un-murder Patches. It balanced injustice with injustice. It wasn't enough, but it was everything. That is all Abel had meant.

"So why are you smiling?" I shouted. "Aren't you sorry?"

He only grinned.

I was so tired; my anger exhausted itself like a spark cast off from the fire. I had seen him that day in the camp. I had looked into his eyes as I struck him across the face with my full strength.

"Sorry doesn't fix things. Didn't Abel tell you? You're dead and nothing's fixed. Why did you do it?"

Kodiak grinned on, unperturbed. "Crank you, you great bear."

I rubbed a hand across my face, pulling it away and finding it black. I rubbed my face on my shoulder, not knowing if it was as filthy as the rest. I didn't want to see his face anymore, so I rose and stood between his great hands, gazing at the back of his head.

"I know. You did it because you could. You aren't like Crisp, dying proud, or Oyster, dying stupid. But you're still dead. I don't know, Kody. You told me we aren't meant to die Unforgiven. Did you?"

He now looked sad where he lay in the earth. There was only one answer to all my questions, the one he had given when he ran back into the settlement, when he drew his knives.

It is well.

"Yeah. I know."

I rubbed my face again, heedless of the ash. I was already covered.

"Thank you, Kodiak. For what you did."

I wanted that to be it, but it wasn't. I had wanted him dead for so long.

He lay there like Patches had.

"I forgive you."

I reached out a hand but found myself unwilling to touch him. Straightening, I turned my back and began walking again, into the heart of the desolation.

*

The great, charred pillar rose from the ground across the ashen sea from me. There was nothing, no one left but that. From afar, its blackness blended into the ground; as I drew near, the sunlight caught angles in the wood, glaring in points of white.

Around that pillar, even the faint outlines of huts disappeared. There were no more skeletons, though Outlanders had certainly been here. Nothing remained but the trunk of wood.

Here I was. At the tree. It was dead center, marking it true as the support for the great hall that held the beacon. Marking it as Abel's resting place. The wonder of what tree could withstand the wrath of heaven was lost on me.

I drew near and placed my hand on it. The tree was smooth and hard as rock when I ran my hand across the surface. I leaned my forehead against it, aware again of how tired I had become.

I gave it an awkward pat and turned to survey the tree line, several stones' throws away. I touched my leg again, feeling the cylinder that could take me home. I turned to the tree.

"I don't know how I thought this would end. Maybe I thought… you know what I thought. I didn't deserve this punishment and that, when what was done to me outweighed anything I had done, I'd deserve a place back at the table." I rubbed my hands together, and some of the skin showed through the ash. "Stupid."

I unslung my pack and set it before the pillar, then sat on it.

"I don't know what to do."

With my feet, I made ridges and valleys in the soot and dirt at my feet. I tried to make a big mound, but the hill collapsed, little grains tumbling down over each other. I squinted at the sun; it was either morning or afternoon. I didn't know which way was North.

"It should be you, Abel," I said. "I know, you have nothing left back home. But you didn't deserve to die. It should be you."

Yet even if I'd been capable of getting to the beacon, of that run through a gauntlet of hostile men and women, my heart would have quailed. I would have waited for another path. I would have waited until one more needed thing had broken in my hands.

I leaned down and let the ash run through my fingers, the remains of all that had been here. The evils wrought by the cracked souls of the Outlanders. The crushed innocence of the whole ones. The sins and sacrifices of the Unforgiven. Sifted together, indistinguishable.

I jammed closed fists against closed eyes. "I need to tell you something: It was my fault. I told you it was Ivan, but it was me. I killed you." I rushed on, as if afraid the blackened tree would interrupt. "You didn't know, you saved me but you didn't know, I broke the beacon's antenna. It was me."

As the words fell, I knew that, to him, it wouldn't have mattered. It would have changed nothing.

"So, it comes to this. You should be alive, but you're dead. I should be dead. Here I am."

So many times I had walked away when Abel tried to speak. I had dedicated myself to fighting back, so afraid that someone might suspect I didn't have the answer. I didn't have the answer.

"Freely given?" My voice grew, cold and loud, like the wind atop Abbey Spire. "Do you know what you've given me?

"How do I wake up for the next fifty years knowing that the only good man in this God-forsaken place was burnt to nothing because I got it wrong?

"You want me to go home and just live under that? Walk back into the unfixable failures that got me here, and live under that, too? They don't want me! I can't do anything for them anymore!

"Is this supposed to be a gift?"

I pulled out the knife. It lay heavier than the screwdriver in my palm, and mismatched pieces began twisting together.

The blue button would end this. It pulled me from here and took me to a place I no longer belonged. It was a passage I had not earned, and I did not fit the door.

But the knife...

The knife. Something pulled tight inside me and strained against my chest. I couldn't breathe. It snapped.

"Is it supposed to be a gift? I can't carry it! Add it to the pile, Abel! Add it to the pile, next to Pope's medicine, and Happy's glasses, and Oyster's juice, and every spragging thing littered through this jungle!"

I stood and stalked past the log, but I felt its blackened eyes on my back.

"Every cracked thing I do will remind me that I'm only here because you aren't! What do I do with that? I'll tell you what I do!"

I looked at the knife again. With effort I closed my fingers around the hilt, until my knuckles turned white.

It fixes nothing.

Yet it may be necessary.

I considered all my softest bits. The neck was too close to my head. They said the thigh would do it, but I did not know where the blood ran. I held the knife before my belly.

It would not move.

I took the knife in a second hand and squeezed tighter.

It came toward me, a centimeter, then several. I screamed at my hands to drive it home, but they would move no farther.

They would not move.

I turned and hurled the knife into the pillar. "What have you done to me?" It struck handle first and bounced off to lie in the ash.

"Drown it, Abel! Taj said he could do it! Taj said he wanted to do it! I only said I thought I could do it! And now it's my fault you're dead!"

My pulse pounded on my neck, on my scalp, the words tore my throat.

"You chose this, Abel! You chose this! I didn't ask you to die!"

I pounded the words into the wood with my fists until my knuckles bruised. No amount of blustering, pounding, wheedling, or begging could wrench one word from that dead wood. Rage was the only thing strong enough to hold my tears at bay, to deny passage to the guilt that wound through me. I was afraid that if the pain stopped, if the rage stopped, I would hear the words that even then clattered in the basement of my soul.

I'm not worth this.

I was out of breath, and I bent over with hands on my knees. "Do you know what you've done?"

The words echoed and fled. Apart from me, nothing moved. As I threw back with curses the weight pressing on me, I knew what Abel's quiet words would be.

I do.

I straightened, taking deep breaths, then leaned forward and rested my head on the tree. I reached my hands up to find small holds for my fingers, and stretched my weight upon it. "Then why?"

The silence brooded, patient and curious. And the tears came.

They came warm, tracing lines from my eyes to my nose where they fell, grey, to the ground. I don't know what well they flowed from; it all lay on my heart. I wished I had it all back, that I could do it again, everything. Everything. I wanted to do it right. I wanted to do it better. Hollow wishes, everything wrong would remain wrong, and only I would escape.

I hated Abel for the gift, and I held it tight.

"I'm so spragging sorry."

I had no right to any other words.

"I'm sorry, Abel, it's not your fault. I tried."

It was enough. Abel had granted those words to Kodiak, and in shame, I knew he would have said the same to me. But they were a lie.

"It isn't enough!" I said, pressing my head into the tree. Perfect would have been enough. "It wasn't enough."

The evidence was final. Everyone died. I knew now why he had pulled me so close that his breath was on my face and spoken to me; he knew what this was. Now I knew, I didn't understand, and it was already done.

"Abel, I'm not worth it," I pleaded one last time. Nothing moved, nothing spoke.

*

In the end I sat in the ash, my back against the last thing standing in the desolation. I drew the stick and its blue button from my pocket.

I didn't want to go home.

We could not be forgiven, any of us.

If there was a path ahead, I couldn't see it. But all other doors were closed.

I twisted open the lock, held it aloft, and pressed the button with my thumb.

Forgiven. I barked a hollow laugh.

I was the guiltiest man on the planet.

– FORTY SEVEN –

I squinted in the sunlight. The sterile air of the Hall had a distinct scent, one I hadn't noticed before. It was now striking. It smelled like the absence of Outlands; no water evaporating after midday rain, no tree decomposing in the soft dirt, no dust in the air or animal dens diffusing from the ground.

Over and over I sucked it in, testing the novelty as I squinted out the window and pretended I was alone. The light through the window turned the spires gold as the sun began to drop toward the horizon. Everything moved slowly and lazily in the distance, spread out below me. It looked like a city trying to struggle free of its cocoon.

A throat cleared next to me, and I stilled the reflexive glance. Henry stood patiently beside me, watching machines and figures trundle across the landscape. I didn't like making him stand in silence. It had been days, and I had said little to anyone. I didn't know what to say.

A few hours had passed before the aircraft came for me, the soft drone building until it roared above and whipped the ash to a maelstrom. I had sat against the great log, heart spent, words spent, waiting. As the time stretched, I again wondered if they were coming at all. I wondered if maybe this was all there was, to wait until I died, the last of us.

It was a comforting thought. The resolution. It was the simplicity of it that comforted, to wonder no longer how it all might play out and what I must do.

And then the flyer came and dropped a line. I hooked it onto my pack, as I had the day I jumped, and in moments I was inside. There were four doctors waiting for me. Four. I spread my arms and opened my hands, empty. They looked confused.

"It's just me."

I had pushed away their inquisitive hands until they left me alone. The men who had needed them were lying under the trees below.

I showered for a long time. Afterward, I stood before the mirror. My eyes were unfamiliar. I stared, hoping for some spark of recognition, but the longer I looked, the more alien I seemed.

The sergeant major had shown me slides of the settlement, before and after, lit up in little dots. 923 Outlanders, he had informed me. 920 or 921, I had corrected to myself, plus Abel, Kodiak, and maybe Stump. It wasn't important now.

"Congratulations," he told me. I never learned his name.

And then today. It was the second day I had spent in Henry's office. I had not yet spoken a word, nor had he. He stood with me by the window. At midday we ate.

Now I watched a train traverse the landscape, taking minutes to pass from left to right and minutes more to disappear. As the end of the train rolled into view, Henry cleared his throat again, and this time I did turn. Henry waved a hand, apologetic.

"I'm sorry, Henry," I said.

He waved his hand more emphatically and coughed again before straightening to look back out the window.

The broken silence tried to enfold us again before anything else could escape. I did not turn back to the window, though. Henry adjusted his glasses and squinted at something in the distance.

"Henry," I said again.

He looked at me now. His features fell still when he saw my face, and he held my eyes, at whatever he saw there. I wanted to speak. Words flew by me, but they did not fit together.

"What happened?" Henry asked.

"Patches hated flying," I said, snatching at the closest thought.

Henry looked down, releasing my eyes. More words came, and they tumbled out like the broken parts they were.

"So did Kodiak. They panicked. Kodiak killed him. Just bled him dry, left him there in the grass."

Henry put his back to the window and slid to the floor. He crossed his legs and watched the space between his feet.

"Oyster tried to hoard the bug juice. He wanted a new life. A parasite killed him on the first night.

"But Ivan wanted to take control, to be Leader. Crisp, some of the others liked that. Ivan promised us everything, as if he could actually give it. Others looked to Abel. So we fought.

"Outlanders found us in the night, and we shot them. Only Pope was hurt. I hadn't fixed the Eyes in time; that's when it began. I broke Happy's glasses to get the Eyes working.

"The next day Ivan tried to take over. Maybe that's when it began...that's why he stole Happy's glasses. He abandoned Crisp the next time we fought the Outlanders, and Crisp was chased down. He took Duck away from us and left him to the Outlanders too. He tried to kill us all, but he couldn't. Taj shot him in the night. Said it was an accident."

Henry had not moved from the floor. I raised my hand to the window and traced a shape against the glass. The train had disappeared, and the world again looked still. The gold was deepening and coloring everything, polished windows glinting and throwing the light back and forth across the city.

"One of us killed Crow, stabbed him in the chest during an argument. I never found out who.

"The next time we found the Outlanders, I killed one. Pope got hurt again, with toxins. Kodiak saved my life. I still hated him.

Henry leaned his head against the wall. His eyes were closed.

"But Pope died in the end, and Happy, when Ivan brought the Outlanders on us again. We ran, and Happy was blind..." I trailed off. "I broke the glasses before Ivan stole them. Henry, there's so much blood on my hands."

A bird wheeled in the thermals, watching the landscape as I had. The hunter turned in ever twisting circles, no sign of prey to call it back to earth.

"Come, sit," Henry said. He rose and shuffled to his worn chair, as he had less than two weeks ago. So long ago. I saw tightness in his eyes before a forced smile hid it. In a dormitory, I'd seen two new shaved heads and two pairs of hollow eyes looking out at me. No Abel. How often must Henry have this conversation?

Henry seemed to follow my splintered narrative. He knew the story well enough, it seemed. "What else?" he asked.

I'd just been listing the dead. What else? "The day Ivan first betrayed us Kodiak beat him to a pulp. He deserved it. But Abel stopped Kodiak anyway. I thought Abel was trying to protect Ivan. I thought… but he wasn't. It was for Kodiak. Kodiak wasn't the same after. I punched him in the face, I looked in his eyes, and he wasn't the same.

"Abel wanted to save Duck, too. We all did. We didn't try hard enough, though; I didn't try hard enough. Duck went with Ivan, hoping in that promise. Ivan's promises came cheap. What he got was strung up in a tree and mutilated by the savages." I let that lay. There is no more I will ever say about it.

"But Taj shot Ivan. Taj was a brutal man. I called him a necessary evil. I accepted him because I needed him. I thanked him when he shot Ivan. Even if that saved our lives… or in the end, just my life… Even if it had, it doesn't change what Taj was. And I accepted him.

"I shot a man, too, Henry. Not an Outlander, not what you think of when you think of an Outlander. Just a man living in the jungle. Call it a necessary evil too, if you like; I was scared and lost, and I wanted to live. I thought we were fighting for our lives, but then I took one. And my gunshot, when I shot him, called all the savages in the Outlands down on us." I held out my hands, washed and clean since I'd been pulled from the jungle. But I could feel the blood running off my screwdriver, still.

"They came to us on the hill, and we killed them. We killed them all and went to find the settlement and kill the rest."

"What else?" Henry asked, when my words trailed away in the darkening room. It was dusk, but neither of us moved to turn the lights on. I let the silence stand; my narrative had crossed the space at all the wrong angles, and I could not remember what was left. It was all before me.

"And Stump. When we were in the Hall, when we went into battle, when Ivan and Kodiak and Taj were storming, he never flinched. But he was afraid his whole life, like a man standing before a fire. Before the end, he up and walked through the flames. It hurt him, and there was nothing waiting on the other side. What he'd longed for was years gone. But he walked through.

"They got him, because he wouldn't stick a knife in a child. That child gutted him. Stump died on his feet. If that makes any sense."

Henry looked up. "And Kodiak?"

I rested my head against the soft chair back, and against the darkness of closed eyes I saw Kodiak again: the mountain, the avalanche.

"You all fight the Outlanders with your Unforgiven, with your satellites. We fought them with guns. Kodiak fought them with his hands. All nine hundred twenty of them."

"Alone?" asked Henry.

"And they ran from him."

Henry breathed, slow breaths in the dimness, in and out. "How did this happen?"

485

"There were innocents locked in a cage. Kodiak wanted them free. When he did something, it was done. In the end the Outlanders were too many. They turned, they came at him, they climbed over him, and even so it was barely enough."

I looked up and Henry was studying his hands again, lips pursed. The shadows fell deep across his face; I hadn't noticed the wrinkles before.

"And Taj wandered off and died cursing Abel with his last breath."

There was pain in each memory. But with each word came lightness, another shoulder carrying the weight. Yet now I had come to the brink; and even summoned, words would not come. We sat.

At last Henry asked. "What happened to Abel?"

"Abel was a good man."

"A good friend," Henry added. And I left it at that.

*

Henry asked more questions, and slowly we rewove my tattered account. The city flamed to light. Dinner was brought and cleared away.

As we spoke, I remembered other things. I remembered laughter. I remembered sitting around the camp lights at night, eating meager suppers. I remembered the wind in the trees and the light dappling the leafy floor, the bird song and the harmony of beetles and crickets.

Henry listened, and he understood. He understood enough. In the end I told him about Abel. I told him how I had broken the beacon, and how Abel had run.

When I finished, truly finished, he sat back in his deep chair, fingertips pressed together as if to make a cage. He gazed into it, seeing shadows inside. I also sat back, I also looked at my hands, but they lay open and empty.

"And now, here you are," Henry said.

"I don't belong here," I said, softly.

"All will be well," Henry said.

The words fell like a half-hearted pat on the back. The nod I gave was reflex. The lines on the rug twirled around each other, making stylized flowers against a cream background. Again, I tasted the sterile air.

"Callie Joan Mendes. Winter Joseph Odel."

"The children…" Henry said.

"Nothing is well."

I saw his shadow move on the floor, crossing the twisting lines, and felt his eyes on me. "How little you resemble the man who sat here before."

"Nothing has changed," I said. "I thought I could climb this mountain, attain perfection by will. I still think it. I know I can't, but I don't know what else to think."

This time Henry said nothing.

"I used who I had to, to live, and blamed who I had to, to live with myself. Happy did when I didn't, and it cost his glasses. Ivan did when I didn't, and it cost us Duck. Kodiak did, Abel did; I did not. The machine ground the best men back to dust, and here I am. The top of my mountain."

"You did so much for the men out there," Henry said.

"You know all I've done."

His eyes flicked to the desk behind me. My file was still there.

"It should be Abel," I said, recalling words, thoughts from the smoking basin. My voice hardened, forcing Henry's probing questions back into the ash. "Well, the fire took him and left me behind."

"All will be well," he said again. Again, the words fell lifeless to the floor.

And we sat. I wanted to look out the window, to watch the lights move slowly in and out of the Spire shadows, to fall ever more deeply into silence. I was so tired.

"Thirteen," he said.

"Don't call me that anymore."

"Timothy," he said, more gently.

The word settled. For a time, I had not heard it. For a time, no one had known it.

"Nothing has changed," he echoed. "But you are Forgiven."

"State's Forgiveness." Leaning back, I stretched my neck over the rounded chair. With an effort, I released the tension in my shoulders, my chest, in my fists which had closed. "It doesn't mean anything."

"The door, there, is open." Henry adjusted his spectacles. "There is no one standing between you and the rails. Surely that means something?"

"That's not how it works."

"The State set a price."

"Five hundred bodies."

"The price was paid."

I leaned out over my knees, coming close to him. "So *spragging* what!"

I rose and stood above him. He only pursed his lips again.

"Where out that door do I go, Henry? What right does the State have to take everything behind me, and everything before me, and say, 'it's all right'? I'm still the man they condemned, Henry. I'm not fixed. My wife isn't fixed. My wife's mother isn't fixed. I told you, nothing has changed. More is wrong than there was before."

Henry slowly nodded, saying nothing. I walked to the window. I expected no answer. There was no answer.

The city had changed, dark and sleepy. Bright lights washed the spires with their glow. Smaller lights moved here and there on invisible tracks.

I spoke quietly. "What do five hundred Outlanders have to do with me?"

Henry's quick voice met mine. "Nothing."

"Nothing! Patches paid the price," I said, pressing fingers into the glass, one by one. "Happy paid the price. Pope paid the price. Stump paid the price. Kodiak paid the price. Abel paid the price." My anger had already guttered. It could barely make itself heard over fatigue and grief. "So why am I the one called Forgiven?"

Henry rose behind me. He approached with patient steps as he spoke. "Do you wish you had died?"

Looking down the glass, I saw the land far below, and my reflection. I did not know.

"To die, or to fix. Are those the only paths for you?"

I thought of ferns and shadows, roots and black packs beneath a green canopy.

"There is no path."

His soft *hmph* came at my shoulder.

"Why do you want to fix everything?"

Because I broke it. Because the cracks kept spreading, spreading, and people were dead. Because I hated the grief I'd planted, and it had no cure. Because I could not shoulder life ahead with this behind.

"So that you will be worthy," he said for me. "Worthy of life," he repeated, quietly, and nodded to himself.

"Worthy of forgiveness." And he stopped.

I rested my head on the window, the cool of the night seeping through like a kiss to my forehead. I'd already had this conversation with Abel. With Kodiak, with Happy, with Patches. I'd found the stone at the bottom of all the murky water.

"I'm not worth this."

"And that isn't how it works," Henry said.

For a moment, we were back where we started. Side by side, staring at the city. Silent.

"How does it work?"

"You are forgiven."

"I told you, I'm—"

"You are forgiven," Henry interrupted, his words firm.

He raised his head as I met his eye, and his chin quivered. He held me in a fixed gaze; the lights shining through the window turned his glasses to twin moons.

His words stood.

"There's no justice to it," I said, at last.

"No! There is mercy to it!" A sudden urgency took his voice and quickened his breath. "Do you not see it?"

I took his word, tested it on my lips. I turned it by degrees, tried to fit it in. It had a weight, but there was no place for it.

"I'm not worth mercy either."

"Then why did Abel run to that hut?" His hands opened and closed, the knuckles briefly whitening with each squeeze. As if he wanted to gesture in anger but had forgotten how. As if he wanted to take my shirt and shove me against his glass.

"Did he say anything?" Henry pressed. "Before the end?"

In the dark, I could still hear Abel's voice. I could still hear the strain. But also lightness. When he left me, he'd already let go.

"He said 'freely given.'"

Henry stilled, turning the words over, as I had turned his. "And was he talking about his life," he said, "or was he answering all your riddles?"

"I don't know, Henry."

Abel had spoken, and he'd gone. I remained. In the junkyard of all the sins and bruises I'd piled, it somehow felt the heaviest. It was no accident, no entanglement and escalation, no unintended consequences. Just a moment, and I'd done nothing. He went, and I remained.

"And I don't know why he did it."

The small lamp on Henry's desk was insufficient and could not raise the room above a dusk. He pulled his glasses from his face and worried at an earpiece before putting them back on. The beginning of a smile touched the corner of his eye as he did. "You said you found Kodiak. In the ashes."

"I did."

"Tell me about him."

"What about him?"

"Did you forgive him? Before the end?"

"I did."

"Why?" Henry asked.

Because he had run into a mass of cracked Outlanders. Because he had died. Because I was sorry. Because I liked him. The harder I thought, the blanker my mind became, none of it was deep enough to cover Kodiak.

Henry pressed. "Did anything he did un-terrify you in the days come and gone? Did any of it fix Kodiak's bloodied past? Did any of it bring back Patches?"

"No," I said.

Henry pressed. "So why? Why would you forgive him?"

"I just did."

Henry wasn't looking at me. He was watching the lights out in the city; one hand rested against the cool of the window, the other in his pocket. His voice grew soft. "Freely given?"

I bowed my head.

"Timothy," he said. "There is nothing more to do. There is no mountain, nothing to climb. Only what is given to you."

I again studied the lights reflecting from his glasses, making him luminous in the half-dark. That was it. Not the stamp of the State, not the work of my hands. What I needed, out of reach, freely given. And I understood, at last.

"I'm not worth this," I said again.

"It is done."

*

I didn't speak for a time. He led me back to the chairs. A man brought tea, and Henry whispered a thanks to him before handing me a cup. I watched the curling vapor float before me until the water cooled.

Perhaps Henry was right, perhaps something had changed. As we poked at the ashes left by the desolation of the Outlands, pieces were turning over.

More and more, I glanced at the doorway. It seemed to grow larger and larger in the dark. I feared it.

"Henry," I said at last, and he stirred. "Where do I go?"

"Where now?" Henry said and tucked his chin to his chest with a frown. "Yes." He removed his glasses to polish them self-consciously. "I suppose you go back."

The polishing continued, and his voice grew more certain. "Let it all go, everything you've wound around yourself, and run. Run, Timothy. Heal. Things will never be right. You may never be right. You say nothing has changed but I tell you," and glasses on, he peered at me. "Everything has changed. Your life is not fixed, but neither is it destroyed. It is before you."

His words flickered like firelight, dancing on the wall. The shapes flashed, warm and welcome, brief and beautiful, and the great machine finally stretched itself out before me. Invisible threads ran on into the infinite, the choices, the pain, love, victory, and disaster. Even my own small life, woven into the fractal, a mosaic of failure bound together by mercy.

"You want to know if you can be forgiven? Go home."

"I have no defense," I protested. "I have no apology. Henry, I put her through hell, and she walked straight through just to stay by my side. I have nothing to say."

"Then you are finally ready," Henry said.

I caught his eyes, shook my head, pleading. "What can I bring her?"

"You will have what is given to you."

"Is there hope?" I asked.

Hidden wrinkles took shape around his quick smile, and he nodded. "All will be well."

His smile held me, like my father's hand on my shoulder, as commuters on the train docks crowded us.

"Do you want to know if you can be forgiven?"

"I do."

Henry clapped his old, warm hand on my shoulder and, side by side, we watched the small lights of the city move through the night.

– EPILOGUE –

She had not said a word.

Red-gold light of the dying sun slanted sharply through the curtainless window, kindling the dust floating in the barely furnished room. In the middle, the chair, table, and sofa stood alone, islands in the otherwise stark residence.

She held an empty mug in her hands, her feet tucked under her in the chair. She looked at him where he sat, in the middle of the sofa. He did not look back; he was studying a spot on the floor. He had fallen silent.

"Why tell me all this?"

He did not immediately speak, though rumors of thoughts, words flickered on his face. "I don't how else to say what I need to say."

"Why not just say you're sorry?" She did not blunt the edge in her voice, tired of the effort.

"I've said I'm sorry a thousand times before, and every time it was a lie. You knew it. I knew it. I came here to say something different."

"What did you come to say?"

"I'm sorry." His head came up, and he met her eyes.

She turned her chin but did not look away. Then she shook her head.

"You killed my mother."

He did not respond. He looked away, studying the floor again. Then he nodded.

Her fingers knotted on the empty mug, brown lines stained into each crack in the enamel. Her hair fell forward, and she reached up a hand to run it behind an ear again.

"I mean, what you did. My mother died."

He nodded again.

"I understand," he said. "I didn't before."

Now her face flickered, indecision, but she gave voice to none of it.

"I wish there was something I could do, actually do. All I can do is ask you to forgive me. If that is too much, I understand."

"What about all the things you said? What about everything else?"

He nodded slowly, and again studied the floor.

"Truth, it had nothing to do with you. It was about what I wanted. What I thought I needed to get by." He turned the empty cup on its side like a barrel, turning it over and over, tracking the handle as it clicked past. "I was thinking about myself. Every time. I'm sorry."

She turned her head to the window, catching the rays of the sun and squinting into them. Sounds came from her throat, unformed words, rejected sentences.

"And I wanted to say thank you."

"Do you want more water?" She spoke quickly. He gave a polite smile and held out his cup. When she disappeared into the next room, the man turned to his fingernails, scratching at the last dirt, fully fused to the dents and scratches he'd collected.

She slid back into the room and stood over him, holding out the wet mug. His fingers rested on hers on the small cup and neither let go. Sad eyes looked into sad eyes.

"I've missed you," he said, the words breaking as they fell to either side of audibility.

She let go of the mug and backed away, sitting down and sending a new plume of dust to catch the sunset. The two sat alone while the movement slowed and then stopped, the lightest dust suspended in the dim air, lazily drifting.

"I'm building a house in the outskirts. There will be enough room for… But there's also enough money for a second house. Or for this place. I don't know. Whatever you need. And Henry's given me a list of places to look. I need to see if I can find Abel's family."

His throat was sore, having spoken through long hours. He returned to a study of the floor, casting about for anything else he could say to her. He did not want to leave. She studied the same spot on the floor and also found no help.

He finally stood. "Thank you for letting me come. Thank you for listening."

She stood as well.

"I'm…" He paused. "I'll be nearby next week. I'll stop by. If you're busy or aren't here, I'll understand. I will."

She nodded. He handed her the cup. She held the door.

"Be safe," she said as he stood in the doorway, the words escaping suddenly. He turned, a smile, small, but enough to soften his eyes, on his lips.

"You too."

She stood in the open door as he walked down the hall. He looked smaller than before. Small yet solid in a way that suggested he could be leaned upon.

At the turn in the corridor, he stopped, looking back to her doorway, and their eyes met again. A fleeting smile appeared at the corner of her mouth and was gone. She raised her hand in a furtive farewell and ducked inside the doorway.

Outside, he allowed a sad smile, let out a heavy breath, and walked to the spire's maglift.

Inside, she leaned against the closed door. Her thoughts swirled with fire, words, death, tears, rooms empty at home and full at the Hall of Judgment. The wounds ached. And she saw a man, all wires and lights, quick words and a quick laugh that had slowed over the years. She saw the man whom she had loved. She saw what he had been, saw what he was becoming.

Her smile was weak, mingled with sorrow, with doubt, but it held.

One week.

AUTHOR'S NOTE

This is an old-fashioned book. I can hear the question mark as I write that – light dystopia? Environmental apocalypse? Made-up words for digital paper and classist slurs?[1]

What I mean is that the book does not hold your hand, does not draw you passively through its narrative. It asks you to stick with it, to invest, until it gives back. Thank you for persisting, for finding the inflection points where the tinder catches fire, and the story begins to roar.

And I invite you to read it again. There is more. Something unnoticed will fall into place. Events separated by hundreds of pages will connect. It is my hope that you will come back and find something new woven into these pages with each journey.

*

If you enjoyed this book, if you found it of worth, there is no greater accolade than a recommendation to a friend. The most valuable gift to an author is a new reader.

Lastly, honest reviews on Amazon or anywhere around the internet are like gold. I would be indebted if you would leave a note somewhere to let us all know what you thought.

---

[1] Spragger (horse cart valet or wheel maintenance) and Nedder (needle maker) are real words. I thought pre-industrial occupations appropriate slurs for a technocratic society with a savior complex.

ACKNOWLEDGEMENTS

The cost of writing is hours. Often long, categorically solitary, with flashes of exhilaration scattered through the plodding. I am so grateful to Three Cord Press, to JB Simmons and Michael W Andersen, who shared this journey over the 12 years that passed between word one and final formatting. Their fellowship, experience, encouragement, and critique carried me along. Thank you for sharing the journey and showing the way.

To my wife, Grace, who watched me silently sit at my desk and work at this for years. Who rode the emotional ups and downs with me, who kept me fed and watered when my head was miles away, who always had the answer for contextless questions like, "what's a good name for a made-up disease?"

To Danny Lee, Grant and Heather Hollis, Lorene Eberhardt, and Emily Adelizzi for reading this half-baked and seeing what it could be, and mercilessly driving me toward it.

For the ongoing prayers of my mother, my father, my wife, and a great crowd of encouragers who have done the greatest work to make this book more than I could make it on my own.

And to all that asked how it was going, if it was done, and when they would be able to read it. It's ready.

Thank you.

Made in the USA
Las Vegas, NV
21 February 2025

18474216R00296